OF BLOOD & STONE

A.J. BRAUN

This book is a work of fiction. Names, characters, places, and incidents are the product of the author's imagination or are used fictitiously. Any resemblance to actual events, locales, or persons, living or dead, is coincidental.

Cover Art by FlavulousArt

Map Art by A.J. Braun

TRIGGER WARNINGS

Child abuse (flashback), suicidal ideation, near attempted suicide (flashback), PTSD symptoms, vomiting, on-screen torture, depressive symptoms, blood & gore, incestuous relations (not romance-related), dub con (brief, not romance-related), religious trauma, glorification of self-harming practices, misogynistic systems of power, manipulation/gaslighting (not romance-related), profanity, and explicit sexual content.

To the readers who left everything they believed in to find themselves:
may this story, in all its meagerness, reflect even an ounce of your bravery.

DRUENIA
COASTAL VILLAGES
VUTROR
ESTEA

PART ONE

CHAPTER I

THE RITE

The price for life would always be pain. Sylzenya breathed in deeply as she reminded herself of this truth—the first she'd been taught as a child. Yet it proved difficult to keep the scream in the back of her throat while the cut on her back burned from her goddess' power.

"Come on, Syl, don't be a baby," Her friend Nyla seethed as they pushed their palms into the earth.

Sylzenya huffed a strained laugh. "You're the one sweating, not me."

Their goddess' golden power encircled them, swirls of light wrapping around their arms and torsos, diving deep into the open flesh of their backs. Sylzenya let out a triumphant shout as a sprout poked from the ground, green and vibrant. She pushed harder into the soil—listening.

Thump.

Thump.

Thump.

The earth's heartbeat thrummed against her palms—her *goddess'* heartbeat. Pain mingling with excitement, Sylzenya beckoned the sprout to rise. It obeyed, a trail of golden light pushing it up until it was high above her head. Before it could reach the tops of the willow trees, Sylzenya curled her fingers into the dirt. The sprout bloomed, yellow petals unfurling, a rain of pollen floating through the air.

"Finished," Sylzenya said with a smirk, releasing her hands from the ground. The golden light retreated into the earth. Warm blood trailed down her back, soaking into the white fabric of her robe and dripping into the soil.

Nyla grunted, following her lead, a green sprout poking its head through the dirt right before she released her hands.

"You know, I really hate you sometimes," Nyla mumbled.

Sylzenya raised a brow. "You said to not hold back, so I don't."

"Doesn't make it any less infuriating."

"If you want, I can go easy—"

"*Never* go easy on me."

Sylzenya leaned forward, a playful joke sitting on her tongue, but then the glimmer in her friend's eyes faded.

"Nyla," Sylzenya said, "you're going to do just fine."

"Easier said than done," she replied, staring at Sylzenya's flower stalk, "Tell me again why you, of all people, still need to participate in the rite?"

Sylzenya touched the stem of her flower, the stalk soft as a bird's feather. "Because unlike you, of all people, I actually enjoy our traditions."

Her friend smirked. "You just want the attention."

"*Me*? Attention?"

They stared at one another, grins peeking through feigned seriousness. Sylzenya broke first, her laughter bubbling up like a fresh spring as Nyla joined her.

"You're not completely wrong," Sylzenya admitted. "The High One wants me to debut my power so word can spread."

"The High One certainly likes his displays, doesn't he?"

"He does," Sylzenya agreed.

She dug at the base of her newly created flower, dirt gathering under her fingernails until she found what she was searching for. The orodyte stone she'd buried and used with her goddess' power glowed a bright yellow. Gently, she took it in her hand and then placed it in her pocket. Nyla dug out her orodyte, the stone still clear as crystal.

"Nothing like an empty piece of orodyte to bolster my spirit." Nyla scoffed with an irritated smile.

"Now you're just being dramatic." Sylzenya said.

"Are you blind?" She pointed to her small green sprout and held up her clear stone. "My power hasn't grown since the day I arrived at the temple, and there's no changing that."

"Restraint isn't weakness," Sylzenya argued, "you might create less vegetation in one day, but you have one of the highest monthly harvests. Your consistency is what our kingdom needs, not sporadic moments of brilliance followed by days of dryness."

Nyla stared into the blue sky. "I hope you're right."

"You know I'm right. Besides, you've gotten much quicker," Sylzenya said, brushing her finger along the green sprout, "You'll do fine in the rite today."

"*Today.*" Nyla shot to her feet. "What time is it?"

Sylzenya grinned as she used her friend's arm to pick herself up. "Calm yourself. The sun's almost up, so we're right on schedule."

They grabbed their green cloaks, running out of the temple's gardens and falling in step with the other women acolytes wearing the same green cloaks. Sunlight spilled on the dirt path like a river of gold, leading them towards their final ceremonial rite. Sylzenya's white robe, hemmed with golden thread, peaked through the heavy green material, catching the light and reflecting its glimmer on the surrounding branches.

Smile widening, she wrapped her fingers around the clear orodyte hanging from her neck.

"Are you ready to see your parents?" Nyla asked.

Sylzenya's mouth fell flat.

"Ready as I'll ever be, I suppose," she replied, a fingernail scratching along the stone. "And what of your Aunt?"

Nyla's nostrils flared, her smile fading as she gripped her own piece of clear orodyte. "Ten years changes a lot of things. I've wondered if I'll recognize her." Her warm amber eyes turned to Sylzenya's, "Or, if she'll recognize me."

They walked in silence, the branches brushing softly in the breeze.

"She will," Sylzenya replied.

Walking barefoot on the damp soil, she breathed deeply as she felt for her goddess' power in the earth. It sang back to her, sparks of light singeing into her palms and up her forearms. The scar along her back stung, but Sylzenya didn't fear the pain.

She embraced it.

The familiar tall atrium stood before them. Green vines looped in and around the white stone structure. The willow trees bent in reverence towards the white marble throne, their presence encasing the ancient grove.

The High One, their kingdom's leader, sat on the throne, elevated above the small crowd. He was surrounded by four priestesses in golden robes. A willow grew behind the throne—the one she'd created ten years ago, when she was only fourteen years old. Her heartbeat quickened. The willow was fuller now, leaves bright and branches drooping like a waterfall spilling over a cliff side.

The High One's yellow gaze found hers.

"Welcome, acolytes of Aretta's temple," he announced as he stood. Long white hair fell to his waist, his straight nose carved like the marble statues lining the grove. "Please find those who dedicated you to our goddess' temple. We will begin the Kreena Rite shortly."

Sylzenya's mouth went dry.

Standing at the bottom of the dais were people in white and brown linens. But, it was the man with her same dark blue eyes and the woman with her same ash-colored hair that caught her gaze. The lines around their eyes had deepened, her father's forehead more creased than the last she'd seen and her mother's mouth thinner than before.

She should smile like the other acolytes, greeting her parents warmly. And then, she should thank them for leaving her at this grove after she created her willow all those years ago, her connection to her goddess the only reason she cared to wake up anymore.

She should tell them she loved them.

But then she'd be lying.

Muscles tensed and chin tilted up, Sylzenya approached her parents. They stared at her, eyes welling with tears. Heat rushed through her body as they embraced her. She wanted to yell, to force them off of her, but then she'd cause a disruption.

And there was nothing she hated more than displeasing the High One.

"Oh, my flower bud," Sylzenya's mother choked out as her thin fingers curled around Sylzenya's neck. "We've missed you so much."

Her father said nothing as his breaths trembled, his strong hand gripping her shoulder tightly to him. Hands shaking, she forced her arms down at her sides. She hated how she yearned for their familiar scent—like a spring's first rain; a cold piece of linen on her forehead during hot summer nights; warm blankets in front of a dancing flame.

She thought she'd buried such feelings years ago, but here they were—fresh and potent—as if her body had forgotten the sting of abandonment.

"Welcome," Sylzenya managed as they finally released her.

A tear fell down her father's cheek, his brown hair now a gentle shade of gray.

"It felt like this day would never come," he whispered, his calloused hand caressing her face.

Sylzenya flinched. His eyes widened, smile fading as he dropped his hand. She turned to the High One, his yellow eyes sharp, a comfort in this otherwise dreaded moment. She quickly stepped away from her mother and father, wiping nonexistent dirt off her cloak.

"Yes, well, it's wonderful to see you both," she said, not looking at either of them.

Her parents opened their mouths to say something, but the High One's deep voice boomed through the grove.

"Today is a celebration," he announced, hands outstretched. "Our goddess continues to protect us from the famine ravaging the continent, a curse her brother, Distrathrus, had meant to impose to destroy us all. Aretta blessed our kingdom in her final moments centuries ago, granting our women with the power to connect with her mysterious power stored within the earth. May we never know hunger or thirst because of it. Praise be to Aretta."

Everyone echoed the prayer.

"Each acolyte will approach the sacred soil with the leader of their household. The leader will then grant their blessing by opening the wound by which our acolytes and Kreenas connect to our goddess. You must then create what is requested of you. If you succeed, then you will be declared a Kreena." He paused, smoothing out his robe. "If you don't, then you will remain an acolyte, for our richest earth is meant for Kreenas capable of sustaining our people."

The High One found Sylzenya's stare, his outstretched hand forming a fist.

"Let us begin the ceremony," he said.

Women approached the sacred soil one at a time. Out of the fifteen preceding Sylzenya, nine of them failed. Thankfully, Nyla wasn't one of them. Her ability to create a bush of blueberries had been enough for her to gain her Kreena title.

Grief filled the grove as a tenth woman failed. With each passing year, fewer acolytes were able to become Kreenas. Yet with each passing day, the famine grew closer. A silent tension hung in the air, a quiet question seeping through the leaves:

Would their people survive?

"Sylzenya Phatris," the High One finally announced, "Your power has grown beyond any acolyte this kingdom has witnessed in centuries, and so, I would like you to create our goddess' most sacred of creations—a willow."

Everyone in the grove murmured. It was an advanced power, creating a willow, and it was never performed at a Kreena Rite. Sylzenya smiled. This would be the opportunity to show how vast her power had become over the years—to provide hope for her kingdom, just like the High One had requested of her.

She would save her kingdom from the encroaching famine.

Her father joined her in approaching the patch of earth lined by white marble. She unlatched the golden pin that held her green cloak at her sternum, allowing the heavy material to pool around her. Her white Kreena robe wrapped around her body, its design leaving open skin at her hips and chest; two long slits down the sides exposed her sun-kissed legs. A large gap revealed the cut on her back, already scabbing over from the morning's practice.

She looked like a woman.

A Kreena.

Sylzenya turned to her father, hating how the rite called her to kneel before him, towards a man who gave her away as a child.

Breaths shaking, her father revealed the branch he had chosen to carve the wound into her back. It was a white birch, a strange choice of wood for this rite as willows were the more traditional choice, but Sylzenya didn't question it. All she desired was to connect with her goddess' power—to finally become a Kreena.

"You may begin," the High One commanded.

A single calloused finger brushed her shoulder, her father's breaths short while he whispered a quick prayer. He carved the pointed tip of the branch along her scabbed scar. Sharp and shallow, Sylzenya clenched her teeth, closing her eyes as the warmth of her blood dripped down her shoulders and her back, soaking into her white robe.

"Praise be to Aretta." Her father's voice wavered as he spoke.

Slowly opening her eyes, Sylzenya echoed the prayer.

Turning to the patch of soil bordered by marble, she unclasped the clear orodyte from her necklace. She dug a shallow hole and buried the stone, careful to cover it in its entirety. She took a deep breath as she placed her palms upon the earth.

The soil grew warm. Her fingers ached as she breathed in the earth. The energy from the dirt beckoned to her, begging to become one with her.

Thump.

Thump.

Thump.

Aretta's power thrummed against her skin, a living heartbeat as familiar as her own. She grasped for her goddess' power. With a single breath, golden light released from the ground, trailing wide circles around her wrists, up her forearms, and slicing deep into the soft open flesh of her back. The familiar pain started at her shoulder, dragging down and across until it reached her hip, as if a thin dagger were cutting into her skin.

She breathed out.

The energy circled back the way it had come, crawling under her arms, releasing out of her palms, and retreating into the soil. She gulped, breaths steadied as she placed every thought into her connection between skin and earth.

Blood and blood.

Life.

Maintaining focus on her hands, she waited for the green sprout to poke between her fingers. She imagined the bright leaves unfolding from its center, slow and graceful, the stem rising on a golden trail of light, just as it always did.

Suddenly, the heartbeat ceased.

Sylzenya tilted her head. It'd been years since she'd lost concentration so quickly. She closed her eyes as she reached for the power within the earth again.

Instead, she was met with an icy chill under her fingers… and silence.

Sweat dripped down her arms. Shaking her head, she redirected her focus deeper into the soil. She coupled her focus with a seed of truth; she was to be the hope for her people. Without her, there wouldn't be enough Kreenas to sustain the kingdom. She needed to push more, to concentrate more, to *feel* more.

The need consumed her as the earth grew warm against her palms, her heart racing fast as she dug her fingers deeper and deeper into the soil. She grasped for power, for life—for pain.

Silence consumed her instead.

Blood seeped from her back and onto the soil, the steady flow causing her vision to blur. Something was wrong. She lifted her head to the High One, his brow was deeply furrowed as he stared at her hands.

The orodyte.

Sylzenya dug out the piece of orodyte. The stone was crystal clear—pure and without cracks or defects, just as it was supposed to be prior to its use.

The ominous silence heaved onto her chest as if a tree had fallen on her.

If the orodyte wasn't the problem, then that would mean…

A priestess stepped in front of her, the holy woman's arms spread out, her golden robe blinding as she began to recite the words that would reject Sylzenya's Kreena title.

Announcing her failure to the entire grove.

"*Wait*," Sylzenya begged, burying her hands into the soil, searching for her goddess' heartbeat—but it was gone.

"*Enough*, Priestess," the High One's voice boomed.

Silence thick as fog filled the grove. The priestess stopped, her words melting into the air.

"Theraden," the High One called, "bring me the branch you used for your daughter's back."

Her father stiffened.

The High One stepped forward, arm outstretched. "The branch, Theraden."

Sylzenya stood, staring at her father. Wide pleading eyes and a color-drained face stared back. Something twisted inside her chest.

"It wasn't supposed to happen like this," her father whispered, his knuckles a painful white as he gripped the branch.

Heat rising along her neck, she snatched the branch from his hand. Her heart stilled. A yellow substance coated the branch, its color so faint against the white bark she'd missed it completely.

Orodyte serum.

Poison.

Though this one didn't kill or maim humans, it stripped her people of their divine connection to Aretta; it stripped Kreenas of their power. Only their kingdom's warriors were allowed to handle the substance, all ordained by the High One.

Sylzenya's father wasn't one of them.

"No," Sylzenya breathed, looking to her father, "You wouldn't—"

"Sylzenya, listen to me, please."

But nothing he could say would make a difference. She could sense it clearly now, a loss within her fingertips, an emptiness where a heartbeat used to thrum with assured steadiness.

A part of her… lost.

"You—" she whispered, spit thickening in her mouth, "You *bastard.*"

"We never wanted to give you to the temple. Sylzenya, we love you—"

"*Love?*" she shouted, the branch's splinters piercing her skin. "You call this love? Stripping me of our goddess' power? Dooming our people?"

Sylzenya regretted the words as she said them. Everyone in the grove gasped. She shouldn't be reacting this way; she was supposed to bring hope, not fear.

"Sylzenya, please—" her mother whispered, reaching for her arm.

Sylzenya held up her hands, tears streaking her face. "You're no parents of mine."

"*Seize them.*" The High One commanded.

Bright power erupted in the grove. Shouts rang in the air, warriors entering the ancient sanctum. Her mother and father didn't fight as they were secured, hands tied behind their backs, pieces of vines secured around their mouths. Their muffled cries muted in Sylzenya's ears as a soft breeze brushed her face, the earth beneath her nothing but dirt and ash.

She dropped the birch branch.

"Sylzenya," Nyla called, "come on, let's get out of here."

But her friend's voice spoke to her as if from a distance. Everything around her had blurred. Numb and chilled to the bone, she wrapped her fingers in her robe. The life she'd worked for—*breathed for*—these last ten years… taken with a tree branch to her back. She should've known better than to trust her *father*, her holy cut now defiled by his hands. Tears wet the earth at her feet; heat spread to her limbs; a sting ran up her nose into her forehead.

Aretta, please, hear me.

She waited. No answer came.

Someone started to yell. She jolted from her stupor, realizing the person yelling was her. As she beheld the grove, people kneeled before her.

Weeping.

Without her power, the famine would take her kingdom. Her *home*. Sadness quickly gave way to anger. It burned hotter than the pain of the orodyte serum in her back. Picking up the branch, she silently walked the only path she knew by heart; the path to the temple.

"Syl, where are you going?" Nyla questioned.

"The altar room," Sylzenya stated. "I need to commune with Aretta."

"Hold on. Let's take this slow—"

"*I need to commune with Aretta.*"

The earth felt dead under her feet as she broke into a run, her robe billowing as cold wind whipped her face. Grief threatened to choke her throat, but she held it back. Now wasn't the time to cry. Her people needed her to be strong, they needed her to *fix* this. Willow branches scraped her face as she rushed out of the grove, mumbling prayer after prayer, begging her goddess to meet her through the ancient roots in the altar room. She needed a cure, a miracle—*anything.*

Without her power, there wouldn't be enough Kreenas to fend off the famine.

Without her power, her people would die.

CHAPTER 2
SICKNESS

Gray skies and dark shadows covered the fishing village in a heavy silence. It was that rare moment of quiet before dawn, where all the babes were finally asleep and the crows had yet to wake; even the tumultuous waves surrendered their battle to the jagged rocks guarding the shore. A delicate silence as thin as a spider's web, easily broken by the scuff of a boot or ping of pebbles on glass. As Elnok moved through the shadows and leapt onto a nearby rooftop, one might think he threaded the thin web himself.

The silence split and fell as a loud ring of a bell echoed throughout the village. Elnok crouched low as he steadied himself on the sloped roof, the tiles rickety and cold as they wobbled beneath his black leather boots. Doors opened one by one, people sticking out their heads and checking both ways, their hesitation palpable as a different sound echoed throughout the village.

Laughter.

Not the contagious kind that brought smiles, but the kind that caused skin to ripple and the spine to tighten. Laughter from the pirates who had rampaged the village last week and now considered it under their rule. An unfortunately common practice in these coastal parts.

Elnok scoffed. If this village had guards who knew how to wield a sword, these idiotic marauders would've run off with their watered-down mead the moment they stepped foot on this shore. Yet who ruled the village mattered little to him.

Cold metal circled his eye as he peered through his monocular out to the unruly sea. White caps clipped against the horizon while a pelican dove for its breakfast, the bird narrowly dodging the fast-approaching ship. Billowing white sails and a gold maiden statue sent waves of relief and panic in Elnok's chest.

They came.

Elnok returned his monocular to his pocket. He had less than an hour before the royal vessel docked. Thighs burning from crouching, Elnok maneuvered to the side of the roof with a huge gaping hole, one he'd been diligently widening all week. He'd covered it with straw from a nearby stable that'd been empty the past few days, the last of the horses having mysteriously disappeared.

It didn't surprise Elnok when he learned a few days later that the butcher wasn't just selling fish, but animal meat.

Livestock had become a rarity.

He removed the straw, the smell of diseased meat flooding his nostrils. Cursing under his breath, he quickly placed his black cloth over the bridge of his nose. The wooden ceiling beam shuddered under his weight as he slowly lowered himself. Soundlessly, he stalked along the beam, stopping once he was above the meat counter. The shop's toothless owner caught flies with his hands and, to Elnok's dismay, ate them.

"Boss," a gruff voice sounded from outside. "It's those damned kids again. They're taking off our wood panels on the alleyway side."

"Well, go take care of it," the fly-eating, meat-shop-owning man demanded.

"Can't. Guard said it's your job, not mine."

Grumbling something about the "absurd laws of this wayward town", the shop owner joined his hired hand out of the shop, leaving Elnok with his prize. Elnok smiled, knowing full well he'd have to find the coin he promised the young girl who agreed to be his distraction.

One job at a time.

Swiftly, Elnok tied his trusted rope around the ceiling beam. He gave the knot a hefty tug, and then lowered himself while the shop owner became occupied with the town's deviant children.

He searched the stained display case. Intestines, hearts—oh gods, *bladders*?—kidneys, and tongues hung in their typical spots…

And then he found it. A locked cabinet.

"Here we are," Elnok whispered.

He pulled out his pick and wrench and wedged them into the lock, searching for the tumblers, each click a sweet ping of satisfaction. One final click and the cabinet opened.

Elnok let out a low whistle, grinning at the half-eaten loaf of bread.

"Tell those guards they should be the ones taking care of those roaches, *not* me," the shop owner bellowed.

Elnok's heart sputtered as he snatched the bread, stuffing it into his bag and ducking behind the counter.

"I swear to the blubbering gods," The shop owner entered the shop—a far larger man than Elnok had taken into account—and stopped, staring at the dangling rope.

"What in the hell is this?" the man grumbled.

Elnok cursed. He should leave the rope, run out of the shop, and get a new one. But he'd had it for years. It'd been through his best of times and worst of times—it was a part of himself, really. He couldn't abandon such a fine piece of corded straw, least of all to a man who ate *flies*. Elnok grimaced as he picked up one of the bladders, quietly walking with bent knees to the other side of the counter until he was directly behind the shop owner.

"Strange, isn't it?" Elnok said, "You'd think a hanging was about to take place."

Eyes wild, the shop owner spun around, his attempt to grab Elnok by the throat dodged as Elnok stepped to the side, holding up the bloodied bladder.

"*Thief*," the man growled.

"Actually, I was hoping we could do some business—"

The man lunged for Elnok. Instincts threading through his muscles, Elnok jumped, narrowly missing the tackle that would've surely broken a few of his ribs. Without missing a step, Elnok threw the bladder at the man, grabbed his rope, and climbed.

"Guards! *Guards*!" the shop owner yelled.

Splinters piercing his fingers, Elnok gripped the beam, balancing and unraveling the rope in one swoop. Tying it up and wrapping it around his waist, Elnok ran across the beam.

"*My bread*! You low-life bastard!"

Elnok didn't have time to refute the man's rather rude statement. Instead, he jumped up through the roof's hole. Chilled air whipped his face as he leaped onto another rooftop, and then the next. Armor clanked loudly as guards pursued him on the ground. He circled his way out of sight, finally sliding flat onto the familiar tiles of the infirmary's rooftop.

He waited, ears straining, breaths heavy.

Distant shouts rang through the town while seagulls squawked, the sounds of pursuit fading into the opposite direction.

Not my best work.

Elnok crawled across the cold roof tiles. He removed his other stash of hay, exposing the hole he'd made last week for his other frequented destination. He silently jumped down onto the wooden rafter.

The familiar stench of rotten corpses and bloated fish assaulted his senses as he ran across the flimsy beam. Cots lined the infirmary floor, people with graying skin sending watery coughs into the air while nurses rushed to and fro, more than likely offering their morning "delicacy" of ground fish with lentils. But Elnok doubted if it was anything more than rat intestines and bile.

Elnok stopped as he found the familiar mop of dark brown hair. Smiling underneath his face cloth, he jumped off the beam and fell through the air.

A woman yelped as he landed with a light thud, straddling Orym, his closest of friends and most trusted companion.

Orym stiffened in fright only to give way to a loud cackle.

"You brutish man!" Orym laughed as he coughed into his fist, blood dribbling from the side of his mouth. "You nearly killed my nurse."

Elnok smiled as he said, "I would never do such a thing to sweet Yenna."

"How *dare* you?" The nurse, Yenna, scolded him from behind.

Elnok turned to find her in her usual garb, beige linens and a matching face scarf. Her green eyes and dark eyebrows were set against brown skin.

She grabbed his arm and shoved him to the side, forcing him to sit on his ass next to Orym's cot. With anyone else, he would grab their arm and twist until the bone broke, but he did no such thing to Yenna. She took good care of Orym.

"This needs to end, Jasper," she whispered, her grip strong despite her small arms.

Jasper.

The alias by which Elnok was known in this coastal village, for his true name would only render unwanted suspicion. Better to remain anonymous under the guise of an unimportant, petty thief than someone of importance. Although, with the ship docking soon, it wouldn't matter much longer.

"My dramatics wouldn't be needed if you'd inform the guards to let me through," Elnok replied as he raised a brow, "But I think you rather enjoy a good show."

"What I would enjoy is if you let us do our jobs and not frighten our patients," she hissed.

"Oh come now, Yenna, he's just bringing some much-needed excitement to our otherwise dreary lives," Orym teased as his brown eyes shone against his pallid skin, "Isn't that right, *Jasper*?"

"A duty I take more seriously than most," Elnok said with a wink, readjusting his face cloth over his nose.

He tossed the bag to Orym, his friend laughing loudly as he held the piece of bread in his hand, ripping off a bite and stuffing it in his mouth.

"I won't lie," Orym said, crumbs falling from his mouth, "I had my doubts, but I suppose you *are* the better thief."

Yenna groaned.

Elnok patted the nurse's shoulder. "No need to complain, seeing that Orym will be walking out of this piss-stained infirmary and joining me for some shitty ale come nightfall."

Orym's eyes widened. Yenna batted Elnok's hand off her arm.

"You found medicine?" Orym whispered.

"The Vutrorian ship will be docked within the hour," Elnok replied, "and with it, the request I sent weeks ago."

Orym's face stilled.

"A Vutrorian vessel?" Yenna said, desperation in her voice as her brows knitted together, "Perhaps the gods have heard our prayers."

"Or perhaps my letter was well-received," Elnok countered as he gripped Orym's shoulder. A well of emotion rose in his chest, the blood dripping down his friend's chin was a sure sign the sickness would take him in the coming weeks.

But Elnok refused to watch his friend die.

Orym struggled to raise his arm as he gripped Elnok in

return. What had once been thick, corded muscle under golden skin was now small and frail, having lost all its color. His eyes were the only part of him that still looked alive.

"The medicine is only a rumor," Orym choked out.

Elnok clenched his jaw as he said, "If Vutror wasn't sourcing it from Estea, I wouldn't believe it either."

"*Estea*?" Yenna interrupted, "Those magical imbeciles wouldn't help anyone outside of their godsforsaken forest even if they knew we were all to die tomorrow."

"Did someone say Estea?" a woman lying in a cot next to them said as she lifted herself to face them. Her skin was sheet white and blood stained her chin.

"Now's not the time for your stories," Yenna said in a singsong voice, "Go back to sleep—"

"My brother wanted to go to Estea. He braved Lhaal Forest two years ago to do it." The woman continued, her arms shaking, "Our family's grain field had finally withered; the last one in our village. But my brother refused to accept it and made to demand food from Estea. He'd been told their women could create crops from the ground with their magic—crops that were ready to *harvest.* Can you imagine? Growing grain to bake it that same day? What I would give for a single fucking piece of bread again!" Tears began to well in her eyes, "But he never returned."

"No one returns from Lhaal," another person voiced, a man on a different cot, "Your brother was a damned fool for such a venture."

"Everyone," Yenna pleaded, "Please, go back to sleep—"

"He was one of our best fighters," the woman argued.

"Doesn't fucking matter how good of a fighter he was," the man replied, "Nothing can get past the monsters that live in that devilish forest."

"A Dynami can," she argued.

The man on the cot laughed bitterly, "Magical, blubbering

Esteans. Disgraceful to call them warriors. If it wasn't for their magic, they'd be useless."

"I heard a Dynami was spotted along the coast," Orym said as he coughed.

"What?" the woman replied, "But they're only meant to go as far as Vutror. Why would they be on the coast?"

"Bet someone stole a piece of that stone while they were sleeping," the man cackled.

"Someone stole a piece of orodyte from a Dynami?" the woman asked, her voice rising.

"I've heard they kill for that sort of thing," Orym said.

"What if they're going on a killing spree?" the woman said, eyes wide and shaking, "Are we all going to die before this sickness takes us?"

Suddenly she erupted into shouts. Surprise took over the infirmary as others joined in the woman's panic. Nurses rushed to their patients' sides with calming words and bowls of gutted, cooked fish.

"This is your fault," Yenna hissed to Elnok and Orym as she stood.

Elnok didn't have time to reply as she left, aiding her fellow nurses as they fought to maintain the peace in the infirmary.

"I think she's rather fond of you," Orym said with a small grin.

"Her consistent threats are certainly charming." Elnok smirked.

"She doesn't talk much until you show up, you know."

"And you don't seem to notice the way she can't take her eyes off of you."

He grinned, more blood sliding down his chin. "I suppose I'm quite the looker at the moment, aren't I?"

Elnok scoffed, ignoring the way his chest tightened. It'd only been three weeks since their stay at a nearby village, staking out an expensive jeweler and enacting one of their best, most elaborate heists in years. They'd ate well those next few days and drank like royals, wearing one of the crowns they kept for themselves.

The next morning, Orym vomited blood.

"But you're serious?" Orym continued, "You sent a letter to Vutror? For medicine?"

"I did."

"So you're telling me they're docking a ship that carries a medicine coveted by *everyone* in response to a common villager's request?"

"I can be *quite* convincing."

Orym fell silent, his smile fading as his eyes turned to the ceiling.

"If you go on that ship, Elnok, I'm going to kill you."

"That would certainly put a damper on things," Elnok replied.

"You can't risk being recognized."

"And you can't die."

They stared at one another for a long moment.

"I'll recover," Orym said, his body too sick for him to lift his head, "I'm young—*we're* young—a mere twenty-six years of age. And besides, there are people in here who are faring far worse than me. They need the medicine."

"There's no recovery from the sickness without medicine, Orym. I don't care how optimistic you are. And I can't get enough for everyone, so if I give it away to one person, then more will want it and—"

"You don't understand what this is like," Orym snapped.

Elnok dropped his hand from his shoulder.

"Gods, just… listen to me for one fucking moment before you get yourself killed, alright?" Orym continued, "This sickness has had me for only two weeks, and it's been nothing short of torturous. Others have been in this pain for months; I can't take the medicine in good conscience." He stared at

Elnok with steely eyes, "Even if you bring it to me, I'll refuse it."

Elnok flared his nostrils. Damn his friend and his high morals.

"Damn my high morals," Orym said with a sly smile, "That's what you're thinking, innit?"

"You really are a worthless thief, and an even worse fisherman," Elnok replied. He knew any further argument wouldn't get them anywhere. His friend had made his decision, and Elnok hated and loved him for it all the same.

"You surpass the master and what do I get? Insults," he said with a wink.

Orym shut his eyes and feigned a snore as Yenna made her way back to the cot. Elnok restrained himself from slapping his friend in the face as he caught her stare, her hips swaying to and fro as she crouched down next to them.

"Sang him to sleep again?" she inquired, a mischievousness in her tone. The infirmary was back to its usual lull. "Perhaps we should hire you, if you weren't such a bothersome fool."

"I'm afraid my earnings would take a real dive if I switched occupations," Elnok replied.

She clicked her tongue as her gaze roamed his chest then back up to his eyes.

"I know your name isn't *Jasper*, by the way. No one else cares enough to realize it, but no common man could convince a Vutrorian vessel to his aid." She paused. "Whoever you are, just make sure you actually start… doing something."

"And what exactly do you mean by *doing something*, Yenna?"

"I followed you for a few nights when you first entered town, but from what I saw, you don't do much." The woman raised a brow, "You just… run around, steal food, and bring it back to your friends."

Heat rushed into Elnok's face. He hadn't been careful these past few weeks, his desire to see Orym healed overshadowing his typical pattern of staying close to the shadows. But perhaps it was more than that. After he sent that letter to Vutror, he'd grown careless. There would be no point in hiding much longer.

"There's something else you should know," she whispered, "everyone's trying to say this sickness lasts for a few months, and according to past cases, it did. But more and more cases are proving otherwise. Now, it's taking people in three weeks or less."

Elnok's breathing faltered. "That would mean…"

"Orym has a week, maybe less."

He formed his hands into fists, his fingers digging into his skin.

She continued, "Whoever you are, this town could use your help. In fact, this entire continent could, so if you have any kind of power that could change things around here—"

"I'll be back tonight." Elnok avoided her gaze as he stood. "Keep him out of trouble."

He ignored the wounded look in Yenna's eyes as he left the premises. The guards sputtered, questioning how he'd gotten into the infirmary. Elnok ignored them as the Vutrorian ship approached the harbor.

He knew Orym wouldn't like his plan, knew the man's heart was too wide and too deep to accept a cure that others wouldn't have access to. But Elnok found no qualms in letting others fall to misfortune if it meant those he cared for lived.

It didn't matter if Orym had one week left or three months. He'd get him the medicine today.

Orym would be cured by sundown.

CHAPTER 3
A PRICE

Torches lined the high sandstone walls of the temple's altar room. Sylzenya's bare feet slapped against the cold marble floor. Yellow and orange stained-glass windows covered the ceiling, casting a warm glow onto the willow growing in the center of the room. Large roots protruded from the ground, like ripples in a pond before they dove deep into the earth.

She would seek her goddess, Aretta, through these roots, but she needed to calm herself first. The anger from her father's betrayal swelled inside her veins, burning against her skin, causing the cut along her back to ache. It was his fault she'd lost her connection to Aretta, his fault their people would starve to death.

"No one's communed with our goddess through these roots in centuries, Syl," Nyla spoke from behind, her friend's voice echoing along the sandstone walls.

Sylzenya closed her eyes tight. "I'm aware."

"Then why do this to yourself?"

"Because I don't have another choice."

Nyla shook her head. "I know you're upset, but you know orodyte serum can't be extracted from our bodies once it's entered our blood." Her friend's warm hand gripped her shoulder. "Let's take this slow, alright? You've already lost too much blood to accomplish this rite properly."

Sylzenya turned, body rigid.

"My father poisoned me, Nyla."

"I know—"

"He *stole* my power from me. He's doomed our entire kingdom."

"Sylzenya, please—"

"They sacrificed my childhood for this, and they take it away without a second thought? Dooming not just our people, but their daughter with it?" Sylzenya's face burned hot as she curled her fists.

Nyla stilled, her amber eyes filled with pity. "Your parents are… unwell. But this doesn't mean we need to find a solution right now."

"I still might have some power left, and if I do, I intend to use it." Sylzenya peeled her friend's hand off of her shoulder. "If you're truly my friend, you'll stand with me, not against me."

"I am *always* with you, Sylzenya," she retorted, "but there's a lot to consider. It's why I urge you, at the very least, to delay what you're about to do."

"There's no time," Sylzenya replied, gaze turning to the willow's roots, "I need to make this right before word gets out that my power is…" she paused, clearing her throat, "I'm going to seek Aretta's Willow. Its sap can heal any ailment, so it should be able to do the same for this poison."

A taut silence spanned between them.

"Not only is the tree a myth, we don't even know if it's capable of restoring power."

"And that's why I'm going to seek Aretta—for her direction and counsel."

"Is there nothing I can say to dissuade you from this?" Nyla asked.

Sylzenya's jaw hardened. "Our life's path is that of a Kreena, our sole purpose to provide for our people. And pain is merely the price we pay for it."

"This isn't the time to use scriptures."

"Then what times are they made for? When everything is bright and good? I'd thought they were meant for times when we needed hope."

Her friend stared long and hard at her. Letting out a deep breath, Nyla finally stepped back, placing both hands over her heart and bowing. Sylzenya returned the gesture, one of respect and honor on behalf of their goddess.

Kneeling before the tree and its roots, Sylzenya bowed her head. She heard Nyla's whispered prayers echo along the walls behind her.

Smooth, cold bark slid underneath her palm. Bright green leaves brushed against each other. Closing her eyes, she listened for her goddess' heartbeat. The familiar rhythm she sought out not only when she was creating vegetation in the gardens, but also in the cold nights when she yearned for her parents.

Please, Aretta, don't abandon me just yet.

Something soft sounded in her ears.

Thump.

Sylzenya dug her nails into the root, splintering the bark.

Thump.

Desperation gave way to searing pain, the cut along her back reopening.

Golden threads twirled out of the ground, slow and unsteady. Circling her arms, her goddess' power faltered, the threads flickering in and out of focus.

She was running out of time.

Everything around her swirled into bright colors—purples, oranges, greens, and blues—like a clear piece of orodyte reflecting the sun.

Sylzenya's head spun.

She willed herself to remain present as the colors brushed past her vision, illuminating before her a willow as tall as the temple itself. But unlike the willow inside the temple, the tree was as clear as crystal. Thin lines of gold ran up and down its base, into the limbs, and filling the leaves.

The mythical tree—Aretta's Willow.

Aretta, hear my prayer, she pleaded. *Where might I find your tree?*

Only silence answered her, the golden light continuing to run up and down the tree.

A flapping of wings brushed by her ear. A bird landed on one of the tree's many limbs, its gray and white feathers paired with deep blue eyes. It sat on the branch, staring at her, a thin gold object held in its beak.

A ring.

A bold question to ask, a voice whispered.

Sylzenya's back ached. The strange voice filled her ears, neither male nor female, caught in between a song and a growl.

Please, Sylzenya begged the voice. *I've been poisoned and require healing, or else all of Estea will starve.*

For life there is a price, the voice answered. *And only in pain can it be made whole.*

Sylzenya flinched at the use of the scriptures.

Before she could reply, the bird flew from its branch and landed in front of her. Its gaze pierced hers, and she knew the voice belonged to the creature.

I do not fear pain, Sylzenya replied.

A lie.

I would not lie about this.

There is more pain than that which carves into your back, Sylzenya Phatris.

The bird flipped the ring in its mouth. Sylzenya's vision blurred, but she quickly called the tree back into focus. The last remnants of her power were fading, and she wouldn't let this warning deter her from her path.

Are you Aretta? Sylzenya inquired.

Aretta sacrificed herself centuries ago to destroy her brother, the god of chaos, Distrathrus. I would think you, a daughter of her temple, would know this, the bird answered. *Ask your question, Sylzenya.*

Does Aretta's Willow live? she asked.

It does.

Her heart pounded hard in her chest. *Do you know where it lies?*

I do.

Can it restore my power?

The bird blinked. *Yes.*

Please, show me the way.

There is a price for such knowledge.

Sylzenya took a deep breath. *Is there another way to restore my power? To save my people?*

The bird blinked twice.

If you are to restore your power and protect your people, then Aretta's Willow is the only way.

Name your price.

The price for life will always be pain. The bird tilted its head. *But you will regret choosing this path. I have seen it.*

Sylzenya gripped the splintered root until it pierced her fingers, the crystal willow fading before her. She didn't have time to consider consequences, for nothing could be worse than her purpose ripped from her body.

The only regret I would have is failing when I'm needed most.

The bird blinked again before dropping the gold ring onto the dirt.

Very well, Sylzenya Phatris.

It used its beak to draw a circle the size of Sylzenya's palm. The piece of earth flashed a bright gold, the circle rising up from the soil, becoming something solid and beautiful: A gold compass, overlaid with a thin piece of glass. Inside it, there were no etchings, no directions—nothing but a thin stream of light as its needle.

A compass made by Aretta's hands, its needle crafted from the bark of her willow, the bird said. *Find the compass, and you will locate the willow, for the tree refuses to stay in one place for too long, and the needle will always point towards its home.*

Sylzenya's eyes widened, *Where is this compass?*

It resides in the temple. As the compass points to Aretta's Willow, so it rests within the form of another.

It resides in a willow?

The bird nodded. *This is all I know, for it was hidden centuries ago by someone else's hands.*

Sylzenya frantically thought of every willow in the temple. The trees were in every room, on every corner. There were hundreds.

Whose hands?

There are many things that I cannot say, even if I wish to. But I will say this—be wary of who you trust.

Sylzenya shuddered. *Who are you?*

But the bird only hopped closer to her, its thin clawed feet planted in the center of the ring.

For life there is a price, and only in pain is it made whole, Sylzenya Phatris. Your choice has been made, and so your consequence is set in blood and stone.

The gold ring erupted into a harsh light. She turned away, eyes watering from the spectacle. But when its light ebbed, she looked again, its golden sheen turned crimson, slowly melting until it became blood. It seeped into the soil, the ground becoming translucent, exposing a clear piece of orodyte hidden beneath the earth. The blood filled the stone until it burned a bright gold.

Suddenly, the bird shrieked.

Sylzenya gaped as a webbing of twigs sprung from the earth. It circled the bird like a claw, crushing it. Blood dripped from the ball of twigs, the bird's neck bent in an odd shape, its white and gray feathers poking out at strange angles.

"What is this?" Sylzenya shouted, eyes wide, "What price must I pay?"

Pain as sharp as a dagger sliced across her back as everything swirled, her vision causing her head to pound as she shouted for her goddess.

Then everything gave way to darkness.

Sylzenya.

Her name echoed through her ears like a whisper.

Sylzenya.

The voice grew louder.

"Sylzenya!"

She opened her eyes, fresh air filling her lungs as she sucked in as much of it as she could hold. Her body ached as if a tree had crushed her.

"By Aretta's blood," Nyla cursed. "If you *ever* do that again, remind me to strangle you first."

Sylzenya coughed while Nyla held her like a newborn babe. Despite the pain and the death of the bird, hope bloomed in Sylzenya's chest.

"It worked, Nyla," Sylzenya said, voice hoarse and lungs burning.

Nyla's brows rose to her hairline. "You found the tree?"

"Not exactly." She coughed again. "But I might be able to find it. There's a comp—"

Doors slammed against stone, interrupting her. Voices of all kinds echoed through the room, but one of them stood out from amongst the rest.

"You will see to it that Theraden Phatris and his wife remain in the dungeons under stern watch," the High One said to the priestesses that followed him into the sanctuary. "There will be no trial, for we all saw his treason with our own eyes. Now go and make sure the newly ordained Kreenas are accounted for. Have each of them checked thoroughly. We will save the celebratory banquet for another day."

The priestesses turned and left, but the High One's gaze

latched onto Sylzenya, and she saw something she'd never witnessed from him before.

Panic.

"What is this?" The High One questioned as he took long, quick strides towards her and Nyla, "What's happened?"

Sylzenya couldn't find the words so Nyla spoke instead.

"She tried to commune with Aretta."

The High One kneeled before them, his cold hand running along Sylzenya's face. The chill caused her to flinch.

"She's lost too much blood," the High One replied, "I'll take her to the infirmary. Nyla, go ahead and return to your chamber. There will be a priestess waiting for you."

"Yes, Your Grace," Nyla said as she passed Sylzenya to the High One's extended arms. "We'll talk later, Syl, alright?"

Sylzenya forced a wary smile. "Alright."

Never had the High One done anything like this before. He'd walked alongside her, talked with her, but never had she experienced any kind of touch from him except a pat on the shoulder. She meant to steady her posture while he carried her through the temple's halls, winding through the many corridors decorated with torches, vines, and flowers, but her strength was gone. She slumped against his chest instead, which was somehow just as cold as his hands.

"You must rest, Sylzenya, understand?"

The concern in his voice surprised her.

"I understand," she wheezed.

They finally made it to the infirmary, a room full of shelves lined with glassware of all shapes and sizes. Vines and roses wove up and around the walls and ceiling.

He instructed one of the nurses to fetch herbs for Sylzenya's cut as well as for sleep. He placed her face down on a cot made of feathers and covered in soft satin. When the High One crouched down to her eye level, she couldn't help notice how his yellow gaze looked brighter than usual–more alert.

"Were you able to commune with Aretta through the roots?" His voice was a low whisper.

That same hope from earlier filled her chest, but then it doused like water on flames.

What was she going to tell him? She saw a bird and it told her to find a legendary willow with a compass? It sounded absurd. It *was* absurd. She'd just been poisoned, and now she was bleeding so much she couldn't see straight.

Explaining this would be impossible, and she needed to know for certain if she believed what she'd seen with her own eyes before burdening her leader. When her parents had left her to the temple, the High One had been the one who recognized her power. He'd been there when she needed comfort. He'd been the one who stood by her when she needed it most.

He'd given her a purpose.

She didn't need to worry him more after today's events.

She heard herself answer as if she was somewhere far away, "I don't know." The pain in her body ached and scraped against her bones.

The High One's ageless face didn't change, his eyes still steadied on hers.

"You'll get your power back, I'll make sure of it," He stood. "I'll be holding a dinner for all the Kreenas tomorrow evening. I will need you to be in attendance as well, so please, get as much rest as possible."

Silence.

"Yes, Your Grace," she finally whispered.

As Estea's leader left the infirmary, Sylzenya ingested everything the nurse offered her. And as sleep slowly took her away from her despair, she saw the bird's deep blue eyes as it held the gold ring in its beak. It stood upon the compass, the needle bright and pointing towards a glowing, crystallized willow.

Your choice has been made, the bird's voice echoed as she drifted to sleep, *and so your consequence is set in blood and stone.*

CHAPTER 4

ELNOK'S DECISION

Elnok spun the gold ring around his pinky finger. The distant familiarity of its weight brought memories of dark gray stone and gilded chalices, deep blue jewels and the reek of wine. It'd been over a decade since he'd worn it, and while a part of him wished he'd thrown it into the sea all those years ago, he'd known better.

It was the reason he could request Orym's medicine.

Elnok flexed his hands as he and his group of thieves approached the blood-stained dock. The high noon sun shimmered on the white-capped waters as the gangway creaked underneath their weight. His black cloak billowed around his knees, the rope tied to his hip lightly patted against his leathers, and the blade of his short sword glinted in the sharp sunlight.

Dockworkers lined the gangway, their ragged beige clothes topped with thin sheets of metal. Their backs straightened and their eyes faced the ground, the sky, the brown-husked ship, anywhere they wouldn't catch Elnok or his crew's gaze.

The stench of their fear lined the stains of their armpits.

These weren't warriors—not even close. They would sooner squeal and abandon a fight than attempt to draw their poorly crafted swords. Yet Elnok still narrowed his gaze and unsheathed his small dagger, making sure each dock worker acted accordingly.

In a world where resources dwindled and food had become scarce, survival was a privilege easily squandered. If Elnok was to protect himself and his crew, he had to be seen as heartless—ruthless. Everyone did. It was a mask he hated, but he'd worn it for so long, he often wondered if he'd lost himself to it.

Then again, perhaps everyone had.

"What's this?" a scratchy voice said from behind, "Someone tryin' to steal our spoils?"

Elnok stopped on the gangway, turning to face the band of pirates that had *laid claim* to the village.

"Merely retrieving that which has been requested," Elnok replied with an air of nonchalance.

"*Right.*" Their captain laughed as she chugged the remainder of her beer, throwing the mug into the dirt afterward, "And I'm the long-lost Prince of Vutror. Now that we've acquainted ourselves, why don't ya pay yer mind and step away from what's ours, *boy*."

Elnok raised a brow, the heated gaze of his crew falling on him. Slowly, he made his way back down the gangway, sliding his fingers through his shoulder-length black hair.

"And where did you just hail from? The Northern Sea?" Elnok inquired as he stepped in front of the pirate.

The woman met him with a smile full of silver and gold.

"Yer dumber than ya look, boy. Course it was the Northern Sea. Years on end in its unruly wake." She spit on the ground as her posse laughed. "Seen more pillages and battles than ya've probably encountered yer small little life. Now, if ya wouldn't mind—"

Elnok steadied his dagger underneath the woman's chin before she had the chance to counter. She lurched back, eyes wide, but Elnok grabbed her shoulder and brought her close.

"I'd reconsider your next move," Elnok whispered.

The pirates went for their weapons, but Elnok's crew drew theirs first, a warning for the pirates to step away.

They obeyed.

"Here's how this is going to work, Pirate," Elnok whispered, "I'm going to let you waddle on back to your riches and spoils this village has brought you. I don't care what you do to this place, but I promise you, you'll only find death if you attempt to board this ship." Elnok leaned in closer. "Understood?"

The pirate coughed, her throat bobbing on the pointed blade.

"Yer not just a common thief, are ya?" she questioned, sweat beading at her temple.

Elnok smiled. "Not quite."

The pirate backed away, eyes frantic as she readjusted her gaudy hat and puffy laced shirt.

"They can have this load of shit," she yelled, loud enough for every passerby to hear, "Vutrorian vessels aren't worth the damn trouble anyhows."

Elnok's crew laughed as the pirates scuttled away, but he couldn't manage anything more than a thin smile as he turned back to the ship.

"Stay on the gangway and make sure no one else boards," Elnok instructed, "This won't take long."

"Orym said we should accompany you," one of them stated.

"Orym's ill and doesn't know what he's saying," Elnok retorted.

"Don't think we haven't taken note of your comings and goings these past few weeks. We know something troubles you beyond Orym's sickness, and we've all agreed we aren't going to leave your side—"

"This is not up for discussion," Elnok snapped.

Their eyes grew wide as each of them lowered their

weapons. Elnok's head pounded as he dropped his shoulders. Nerves rarely got the better of him, but this day was never supposed to happen. Necessity overruled preference.

"Orym is dying and this could be his only chance of survival; I need to know you will follow my orders," Elnok said. "I need to know I can trust my crew."

A moment of silence was followed by a group of wary nods.

"I'll issue my signal if I need assistance," Elnok said.

Salt and wind filled his lungs as he walked the remainder of the gangway, meeting a lone guard at the ship's entry.

"Away, scum," the guard said as he blocked Elnok's path, his grotesquely clean armor causing Elnok's eyes to water. "Or your blood will join the stains on your village's flimsy dock."

Elnok grinned. "Are these the manners the royal guards are taught nowadays? A shame."

"Watch that mouth, boy—"

"Everyone today keeps calling me that: *Boy*. But I daresay I stand a good few inches taller than yourself, not to mention my arms are twice the size of yours. Are we certain you didn't sneak on this ship to fulfill some boyhood fantasy of yours?"

The guard gripped his hilt as he stepped forward.

"One more word out of you and that mouth of yours will be wiped clean off—"

Elnok raised his hand, the glint of the ring shining in the guard's eye.

"And what exactly is this supposed to…" His voice trailed off, his eyes studying the ring. His pale skin turned sheet white. "You—You? But it can't be—"

"Will you continue to make a member of Vutror's royal family wait outside his own ship?" Elnok questioned, "Or must it be *your* blood I spill on this dock?"

The guard gulped, eyes frantically glancing from Elnok's ring to his face. But the truth was as undeniable as his royal signet ring. The guard whispered a flippant apology as he stepped to the side, welcoming Elnok, the long-lost Prince of Vutror, onto his family's oldest and most prized of vessels.

"Now," Elnok said to the guard, "Where's my brother?"

The guard gave Elnok an unruly amount of apologies as he left him at the gaudy entrance to his brother's quarters. Elnok spun the ring faster and faster on his pinky finger, clenching his jaw as he ground his teeth. Ten years since he'd last seen his brother. Ten years since he'd had anything to do with Vutror.

And yet, it still didn't feel long enough.

Sucking in a deep breath, Elnok pushed open the doors, the large pieces of hand-crafted wood bowing before him.

Windows looked out over the rippling shore. Waxed candles lined the sills, dripping onto the floors and pooling around the metal legs of a telescope pointed skyward. A green velvet chair, placed behind a great oak desk covered in tattered parchments, bent quills, and countless empty glasses, faced the wide windows. Above the chair and against the wall hung a gold-laden frame with the unmistakable artwork depicting his brother. Dark hair, a wily grin, maroon clothes stitched with jewels, and the same pale green eyes as Elnok.

Tosh Rogdul, the King of Vutror.

"It's been some time, brother." Tosh's grating voice echoed through the room.

Elnok tensed as his brother's dark figure stood from the chair. Tosh's back faced him, his oily black hair longer than that of the portrait. His silk tunic hung loosely off him, as if it were far too large for his frame. In his hand was a glass of wine.

Elnok spun the ring faster.

"So it has," Elnok replied, his voice cold as ice. "You received my letter?"

A pause.

"I wouldn't be here otherwise," Tosh said, taking a sip of wine.

The sharp stench of it swept into Elnok's nose. He choked on his saliva, refusing to allow the memories to push into his mind.

He fucking hated that wine.

But then Tosh turned, and Elnok's face fell. His brother's skin appeared waxen, like a skeleton donning a piece of thin flesh. His eyes were large and stained red, his green irises bright and unsettling. Elnok now realized his clothing wasn't too large, but Tosh was too small. A walking thing of death. This looked different than Orym's sickness. Worse, somehow.

He couldn't help but take a step back.

"All this time," Tosh whispered, "I thought you were dead."

Elnok's mouth curled downward, his fists clenching. He had no reason to feel sorry for his brother's current condition, whatever it may be. Tosh deserved nothing from him, especially his pity.

"Apologies for the disappointment," Elnok replied.

His brother's lip quivered, opening as if to say something only to take a long gulp of wine. He set the glass down with a clink.

"I come with an answer to your letter," Tosh said, "The medicine you requested is only a rumor. Estea has not graced us with such providence."

Elnok's chest hollowed.

"However, we have physicians back in the palace who have found ways to delay the sickness. If you wish to bring your friend aboard, we'll take him with us—"

"I'd never put Orym through your torment," Elnok interrupted.

He turned to leave.

"Elnok, wait." Tosh's voice cracked.

A rush of wind caught Elnok's hair as a large man appeared from a shadowed corner. He moved in front of him, blocking his way out. The man removed the hood of his long brown cloak, revealing golden-blonde hair that fell to his chest. He didn't look much like a Vutrorian guard, far too tall and muscular for the training they went through. But perhaps Tosh had been in need of more strength.

"The king is not finished," the golden-haired guard said, voice like thunder rumbling against the sky.

Elnok danced his fingers along his sword's hilt.

"I would hate for my long-awaited reappearance to result in bloodshed."

The man smiled. "I agree."

He didn't move.

"Perhaps I need to be more forthright with you," Elnok said as he unsheathed his sword.

The guard's smile widened as he removed his cloak and drew his long sword, the weapon twice as long as Elnok's shortsword. He didn't think much of it, having been trained in such combat, until he noticed the glowing yellow stone on the man's chest.

Sparks of gold shot up along the man's veins—his legs, arms, and neck—like lightning, crackling across his golden skin, his eyes burning brighter than the sun. Green and brown leather armor with intricate swirl patterns wrapped around his body; not the silver armor or black leathers of a Vutrorian soldier.

Elnok's blood turned cold.

"No outlander has ever fought me before," the magical Estean warrior—the Dynami—said, his magic causing the room to flicker with light.

Elnok should've known better, should've foreseen his brother's bloodlust after finding out he had lived. He'd somehow hired this Dynami to kill him; it would always be about Tosh maintaining the Crown, no matter how many times Elnok voiced never wanting it.

"Kharis," Tosh's weak voice said, "This isn't what we agreed upon—"

Blood pumping hard and fast, Elnok used his brother's distraction to slash at the Dynami's stomach. The Dynami parried without so much as a look, catching Elnok's swift movement with ease. Power heated against Elnok's skin as the magic sparked off the Dynami and onto his arm. He pushed away from the warrior's sword, readying his stance as Kharis laughed with gusto.

"*Clever*," Kharis said, "One move and I can already tell you fare better than most outlanders." His glowing eyes narrowed, "But I'm curious to know what you think of this?"

Elnok's footing faltered, his focus caught adrift as the Dynami rushed for him, but it was as if he'd melted into the air, only a streak of light until Kharis appeared in front of him, his sword leveled beneath Elnok's throat, the magic searing into his skin, the blade drawing blood.

"If you spare me, Estean, I'll owe you a great debt," Elnok offered, "Money, jewels, fish that won't cause your stomach to revolt—name your price, and I'll retrieve it for you."

The Dynami huffed a laugh, "I have no need for such things."

"Then name your price."

"Listen to your brother and accept his offer."

The glowing blade was like flames licking at his neck.

"I suppose you'll have to kill me after all," Elnok replied.

The warrior frowned. "Is death truly a better option than simply listening to what he has to say?"

Elnok flared his nostrils. "Quite."

The Dynami's frown deepened.

"Kharis," Tosh said again, "Release him."

Eyes still narrowed, the Dynami released his hold. His magic vanished, the yellow stone on his chest losing its color, looking like clear quartz—hardly worth anything around these parts. Elnok dusted off his cloak, using this brief moment of respite to swerve around the warrior and get off this damned ship.

"Elnok," Tosh called after him, "If it's medicine you want, then there might be a way to get it."

Biting the inside of his cheek, Elnok stopped. It had been a mistake to call upon his brother for assistance—a desperate, impulsive attempt. And yet, he heard the pain in Tosh's voice; he hated how it made his skin crawl, almost as if a part of him still cared for the monster.

He couldn't stop himself as he turned.

Tosh's large reddened eyes stared at him. He gripped the desk as if he were in pain, the wine glass he'd been nursing having tipped over, spilling its contents onto the floor.

"And what would that be?" Elnok questioned, his grip on his sword so tight the skin of his knuckles cracked; a warm drop of blood ran down his hand.

Tosh looked towards the Dynami.

"There's a legend in our land," Kharis began. "In our goddess' last breaths, she saved our kingdom from her brother, Distrathrus, whose poison infected the continent and was about to infect Estea. To destroy him, our goddess had no choice but to sacrifice her life in the process. In her place, a great willow tree formed. The tree was imbued with her—the goddess of life's—power and has the ability to grant many things, one such thing is that of healing. One can surmise it could heal the sickness that sweeps this land."

Elnok took a deep breath, sheathing his sword. "And where is this tree?"

The Dynami crossed his arms over his chest. "That's what makes it a legend, Prince of Vutror. No one has seen it with their own eyes."

Tapping the hilt of his sword, Elnok leaned against the door frame.

"A mythical healing tree that no one knows the location of?"

The question hung in the room like the stench of Tosh's wine.

Elnok pushed off the wall. "If that's all there is, then I'll be taking my leave."

"The tree is real, and I plan to find it," the Dynami said, "but I need assistance."

Elnok laughed bitterly. "And where would you have us start? A journey through the entire continent? I've not enough time nor coin for such a venture."

"I believe it to be somewhere in Lhaal Forest," Kharis replied.

"The terrain filled with monsters? You do see how this is a terrible way to recruit someone to assist you, yes?" Elnok shook his head. "But what I'm wondering is why *you* are searching for it, Dynami? If the rumors are true, your people don't suffer from the sickness."

The warrior's smile faded. "I care for more than my people, Prince. Your side of the continent deserves to be in good health—"

"Spare me the heroics. At least explain to me why you would need *my* assistance in this endeavor?"

Tosh lifted a piece of parchment. "Vutror receives food and water from Estea while Vutror trades our weapons. We're in the middle of revising the negotiations, and I'm unfit for the journey to Estea to finish them."

Elnok straightened his back. "So *that's* what this is about. You're asking me to go be your placeholder for political machinations?"

"The High One will not accept negotiations from anyone who isn't in the Vutrorian royal line," Kharis countered. "And as a neighboring ally, you would be granted access to parts of the temple I'm not allowed to enter, parts where there could be historical information about the tree."

"I have no interest in playing as a political pawn, especially with a leader who refers to himself as *the High One*."

"Do you not harbor any compassion for your brother's current state? For the affairs of the Vutrorian people?"

"My own affairs are enough to handle at the present moment."

The Dynami shook his head. "If we do not try to find this tree, then your friend will die."

Elnok's fingers slipped from his sword's hilt. That was the point of this whole endeavor—to save Orym. But, to play politics in order to gain information about a legendary tree sounded like madness.

He spun the golden signet ring on his finger. There were no other options.

And Orym only had a week left.

"Well then," Elnok said as he leveled his gaze with the warrior's, ignoring Tosh whose gaze fell to his spilled wine. "You've won me over with your fool-proof plan. Now, how soon before we depart?"

CHAPTER 5
DESPERATE TIMES

Yellow stained-glass ceilings covered the temple's dining room in a warm glow, casting long shadows on the looping vines draped along the sandstone walls. The long oak table was simple in its natural cut, decorated with white candles in intricate gold casings and all sorts of fruits and vegetation from the temple's vast gardens. Greenery weaved in and out of the display, flowers still blooming as Sylzenya's fingers curled tight around the stem of her wine glass. It was made of the same crystal as the temple's stained glass, causing the red wine to appear black as she gently swirled it.

"Something amiss with the wine, Sylzenya?" the High One asked as his yellow gaze drifted to her glass.

His voice echoed in the vast hall. He'd requested her presence alone before the banquet began, and if she knew anything, it was to wait for him to explain why when he deemed it right.

Sylzenya feigned a smile. Ever since she woke a few hours earlier, the vision hadn't ceased playing in her mind. Aretta's healing willow. A compass with a piece of its bark. The bird with white and gray feathers. A gold ring turning to blood, filling an orodyte.

The knowledge had come with a price, a price she didn't understand.

She picked up her glass. "This is an event for the newly ordained Kreenas."

The High One smiled. "That's why you must drink."

"Your Grace," she replied, keeping her voice steady, "I'm not a Kreena."

He gripped her hand. "You will be."

Tears welled behind her eyes. The greenery on the table didn't respond to her fingertips brushing against its soft leaves. The faint sound of her goddess' heartbeat had faded after the vision, and she hadn't heard it since. Life around her felt cold and silent. And despite the vision, she still didn't know where to find the compass. If it truly resided in a willow, it could take months to find it. Years, even. But more importantly, she didn't know if the vision was even true.

"It's orodyte serum," Sylzenya said, "There's no cure, no herbs, no way of getting back my connection with Aretta."

"Sylzenya, you must trust me," the High One pressed, squeezing her hand, "I've invited you here because I'm going to announce to all the Kreenas and guests there's nothing to fear."

Her eyes widened. "Is the famine no longer a threat?"

He furrowed his brow, "Quite the opposite, I'm afraid. But only you and I will know this."

"What do you mean?"

The High One straightened, his posture mirroring his long nose. "I'm currently working on a cure for the orodyte serum, and the results are more than promising. Because of this, I'm going to announce tonight that you're on the mend."

The bird's voice echoed through her mind. *If you are to restore your power and protect your people, then Aretta's Willow is the only way.*

"I thought—" Sylzenya paused, her fingers stiffening. "I didn't know it could be extracted."

"Desperate times have called for creative measures," the High One replied, "You are Estea's greatest of Kreenas, and your parents stole this from you. Your title, your power, your provisions for our people—we can't let their failed attempt to ruin this kingdom come to fruition. Nor can we let them take away what's rightfully yours."

The wine swirling in her glass steadied, potent and thick. Ever since she woke, she had refused to think about her parents, and she didn't plan on discussing them now.

"It's going to take some time to make sure this cure is ready for you," the High One continued, "But we mustn't create any need for panic, so you're going to follow my lead. Do you understand?"

His cold hand gripped hers tighter, her heart battering against her chest.

Be wary of who you trust, the bird had warned.

"Even though your power is absent in this moment, you can still offer hope to our people. What happened at the Kreena Rite yesterday can be smoothed over. Assure them that you're on the mend. Let them know Aretta is with us."

She finally looked into his yellow eyes.

Be wary. But, this was the person who treated her like a daughter all these years. He offered her hope; encouraged her to find purpose; helped her find her way when her parents left her at the temple's steps. Even now, when her mother and father ripped her life away a second time, he invited her to the Kreena's table and offered her food and drink.

He offered her a *cure.*

The search for Aretta's willow was pointless. Even if she found the compass, the tree moved on its own accord. Who's to say it wouldn't attempt to evade her pursuit? Her people needed to outlive the famine, which meant she needed her power back as soon as possible.

Time would never be on their side.

"I'll do whatever I can to provide our people with hope," she replied.

His face relaxed, a smile pulling at his mouth. "Estea will survive this famine, and it will be because of you, Sylzenya Phatris," he lifted his wine glass. "To hope."

Sylzenya raised hers as well. "Hope," she whispered.

A soft clink followed by a sip. The wine stung her throat, its potency filling her nostrils and mouth. As she drank deeply, the bird's dark blue eyes flashed before her, its chilled voice echoing through her mind.

Your choice has been made.

She took another deep sip, ignoring the voice and the way her body tensed under its undeniable pull in her chest.

And so your consequence is set…

She drank more, more, more.

In blood and stone.

As she slammed her empty glass onto the oak table, the doors opened, and the banquet began.

"Welcome," the High One announced as he stood, splaying his hands wide. His long white robes etched with gold designs spilled like a waterfall to the marble tiles.

Sylzenya took a long gulp of wine. Kreenas and the guests silenced themselves, some of their faces stained pink while others a subtle red, the wine having already taken them into a state of blessed delirium.

"Tonight we celebrate the success of all the years you have spent learning and providing for Estea. Our kingdom would be nothing without the power Aretta bestows on Kreenas."

Everyone shouted in agreement.

Sylzenya took up a new glass of wine and drank.

"As you all know," the High One continued, "The famine

continues to spread across the continent of Druenia. Estea has been able to withstand its ravenous reach all these years; we remain blessed by our goddess." He paused, turning to Sylzenya. "There were eleven failures at yesterday's Kreena Rite, one of which, I'm happy to announce, failed due to a mistake that is already on the mend."

Whispers echoed in the large room.

Nyla kicked Sylzenya's leg under the table. Sylzenya widened her eyes in warning, but her friend didn't hide the shock in her features.

"Thanks to the work of our people, there's now a cure for orodyte serum," the High One announced. "Sylzenya Phatris will be back with us soon. Praise be to Aretta!"

Everyone echoed the prayer, clanking their cups in celebration. Kreenas turned to her, eyes wide and smiles even bigger as they asked question after question as to why and how. But the High One ceased everyone's chatter, outstretching his arm to Sylzenya—requesting her to speak.

Clearing her throat, Sylzenya stood, hands sweating and heart pounding as she raised her wine glass.

"Let it be known that Aretta has gifted us her favor from the very beginning," Sylzenya said, the expectant eyes of her fellow women urging her to continue, "She has blessed the High One with knowledge to restore the power stolen from me; I can already feel her power sing to me from the earth."

Small shouts of excitement and praise bounced through the air. Sylzenya refrained from gritting her teeth; she hadn't lied this blatantly before. Gathering herself, she forced her smile to her lips like she always did.

"But until my return, Estea has each one of you to look towards for strength. I believe you will do our people justice with the crops and waters you choose to create." She paused. "I will be back with you soon, and we won't let this famine touch Estea—not now, not ever."

Everyone raised their glass.

"*Praise be to Aretta!*"

Boisterous laughter filled the hall as Sylzenya returned to her seat, face hot and legs shaking. Nyla clanked her glass with Sylzenya's, giving her a nod and a smile.

The High One stood. "The kingdom-wide banquet isn't for another two harvest cycles. However, I've decided now is a perfect time to celebrate all your hard work. We will have it tomorrow night instead so we might bolster hope in our kingdom's faith. You will each work diligently in tomorrow's gardens to ensure there's enough food for every citizen of Estea for the event. Is that understood, Kreenas of Aretta's temple?"

The women responded with a resounding, "Yes, Your Grace."

"Excellent. Now, continue to eat and drink to your heart's content. Tonight we celebrate. Tomorrow we work."

Laughter and excitement took over the dining hall once again as the women obeyed the High One, returning to their plates full of steamed squash, bright greens, and dripping fruits.

"Sylzenya," he whispered, leaning close, "I must ask a rather important task of you."

Sylzenya straightened. The lie of her power returning made her stomach sick, so she drank another deep gulp of wine.

"Of course, Your Grace."

"The King of Vutror, Tosh Rogdul, will be arriving any day to discuss the trade treaty between our kingdoms. While we will supply him with armed escorts, I would like for you to accompany him whenever he requests access to the temple."

Sylzenya couldn't help but notice Nyla's amber gaze sharpening on her. The High One was quiet, but not enough for her friend's notoriously good ear.

"You would like me to acquaint him with our culture?" Sylzenya asked.

"Yes," the High One replied slowly, "and I would like for you to watch him closely."

Sylzenya narrowed her gaze. "Is there a particular reason he is in need of watching?"

"I will be rather busy these next few days, and I need someone I can trust to observe and relay any suspicions to me." He leaned in even closer, the sharpness of his yellow eyes piercing hers, "Outlanders can be… unpredictable. Their motives not always as clear as they present."

"I see," Sylzenya said, "This is quite the task, Your Grace."

"Indeed." He smiled. "I would not trust anyone else with it."

Heart pounding, she nodded. "I will do as you say."

"Very good."

The High One left his seat and made his way to the end of the table, conversing with other Kreenas.

"*I would not trust anyone else, my most powerful Kreena*," Nyla mocked in a low voice.

Sylzenya kicked her shin under the table. Nyla's yelp turned into a laugh.

"So while we work under the burning sun, you get to prance around with a king?" Nyla asked. "How unfair."

"Can you ever learn to mind your own business?" Sylzenya asked as she leaned forward, "Or better yet, can you ever just let me be?"

She smiled. "Where's the fun in that? Now, drink up. I don't want to be able to remember a single word I've said by tomorrow morning."

Sylzenya grinned, finishing her third cup. Everyone drank well into the night, the final wine bottle emptied, their white robes stained crimson.

Despite the High One's confidence, Sylzenya had difficulty ignoring the direction given to her in the vision. The bird had given her a path and spoken of a price. What could be more torturous than her current state of powerlessness?

The search for the compass was wishful thinking anyways.

Absurd.

Aretta's Willow had either been lost for centuries or was a simple myth. Searching for it would only be a distraction, and her people had survived this long without it. She had a cure on the way and a new task.

All she needed to do was focus on the Vutrorian King and his whereabouts. She'd keep a careful eye on him whenever he chose to see the temple, would report all his comings and goings, and anything he said or chose not to say.

Sylzenya's task was to protect her kingdom, and she would not fail again.

CHAPTER 6
A PLAN

Waves rocked the royal vessel as Elnok balanced a plate of grilled fish in his hand. His brother's crew did a fair enough job pretending the long-lost Prince of Vutror didn't just board the ship with his group of ragged thieves two days ago, but wary eyes found him nonetheless, their whispers just loud enough to carry on the wind.

I heard he went mad after the king and queen's death.

I heard he'd always coveted his brother's crown.

I heard he killed a guard during his imprisonment.

Rumors tossed to and fro like the sea crashing into the ship, but Elnok had little care for such talk. If they believed him to be the one who was mad, then so be it. After he found the healing tree in Estea, he'd never see these people again, for he had no intention of reclaiming his royal position. All he needed was his crew in good health, and he would be satisfied.

"Pay no mind to them, Your Majesty," the woman steering the ship called from above. "They're just bored, is all."

Elnok took a bite of the fish, the taste of salt and the sea causing his stomach to grumble for more. He'd been approaching a week since he'd eaten anything that wasn't dried seaweed.

"And what of you, Captain?" Elnok inquired.

The woman smiled, black hair sweeping across her deeply tanned face.

"Difficult to find boredom when steering this hefty of a ship."

"There are days that require far less effort, I'm sure."

She raised a brow. "I was told you'd been killed by pirates."

Elnok swallowed another bite of fish. "A worthy conclusion."

"Not really," the captain replied, "because if you were able to escape those Vutrorian dungeons as a young lad, then I found it hard to believe one of those lousy groups of marauders brought your end."

Elnok huffed a laugh, but then a cabin door slammed open, and his heart stalled in his chest.

Across the deck stood his brother, the King of Vutror. Tosh's eyes were wide and bloodshot, the remnants of wine dripping from his mouth, staining his white satin shirt. Elnok pulled a dagger from his belt and flipped it in his hand. Everyone on the ship ceased their work. Blood pumping loudly in his ears, Elnok took a step back, the plate of fish in his hands falling to the deck, shattering into pieces.

"*He's going to steal it from me*," Tosh yelled from across the deck.

Grab your sword.

But Elnok couldn't move. After all these years of training his body to obey in any circumstance, his arms and legs refused. No longer did he smell the brine of the sea, but that of damp stone. And no longer were there open skies with passing clouds but dark gray bricks and a rod of hot steel.

No longer was he a grown man, but a scared boy.

"Tosh, get back inside." The Dynami's thunderous voice came from inside the cabin.

The large Estean man walked out of the double doors, approaching Tosh like he was a newly caught fish about to slip from his grasp. But Tosh didn't respond as he drank the last of his wine, throwing the glass on the deck.

Fight. Run. Do something, dammit!

"He says nothing to deny it," Tosh shouted, "But I'll burn the truth out of you, won't I, Elnok?"

Elnok stood motionless, sweat pouring down his neck, the scars on his back searing with dark memories.

"Tosh, that's *enough*," the Dynami said, grabbing his wrist.

Tosh's eyes grew wild. "Away from me, Kharis, this isn't about you—"

"Tosh, listen to me—"

"I will not be handled like a common *peasant*!"

A burst of light erupted from Kharis, blinding everyone on the deck. Elnok staggered back, his scars aching with pain as he hit a wall. Limbs nimble once more, he found a doorknob and ran into a musty closet, slamming the door and locking it.

A thin stream of light filtered through a small round window. Brooms, mops, and cloths were organized in a neat heap. Elnok took one of the cloths and wiped his sweat-stained face. Breaths ragged and heart pounding, he leaned both hands on the wall and shuddered. His back still burned, memories of his time in Vutror's dungeons on the cusp of drowning him. Tosh stoking an iron rod, the tip a bright orange.

No.

He wouldn't allow himself to think on it. Not here.

Elnok removed his cloak and tunic, retrieving the pot of salve he'd stolen from a merchant three weeks ago. Dipping his fingers in the cool substance, he gently covered the rigid scars lining his upper and lower back. Flexible as he was, he could never reach the scars settled in the center, and so they continued to burn while the rest fell to ease with the salve.

He waited until Tosh's shouts ceased before emerging from the closet, his tunic sticking to his back from the salve.

All eyes on deck turned to him.

Tosh and Kharis were gone.

"I told you I was going to kill you for getting on this ship, Elnok," Orym wheezed as he laid on a cot in one of the ship's main cabins.

"Quite the threat for someone who can barely lift their head," Elnok replied.

Orym ignored him as Elnok helped Yenna with folding his friend's dirty sheets and supplying him with new ones.

"If it wasn't for him, you'd still be coughing up dust in the village's infirmary, and I'd still be feeding you whatever kind of disgusting gruel we scrounged that day," Yenna scolded.

"Don't encourage his behavior," Orym retorted.

Yenna's hands stopped their work. "Talk to me like that again, and I'll let that Dynami handle you instead."

Orym's pale face stained red.

"Apologies, Yenna, it's just…" He trailed off as he locked eyes with Elnok. "I was told your brother threatened to burn you."

"He's never been the best with his words," Elnok replied, ignoring the way his back still ached.

"Has he done so before?"

Elnok shrugged.

"*Elnok.*"

He raised a brow as he replied, "Orym."

His friend sighed. "Yenna, can you give us a moment?"

The nurse eyed Elnok as she left the room.

"We need this ship docked at the next closest port," Orym said as the door closed with a thud.

Elnok continued to fold the sheets. "Are you in need of something this ship doesn't have to offer?"

"You told me you were a fugitive of the king."

"I was."

"You're a fucking royal of the Rogdul line. You lied to me."

"Omitting information that no longer reflects my life isn't lying."

"Can you just be real with me for one godsdamn moment, Elnok?" Orym snapped, his brown eyes wide, "Ten years we've lived our lives on the run and not once have you mentioned your family. I never pushed because I assumed you would tell me when you were ready, but now I see it for what it's always been." He turned his pale face to the ceiling.

"And what is that?"

"You never really trusted me."

Elnok scoffed, "I'm putting my life on the line so this sickness doesn't kill you."

"I didn't ask you to do that."

"You didn't need to."

"What the fuck is that supposed to mean?"

"It means I *care*, Orym," Elnok replied, the sheet he'd been folding now in a clump on the floor. "I never talked about my family because I wanted to forget them—needed to. But if it really means that much, I'll let you know that after my parents were murdered, my brother drank himself mad and aimed all his anguish towards me."

Orym opened his mouth to speak, but he stopped, eyes softening.

"So when I escaped," Elnok continued, "and found you and our crew, I swore I'd never look back."

His friend took a wheezing breath. Blood dribbled from the side of his mouth and down his chin as his brows dipped.

"What did your brother do to you?" he whispered.

Elnok said nothing, allowing the silence to be his answer. Orym gave him a knowing look, his eyes roaming to Elnok's back—his scars.

"He's a cunt, then," Orym growled.

Elnok huffed a breath. "I've never taken to using one of my favorite parts of a woman as an insult quite like you have."

His friend paused, a small smile. "Fine. A bastard."

Elnok nodded. "A cunt-ish bastard."

Orym sat up, his laughter turning into a fit of watery coughs.

"Even cunt-ish bastards die some day, you know," Orym said.

Elnok stiffened.

He continued, "I don't think I would've laughed half as often during this godsdamned famine if it wasn't for you and all our misadventures." He paused. "But good things must come to an end, even if it's sooner than we had hoped. And just because I'm gone doesn't mean your life stops too, Elnok."

"What about Yenna?" Elnok asked, ignoring the way his chest squeezed far too tight.

"She'll be fine."

"The woman clearly isn't made for sea travel. She's puked every other hour at this point."

"Then let's get docked at the next port—"

"You know that's not what I meant."

His friend's face turned a pale red.

"None of us are ready to say goodbye to you, and we don't have to. I'm going to find this healing tree and you're going to be cured, alright? And right now, you're only wasting what little breath you have left by trying to convince me otherwise. Best we spend these last few hours together in shared happiness instead of anger."

Orym's gaze softened right as the door opened, the rest of their crew spilling in with plates of fresh fish and watered-down ale. Yenna joined shortly after, wiping what must've been a remnant of bile from her mouth as she smiled at Orym. He smiled back. Elnok joined in the eating and drinking with his crew, retelling old stories of their comings and goings along the coast over the past decade.

Laughter filled Elnok's heart until Kharis entered the cabin, his green and brown leather armor still on, the yellow stone on his chest aglow.

"Excuse me for the interruption, Prince Elnok," the Estean warrior announced, "but it's time we discuss our plans before our departure."

Everyone stiffened at the Estean's intrusion, but Elnok bade everyone to continue telling their stories. He followed Kharis to the main deck, the hot sun baking an intense heat into the wood of the ship. They approached the side of the vessel, the Dynami resting his forearms on the railing. A brisk wind swept Elnok's hair across his face, so he fastened it at the nape of his neck.

"Tell me what you know of Estea," Kharis said, his golden-blonde hair waving in the breeze.

"I thought you wanted to discuss a plan."

"I do. Understanding your perception of Estea will help."

Despite the sun glimmering along the calm waters, a dark storm cloud slowly approached from the horizon. All Elnok wanted was to spend these last few moments with his crew, but he joined the warrior and leaned his arms on the railing.

"Your kingdom only trades with Vutror because of the special weapons they provide. In return, your kingdom provides Vutror with shipments of food and water." Elnok paused, considering the days he'd spent with dust in his teeth and his stomach growling for anything other than seaweed. "But this also means your people willingly leave the rest of the continent in famine when you have the means to do otherwise."

He expected Kharis to counter, but the warrior only stared

forward, his dark eyes focused on the approaching storm cloud.

"What else?" he asked.

"I've heard rumors it's your women who tend to your crops through magical means," he replied, "but it's Dynameis like yourself that are the only beings capable of surviving Lhaal Forest."

"And what of the monsters that dwell in Lhaal?"

"There's little I'm certain about. Only that legend says those monsters were born of the bloated earth and carved with the intent to kill. And, if it weren't for these creatures, the people of this continent would've taken your people to war when the hints of famine and drought showed themselves ages ago. You Dynameis would've killed them with ease, but they would've done it anyways."

Kharis' expression remained unchanged. "Would you have joined such wartime efforts?"

"No."

His brows raised as his mouth thinned. "Interesting."

"What is?"

"You speak about Estea with disdain, but you wouldn't jump at the opportunity to fight us if given the chance?"

"I'm not a fool, Dynami. While war against your kingdom ushers excitement just as much as strong ale and passionate cries for blood, it would only mean a quick death. Yet, I imagine that's what most people are desperate for nowadays—a way to feel like they did something at the end of it all." Elnok paused, voice lowering, "Not just sit in this dust and slowly waste away."

"And that is what you would prefer? To slowly waste away, as you say?"

Elnok paused, the salty breeze filling his lungs.

"I wish to survive."

They stood in silence as the storm cloud expanded its reach across the sky.

"It will take a day and a half to make it through Lhaal Forest. While the monsters will prove an obstacle, it's Estea that will be far more dangerous for you. So if you truly wish to survive, then you will heed my warnings with utmost caution."

Despite Elnok's efforts, sweat formed on the back of his neck.

"First, the High One, our leader, will not be pleased that you are arriving in Tosh's place."

"You said he wouldn't accept anyone besides those of royal blood."

"Correct, but it doesn't mean he wants to undergo trade revisions with someone who's been supposedly dead for ten years. He'll more than likely delay the meetings and gather as much information about you as he can, but I believe this will work well for what we need to accomplish."

"We're looking for a tree that heals people, and yet you speak as if we're inciting a revolution."

"Perhaps we are."

Elnok's muscles tightened as he pushed back from the rail.

"Our goddess, Aretta, died centuries ago, leaving the High One as her vessel of sorts. But if her tree remains, then this could challenge his position; it would mean a piece of her survived in the battle between her and her brother, Distrathrus."

"Seems like information you could've shared with me two days ago."

"I didn't think such a factor would deter you."

Elnok worked his jaw back and forth. "It might if it means this is an impossible task."

"I wouldn't be considering this if it was."

Elnok leaned back on the rails. "Then being under your High One's scrutiny sounds like a disadvantage."

"Not entirely. Since Vutror is an allying kingdom, you have free access to parts of the temple many of our people don't. Yes, you will have guards with you, but simply be under the guise you're interested in our history as you search for information about the goddess' tree; it will be your first time in Estea so I doubt it will cause much suspicion if you play it right." Kharis straightened, leaning an elbow on the railing as a smile peeled across his mouth. "And given your occupation this last decade, I'm guessing you're rather talented at such games."

"So it would be folly to inquire this High One about the mythical tree?"

Kharis' smile faded as he tapped a finger on the railing. "You said it yourself, Estea has the means of providing for all of Druenia if we so wished. And yet, we don't."

Elnok raised a brow.

The Dynami continued, his gaze narrowed, "While the High One is a pious man, he is prideful above all else. Your worries mean little to him. All he wants are the Vutrorian weapons. Wield that knowledge carefully, Prince Elnok, for even I'm uncertain why he covets them so greatly."

Elnok's brow creased. "Is there anything else I should know?"

"Be wary of our kingdom's Kreenas."

"I'm sorry… a what?"

"A Kreena. It's what we call Estean women who use our goddess' power to produce food and water. They're the most pious of our people. They've been dedicated to our goddess since they were young and know little else. My people, especially the Kreenas, are steeped in tradition; if you question anything in regards to our kingdom in front of them, they might report you to the High One."

"They sound like my personal hell."

"Except they're the most educated in subjects such as Aretta's Willow. Gaining the favor of one could be a tremendous help in finding the tree," Kharis countered.

"Let's hope it doesn't come to that," Elnok replied. "So that's the plan then? We make it through Lhaal, your High

One will observe me ruthlessly for days, and I'll scour the temple to find information about the tree?" Elnok tipped his head to the sky. "And what will you be doing through all of this?"

Kharis smiled. "Doing what I can to make the High One's observations of you… difficult."

Elnok couldn't help but smile in return.

"We've only got a week left before your friend's sickness takes him." Kharis held out his hand, "But I believe that in our joint effort, we can find Aretta's Willow."

Elnok stared at the open palm, still wary of the warrior's motive in all of this, for he knew even the most noble of acts were spurred by personal gain. He needed to be cautious in case betrayal lay ahead. Either way, he needed to get into Estea to find the tree, and there was no way of making it past the forest's monsters without a Dynami.

Elnok shook his hand.

"Here's to finding that tree, Dynami."

The warrior smiled, "Call me Kharis."

CHAPTER 7
NOTHING'S THE SAME

Willows covered the temple's gardens in a cool, green shade as the morning sun continued its journey into the sky. Golden power shimmered in the small grove, the threads of light wrapping around hands, forearms, and shoulders, slicing into freshly marred backs.

Sylzenya's own scar along ached as she stood—watching. The High One had asked her to assist the Kreenas that morning since the kingdom-wide banquet would be tonight. He told her that, although her power was gone, her presence would provide stability.

A sense of normalcy.

Yet nothing felt normal.

Aretta's Willow continued appearing in her dreams, its crystallized trunk and limbs streaming with her goddess' power. The bird, the compass, the gold ring—they haunted her, causing her to wake in fits, drenched in sweat. She ignored it; all of it.

Normal.

Everything needed to go back to normal.

Hands laced together, her fingernails cut into her skin, a

drop of blood running down her lightly tanned hands the same way Nyla's back bled as she created her fourth plum tree of the day. As Nyla focused on their goddess' power, Sylzenya stepped forward, picking one of the swollen fruits off the branch, swiping her thumb up and over its soft skin.

"Well?" Nyla asked, sweat shining on her pale skin while her disheveled black hair covered her eyes, "Does this one taste right?"

Sylzenya sank her teeth into the plum. Tart and sweet, the stone fruit's juice dripped down her chin, staining her skin a reddish purple. It was far better than the other three, which were either too sour or painstakingly bland.

"I'm impressed," Sylzenya replied, "I might even say it's delicious."

Nyla laughed, her smile mixed with an unmistakable look of pain.

"If you could tell the High One, I'd fancy myself a break."

"You're a Kreena now," Sylzenya replied, "you're free to rest as you find fit."

"*Sure* I can," she said through strained breaths.

"You need to take care of yourself, Nyla. He knows that."

"Look, you might be here because you enjoy the traditions, the rituals, and everything else we're asked to do, but you know why I'm here."

Sylzenya paused. "I thought your aunt's shop was doing better?"

"Just because she's doing better doesn't mean she can suddenly afford the crops she needs for her shop to make ends meet," Nyla grunted. "So, if you can put in a word for me with the High One, I'd appreciate it."

Her friend let out a long breath as she broke her palms from the ground, golden light retreating into the soil as the plum tree's growth stunted. She clawed through the dirt and grabbed the now yellow orodyte. As her friend stored the stone in her pocket and drank greedily from her waterskin,

Sylzenya took another bite of the plum, uncertain what she could possibly say to provide comfort.

With her power gone, there wasn't much to offer. The thought sliced through her deeper than her Kreena cut. Pain was a small price for the wellbeing of their people, and while her friend and companions still offered their power sacrificially, all Sylzenya could do was stand and watch.

Helpless.

She blinked away the tears forming in her eyes.

"If you're headed towards the healing baths, I'll join you," Sylzenya said as she helped Nyla to her feet, "My back hasn't healed properly since…"

Her throat closed, unable to say those final words.

"Since the rite," Nyla finished, dipping her brows.

Sylzenya brushed at her robe. "Whenever it's about to scab over, it breaks open again. It's not bleeding enough to be a true concern, but even the medicines the infirmary gave me haven't been able to help."

"I didn't know orodyte serum could prevent natural healing like that." Nyla paused, leveling her gaze, "I still don't understand why your father did it."

Mouth thinned, Sylzenya didn't respond.

Silence spanned between them as they walked along the dirt path towards the temple.

"Are you…" Nyla took a deep breath, "Are you going to visit your parents? In the dungeons? I'm sure the High One would let you if you want answers."

"*If* is the important part of that question."

Nyla frowned. "Why wouldn't you?"

"Because I don't want to see them."

"Syl, they're your parents. There must've been some twisted reason behind this inane act."

"They're unwell. Delirious. *Deranged.* I believe those are the words you're looking for," Sylzenya replied, fingers digging into the plum, piercing through its skin into its soft flesh.

"Whatever it was they tried to do, it didn't work, praise Aretta that the High One found your cure." She patted her shoulder. "A true miracle."

Sylzenya's spine tightened at her words. She hadn't told anyone, not even Nyla, about how he hadn't found a cure, but was *finding* one. While a part of her ached to tell her—for someone to know how deeply this emptiness consumed her—Sylzenya reminded herself it wouldn't be long before she was on the mend. The High One had promised to have it ready soon, and she trusted him. No need to cause panic for anyone, especially her closest friend.

Nyla continued, "If you're certain it wasn't out of some misplaced sense of love, then why not go get answers?"

Rolling the sticky plum in her hand, Sylzenya stopped walking. "It wouldn't change anything. The damage has been done, and seeing them would only cause me unnecessary grief."

She turned to Nyla. Her friend's face faltered, hands deep in her robe's pockets as she nodded her head, gaze averting to the dirt.

"I don't want answers from them. I just want my connection to Aretta restored, and things to go back to the way they were."

Nyla let out a long breath, her hands fiddling with her robe. "I'm not sure that's possible."

Sylzenya's eyes widened, worried Nyla might have guessed the High One's cure was untrue.

Frantic, Sylzenya said, "The High One's cure *is* working—"

"No, not that." She turned, her amber gaze piercing. "Syl, before the rite, no one outside of the temple knew your power was strong enough to sustain our entire kingdom. And yet, it was *you,* of all Kreenas, who was sabotaged." She lowered her voice to a whisper, "The High One's requested each Kreena be monitored tonight, but not by a priestess like usual, by

Dynameis. He's asked them to wear their full uniforms—swords, shields, orodytes…"

Sylzenya's stomach soured.

Nyla continued, "Nothing's going to be the same after this."

Mouth open, Sylzenya found herself at a loss for words. She'd been so focused on gaining her power back, she hadn't considered the implications of her parent's sabotage. It wasn't just an act against herself—it was an act that called something else into question.

Were there others who would've jeopardized their own people?

And if so, *why*?

A scuffing of dirt and metal interrupted her thoughts.

Men in green and brown leather armor entered the willow grove, each of the Dynameis wearing an orodyte on their chest plate. All of their stone's impurities had been depleted, each of them clear as crystal.

Nyla sighed. "Seems the Dynameis are here to boast of their latest adventures."

"Oh please, you love hearing about the monsters in Lhaal. Besides, they're only here to exchange their orodyte," Sylzenya said. "*Then* they'll talk for hours about their adventures."

"Just because the forest interests me doesn't mean I want to hear them boast for an eternity," she said, "And just when I was hoping to get a break."

Sylzenya rolled her shoulders back as two Dynamies approached. She recognized them, one with black hair and golden skin, the other with long red hair and a pale complexion covered with endless freckles.

Nyla's face flushed while Sylzenya cursed under her breath.

"Morning, Nyla," Marlo, the Dynami with black hair, greeted. "And you as well, Sylzenya. It's been a while, hasn't it?"

Sylzenya smiled with everything but her eyes, while Nyla crossed her arms.

"It has," Nyla replied, "seems you two have been busy. Are days like this ideal for swinging swords at monsters?"

"Fancy you say such things, because we *did* just get back from a mission in the forest." Westley, the Dynami with red hair, said with a broad smile.

"You don't say?" Sylzenya said, looking at the blood and gashes on their arms, "I would've never known."

"Not a fault of yours by any means," Westley replied, "We know living life in the temple must be limiting in your understanding of what happens outside of it. Perhaps, one day, we might be able to convince the High One to let you leave these grounds and experience something… a bit different."

In your dreams, Westley.

Memories of their night together three years prior flashed through Sylzenya's mind. Sweat-stained skin, clumsy touches, and a naivete she wished she could forget. Despite the celibacy law for both Kreenas and Dynameis, it was rarely followed. It'd been the first and only time she'd done anything outside of the High One's rules, an experience Nyla had convinced her needed to happen at some point to "get it out of the way." When Sylzenya had returned that night, she promptly decided she preferred the rule, which is why she'd denied Westley's advances ever since.

Whenever she found pleasure, it would be by her own hand, which proved far more skilled. So, despite Sylzenya's instinct to throw her disheveled plum at the Dynami's oversized head, she smiled.

"Afraid we're rather busy nowadays," she replied.

Westley's confident demeanor faltered. Sylzenya took another bite of plum.

"Anyways," Marlo interrupted—*thank gods*, "Do either of you have any fresh orodyte we might be able to take off your hands? Ours have run dry."

He revealed two pieces of clear stone, a myriad of colors reflecting in the soft sunshine.

"You ran out of *both*?" Nyla asked, reaching into her robe's pockets, which Sylzenya knew held four pieces of glowing orodyte.

"We went up against an ichthys," Marlo replied, "nearly lost one of our newest recruits to it."

Marlo looked at Sylzenya and Nyla expectantly.

"Never heard of an ichthys," Sylzenya finally said.

"You don't know what an *ichthys* is?" Westley asked. "By the gods, it's only one of Lhaal's most deadly creatures. Surely even Kreenas know that."

"Then how'd you manage to escape it?" Sylzenya asked, a genuine question, yet she knew her tone would cause Westley to bristle.

It worked.

Marlo replied, "An ichthys is an aquatic creature invisible to the naked eye. They're the rarest in Lhaal, but not extinct by any means. Westley and I hadn't encountered one before. We were just filling our waterskins at a pond when someone pointed out a strange black cloud in the water, but one of our recruits had already drunk his fill."

"Dying by infected water sounds like a rather unimpressive way to die in that place," Nyla said, pulling out two of the glowing orodytes.

Nyla offered two of her orodytes, keeping her other two in her pocket, sticking to the Kreenas' codes of creation. If Dynameis seek to exchange their orodyte during their shifts, Kreenas may offer half of the orodyte stones they filled. The other half must be brought to the temple to be distributed fairly amongst the warriors.

"Oh, no, the ichthys' poison doesn't kill you," Marlo said, accepting one of the stones. "It controls you."

Sylzenya and Nyla stilled.

Westley took the other piece. "It's true. The ichthys

secretes a toxin into the water, and you don't even have to drink it to be infected. If it gets in your mouth, eyes, what have you, then the ichthys has control over your whole self. Mind, body—even soul."

"It took control of the recruit's mind, manipulating him against us," Marlo added, "even used his orodyte to access Aretta's power through him. I didn't know they could do that."

"And you didn't end up killing him?" Nyla questioned.

"Didn't have to. The ichthys loses its invisible quality when it possesses another, and so I was able to find it in its watering hole and spear it through the gills with my sword." Marlo raised his longsword, stained in black blood. "Once the ichthys is dead, its control over its subject is broken. It was a nasty battle, though. Those monsters are slippery things, and it took me a while to find its gills. I had to use power from both of my orodytes to finally kill it."

"And where were you in all of this, Westley?" Sylzenya asked.

His earlier intrigue in her had clearly depleted as he replied, "Keeping the recruit from *killing* everyone."

"And you only saw it because of the water changing color?" Nyla asked.

"Like I said, we were lucky," Marlo replied, "I'd only heard rumors of its true appearance, but they barely did it justice. It looked like a large fish without fins, and had sharper teeth than a serpentum's fang."

Westley added, "Distrathrus' creatures are far more than just armored skin and hulking strength."

The grove fell silent at the mention of the god's name. So rarely did anyone utter it. The name was like a distant curse, one that had almost taken Estea in its monstrous claws centuries ago.

"Praise Aretta for ending him when she did," Sylzenya

replied, "Who knows what other monstrosities he would've created in that forest."

All of them echoed the prayer.

"Well, Nyla and Sylzenya, we're grateful for the orodyte. I'm sure we'll be able to utilize its impurities to slay a serpentum or arachni on our next mission. Maybe even an ichthys," Marlo said, a broad smile on his face, "Perhaps we'll see you later tonight at the banquet?"

His eyes shimmered as he locked his gaze with Nyla's. Sylzenya didn't miss the rush of red blooming on her friend's face.

"I'm certain we will," Nyla replied, looping her arm through hers.

The men bowed again, Marlo staring at Nyla, Westley's eyes trained on Sylzenya. Without another word, Sylzenya turned and led Nyla towards the temple, leaving the other Dynameis and Kreenas to exchange orodytes, stories of Lhaal Forest and, perhaps, fleeting glances with unspoken promises.

"I swear on Aretta's blood, if you fall for that little act of his, I'll have to lock you in the temple until your mind is washed clean," Sylzenya whispered as they left the grove.

Nyla laughed. "A little playful talk and suddenly you assume I'm swayed into his affections?"

"You know why he was talking to you like that, don't you?"

"He's a man with a sword. His reasons are obvious enough."

They approached the temple, its sandstone walls reaching to the sky, curving into a dome made of stained-glass. The guards opened the doors, the crisp scent of rosewater fresh and light as their bare feet slapped against the marble floor.

"Just have some fun tonight, Syl. You deserve it after everything that's happened."

Sylzenya shook her head. "I wouldn't say time spent with Westley is *fun*."

"Then find someone else. You're the most *powerful* Kreena in all of Est—"

"*Was*," she corrected.

"Are going to be *again*," Nyla said, "All I'm saying is that you could choose any Dynami, and they'd be more than happy to… swap orodyte."

They stopped at a wall made of dark ivy, pulling aside the vines to reveal a dark, damp room with a single torch.

Sylzenya's brows rose to her hairline. "You think other Dynameis want my orodyte?"

"Oh, I *know* they want your orodyte."

Furrowing her brows, Sylzenya stared at her friend. Nyla opened the gold door to the sanctuary of Aretta's healing waters. Steam assaulted them, filling her lungs as the warm layer of water met her cold feet.

"My orodyte isn't any different from yours, let alone other Kreenas'," Sylzenya argued as she stripped, the back of her white robe damp with blood. She hung the cloth on a thorned vine draping the wall.

"It is to them," Nyla said.

"Then they're painfully simple-minded."

"Alas, the fault of men with swords."

Their laughter echoed along the sandstone walls as they stepped into the large circular pool. Despite the heavy steam, the faint golden light from the water pulsed as it always did, the intricate tiles lining the pool's floor depicting a willow, matching the yellow stained-glass stretched across the ceiling.

Every nerve of pain in her back melted away as if a swath of mint salve had been rubbed into her skin. She let out a low moan. The pool had been blessed by Aretta centuries ago—the last source of healing magic—weak, but effective enough for Kreenas' bleeding backs.

Purpose surged in her limbs as she slowly submerged herself. Perhaps they wouldn't need the pool if Sylzenya could find Aretta's Willow—a tree capable of healing *every* ailment.

"Syl, will you at least consider what I said earlier?" Nyla asked, her face lost in the glowing steam.

"About giving away my orodyte?" Sylzenya replied, a small laugh on her lips.

"No, not the orodyte," Nyla strained.

Her laughter faded. "Once I'm cured, I'll consider confronting my parents, but for now," she sunk lower into the pool, "I just need to survive this banquet."

"Fair enough," her friend replied. "But also, don't give your orodyte to another idiot like Westley."

Sylzenya's smile slackened as she stared at the glowing water, considering the words Nyla had shared earlier, hating the truth it called forward—*nothing's going to be the same after this.* Even if she regained her power, life would look different. More guards, more protection, more uncertainty… acolytes and Kreenas wouldn't be able to live in peace, and neither would her people.

Suddenly, her eyes brightened and her heartbeat quickened.

Even if the High One's cure worked, having Aretta's Willow's location could prove invaluable. It could heal, yes, but perhaps it could do more—perhaps it could provide power for Kreenas besides herself. It could heal them quicker than these waters, they could make more food than ever before, and the famine would cease to be a threat. Perhaps it could even provide more strength for the Dynameis, allow their orodytes to last longer, and give them abilities to avoid mind-controlling monsters like the ichthys.

Perhaps if the vision had been right and she found Aretta's Willow, Estea could have more than just hope—her kingdom could have a future.

She needed to tell the High One about her vision.

CHAPTER 8
LHAAL FOREST

The large Vutrorian ship had been anchored a ways out from shore. The dark trees of Lhaal Forest, the woods surrounding Estea, reached for the sky like thin, black spikes.

Elnok had never been one for farewells, so he knew it would be futile to hide the tears welling in his eyes as he embraced each of his companions. They offered him words of encouragement and humorous reminders to behave like a royal, not a thief. But it was when he approached Orym, supported on either side by other crew members, that a lone tear stained his cheek.

"Elnok, if you don't make it back in one piece." Orym paused, his jaw clenched as his lip quivered.

"I will," Elnok replied as he gripped the back of his friend's neck. "And you'll be back in one piece once I give you the medicine."

His friend's pale mouth thinned. "You can still stay."

Elnok took a deep breath. "I can't. Knowing there's a cure for you out there… you saved me all those years ago. Let me do the same."

"But—"

"I'm going to come back," Elnok stated, embracing him, "I promise."

Orym held him tight. "I'm holding you to it."

"Good." He let him go, turning to the nurse, Yenna, and said, "I know you'll take care of him."

She nodded, her hand gripping Orym's frail wrist.

They parted ways, Elnok climbing into the small boat hung by pulleys on the side of the large Vutrorian vessel. The Dynami, Kharis, walked out of the main cabin. Elnok's brother, Tosh, followed, a glass of wine in his hand. The two men stopped, seeming to whisper to one another. Elnok strained his ears but heard nothing. Finally, Kharis left Tosh's side and joined Elnok in the boat.

"Do you wish to say farewell to your brother?" Kharis inquired.

Elnok glanced towards Tosh. His brother's hand shook, his wine spilling onto the deck. His black hair appeared newly washed, his maroon shirt still hanging off of him. Elnok gulped as Tosh took a step forward, as if he was about to say something. Instead, Elnok turned back to Kharis.

"There's nothing to say," he replied flatly.

Kharis didn't respond, orchestrating the Vutrorian crew members to lower their boat into the choppy sea. Orym's pale face disappeared from view. The waves bumped their boat as Elnok and Kharis paddled to shore. Facing away from the royal vessel, Elnok couldn't help but notice Kharis' hard stare never leaving the ship. Elnok turned and found his brother leaning on the side of the railing, a look of yearning burned into his sickly features.

At first, Elnok thought his brother was looking at him. But, when he turned back to Kharis, he realized it hadn't been him at all. Elnok's stomach dropped as understanding crashed into him like a thick wave during a storm.

He finally knew why Kharis wanted to find the goddess' tree.

Elnok said nothing to the Dynami during their short paddle to shore, and Kharis kept his mouth closed. It was just as well, because Elnok only had words of accusation.

Once they arrived at shore, Elnok craned his neck towards the forest sprawled before them. Large, dark trees reached for the sky like broken, cracked fingers. A filament of darkness hovered on the tops of the spindly branches, a blanket of perpetual night, preventing the sunlight from piercing through its veil. Opaque mist crawled out of the dense forestation, curling at his boots like claws digging into the sand.

He examined his black leather armor for any defects, sheathing his shortsword into his scabbard with a deafening scrape.

Shit.

He needed to remain calm. So what if he was about to trek into a forest infested with flesh-eating monsters, being guided by a magical warrior who he'd just lost all trust in?

Double shit.

"I'll need that," Kharis said as he pointed to the sword, "There's no killing monsters without properly preparing Vutrorian steel. It's our only means of doing so."

"I thought you said you didn't know why your High One wanted Vutorian weapons?"

Kharis donned a pair of brown gloves. "Vutrorian steel itself is not what we want—it's what it's capable of withstanding that makes it valuable. The metal is so strong that us Dynameis rarely need our weapons replaced, and yet the High One continues to request vast shipments. That's where my concern lies."

Elnok warily handed Kharis the sword. "I see."

Kharis took a vial from his pocket. Yellow glowing liquid sloshed in the small vial, bright as sunshine. He popped it open, leveled the sword with the earth, and tipped the vial onto a small groove that ran down the entire blade. The liquid spilled into the thin groove, coursing along the blade like a river of gold on a silver piece of land. The sword pulsed a sudden bright white as the liquid turned solid.

"Orodyte serum," Kharis said. "It's a source of power that's full of impurities, collected by Kreenas when they create food. It allows our swords to slice through the monsters with ease. Without it, steel would bounce off their bodies as if the creatures wore thick armor."

Elnok furrowed his brow. "What about the orodyte you always have on your chest? Is it not the source of your own power?"

"Yes and no." Kharis explained, "Aretta gifted Estean men with the power to protect ourselves and our people. This power is the ability to harness the orodyte stone's impurities, which supply us with heightened strength, speed, and hearing while fighting."

Elnok said nothing as he accepted the glowing sword, arcing it through the air once, twice. Its weight hadn't changed, but he could feel the power in the steel; he dared not sheath it into his scabbard.

As Kharis poured the serum onto his own sword, Elnok couldn't help but remember how the man had looked at Tosh that first day on the ship.

He'd been blind to miss the affection.

"So, how long have you been fucking my brother?" Elnok quipped.

Kharis' golden-tanned face turned pale. "I don't know what you speak of."

Elnok scoffed. "Please, save the lies for your people."

"I'm sure someone of your caliber often enjoys finding meaning where there isn't any to be found."

"Someone of my caliber?" Elnok balked, "I know bullshit when I step in it, and I seem to be drowning in it right now, thanks to you."

Kharis sighed. "We have more important things to worry abou–"

"The one person who can help me get to this damned tree is *also* fucking my deranged brother," Elnok interrupted, "I'd say that's worth worrying about, don't you?"

The warrior retained his focus on his task, the blade glowing as the liquid traveled the groove.

"We aren't just fucking, if that's where your concerns lie."

"If you think that's my concern, then you're missing the point entirely."

"Suppose bigotry isn't dead."

"Bigotry?" Elnok exclaimed, "My brother's a psychotic madman who tried to *kill* me when I was a child, and *you* are in love with him."

Kharis took a deep breath as he sealed the vial and swung his blade in a full arc.

"He didn't try to kill you, Elnok. He wasn't in his right mind."

"Ah yes," Elnok said, standing, "Let's pretend Tosh's apologies actually mean something for once, hm? Do you know how many times he told me the same thing? And then the next day he forgot every word and tortured me until I passed out."

"Look, I know this a lot for you, and that's why…" Kharis let out a controlled breath. "You weren't supposed to know."

"Well, you did a piss-poor job hiding it. I should've seen it the other day, when he'd threatened me. You came out of his cabin where you'd probably been inciting his madness." Elnok stepped back, hand on his hilt. "Are you taking me into the forest to dispose of me… for my brother?"

"Elnok—"

"Fuck," he whispered, heart pounding and blood pumping. The gray stone walls of the dungeon closed in on him again, his brother's laughter echoing off the empty space. "*Fuck.*"

Kharis turned to him, grabbing his shoulders as his eyes flickered with a yellow glow. "Elnok, I'm *not* going to harm you. I swear upon Aretta herself."

Elnok stilled, sword steady, body rigid. "Your power says otherwise."

Kharis released him, his yellow eyes doused. "I'm sorry, I just… Elnok, when he almost attacked you on the ship, he hadn't been drinking his wine. We've recently learned that when he doesn't drink it, his madness increases tenfold. One of the guards informed me he hadn't drunk any for an entire day, so I went in to coax him to, but he wanted to believe he didn't need it. He hated the way you looked at him, could tell you disapproved of it, and so he convinced himself he could do without it. Instead, he relapsed."

Lowering his sword, Elnok took a long deep breath, the warrior's gaze softening with it. The gray stone walls melted away into blue sky and the steady ocean spray.

"I held him back to make sure he didn't hurt you," Kharis said. "Once he came to, he made the decision to stay away from you the rest of the journey."

A cold wind whipped across his face. Elnok avoided the warrior's gaze, tapping his hilt.

Kharis continued, "What he did to you was wrong, Elnok. Horrifying. I'm not going to defend his actions even if he wasn't in his right mind. And I'm not asking you to forgive or reconcile with him, either. But whether you came to know or not, our plan is the same. We're going to find this tree so we can get back and heal the ones we care about. Once we're done, you never have to see him again. Can we at least agree upon that?"

Elnok turned to the warrior, eyes narrowed. There would be no turning back, not now that they were just outside of Estea—not now that they were this much closer to the healing tree.

"Fine," Elnok said. "We can agree on that."

Rot and sulfur burned Elnok's lungs for hours as they traversed through the crooked trees of Lhaal Forest. Mist swirled just above their thighs, like wading through high tide in the summer. Elnok steadied his sword in front of him, the blade pulsing with an ethereal glow, his and Kharis' weapons the only sources of light as the warrior led the way through the deadly terrain.

Elnok cracked his neck. He wasn't used to wearing armor, his strengths centering in stealth, not brawn.

"We'll need to set up camp for the night," Kharis said as he came to a stop at a clearing. "I'll take first watch."

Elnok didn't argue as he sat in the grimy dirt and leaned against a fallen tree. He ate a rock-hard piece of potato bread, his molars aching after he finished. Tilting his head back, he tried to fall asleep, but the noises were unlike anything he'd ever heard. Metallic chitters and nails scraping against bark echoed through the dark leaves.

"I might as well take first watch," Elnok said. "Won't get much sleep tonight."

Kharis raised his sword. "Nothing will harm you in here, Elnok Rogdul. I swear on my life."

"Your nobility is contagious," Elnok drawled.

The warrior ignored him as he placed his weapon down, folding his arms across his chest and closing his eyes.

Elnok spun his gold signet ring around his finger as the hours went by, attempting to keep himself calm despite the sounds seeming to get closer. His grip on his hilt tightened as he turned around, something moving through the trees—something glowing the same way their swords did.

He took off his ring and placed it inside his chest pocket.

"Kharis," Elnok whispered, raising his blade.

But the warrior didn't budge. Elnok looked through the trees again, the golden glow shimmering through the branches. He strained his eyes as he stood, moving closer. Yellow light burned brighter as he brushed a branch to the side.

In the distance, through the brush, a golden light pulsed. Elnok strained his eyes. The light condensed, giving way to a shape. A tree. But this tree was different from the rest. It wasn't thin and sharp, but lush and full, the light streaming up and down its bark and spilling into the leaves.

It couldn't be.

Could it?

"*Kharis*," Elnok said louder, "Kharis, do you see this? Is this the goddess' tree we're trying to fi—?"

All at once, it disappeared.

Elnok blinked his eyes multiple times. He swore he'd seen a glowing tree, had no doubt in his mind; and yet, only darkness stood in its place. He stepped forward, but instead of dirt meeting the bottom of his boots, a loud crunch sounded instead.

Air rushed past him as the warrior suddenly stood by his side, body glowing and weapon raised. The light reflected something large, clear, and shiny.

"Serpentum skin," Kharis whispered as he cut his sword through the translucent material. "Only a day old by the looks of it. Best we not wait around to find out."

Elnok didn't argue, any sleep that had held in his eyes gone as they no longer walked, but ran through the trees.

"*Fuck*," Kharis said as he held out his arm, stopping Elnok.

"The serpentum?" Elnok questioned, his heart beating fast.

"No, thank Aretta herself," Kharis replied. "But we're not alone anymore."

Elnok followed his gaze, gulping as something thin and glossy shimmered against the light of their blades.

Webs.

"We need to hurry," Kharis whispered.

Elnok followed his swift movements as they changed direction.

"Arachnis are tricky," Kharis explained as they jumped between black thickets, the mist swirling as their legs pounded through the darkness. "Their venom's slow-working but fatal. And where there is one, there are many not far behind."

Elnok's breaths came up short. He'd fought some of the most gruesome of thieves and most tactful of guards, but when it came to monsters, he felt small—useless.

Like he was already buried in the ground.

"They can move in and out of sight," Kharis continued as Elnok ran faster, hopping over dead branches and pushing through sharp thorns that pricked his face. "It's not due to swiftness, as they're rather slow creatures, but they're able to render themselves invisible."

Elnok stopped running. Kharis grunted as he caught himself against a tree trunk.

"Invisible?" Elnok repeated.

Kharis panted as he replied, "Only a single moment, but it's just enough to throw off its attacker… or its prey."

Elnok laughed hysterically, his body shaking. "Am I a joke to you?"

Before Kharis could respond, a high-pitched shriek from somewhere close behind pierced Elnok's ears.

"*Come on*!" Kharis shouted as he grabbed Elnok's arm, pulling him forward with a force that almost sent him into the ground.

Elnok sprinted. Arms pumping, legs pushing, heart crashing into his lungs as he stayed in step with Kharis as best he could. More shrieks filled the air, branches and twigs breaking all around them, trees shaking, the air's rotten stench mixing with something sweet.

Deadly.

"Their eyes as well as the space where their legs connect to their bodies are the softest and easiest to slice," Kharis instructed through harsh breaths, "But dodge whenever you can—"

A large obsidian body crashed into Kharis. Propelled forward, the warrior thudded against a tree, the crooked elm toppling over and landing with an earth-trembling shudder.

Elnok skidded to a halt, sword raised.

Yellow light pulsed into the darkness, revealing eight long legs as they struck into the earth like spears, the limbs connected to a large bulbous body. Glossy eyes blinked at him, as if the light were foreign in this perpetual darkness. The monster—the arachni—clicked its pincers together, the fangs as long and sharp as short swords. Dark liquid dripped from its points.

Elnok gripped his sword, digging into his instincts as the memories of escaping Vutror's dungeons flooded him, stoking a ravenous flame inside his body. The same ferocity he'd used to kill those guards consumed him. He may have never fought a monster before, but he knew what it took to become one.

He knew how to survive.

The arachni launched forward. Instincts threading through his muscles, Elnok jabbed for the arachni's glowing eyes. The monster dodged his attack, rushing past him and slamming into a tree. A dark hiss splintered the air as the monster crunched bark in its mouth.

A metallic chitter breathed down his neck.

Hot panic sliced through his veins as he immediately dodged left, spinning around to see nothing but forest—until it appeared out of thin air.

The arachni lunged, sharp fangs aimed for Elnok's head, but instincts overcame fear; he struck up into the creature's mouth. The sword pierced through its jaw, the tip of the glowing weapon splitting the arachni's mouth. Elnok's breathing was ragged as he ripped the sword out, hot blood spraying his face. Dark fear rushed through Elnok's veins as he stepped back, numerous beady eyes glinting against the glow of his sword—in front of him, in the trees, skittering closer and closer…

"*Kharis!*" Elnok shouted, his hilt slipping out of his grasp.

Light burst from behind the countless arachnis, the spectacle so sharp Elnok shielded his eyes. Blinking rapidly, Elnok jumped as Kharis stood in front of him—smile wide, eyes glimmering like the sun. Yellow beams of light crackled along the veins of the Dynami's legs, up his arms, and down his neck.

His orodyte shone the brightest.

"I'm impressed," Kharis said with a wink as he spun his sword in a single arc. "You almost killed one."

Before Elnok could take a breath, the warrior flashed before his eyes.

The only sign of his person was left by streaks of light, like ripples of water after the toss of stone. Horrific shrieks filled the air. Elnok kept his sword in front of him as he backed up against a tree, watching in awe and terror as Kharis tore the arachnis apart with his blade, long pieces of tree limbs twitching on the ground—

Not tree limbs.

Arachni legs.

Dozens of their appendages had been dismembered by Kharis' sword, the arachnis' large bodies rolling onto the earth and screaming into the mildew air as they bled out.

Bile rose in Elnok's throat; he turned to the side and emptied his stomach.

"Hold out on that sickness until we've made it through," Kharis' voice called through the trees. "We best keep moving."

Elnok wiped the soured mess from his mouth, the metal of his armor mixing with the acid on his tongue. He ran through the graveyard of arachnis, their legs still twitching, screeches piercing the air until their glossy eyes froze over.

Kharis stood over a dead arachni, twirling his sword as if

he hadn't just slain what must've been at least twenty monsters in only a few moments.

"Let's go," Kharis said as he turned, "that wasn't even the whole nest."

The rest of the journey was quick, Elnok's fear driving his body forward despite his exhaustion. He couldn't imagine why anyone would attempt to cross this forest without magic, even with the promise of Estea's provisions on the other side.

Surely, there was no worse way to die.

Warm sunlight caused Elnok's skin to pimple as they made it through the last line of trees. Relief washed over him like a salty wave on the shore as they approached a sandstone wall, towering at least five stories high and stretching as far as Elnok could see.

"*Kharis*," a man yelled, "we were beginning to worry!"

Kharis waved as they approached the man at the base of the wall. The guard wore the same green and brown leather armor as Kharis, with a glowing orodyte on his chest to match.

"And this is the King of Vutror, is it?" the wall guard asked, his dark brown skin matching his eyes.

"His brother," Kharis responded. "The king was unfit for travel."

"Brother?" The guard's brows raised. "The one who was said to be dead?"

Elnok replied, "Not as dead as people presumed."

"Clearly so," the guard said with a crooked smile. "The High One will be… surprised."

"Indeed," Kharis replied, "I'll explain it all to him, but for now, the prince needs rest."

"Ah, that will have to wait, I'm afraid; the kingdom-wide banquet is about to begin. I was instructed to ensure you both attend if you arrived on time."

Kharis straightened. "But that's not for another two harvest cycles."

"You've missed an important number of days. More Kreenas failed this year than ever before, and one of them was pois—" The guard stopped, his eyes flitting to Elnok. "Apologies, Prince, but I'll need to fill in Kharis privately as we walk."

Elnok smiled widely. "Of course."

But I can't help it if your whispers aren't quiet enough.

He followed Kharis' lead as the guard opened the gate and ushered them through. Nothing could have prepared him for how many shades of green there were. The leaves seemed to glow against the sunshine, the trees and bushes enclosing them on a winding path.

He followed at a distance, staring in awe while listening intently to their conversation. Retrieving his signet ring from his pocket, he spun it mindlessly on his pinky finger, listening carefully as he learned an exceptionally powerful Kreena—one of those magical women—had been poisoned with orodyte serum during an important ceremony two days ago.

Kharis tensed. Elnok stopped spinning his ring.

"You know what that means, don't you?" the guard whispered, so quietly that Elnok had to strain his ears.

Kharis said nothing, his grip tightening on his hilt.

"It means the famine's coming," the guard said, "Estea isn't safe anymore."

CHAPTER 9
DOUBT

Guards stood on either side of the gold balcony doors as Sylzenya entered the High One's council chambers. Plants and vines crawled across the stain-glassed ceiling, draped along the walls, and spilled onto the edges of the floor. Small willows lined the room, bowing towards the group of marble statues depicting their goddess.

Sylzenya rolled her shoulders back, placing both hands over her heart as she bowed. As is custom, the guards issued the same gesture back, the squeaking of their green and brown leather armor echoing in the large room.

"The High One will be here shortly," one of them announced.

Sylzenya smiled softly as the guards returned to their rigid postures, eyes pointed towards the entry doors.

The kingdom-wide banquet had already begun. Citizens crowded the gardens below, but Sylzenya had requested a private meeting with the High One. She took a shaky breath as she approached one of the willows, letting the drooping branches hide her in its green fold. Tears stung her eyes. She swallowed them. The emptiness in her chest grew with each day, the reminder of her lost power, an ache slicing just as deep as the one on her back.

If you are to restore your power and protect your people, then Aretta's Willow is the only way.

Scratching a nail down the willow's fibrous bark, she let a sharp splinter pierce her thumb. If the compass was inside one of these trees, then she needed to carve into each trunk until she found it. The task seemed impossible, but there had to be a way; if she could find the compass to Aretta's Willow, then they'd always have enough power to make sure the famine never reached Estea.

This was why she needed to share her vision of the compass to the High One tonight.

Stone cracked against stone as the doors opened. Sylzenya quickly emerged from the willow. The High One strode in, his long white robes matching his hair. A twisted gold coronet lined his forehead, the metallic glint brightening his eyes as he held Sylzenya's stare. He opened his arms, a wide smile on his face, causing her shoulders to relax.

"A splendid night when the entire kingdom shows," the High One said as he extended his arm for her, "Now tell me, what honor am I owed to be called upon by our kingdom's most renowned Kreena?"

Sylzenya's eyes widened. "Your Grace, with all due respect, I'm still—" She paused, her gaze shooting to the guards, realizing she shouldn't speak of her powerlessness, "Unable to fulfill my duties as a Kreena."

His smile didn't falter. "Don't sell yourself so short. You're on the mend, soon to be back in the gardens and creating more than all the other Kreenas combined."

She didn't argue with him as she took his extended arm, the gesture unfamiliar. He seemed elated, so unlike the panic she'd seen him wear the day she'd been poisoned. Both emotions were foreign to his ageless face.

"Now, Sylzenya," he continued, leading her towards a

statue. "I'm assuming you're wondering when the cure will take full effect; I'm pleased to inform you it shouldn't take any longer than a few more days."

She took a brief breath, a small smile pulling at her mouth. "That's wonderful news, Your Grace. Thank you."

The emptiness inside her chest ebbed, replaced with a ray of hope.

His grin widened. "It is. If that's all—"

"It's not," she interrupted, her nerves causing her arm to shake.

Cold fingers gripped her forearm. The High One's brows furrowed, his moment of excitement lessened as he looked at the guards, then at her.

He lowered his voice. "Is there something wrong?"

"No," Sylzenya quickly replied, "in fact, the opposite."

Be wary of who you trust.

The bird's deep blue eyes cut across her vision, its warning thrumming inside her chest. She needed to tell him before she convinced herself not to.

"Wonderful," the High One replied, "I'm eager to hear what news you've brought to share—"

"Aretta's Willow," Sylzenya blurted, closing her eyes at her lack of tact. "I mean to ask, what do you know of Aretta's Willow?"

The High One's cold body turned rigid. His smile vanished, and his grip tightened to a point of pain.

"Guards," he announced, "please give us a moment."

The men bowed their heads, faces expressionless as they stepped out onto the balcony, the doors closing behind them with a thud.

"What's the meaning of this?" the High One asked, his voice chilled and grating.

Sylzenya's skin pimpled. "My apologies, Your Grace. I'm not broaching this subject as well as I intended, and I know tonight is a busy night—"

"Yes, it is."

Sweat building along her neck, she gulped. This—impatience and scrutiny—was an emotion she'd seen far more of from him. She'd hoped to avoid such a reaction, but she knew how to talk to him despite it. He always heard her in the end.

"What my parents did was unprecedented and is causing rumors of upheaval to ripple through the kingdom. I'm ashamed, for it was my family that started this, and so, I mean to fix it."

The High One's brows lifted. "Your parents are no trouble of yours. I'm taking care of it."

"I know that, Your Grace," she replied, "But their actions impacted not just me, but all of Estea. I fear that when I get my power back, there will still be questions and uncertainty amongst our people about whether the famine will take us. It's no way to live. I mean to try everything within my power to—"

"*Sylzenya.*"

She stopped, her eyes wide as the High One took his arm away from hers, his cold hands gripping her shoulders instead. His harsh yellow gaze studied her face.

"You speak of things a ruler must worry about, and so I am, more than you know." He paused, a flicker in his jaw. "Your parents proved who they were, who we always knew them to be—delirious, selfish, and hostile. Wasn't it I who told you these very things?"

"Yes, Your Grace," Sylzenya said, tears burning behind her eyes.

"No child should experience these horrors from their parents." He placed a loose strand of her hair behind her ear, his cold fingers brushing her neck. "I should've protected you, and I failed. This is my wrong to right, not yours."

Sylzenya's breaths shortened, a pull in her chest telling her to flee. She ignored it. She couldn't run from the topic of her parents anymore.

"Thank you, Your Grace," she whispered.

He tilted his head, brows furrowed. "Now, why on earth are you asking about Aretta's Willow? As you already know, it's a legend."

"Yes, well," Syzlenya paused, the spit in her mouth thickening, "What if it *were* real? And if we were to find it, then perhaps we wouldn't have to worry about people like my parents sabotaging other Kreenas or acolytes—"

"There will be no other people like that," he seethed, his yellow eyes flaring. "I'm making sure of it."

Her breath faltered, muscles tense as his keen eyes softened along with his grip.

"If the tree was real, then it's been dead for centuries, and as a leader, I can't in good conscience put any of our efforts towards an empty promise." His smile returned. "It is *you* who's our hope, Sylzenya. *You* are going to bring restoration to our people, and I need *you* to believe in yourself. In three days I'll have your cure ready, and I need you to be prepared to take up this mantle."

Heat rushed into her face and limbs. He wasn't listening to her like she'd hoped. Despite all his glorious words, a seed of doubt had settled within her heart.

Perhaps she wasn't enough to save her people.

And if this was true, then they needed something more.

"I understand, Your Grace, and I don't mean to shirk any of my duties. Once I'm cured, I'll do as you say, but what if —" She took a steadying breath. "If it doesn't work, or if my efforts are still not enough, then our people will need more. I've been wanting to tell you, that after I failed the rite, I communed with the roots of the altar room, and when I did, I saw a vision of Aretta's Willow—"

"*Enough.*"

Everything stilled. The room hadn't been moving, no water lapping in fountains, and yet, everything froze, Sylzenya's heart as well. Even if she wanted to speak, she couldn't find the words, the High One's face causing her to gulp.

He leaned forward, his cold finger tilting her chin up.

"After all these years," he whispered, "why are you choosing to doubt me now, Sylzenya?"

The emptiness in her chest grew, her desire to feel her goddess' power in the soil boundless, and the need to feel the power opening her cut unbearable. She desired a pain she understood, not *this*.

"I'd never doubt you," she whispered, tears in her eyes.

His gaze narrowed, mouth thin as he tilted her chin up further.

She stopped breathing. "Your Grace?"

The High One sighed as he released her chin, standing to his full height and lacing his hands behind his back. "Your cure will be ready in three days, but I'm afraid you won't be."

Everything within her—her muscles, her lungs, her stomach—seized , as if he'd dealt a heavy blow to her gut.

"I understand why your faith has faltered, but I expected better than this." He motioned towards the balcony doors. "Your people deserve better than this."

Disbelief and fear warred with heated anger. She doused all of it, biting the inside of her cheek until it bled, forcing herself to meet her gaze with the High One's.

"I'm sorry, Your Grace," she said, her words metallic on her tongue.

He didn't smile or offer recompense. Instead, he turned to Aretta's statue and stared long and hard at the goddess.

"It's my fault you're not prepared."

"Your Grace—"

"If you're to be the hope of our people, then you must prove to me you're capable of handling such a task." He turned to her, mouth thinned and eyes focused. "Until I'm certain of this, the cure will remain with me."

It felt as if the floor had been ripped from under her feet.

The emptiness in her chest widened, threatening to consume her.

"I promise I won't talk about the tree anymore," she begged, her fingers digging into her skin, "I promise I won't doubt myself."

The High One smiled sadly. "If you had said this to me earlier, I would've believed you. Thankfully, there's still time to remedy this bout of uncertainty." He trailed a finger along the marble statue. "Starting now, any task I give you, you must do *exactly* as I instruct. If you're successful in this, then I will give you the cure when it's ready. But, if you don't," he chipped a piece of marble off the statue, "then we will start over."

"But what about the famine?" she asked, sweat dripping down her back, a cold tear trailing down her warm cheek. She hated herself for not being able to hold back this emotion.

"It's like you said last night, we have enough Kreenas and acolytes to keep our reserves full for the time being." He leaned down, his face inches from hers. "Unless you plan on making this difficult?"

"*No*," she quickly said, heart racing and palms sweating. Blood filled her mouth, stinging like acid in her throat, "I'll do as you say."

He clicked his tongue. "Good. First, I never want to hear you speak of Aretta's Willow again, understood?"

Forcing the tears behind her eyes, she rolled her shoulders back. It didn't matter that it didn't make sense to her; his certainty of her position as Kreena overruled her desire to find the tree. She would have to accept this. There was no room for mistakes, uncertainty, or doubt. If she was to restore the emptiness and gain her power back, then she had to comply.

"Understood, Your Grace," she said, forcing the shakiness in her voice to stay in the back of her throat.

He stepped around the statue, motioning for her to join him. She obeyed.

"Next, you're going to make an announcement to the entire kingdom about your return as a Kreena. You're going to bolster their confidence just as you did with the Kreenas and acolytes last night, telling them your cure will be in full effect soon." He stopped in front of the gilded doors, eyes narrowed. "Tell them there's nothing to fear, that the perpetrators have been taken care of, and Estea will live in abundance forevermore."

She wanted to ask questions, such as what if she *did* fail his test and they had to "start over" — would that mean it would be another three days of proving herself until she can get the cure? Or was it shorter, longer? Yet the questions stayed on her tongue, for she could see she'd worn his patience thin. For the first time in her life, she'd fallen from the High One's graces.

For the first time in her life, she didn't share her true thoughts with him.

"Yes, Your Grace," she replied, bowing her head, "I would be honored."

"Good. And lastly, you will regularly report everything the Vutrorian king says or does." He shook his head. "There's much to repair, Sylzenya. Am I clear in these expectations?"

"Yes, Your Grace," she whispered.

He said nothing as he opened the doors, the guards on either side standing tall. Flaming torches and glowing orodytes filled the gardens below, the people ceasing their chatter and movement as she and the High One approached the banister.

"Good," the High One whispered, so low the guards couldn't hear them, "now show me."

Forcing her arms to stop shaking, she accepted the cup of wine offered by the guard. The High One addressed the crowd, proclaiming he had a special announcement from his most blessed of Kreenas. Sylzenya stared into the distance, the view allowing her to see Lhaal Forest—a curse and a blessing surrounding her people—keeping threats out only by harboring monsters within; creatures of instinct, doing whatever they could to stay alive.

She raised her glass to the sky, her people following her lead as she talked of hope, each word widening the emptiness in her chest until the scar on her back burned.

Perhaps she was more like those monsters than she cared to admit.

CHAPTER 10

A THIEF IN ESTEA

The cool night air clung to Elnok causing the hair on his arms and neck to raise. It reminded him of winter nights sitting around the campfire with his crew, telling stories, and eating scraps together with watered-down ale that tasted like piss. Standing before the Estean temple, those days felt like a distant dream.

Sandstone pillars stretched up towards the sky, the reflection of a nearby river draping the building in silver flames. Films of gold cracked along the sandstone like ripples of lightning. A breeze swept into his lungs, smelling sweetly of earth and herbs. He was surprised as a deep well of emotion ran up his nose into his eyes.

When was the last time he smelled something that wasn't dry dirt and rotting fish?

Unlike the rest of Druenia, Estea was *alive.*

"Quite the temple, isn't it?" Kharis asked, the warrior twisting his hair into a topknot, "Wait until you see the gardens."

"I'd rather sleep," Elnok muttered, his eyes drooping while his body begged for respite.

He'd barely slept more than a few hours during their trek

through Lhaal Forest, the fear of monsters coupled with the strange sighting of the glowing tree keeping him awake.

"Your sword, Prince Elnok," the guard who had led them commanded, his hand outstretched.

Elnok raised a brow. "Aren't you all… magical? Can't the royal human without god-like assistance keep his only weapon?"

The guard laughed. "An excellent point, but I'm afraid not. Only Dynameis are allowed to carry weapons on temple and village grounds. But don't worry, we'll take good care of it in our barracks. I'll even sharpen it for you if you'd like?"

He had known they'd strip him of all weapons, so he pretended that the sword was his only, and his favorite. In a way, the sword was a guaranteed form of escape whenever he found himself in trouble, his one-on-one combat more decent than most, but he excelled with his rope and dagger. At first glance, people hardly took notice of either. The sword would always be seen as more dangerous.

But before he could continue his performance of dignified anger, Kharis' strong grip squeezed his shoulder.

"You won't win this argument, only waste our time," the warrior said, "Besides, our men are fantastic at sharpening weapons."

Elnok feigned frustration, sighing in defeat as he unsheathed his blade and handed it to the guard.

"The rope as well."

"My sword isn't enough?" Elnok questioned, real frustration flickering in his gut, "Are you going to ask for my crown too? Are the points too sharp?"

The guard hesitated. "Are they?"

Elnok rolled his eyes. "My rope assists me with inconveniences, as well as…" he ran through every excuse he could make, finally arriving at one that usually did the trick, "…*other* endeavors."

The guard's dark brown skin turned the faintest shades of red. Elnok smirked as Kharis held back a laugh.

"It's not to harm people," Elnok lied, "unless requested, of course. If you understand my meaning?"

The guard opened and closed his mouth, incoherent words and sounds causing Elnok to smile.

"Just the blade is fine," the guard finally sputtered.

"Great," Elnok replied, patting his rope against his thigh, the hidden dagger underneath his leathers still strapped tight. "How long do we have to endure this banquet before we can finally sleep?"

"The High One wishes to greet you both upon your arrival; he'll let you know his expectations for the night and the remainder of your stay."

"Delightful," Elnok replied.

It was anything *but* delightful. Stomach rumbling and throat parched, Elnok and Kharis followed the guard through a protected sidewall, the large sandstone gate lifted by a group of guards and a complex pulley system.

Impressive.

If this had been a mission to steal an item from inside the temple, this entrance would prove useless as an entry point. Heavily guarded, multiple people needed, and a cracking sound echoing for miles. But it could prove a decent distraction. As they passed through the wall and into the gardens, he couldn't stop wondering, even in his tired state, how someone *could* get into this place undetected.

"*Praise be to Aretta*!" a woman suddenly yelled in Elnok's face.

He stepped back, the wine on her breath assaulting him.

"Praise be to Aretta, indeed." Kharis said as he gently redirected the woman back the way she came, "How's your evening faring?"

His voice grew distant as he talked to the woman. Elnok swallowed hard. Damn it all if the wine on her breath didn't smell exactly the same as the kind his brother wasted himself on.

His brother.

Tosh.

Quickly, Elnok forced the memories of his daily beatings away, redirecting his focus to the gardens. Drooping trees stood everywhere, lining multiple pathways flanked by glowing torches. Dynameis stood tall and vigilant, their chests bright with orodytes. Masses of people roamed the pathways with delirious grins and goblets in hand. Breaths strained, Elnok followed Kharis into a large clearing of trees and garden beds. He sucked in as much air as he could, yet the stench of wine only grew stronger.

"Welcome, Esteans, to the annual banquet!" A deep voice rumbled across the gardens.

"That's the High One," Kharis whispered, pointing upwards.

The temple stood over the clearing, a lone balcony stretching out from its side. Green vines draped over the railing, tangling themselves in the light breeze. Standing on the balcony were a man and a woman, both dressed in white robes.

"This evening, we have a special announcement from the most powerful Kreena in Estean history. Praise be to Aretta!"

The garden erupted in a slurred cheer, echoing their leader's words. Elnok grabbed Kharis' shoulder, the scars on his back burning.

"Elnok," he said above the noise, "Is everything alright?"

"She created over half of the willows in this garden, a true testament to her strength and power. Everyone, please join me as we raise our glasses with Sylzenya Phatris!"

More cheers.

Elnok forced himself to stand upright, ignoring the pain and distant memories burning into his back.

The woman stepped forward. While the leader's robes

covered him in one swoop of fabric, hers seemed to be made of one thin strip, wrapping around her body in intricate designs, pockets of lightly tanned skin exposed at her hips, shoulders, and chest. A rather attractive piece to wear, and Elnok couldn't help himself as he stared at her curves, letting her beauty distract him from the pain searing his body.

She carried herself with the grace of a ruler, long ash-colored hair floating behind her in the soft breeze.

A Kreena, the High One had said.

One of the women Kharis had warned him about, the ones who lived in the temple since they were young; women saturated in piety, trusting their High One above all else. But by the way the High One stood next to this woman, she must be something more. A wife, perhaps, or a concubine? Kharis hadn't spoken of the High One having either, but he supposed it didn't affect their goal.

Either way, he needed to steer clear of this woman.

"Welcome, people of Estea," she said, her voice carrying across the clearing and into the gardens, "Two days ago, more acolytes took up the title of Kreena—women who have pledged their lives to see our kingdom prosper during the continent-wide famine. A day worth celebrating!"

Everyone in the crowd clapped.

The woman smiled. "And yet, I know many of you heard of the terrible event which also took place during the rite."

She paused, a falter in her smile. Faint enough for most to dismiss it as a natural break, but Elnok saw something else in her features. His painful memories faded as his curiosity piqued.

A building tension hung in the air, so thick Elnok might've thought everyone had forgotten how to breathe.

She smiled wider—an overcorrection—a common fault for novice thieves, and a habit Elnok tirelessly trained out of his crew. This woman would make a terrible gambler, and an even worse thief.

"My own flesh and blood betrayed me. Betrayed our entire kingdom." She continued, lowering her glass to the banister, "However, in their attempt to strip me of my connection to Aretta, our goddess blessed me with something greater." She stared towards the sky. "*Hope*."

The crowd cheered.

Elnok scoffed.

Bullshit.

"Our goddess has blessed the High One with a cure to orodyte serum, and I'm already nearing full strength."

Cheers erupted in the clearing. People clanked their goblets together, drinking laboriously, dancing and jumping at her words.

"It is good to rejoice!" she yelled over the cacophony, "For where people sought to destroy our kingdom, Aretta protected us yet again. Now please, enjoy the food and wine the High One and the Kreenas have so graciously provided us this evening. Let it be a sign that the famine will never touch Estea: Not now, not ever. Praise be to Aretta!"

The crowd erupted into chants. Elnok grabbed a nearby tree trunk to keep himself steady as people shoved and yelled, wine spilling from their goblets and onto the soil, their clothes, and their mouths. Memories returned, threatening to drown him as he followed Kharis through the clearing towards the temple.

"We'll request a meeting with the High One immediately," Kharis yelled over the crowd, "Then we can leave this place and go to the main village."

Elnok couldn't manage a response, squaring his shoulders against the crowd of drunks instead. He shoved as many of them away as he could, their twisted smiles shaped so much like Tosh's during those nights in the dungeons. He could feel the scars on his back burning hotter with each step.

Someone was looking at him. He could feel it. He turned his gaze skyward.

Hands clenched on the banister's balcony, the woman in intricate white robes leaned forward, her eyes steadied on him. Estea's leader towered behind her, his hands gripping her shoulders as he whispered into her ear. The woman's eyes widened. Before Elnok could make sense of it, someone elbowed him in the ribs, knocking the air out of his lungs. Coughing, he bent over.

When Elnok looked up again, they were gone.

"We're almost there," Kharis said as he grabbed Elnok's arm.

Drooping branches scraped his face as they rushed forward, the mass of people thinning as they emerged on the other side of the trees. A woman in a long gold robe stood in front of the temple's large detailed doors, two guards on either side.

"Elnok," Kharis whispered, "Are you alright?"

Elnok released himself from Kharis' grasp. "Why wouldn't I be?"

"The wine," he replied.

Elnok scoffed, heat rushing to his face. "A bit of wine isn't going to burn me with a rod of steel, now is it?"

The warrior let out a long breath.

"Good evening, Priestess," Kharis announced, "Would you please alert the High One that his Vutrorian guest has arrived?"

The priestess bowed her head as the guards opened the large doors.

"Wait here," she instructed before entering the temple, the doors shutting behind her.

"Say nothing about Aretta's Willow," Kharis whispered.

"Pity. That was going to be the first subject I brought up."

"*Elnok.*"

"Can't take a joke, can you?"

Kharis grunted. "Recite to me why you're here in Tosh's place."

Elnok cracked his neck. "To make sure he wasn't eaten alive by this High One's sharp teeth."

"*Elnok.*"

"I do have a nice name, don't I? Much better than all my aliases."

"By Aretta's blood herself," Kharis cursed, "Answer seriously. I need to know you remember your task for these treaty revisions."

Elnok spun around, smiling widely as he patted Kharis' armor.

"Are you blind?" Elnok whispered as low as he could, "We're being watched."

"I need to know you understand what we're doing."

"And you need to understand how precarious of a position we're in."

Kharis clenched his teeth. "It's difficult to trust someone who offers none to me."

He smiled. "Should've thought of that before getting on your knees for Vutror's king."

Kharis' face turned bright red as the doors opened. Elnok spun back into place, hands laced together as he forced a wide princely smile.

"*Kharis,*" the High One said, striding past the priestess, "This trip took longer than usual, although I now see why."

Estea's leader turned his gaze towards Elnok.

Yellow eyes.

Despite his shock, Elnok didn't falter, keeping his smile wide and beaming. The man's stare was sharp, like a beam of sunlight focused on a singular point, intent to burn whatever it touched.

The High One extended his arm.

The woman in white wrapped robes emerged from behind the priestess. If the High One's eyes were meant to tear through bone, then hers were meant to be its salve. The deepest blue, like the ocean right after sunset—full and endless. But her gaze stayed steady on the High One, her face expressionless as she took his arm. Elnok waited for a reaction from her, wanting that mask he'd seen earlier to fall for even the slightest moment.

It didn't.

"Your Grace," Kharis said with a low bow, "may I present Elnok Rogdul, Prince of Vutror."

The High One narrowed his gaze. "I have treaty negotiations set for King Tosh, do I not, Kharis?"

"The king has fallen gravely ill, Your Grace. He was unfit to travel through Lhaal Forest."

"Are you suggesting you're not fit to accomplish your tasks?"

"My apologies, Your Grace," Kharis said. "You've offered me your trust to return with a Vutrorian of royal blood who can discuss the terms in which we may continue to receive the weapons we need; I found the king unfit to hold such important discussions."

The High One raised his glass of wine and took a sip.

Kharis continued, "But it was a miracle by Aretta's hand herself that the king's brother, Prince Elnok, was willing to take his place and make such arrangements. I don't doubt you two will come to a painless form of negotiation."

"This man was rumored to be dead," the High One said.

"If I may speak for myself, Your Grace," Elnok interjected, "Rumors are simply unverified speculation."

"You never thought to ease this rather dire conjecture?"

"A tasteless prank of mine, I must admit. But it resulted in quite the spectacle upon my return."

"Then where have you been all this time, *Prince*?"

Elnok didn't let his smile fall as he replied, "Touring the continent. My brother was so determined about staying in our family's castle, but I always found it far more appealing to get to know the people of the land on a more personal level." He splayed his hands to the bustle of the banquet, "I'd say we can agree on this notion, wouldn't you?"

The High One raised a brow. "I suppose we can."

Elnok turned to the woman; her jaw remained set, eyes never leaving the High One's face. Even if this woman was a wife or concubine, the behavior felt unnaturally controlled.

"Prince Elnok, this is Sylzenya Phatris," the High One finally said, patting the woman's arm, "She gave a splendid speech, didn't she?"

It took everything within him to keep smiling. "It was excellent."

"We're glad you're on the mend," Kharis said to her.

"You're too kind," the woman, Sylzenya, replied, a thin smile replacing her stoic features.

The High One smiled. "I'm glad you both think so, especially you, Prince Elnok."

"Is that so?" Elnok asked, a tension rising in his gut.

"Quite, because while Sylzenya was originally going to be your guide only if you ever desired to tour the temple, she's extended an even more gracious gesture." The High One looked at her. "She's volunteered to be your guide during your entire stay."

Elnok's stomach dropped.

The woman finally looked at Elnok, eyes glinting in the torchlight as she offered a trite nod.

"Yes. I'll be by your side at every moment, Your Highness, so I can educate you in our people's ways. I'll make sure you receive a rich exposure of our kingdom."

He didn't let his smile falter despite the rising heat in his body. There would be no privacy for discussing plans with Kharis. She wasn't his guide—she was this leader's pet, sent to watch his every move.

My personal godsdamn hell.

The High One smiled, a glint of triumph in his features.

Elnok wished he still had his sword.

"Sylzenya, go ahead and gather your things," the High One said, "Kharis, you're dismissed to the Dynami barracks until your next mission. And Prince Elnok," he paused, a smirk on his mouth, "I'm afraid we won't be able to discuss treaty revisions for the next few days due to my schedule. But you're free to roam the kingdom as you please with Sylzenya during this time."

Elnok offered a low bow, curling his fists until his knuckles ached. "A few days is fine, as long as it doesn't take longer than that. Afraid I've many things to attend to when I get back to my brother."

"Of course, Your Highness," the High One said. "I do hope you enjoy your stay."

Elnok returned with a smile of his own. "I plan to."

CHAPTER II
HOPE

"You're *leaving* the temple?"

Sylzenya grunted as she shoved her only pair of linen pants and her only shirt into a burlap bag. She had little else to pack, every acolyte a devout practitioner of minimalist living. Besides, there wasn't much she'd need for three days out in the village. A couple extra robes would be good enough.

"Yes," Sylzenya replied.

"Right now?" Nyla questioned as she helped her pack.

"Yes, Nyla, right now."

"The High One really trusts you, doesn't he?"

Sylzenya fluttered her eyes closed. The High One *had* trusted her. Now he was testing her. She was to watch the prince and report back any suspicions, yes, but this was just the beginning. She needed to wear her holy, bloodied robe to show her devoutness, she needed to speak loudly and fervently of Aretta's graciousness, and she needed to do so as often as she could. Only if she followed through with these expectations would he give her the cure in three days.

All because she decided to mention the damned mythical willow. She should've listened to Nyla's advice back in the altar room. She should've listened to the bird's warning before she agreed to pay it's enigmatic price.

"Something like that," Sylzenya said with a thin smile, a small well of anger burning in her chest.

Her friend paused, a fresh Kreena robe in hand. "You're troubled by this task."

"I'm out of my depth," she said, the trousers fighting against her as she shoved them into the bag, "I have to keep track of a prince who's been presumed dead for over a decade, and he knows I'm only his *guide* so he can be watched."

"He should've expected it."

"Either way, this isn't what I've been training for all these years."

Nyla set down the robe and looped her arm around Sylzenya's shoulder, bringing her into an embrace.

"You're going to do fine. Great, in fact," Nyla said as she squeezed her, "You're not in charge of his actions, you're just reporting anything you see or hear, and then you'll be back in the gardens fully cured in three short days, alright?"

Sylzenya gulped. She wanted to tell Nyla everything — Aretta's Willow, the vision, the High One's dissatisfaction with her — but she feared the High One's response. He might add more days before he gave her the cure if he found out she'd told someone.

"Thanks, Nyla," she said, a real smile on her lips as she embraced her friend back. "And I've been thinking more about what you said about my parents; I think you're right. The High One says he'll take care of them, but I'd like to hear from their mouths why they did this to me."

"Confront your parents?" she asked, "Why would you do that?"

"You're joking with me, right?"

Her friend tilted her head, amber eyes shining with a

curious glint. "Why bother talking to them? It's like you said in your speech—it's over. Let the past be the past."

"What—" Sylzenya shook her head, "Everything's changed, Nyla, just like you said this morning. We *just* talked about this, and it was *your* idea that I confront them, so don't make me feel crazy."

Nyla scratched her head. "Look, my mind's a bit hazy from the wine, but I don't remember saying those things. If the High One said he's taking care of your parents, then you should let him. "

A chill ran down Sylzenya's spine as she tried to find any humor in her friend's words. But, she couldn't find the usual smirk or upraised brow.

Nyla meant every word.

"What about the increased protection at the banquet tonight?" Sylzenya pushed, determined to make her friend remember, "Dynameis were assigned to *protect* you. That's never been done before."

Nyla smiled wide, patting her shoulder. "And thanks to your announcement, that won't ever happen again. Now anyone who's deranged enough to try and sabotage our kingdom knows they can't succeed; our goddess will always find a way to protect us. Why are you doubting the High One like this?"

Her insides froze. There was that word again: *Doubt.* But she wasn't doubting, never had, not about her goddess or the High One. And she didn't plan on doing so now.

"I'm just confused," Sylzenya replied, "You honestly don't remember?"

She shrugged. "Sounds like a dull conversation anyways. All you need to worry about is this prince and letting the cure do its work."

A loud knock sounded on the door.

"Sylzenya," one of the priestesses announced, "it's time."

Taking a deep breath, she fastened her green cloak over

her bloodied Kreena robe and slung the full burlap bag onto her shoulder.

"I'm kind of jealous," Nyla said as they followed the priestess through the door and down the hallway, "I wish I could leave the temple and see how things are fairing."

Sylzenya bit her tongue hard as she held back the anger swelling in her skin. It wasn't right, this frustration, for she'd brought these circumstances upon herself. Perhaps the bright fire inside her chest wasn't anger at all, but something darker—stickier—like a claw covered in orodyte serum, wrapping around her heart and puncturing her flesh

Not anger, not sadness, not uncertainty…

Shame.

Yes, that was it. She could feel the resonance sting along her bones as she repeated the word over and over, her sandaled feet rhythmically slapping on the marble stone.

For the first time in Sylzenya's life, she felt shame.

Silence swelled in the sanctuary, thin and stretched, as if one wrong step would shatter every stained-glass window.

Forcing her chin up and shoulders back, she approached the High One, ignoring how everything between them felt bent out of shape. It was like a willow burdened with too much weight, its roots tearing from the ground as it tipped. Her parents' betrayal was enough; she couldn't bear the idea of losing the High One as well.

His yellow eyes sharpened on hers. She held her breath, a cool rush of relief flowing through her muscles as he extended his hand. No words needed to be exchanged as she carefully accepted the gesture. His gaze softened, and her shoulders relaxed.

"Sylzenya, you understand this isn't what I want for you,

correct?" the High One asked as he took her other hand in his.

Clenching her jaw, she held back tears and nodded. "Of course, Your Grace."

Cold fingers pressed into her palms. "I'm doing this because you're to bring salvation to our people, and such a task comes with a heavy burden. There's no room for doubt."

Sylzenya held her head high, forcing herself to remain steady despite her knees threatening to wobble.

"I understand, Your Grace."

Tightening his grip, he whispered, "Your parents were jealous of your destiny, jealous that our goddess and our people needed you more than you needed them. Don't let their envious act deter you from your path."

Was that why they'd done it? Out of jealousy?

"I won't," Sylzenya replied, nostrils flaring, "I promise."

He smiled. "Good. Once you've spent these next three days sharing this same message with our people while keeping an eye on the prince, I will give you the cure. Your power *will* be restored, as well as my trust in you."

The pain from her back ached at his words, the deep desire to feel the earth sing through her fingertips and into her veins causing tears to blind her vision.

"Thank you," she whispered.

The High One nodded, staring at her hands. "You're our only hope, Sylzenya. Not just for our kingdom, but for me."

He turned his gaze back to her, a deep emotion sitting in his eyes. Her spine shivered as he carefully dug a hand in one of his robe's pockets, revealing a long golden chain. Connecting the chain was a piece of orodyte—symmetrical, clear in its make, and glinting off of the torchlight.

Perfect.

"This is for you," he said, "Once your powers are restored, I want you to use this piece of orodyte to create the willow I had asked for your Kreena Rite."

Shame and hope twisted inside her chest. Dark and light. Poison and power. She bowed her head, the cold metal of the chain stinging her warm skin as its weight fell onto her shoulders.

"You're everything a ruler could've asked for in times such as these."

Suddenly, the bird's deep blue eyes flashed in her mind.

Be wary of who you trust.

She ignored it. The vision and the bird had done nothing but bring more problems.

"Thank you, Your Grace," she whispered again, lifting her head and touching the orodyte.

"Now," he paused, motioning to the doors, "it's time."

Back stinging and cloak heavy around her shoulders, she offered a strong nod and followed him out into the gardens. The prince and two guards stood underneath a circle of torchlight and willows.

Blood pumping loudly in her ears, her pain sharpened as the royal stared at her with bright green eyes. Dark hair fell to his shoulders, loose strands framing his face as he crossed his arms, his strong build accentuated by a broad chest and formidable arms. He looked less like a royal and more like a warrior, especially with the scars peppered along his arms.

He leaned forward, brow raised in question.

"*Sylzenya*," the High One said, the softness in his face gone.

"Apologies," she replied, pushing the pain as far away as she could manage, "I'm ready."

As the guards led them out of the Temple's main gate, the prince's smile vanished. Sylzenya looked back.

The High One's harsh yellow gaze vanished under sandstone wall.

She gripped the orodyte necklace.

"*Sylzenya*, right?" the prince said, interrupting her thoughts as he stepped in front of her. "Look, I don't mean to rush things, but I am. So if we could find an inn, tavern, anything really, then we can get out of each other's hair and sleep. In fact, I'm not against us staying in separate places for the night either."

She narrowed her eyes. "There's only one inn, and it's not far. We'll go there."

He laughed. "*One* inn?"

"My kingdom doesn't have need for *two* inns," she replied, "That would be unnecessary excess.

"What about travele—?" He stopped, brows furrowed. "Ah, right."

"Everyone in Estea has a home, so there's no need for inns. But we have one for people like yourself." She took a deep breath. "Or apparently people like me."

"I see you're looking forward to these next three days, then."

Sylzenya's face burned, but she quickly collected herself. "I'm happy to do whatever it is the High One asks of me."

"Oh yes, I gathered that."

Sylzenya ignored him. She walked in step with the two guards as the prince trailed behind. The dirt path smelled like fresh roses, the scent reminding her of the many days she had walked it with her parents before her time at the temple. Her mother would pick one of the flowers and tuck it behind Sylzenya's ear.

Flower bud.

Sylzenya's back suddenly stung, warm blood beginning to soak through her robes. Damn this orodyte serum that kept her from healing, and damn her parents with it.

Cursing under her breath, she turned her focus to the prince. He was an easy man to stare at—a strong jaw with some light stubble, thick dark hair tucked behind one ear revealing gold hoops, and a curious gaze drinking everything in its path. His gaze found hers. She looked away, pretending to observe the trees as intently as he had been, but she didn't miss the smirk pulling at his lips.

"We'll be there soon," she announced, "The guards will fetch you some fresh garments while you get yourself settled. The High One knows Lhaal Forest doesn't allow for much traveling gear."

"How thoughtful of him."

Despite his handsome face, she didn't miss the bite of sarcasm in his tone, and it set her nerves on edge.

"It *is* thoughtful of him. More than you know."

"Glad we can agree on it."

She stopped. "Is there a problem?"

He smirked. "Is there? I thought we were in agreement: The High One is *very* thoughtful."

"You—" She caught herself, closing her eyes.

She was tired, hungry, and parched. The last thing she needed was to get in an argument with a man—a royal—she'd just met. He was new to her kingdom, and he'd just gotten through Lhaal Forest. Surely he needed rest as well.

Taking a deep breath, she smiled. "Right. We agree."

He leaned forward and whispered, "*Right.*"

Heat rising along her neck, she quickly turned and walked past the guards, leading them through the last stretch of pathway and into a large clearing.

Sylzenya's heart stilled.

Towering trees createded a canopy overhead, fireflies floating just below like twinkling stars. White stone buildings circled the plaza, each structure covered in twisting vines and blooming flowers. Torches lit the night, providing subtle warmth while people walked, laughed, and drank wine.

A memory brought her to a hot summer night long ago. Her father had crafted two nets, and they had spent hours chasing fireflies until they fell into the tall grass, their chests heaving in laughter.

He left her at the temple two days later.

"Praise be to Aretta!" someone shouted from the center of the square.

Sylzenya jumped, backing into one of the guards, their firm hands tightening around her shoulders.

"It's *her,*" another shouted, their speech slurred, "the one who will save us from the famine!"

"Great," a low grumble sounded in her ear, "more drunks."

She turned to find not one of the guards, but the prince, holding her. His fingers dug into her cloak as his eyes narrowed at the crowd, a look of disgust in his features. A shiver ran up her spine as she flinched out of his grasp.

"It's called celebrating," Sylzenya responded, "Most people enjoy it."

"Not all," he muttered.

She disregarded him, turning to find the guards staring at her. Bodies rigid, they stood as if they were trees themselves, roots securing their feet to the ground.

Waiting.

"Show us!" another person in the crowd shouted, "Show us Aretta's power!"

The orodyte around her neck grew heavy.

"Quite the crowd," the prince said with a sigh, "Anyways, where's the inn? Food sounds like a good place to start…"

Sylzenya didn't hear anything else; everyone in the square had stopped their sauntering and drinking to stare at her in anticipation. An opportunity had presented itself to proclaim her destiny as Estea's security for a fruitful future. She had to make it clear she could take on this burden—had to make it clear so the High One could trust her again.

Taking a steadying breath, she stepped forward.

"…and is there any clean water here?" the prince continued, "Hang on, what are you doing?"

Sylzenya unclipped her green cloak, motioning for a guard. He promptly took it from her grasp and draped it over his forearm. The crowd murmured, conversation increasing as she revealed her Kreena robe, the same one she wore the day of her failed rite.

The proof of power.

"I'm sorry to interrupt whatever the fuck this is, but what are you doing?"

Sylzenya waved her hand at the prince. "Patience, Prince of Vutror. We'll get to your soft royal bed soon enough."

He cursed under his breath as she stepped forward and spread her arms, the crowd falling utterly silent.

CHAPTER 12
WINE RITUAL

Elnok had been right.

This woman *was* his personal hell.

Spinning his gold ring, Elnok glared at her back. The last thing he needed was a detour involving this Kreena putting on a second bullshit act. But here he stood, surrounded by wide-eyed drunkards listening to this woman's "holy" speech about a goddess who died centuries ago. A deity who supposedly "protected their people" from the continent's famine and sickness.

How gracious of their goddess to save Esteans and no one else.

Sylzenya shouted to the crowd, "In Aretta's final stand with her brother, Distrathrus, the god of chaos, she knew she had no choice but to sacrifice herself, for their godhood was intertwined. The only way to rid him from this earth was to rid herself of it as well. Through this display of death, we're taught that pain and sacrifice are the only ways to sustain life."

"*Praise be to Aretta*!"

"And so, behold the robes of every Kreena and acolyte alike." She motioned to the dried blood on her robe.

Elnok's stomach soured. A deep cut spanned her back,

fresh blood dripping from it and adding to the browned stains. It looked as if someone had taken a dagger and sliced her open with horrifying accuracy and intention.

And yet, these people cheered louder.

Sylzenya continued, "Our blood demonstrates how it is through our pain and sacrifice that Estea can survive another day. And we *will* continue to survive."

As the crowd cheered louder, Elnok curled his rope around his hand, wringing it tight, a bloom of pain riding along his veins.

Survive?

These people didn't know the word. Estea was a kingdom flowing with red wine and filled with green trees.

Abundance. Resources. Life.

A fire had been stoking in his gut, fanning into a brighter flame with each word this woman professed—with each praise these people lifted into the air. They talked as if they were on the precipice of death, yet it was clear none of them had known a day of hunger in their life.

"I'll be joining my fellow Kreenas soon," she continued, "My body will be freed from this orodyte serum once the cure has run its course, and I promise you I will do everything within my power to keep this famine on the other side of Lhaal Forest until it's my time to join Aretta in her soil."

The crowd's noise grew deafening.

Elnok rolled his eyes.

"This week we host the Prince of Vutror, Elnok Rogdul; let us show him the sacrifice of our people so he might join us in our celebration."

The crowd jumbled together, moving sporadically until they created a path through the square. In the center of the plaza stood a white marble statue. Squinting his eyes, Elnok's soured stomach churned.

"Prince Elnok," Sylzenya said as she turned to him, any hesitancy he'd seen in her now gone, "This is Aretta's fountain, where the villagers partake of the fountain's wine to promote prosperity. It's my job to ensure you a rich exposure of Estea, so I invite you to participate."

Elnok smiled. "I'm not one to celebrate."

Her eyes darkened. "If you don't, then you're wishing death on everyone in this square."

And what if that's what I want?

He fought back the urge to say it. He needed to keep his mask secure, portray himself as the dutiful prince helping his sick brother with treaty revisions. He needed to bring the least amount of attention to himself as possible if his and Kharis' plans to find the tree were to work, which, thanks to this woman, might be impossible.

Refusing to participate could create an uproar.

"Of course," he said with a stiff bow, "my apologies."

She didn't smile, didn't reply, didn't do anything except turn around and approach the fountain. He considered running, but one of the guards pushed him forward. Gritting his teeth and pasting on a royal smile, he followed.

The last time he'd tasted wine was the day he'd escaped his brother. It'd been forced down his throat then, and it was being forced upon him now. He had no choice but to drink it —not if he wanted to appear harmless.

Not if he wanted to find the tree and save Orym.

Sylzenya lifted her hands towards the statue. The carving was of a woman in a flowing robe, both hands placed over her heart. The wine poured from it as if it were blood.

"May our sacrifices bring her glory," Sylzenya shouted.

Silence hung across the plaza, ominous and holy as she cupped her hands and brought the wine to her mouth. Elnok's eyes widened as everyone in the crowd kneeled, even the children, and bowed their foreheads to the ground. Something between disgust and fear roiled in his chest at the heaviness; he felt crushed under this sense of sacrifice in exchange for life.

Yet, wasn't that what he was doing for Orym?

He shoved the thought away as he finally saw what he'd been hoping for: Sylzenya's hands shook, lower lip quivering as she surveyed the plaza. Sweat lined her forehead, a droplet dripping down her temple as she gulped. A crack in her facade, just like he'd seen earlier that evening on the temple's balcony. The look of someone hiding something—the look of a liar.

The moment she found his stare, her arms stilled, lips curving into a confident smile and dark blue eyes glimmering with purpose as if nothing happened.

As if he didn't see through her little act.

"Prince Elnok," she said, motioning for him to approach the fountain, "if you would."

The crowd returned to their feet, whispers floating through the air, discussion growing the longer he waited. He could try and expose her, although he wasn't sure what exactly he'd be exposing. Besides, these people had no reason to trust him. They *bowed* before her, as if she was their goddess in the flesh.

He'd have to drink the wine, and *then* he'd uncover Sylzenya's secret.

"Of course," Elnok replied, heart racing as he approached the fountain.

The heat in his body chilled as the sharp scent filled his nose. He worked his jaw back and forth. The wine's deep red color appeared almost black in the white fountain. He could smell the burning steel rod as he filled his hands with the wine. He could hear Tosh's voice as he slowly lifted the liquid to his lips.

He drank two sips before his knees cracked against hard marble.

The plaza disappeared. Tosh's angry shouts surrounded him, his brother jeering at him—taunting him.

You're going to steal it from me.

You always wanted the Crown.

You're planning to kill me!

Dark damp stone encircled him—Vutror's dungeons closing in tighter and tighter. Hot iron pressed into Elnok's back, his family's royal symbol branded into his skin. Elnok's throat burned as he screamed. He begged Tosh to stop, tried to tell him he didn't want the Crown. But Tosh wouldn't listen, tempering the steel rod again and pressing it into Elnok's burning flesh.

Bile rose in his throat, the wine stinging as it came back up and passed over his tongue. He gasped for air as Tosh's screams threatened to drown him.

The rod burned him a final time before he lost consciousness.

Elnok woke to murmuring voices. Soft fabric pilled underneath his fingers as he took a deep breath, the mattress he laid on groaning in response. Blinking away the haziness in his vision, he tried to sit, but his aching muscles refused.

"I need to guarantee the villagers you'll be staying with him at all times," an old woman's voice whispered.

"And you can tell them it will be so. I swear on Aretta's blood," Sylzenya whispered back.

"Do you think—?" The old woman's voice caught as she lowered her voice further, "Do you think he's brought the famine with him? Will our people be wrought by sickness? Are we cursed now?"

"He wouldn't have made it through Lhaal Forest if that were so," Sylzenya replied, "You can tell the villagers there's nothing to fear. Our goddess stopped Distrathrus; she wouldn't leave us vulnerable to a man who can't hold his wine."

Elnok's mind fought to catch up. The villagers were frightened *he'd* brought the famine and plague to them. If his chest didn't ache so much, he might've laughed.

"Of course, Your Holiness," the old woman replied.

"Please, Helena, you can just call me Sylzenya."

"Your kindness has been missed since the day you were dedicated to the temple." The woman, Helena, continued, "It's why I was so glad to hear it was you, of all Kreenas, who had been gifted with such power. And as far as your parents…" The woman took a heavy breath. "I should've known something was wrong. They'd stopped coming to the weekly fountain ceremonies, but I had assumed it was because your mother's shop was extra busy due to the springtime bloom."

"It's alright," Sylzenya interrupted, "even the High One hadn't expected it. Everything's been figured out, and I can already feel my power grow stronger each day."

Elnok didn't miss the strain in her voice.

"Praise Aretta herself," Helena breathed, "You know, the villagers would be less frightened by the Vutrorian prince if you were to demonstrate your power."

Sylzenya huffed a small laugh. "I wish I could. But, the High One informed me I can't use my power until this cure has finished its work. I'm afraid a demonstration will have to wait until then."

A silence pulled in the room. Elnok fought his way up to his elbows. Sylzenya stood in the doorway, her back to him. She no longer wore her white bloodied robe but a plain brown linen shirt and black linen pants, her ash-colored hair in a single plait down her back. The old woman stood outside the doorway, the gentle wrinkles on her face deepening as she stared long and hard.

"I see," she replied, "Then I'll let the villagers know you'll be with the prince every hour of every day."

Sylzenya nodded. "Fine by me."

Helena narrowed her gaze. "I hope you find peaceful sleep, Your Holiness."

Sylzenya raised her hand as if to reply, but Helena shut the door. Sylzenya's head drooped along with her shoulders.

Go back to sleep before she sees you.

It's what Elnok had wanted for over a day now: time to get some fucking rest after an entire day in Lhaal Forest, almost being killed by arachnis, playing political pawn for the High One, and drinking the same fucking wine his brother drowned himself in.

But instead, he stared at this nuisance of a woman and felt… sorry for her.

Damnit.

"So I'm cursed now?" Elnok said, his throat sharp with pain.

Sylzenya jumped, missing a step as she stumbled against the door. She cursed as she stood upright, brushing dust off her pants. Elnok laughed, the pressure in his chest turning into a fit of coughs.

"You could've told us you were awake," she replied, blowing a loose strand of hair out of her face.

"But there's nothing quite like hearing what others have to say about you when they think you're unconscious," Elnok said with a smile, "and I must say, I'm rather offended you only see me as a man who can't hold his wine. Being seen as a curse sounds far more interesting."

"And who says that's not how I truly feel about you, Prince?"

"Please, Sylzenya, you can just call me Elnok." He smirked.

She muttered a string of curses as she strode away from the door. Elnok's smile grew wider, finding he enjoyed this crude side of her, until she walked behind a white sheet draped across the room, splitting it in half.

Using *his* rope.

"What is this?" Elnok questioned as he sat up straight, wincing at the pain in his shoulders, "Give me back my rope. If you do it quickly, I'll forget this offense."

She slid the white sheet to the side, poking her face through. "I'd rather not."

She disappeared behind the sheet again.

He let out a long sigh.

"It isn't meant for *decor*," Elnok replied as he tried to stand, but everything became dizzy. He collapsed back on the bed instead.

"Too bad," she responded. "While you slept, I spent hours convincing everyone *not* to arrest and kill you. Thanks to your inability to drink a few sips of wine, we have to share this damned room otherwise everyone thinks you're going to go on a rampage and curse our kingdom with withering crops and dried riverbeds." She popped her head out of the sheet again, "So, your rope is collateral damage for the sake of my privacy."

Elnok rolled his eyes, anger rising in his chest. "Your kingdom is fucking insane."

"Wonderful. I'll let the High One know."

Shit.

Even though he was tired and hungry, he needed to keep in good standing with the High One. He couldn't afford problems if he was going to find the healing tree.

"What I meant was that I'm not used to this sort of thing. All these rituals and customs…" he said, exasperation in his breath as he allowed some true part of him to be seen, "I'm out of my depth here."

He waited for her sharp response, but it didn't come. Instead, she slowly moved the sheet to the side. She was on the ground, legs criss-crossed and face softened.

"Look, let's just get some decent sleep tonight," she finally said, "And then we can try this again in the morning. A fresh start."

"You won't tell the High One I called your people fucking insane?"

"As long as you don't tell everyone you're cursed."

Relief washed through him. "Deal."

"Deal." She motioned to a side table. "Helena made you some salted rice. Should help with your stomach and keep you full."

She disappeared behind the curtain.

Elnok grunted as he ate the entire bowl. It'd been years since he'd had rice, the last of those crops having died out when he was a young boy. Wistful memories flashed in his mind of those days before his parents died.

Tosh and him learning how to fence together, disobeying their instructors and fighting in the hallways, inevitably disrupting courtly meetings. They'd laughed until they couldn't breathe; ate chilled grapes in the heat of summer; and listened to their parent's stories about green trees and bountiful feasts.

Yearning ached in Elnok's chest. If Aretta's Willow could cure Orym's sickness, perhaps it wasn't a terrible idea for it to cure Tosh as well. If they found it, maybe Elnok wouldn't just save his friend, but his brother too.

Maybe they could laugh together. Tell stories. Be a family again.

But he's a monster.

He turned on his side, the bed creaking noisily. Nothing could change what Tosh had done, even if he was cured. Besides, Elnok didn't have any leads for this damned healing tree. Kharis said to start looking in the temple, but would there really be any information no one else knew about? If the High One didn't want it found, he'd make sure of it.

Either way, Elnok needed to try.

He'd start the search tomorrow.

CHAPTER 13
SECRET REVEALED

Sylzenya had known the cut would hurt, every girl's first always did, but she'd been foolish to believe it no worse than that of a bee's sting. While she'd never been bitten by a serpentum, its fangs sinking into flesh, thick and sharp, ripping at her without promise of release, she imagined this to be similar.

Everything within her begged surrender.

Instead, she dug her fingers deeper into the damp soil, the golden light of her goddess' power trailing wide circles around her wrists, up her forearms, and slicing deep into the soft flesh of her back.

Thump.

Thump.

Thump.

A heartbeat. She'd heard of this before, how Aretta's life continued to live on through the soil.

The dirt between her hands shook. Crumbling earth sifted this way and that until a tiny green sprout broke in between her fingers. Eyes wide, Sylzenya leaned forward. The sprout grew rapidly, the golden power of her goddess wrapping itself around what had become a thick tree trunk. Taller it grew until it towered over her. Bright excitement tingled her hands as tree limbs unfurled from the soft brown trunk, leaves blooming like crowded grapes on a vine. The willow tree cast a cool blanket of shade over her heated skin.

"Careful, child," a commanding voice ushered from behind. "That's enough for today."

Sylzenya meant to obey the command, but then a gray and white feathered bird landed on one of the willow's branches. Its bright eyes found hers, an unfathomable blue that pierced deeper than the cut spanning her back. Something about it seemed… familiar. The golden light tightened around her arms, squeezing as the bird continued its unruly stare.

"*Sylzenya*," her mother's voice called.

All in one breath, Sylzenya released her hands from the dirt and fell back, elbows sinking into wet earth. Her goddess' power retreated into the dirt in one quick blink. Head tilting back, she searched the newly created branches for the bird.

But it was gone.

"You have a gifted child," the High One announced.

He approached the willow, his white hair drifting in the breeze with his white robes. His warm yellow gaze found hers. He brushed the back of his hand against the bark, surprise lighting his face. She'd only seen the High One once before, and she'd been just as intrigued by his ageless face then as she was now.

He smiled. "She will make a powerful acolyte in the years to come."

A loud shout of praise to their goddess rang through the ancient Willow Grove. Sylzenya gathered herself as she peered at the all the women lined side by side. Each was draped in shining white robes that wrapped around their bodies in intricate designs, accentuating their curves and exposing part of their chest, stomach, and legs to the warm sunshine overhead.

The Kreenas of Aretta's Temple.

But then she found the gaze of her parents. Her father's dark blue eyes matched his tunic while her mother's ash-colored hair blended in with her white linen dress.

Both wore a sense of pride shadowed by sadness; it felt as if vines twisted around Sylzenya's throat, choking her.

"You may have your final words with her," the High One said.

Just as Sylzenya refused to succumb to the pain, so she refused to shed the tears that formed at the corners of her eyes. Her mother whispered her name, the familiar grip of her father's calloused hand resting on her shoulder. Sylzenya willed herself to breathe.

"It's beautiful, my flower bud," her mother whispered as she crouched next to her, "Your power is greater than we could've hoped for."

Clenching her jaw, Sylzenya shut her eyes tight. "It is."

"Darling, you need not fear," her father voiced, his hand squeezing gently, "I know you worry for us, but we'll be taken care of, as will you. It's best this way."

Her knuckles turned white as her fingernails dug into her palms. Their lives had been difficult. Her father was a lowly guard with such limited power from their goddess that most places of occupation dismissed him after a month or two. And her mother's power only allowed her to keep their naturally grown produce fresh for a single day, unlike most women who could do so for three or four. They didn't make much of a living, but they did it together, relying on their own hands to feed themselves.

But now that she'd proven her affinity to Aretta's power, all of that would change. She would become an apprentice to a Kreena, living in the temple until her dying days while her parents watched from afar. At least they would have access to the temple's plentiful foods, the same kind Sylzenya would be producing for her people in the years to come.

She should be grateful; this day meant her parents would toil less and live more.

And yet, sadness filled her heart.

"Not a day will pass where we won't be thinking of you," her mother spoke, "You understand why this must happen, don't you?"

"I do," Sylzenya whispered.

They'd discussed it extensively. If Sylzenya held great enough power, then she would be needed to keep her kingdom safe. She'd agreed to it then, but now everything felt different.

It felt real.

"Let us see your stone," her father said.

Sylzenya obeyed, pulling away the dirt that surrounded the willow's trunk. A yellow glow fought through the soil, lighting her eyes once she dug far enough to retrieve it. Carefully, she wrapped her fingers around it, the once clear white crystal now pulsing with a yellow light at its center. The orodyte was no larger than a ripe apple.

"Do you understand what this is?" her father inquired.

"Dynameis wear it on their armor," Sylzenya answered. "It's where their power comes from, so they might defeat the monsters of Lhaal Forest."

"Your studies have done you well," her father said, "But there's more. The only way you could create life through the earth is by gathering its impurities and sealing it in this piece of orodyte. In turn, Dynameis can wield the impurity held in this stone through their connection with Aretta's powers, using what was meant to destroy the earth to instead kill those monstrous creatures that threaten our borders." He paused, sliding a finger down the stone. "You've gifted our people a chance to survive in more ways than one."

Sylzenya couldn't stop her hand from shaking.

"Flower bud," her mother whispered as she softly folded Sylzenya's hand into hers, "It's a responsibility that will come with time. You're only a sapling of fourteen years. A Kreena will be your guide these next ten to perfect your skills. You needn't fear this."

Her parents thought she feared the power she held, but they couldn't be further from the truth.

She feared a life apart from them.

"I'll do my best," Sylzenya said as she forced her hand to cease its trembling, "for Aretta, for our people..."

For both of you.

"We know you will," her father said with a gentle voice. "We look forward to the day we see your beautiful, shining face again."

Her mother and father embraced her. Sylzenya dug her fingers into their arms, their warm, familiar scents causing the sobs in her throat to well inside of her. The orodyte slipped from her fingers.

"The time has come, Sylzenya," the High One proclaimed, his voice deep as the thrum of her own heartbeat.

Her parents let her go.

She clung to them, digging her nails into her father's tunic and her mother's dress.

"Please," she whispered, "don't leave me."

Her father's eyes turned glassy, brows dipping as he caressed her face. Hope lit her chest. She knew this face. He would take her back, tell the High One this was a mistake. They wouldn't leave her here unless she wanted it. They loved her too greatly to let her go.

"We'll see you soon, Sylzenya," he whispered, kissing her forehead in goodbye, "I promise."

No.

The High One carefully pried Sylzenya's hands off of her parents. One of the Kreenas came to their side, her long black hair plaited in two strands down her back.

Suddenly, the ground quaked, and Sylzenya's willow twisted into itself.

She backed away, tripping over a rogue branch, hitting the

dirt as the tree grew without her power. Horror filled her lungs as she opened her mouth in a soundless scream. The sun disappeared, casting the grove in darkness. Every tree and person disappeared into shadow, everything except her willow. Instead, the tree grew taller and wider.

Blinding light erupted from the tree. Sylzenya covered her face, tears staining her cheeks as she tried to run, but her muscles refused.

"For life there is a price, and only in pain is it made whole, Sylzenya Phatris," a loud voice echoed from the glowing tree —*Aretta's Willow*, "Your choice has been made, and so your consequence is set in blood and stone."

Pain shot up her back as the gray and white feathered bird flew to her, landing at her feet. The memory of her dedication to the temple had vanished.

"*Please,*" Sylzenya yelled at the bird, "I take it back. I don't need the compass. I don't need Aretta's Willow!"

"If you're to restore your power and protect your people, then Aretta's Willow is the only way," the bird said, "Was this not what I told you, Sylzenya Phatris?"

"I found a cure," she replied, "I don't need the tree."

The bird cawed with laughter. "You found a cure, then where is it?"

Sylzenya gulped. "The High One's almost done making it. I'll have it soon and my power will be restored."

"*Be wary of who you trust.*"

"I should've never trusted *you*."

"I told you you would regret this path." The bird continued, "What has been sealed cannot be undone. Find the compass, Sylzenya, or all will be lost. Find Aretta's Willow, or more than just your power and people will be taken away."

A flower broke through the ground and bloomed, its petals twisting and glowing until it turned into the golden compass, its center glowing with the single piece of bark pointing to the glowing tree. Another flower tore through the dirt and transformed into a golden ring. It shone like the sun, only to turn crimson, melting into blood. An orodyte emerged from the ground, the blood filling the stone until it pulsed a glowing red.

"*The price for life will always be pain.*" the bird echoed, its body snatched by a claw of twigs, its blood and feathers swirling into the darkness.

Sharp pain ruptured along Sylzenya's back as everything around her swirled into a blinding white. She screamed louder, begging the bird to come back and tell her what it all meant—

She jolted awake, sweat dripping down her face. Gulping thick spit down her throat, she remembered herself; she was in the village, following through with the High One's orders, sharing a room with—

"Did you have a nice dream?" a deep voice asked from the darkness.

Prince Elnok. Sylzenya turned to find him sitting on the floor next to her bed, holding a candle, his face tossed in light and shadow.

"My apologies," she said, "Did I wake you?"

She lifted her hands, only to find she couldn't. Confusion pulled at her mind as she tried again only to realize they were secured to her bedpost.

With rope.

"Like I said, my rope isn't made for decor," Prince Elnok said, motioning to the bed sheet no longer suspended between their sides of the room. "Now," he continued, tilting his head, "Tell me everything you know about Aretta's Willow."

Blood raced through her heart and veins, her breaths uneven. She tried to stay calm, but this man's unwavering gaze had her shaking. Wrists chafing against the rope, she wondered why she'd thought to stay in this room with a man who had been claimed dead for ten years.

Be wary of who you trust.

"I don't know what you're going on about," Sylzenya

replied, trying to keep her voice even, "I had a nightmare, that's it. Now let me go, or I'll tell the High One about this."

Prince Elnok stood up. Setting the candle on her bedside table, he took hold of the rope and tightened it. She winced, the rough material biting into her wrists. She wanted to scream for the innkeeper, but the woman might believe this prince *was* cursed.

Rumors would start. She'd fail the High One's tasks, and then he'd withhold her cure. She needed to get out of this as calmly as possible.

Elnok ignored her words, "The issue here is that if you don't tell me what you know about Aretta's Willow and this compass you screamed about, I might just let your little secret slip with one of these villagers. I'm guessing rumors spread fast in this kingdom."

Sweat poured down her aching back. "Again, I have no idea what you're talking about."

"*The villagers would be less frightened if you were to demonstrate your power,*" he said, mocking the innkeeper's voice, "What'd you tell that sweet old lady, again? Something about how the cure hasn't fully developed in your body or some bullshit?" He crossed his arms. "How do you think your kingdom would feel knowing you've been lying to them about this *cure*?"

Her stomach dropped. Everything she'd said in the dream, she'd said out loud.

He had heard everything.

"It isn't a lie," she seethed.

"Gods, your trust in your 'blessed' High One is remarkable. So, according to him, you're going to receive a cure. Why not just tell your kingdom the truth, then?" He leaned forward, his green eyes shifting in the candlelight, "What do you think your leader is hiding?"

The blood drained from her face. She yanked against the rope only for it to tighten more. She cursed.

"He isn't hiding anything," she muttered.

"I'm sure." He smiled. "Now, what do you say? Tell me about the healing tree and compass, and I'll keep this secret tucked away nice and tight? I'd say it's a pretty generous offer."

Sylzenya gritted her teeth, snarling at him as his smile grew.

"Why do you need the tree?"

"Now *that* is privileged information." He leaned even closer, her body shivering as his breath brushed her ear, "And I'd be careful if I were you. I'm exceptionally clever when it comes to identifying lies. So if you choose to do so, I'll know." He leaned back. "Although you can certainly try."

Sylzenya surveyed his face. A roguish grin with severe eyes.

"You're bluffing," she said.

He raised his brows. "An interesting assumption. Would you like to test that theory?"

No, she wouldn't.

"You forget the piece of leverage I still hold against you."

"Ah, yes, how I'm here to *curse* your kingdom. Very well, you tell them I'm cursed, and I'll tell them you don't have any power to save them. Then we'll both lose."

"You'd risk that?" she asked. "Being arrested and thrown in our dungeons for a life sentence?"

"Maybe they'll let us share a cell. Then we can be miserable together."

"A punishment far worse than death," she muttered.

"I'll have you know I make a great cellmate."

"Not surprised to hear it wouldn't be your first time. Are you even a prince?"

He grinned. "I'm what people might call a man of many trades."

"So you're a liar."

"Oh, I'm very much a royal by blood, although my lifestyle may not be a reflection most people expect from a man entitled to a crown."

She stared at him in silence, the single flame burning to its final moments as she cursed this man and his godsdamn rope.

"So," he said, stepping back, "What will it be? Tell me about Aretta's Willow and its compass, or inform your people that their holy chosen one is a fraud?"

Biting the inside of her cheek, she stared into the prince's green unwavering eyes. There wasn't much he could do with the information regarding Aretta's Willow, the excessive amount of willows in the temple making the search for the compass impossible. The consequences were minimal, if any at all, but if the truth about the cure got out… her people could lose their faith altogether.

She'd fail her task.

"Untie me and I'll tell you," she said, her arms no longer shaking, her heart having slowed, "But you're not going to like it."

His confidence didn't waver as he released her from the ropes.

"Try me."

CHAPTER 14

CHANGE OF HEART

It hadn't taken long for the woman to tell Elnok everything regarding Aretta's Willow. And while he found satisfaction in discovering her secret *and* learning vital information about the healing tree, the search only seemed more difficult than before.

She'd said it'd be an impossible task to locate the compass. He'd challenged her limited thinking.

But, since being asked to take off his shoes out of respect for the goddess, and walking along the willow-infested temple hallways, he realized it'd been foolish to misjudge her assessment. Willows lined every blank space, save for the thin path in the middle of each hallway. And according to Sylzenya, these trees were *sacred*, which meant no one was allowed to leave even a scratch.

In other words, no digging through them to find an ancient, enchanted object.

"And this is just the main entrance," Sylzenya said as she motioned him forward, "There's over sixty rooms in this temple, each of them filled with willows."

"Seems excessive."

"They're holy."

"Oh come on," he whispered as they walked through the hallway, bare feet slapping against the marble floor, "You really think it isn't a little overdone?"

Nostrils flaring, she picked up her pace. He followed her in stride.

"Let's work together on this," he said, "You made a bargain of some kind because you wanted a cure, so let's not waste it."

"I've no need for a cure as I have one on the way." She avoided his gaze. "I'm just here to give you a tour of the temple, as per your request."

"And to convince me to give up on finding the compass."

"If you want to tear into one of the willows, be my guest."

"You just want to see me chained up after I used my rope on you," he said with a wide grin.

"A criminal, a prince, and now a child." She jeered, "Man of many trades, indeed."

"Very funny."

She glanced at him sidelong. "Your words, not mine."

He scoffed as he continued to follow her through the temple. He'd hoped her confession would ignite something in her, a desire to find the willow that she seemed to previously have had. But he couldn't match whatever hold the High One had over her.

He'd have to find the compass alone.

Maybe the Estean warrior had some insight… if he could find a way to contact Kharis.

"And this is the healing pool," Sylzenya announced, breaking the silence.

Steam filled his lungs as they entered the large circular room. Warm water slapped against his feet; a tingle sent up into his skin.

"When Kreenas and acolytes have finished their work for the day, they come here to heal their backs." Sylzenya continued, "It's also the only room without a living willow in it, the steam an unpleasant environment for it."

Elnok stepped forward. A pool filled the center of the room—glittering tiles on the bottom glowing in the shape of a tree.

"How's it doing that?" he asked.

"One of Aretta's last gifts to us was a pool of water with healing capabilities. It can't heal anything marred by steel or human tools, only power; power opens our skin, and so power heals us."

"So it's your power that does… that?" He motioned to her back. "That cut and the bleeding?"

She raised a brow. "To create life means we must give life. Aretta's blood lives in the soil; we use it to create plants and vegetation, so our life must be given in exchange. Life for life. Blood for blood."

"Seems taxing. And painful."

"The burdens we bear usually are."

Yellow stained-glass windows shaped like willow trees bathed the massive room in a warm glow, shining light on the pool and the wall's carvings. Elnok approached one of the walls, hands behind his back as he tried to decipher the meaning behind its images.

"This is the story of the Origin, the birth of the continent," Sylzenya said, joining him.

"Let me guess, a god bled all over the earth and life was born?"

"That's a part of it," she replied.

"And what's the rest of it?" Elnok asked, the drawings depicted trees, humans, and unusually shaped creatures. Perhaps the drawings could provide a clue to the compass' location.

Imbecile.

He was grasping for smoke, but he had no other leads, and Sylzenya clearly wasn't going to help him. Better start somewhere.

"Do you actually care?" she questioned.

"I believe you promised me a 'rich exposure' of your kingdom, history included."

Her eyes brightened. Elnok couldn't help the small smile that tugged at his mouth.

"Legend says Aretta and Distrathrus were born of the same star, split in half—brother and sister. They formed two halves of one whole, Aretta spilling her blood onto an empty sphere, creating land and water, while Distrathrus ushered creatures to populate it. According to the legend, they found joy in working together for centuries, their creativity a balance of light and dark, order and chaos."

She moved her hand across the wall, a warm grin peeling across her lips. Elnok leaned forward.

"But then Aretta made humans, and everything changed," Sylzenya said, her hand sweeping across a new image, "She loved them dearly, giving some the gift of her own power. She cared for every human as much as Distrathrus cared for his creatures. Inspired by her decision to try something new, Distrathrus created novel creatures as well."

He walked with Sylzenya as the images wrapped around the room, the carvings evolving into creatures with sharp teeth and jagged tails.

"But his creatures were treacherous. They attacked the humans. Killed thousands."

Blood, spears, and monsters populated the next image.

"Aretta declared he rid their earth of his monsters. But, Distrathrus claimed it was the humans who attacked first, for humans had something his monsters lacked—free will. Aretta disagreed, showing him that humans only killed when protecting themselves from threats. Distrathrus saw humans as beings who'd poisoned his sister's mind and taken her from him. And so, in his unchecked anger, he unleashed his monsters on humans, bending their will to kill so he might have his sister back."

Elnok's brow furrowed. "He made them kill out of bloodlust?"

She stared at the images. "The monsters in Lhaal Forest live off of plants and small creatures. They don't eat humans." She turned to him. "They kill us for the sake of killing."

A shudder ran up his spine.

"And so Aretta and Distrathrus went to war, humans against monsters. The Last Stand, we call it. Thankfully, Aretta won by destroying him and over half of his monsters, but not before Distrathrus placed a curse on the continent. She was able to save Estea in her final breaths, trapping the remaining monsters inside Lhaal Forest. Distrathrus claimed everything else, cursing the ground with dead soil and drying rivers for the years to come on the land Aretta hadn't reached. He was a true monster—the god of chaos." She stopped, the wall's images ending with a bright glowing tree. "And while he left a piece of himself with his monsters, Aretta left us with one last piece of herself as well—the healing tree."

Sylzenya turned, her deep blue eyes shimmering in the golden light. She wasn't wearing a mask anymore. No gimmicks, no performance. The lines at the corner of her eyes scrunched while the corners of her mouth lifted ever so slightly.

Elnok found himself at a loss for words.

She lifted her necklace, the clear stone catching the light.

"Aretta's Willow produces a special kind of sap, crystallizing into a substance that can't be broken by anything other than Vutrorian steel."

Elnok's eyes widened.

"Orodyte," he breathed.

"Yes." Sylzenya smiled. "All it is is sap, but due to its hard exterior, we refer to it as a stone. Aretta's Willow used to lie in the center of our sacred Willow Grove, where ceremonial rites now take place. The day it disappeared, it left an abundance of orodytes in its withering roots." She pointed towards another image, lines mapped out underneath a lush field. "Orodyte is capable of storing impurities, giving Kreenas and acolytes the ability to create vegetation even in our dried soil. And so, our people created tunnels, mining the orodyte for years until we couldn't find any more. This was her final gift to us, that we may survive as a people."

A wave of anger flushed along Elnok's skin. "And why hasn't this been utilized *outside* of your kingdom?"

Her smile faded. "It's been tried before, but with nothing to show for it. It's Estea's soil that Aretta was able to save. Distrathrus cursed the rest. Not even orodyte could store the impurities of his power."

Anger passing, he slumped his shoulders. "How convenient."

"Unfortunately, no one's ever seen the tree," she said, quickly turning away. "Only in dreams or… visions."

Elnok's heart raced. Pitted against him, this woman could ruin his chances at finding the healing tree. But if he convinced her to help? Perhaps they could locate this evasive compass.

He'd have the High One's pet as an ally.

It would require a risk, showing more cards than he'd planned on, but he knew she could be swayed. Judging by the excitement in her gaze as she looked at the wall's images, she admired the tree—found it to be holy.

She'd wanted it before. He'd convince her to want it again.

"I've seen the tree," he admitted, his own tongue cursing at him for sharing information that could get him in trouble with the High One. "Tall, clear as crystal, and filled with magic."

She laughed. "Your one successful attempt at humor."

"It's the truth. When I went through Lhaal Forest with

Kharis, I couldn't sleep. And then I saw something glowing, brighter than this pool." He motioned to the waters. "It was a large tree, glowing with what looked like veins of magic. But just as I was starting to believe what I was seeing, it disappeared."

Sylzenya's stare didn't leave his. He held her there, taking a step forward, lowering his voice. He could see it in her eyes, she was considering his words, wanting them to be true.

"I thought I was hallucinating, but then you shared your vision, and now I have no doubt I saw it. If we work together, maybe we can find it."

As he took another step towards her, she didn't back away.

"Why should I trust you?" she whispered.

He stopped, spinning the gold ring on his finger. "I know I haven't given you much reason to do so."

Her brows raised to her hairline. "No, you haven't."

Shit.

Wrong move.

Before he could say anything else, her mask returned, her brows set hard on her face.

"That concludes our tour," she said, motioning for him to walk out with her.

"Wait—"

"Unless you want more history of our people, I suggest we return to the inn. I imagine you're still exhausted from your travels, especially if you didn't sleep while in Lhaal Forest."

Frustration warred in his chest. "Sylzenya, listen—"

"Ah, there you are," a low voice boomed into the room, echoing off the sandstone walls.

The High One strode in, the light shining on him blinding Elnok.

"Prince Elnok, it's wonderful to see you again."

Elnok couldn't feel more different.

"Likewise, Your Grace."

"Mind if I take Sylzenya from you for a moment? It won't be long."

Elnok turned to her. Sylzenya's mask faltered, a small vein appearing on the side of her forehead as she gulped.

"I believe Sylzenya was in the middle of sharing the lore of your people," Elnok replied. "Perhaps in a few more momen—"

"We finished the tour, Your Grace," Sylzenya interrupted. "Stay here, Prince. I'll be back shortly.

Elnok curled his fists as they left the room.

He should wait, keep looking at the wall, see if there were any clues to find the compass, but a thin layer of panic seized his lungs. He'd pushed her too far too soon. She might report his desire for the healing tree to the High One.

He'd be arrested and put into their dungeons. He wouldn't be able to save Orym, let alone see him before he died.

Taking a deep breath, he left the glowing water and followed them.

At first he'd hated how many willows populated the temple, but now he thanked their goddess for it. Hiding had never been this easy in any of the coastal towns he'd lived in these past ten years.

Slipping between trees, careful to not step on misshapened roots, he caught up to them. The High One looked both ways, missing Elnok hidden in the shadows. The High One gripped Sylzenya's arm and pulled them into a tight grouping of trees adjacent to Elnok.

He held his breath. He'd meant to get close, but not this close.

"Why did you have the prince participate in the wine ceremony?" the High One questioned, his voice sharp.

She took a deep breath, leveling her shoulders. "You told

me to give him a rich exposure to Estea. I thought the wine ceremony a good idea, but I see now it wasn't."

He shook his head. "There's a level of cordialness I must provide when welcoming outlanders into our kingdom—you know this. But what you did yesterday was a risk, and it failed."

"Yes, Your Grace."

He looked around, eyes narrowing as he led her closer to Elnok's hiding spot. Sweat built on the back of his neck, but he kept his breathing quiet, body stilled.

"Show me your orodyte," the High One demanded.

Sylzenya pulled out the orodyte necklace.

"You must remember this symbol. Our promise. You're to bring hope and faith to our people, not render them senseless thinking an outlander has brought the curse to us. It's the very *opposite* of what we agreed on."

Sylzenya's lip quivered. Elnok's hand balled into a fist.

"Yes, Your Grace."

He gripped her shoulder. "*Never* do anything like that again."

Her mouth thinned. "I won't."

"Good."

Despite Elnok's heart pounding in his ears, he remained still, taking slow breaths.

"It'll be more than three days before I give you your cure."

Sylzenya's eyes widened. "But I announced I'll be back in three days."

"You'll be 'conserving your power' until it's needed. What greater way to show our land is prospering by sharing how our greatest Kreena isn't needed at the moment?"

"I promise it won't happen again—"

"*Enough,* Sylzenya. You've made a grievous mistake and with that comes consequences."

She closed her mouth and bowed. Elnok wanted to crush the High One's throat.

"Our Kreenas and acolytes are doing a wonderful job without you; we have time until we need you back."

"I—" Sylzenya stopped herself, gulping, "Yes, Your Grace. How long will that be?"

"One month."

Silence filled the shadowed grove.

"That's how long the cure will take to complete?" she asked, her words slow and measured.

"On the contrary, the cure is ready." He tapped the orodyte. "But you are not."

The silence thickened.

"I know you're disappointed," he continued, placing a hand on her shoulder, "But we agreed to this. You must prove yourself ready, and so far, you've only proven how far from it you are. Do you understand what I'm asking of you, Sylzenya? Or must I repeat myself?"

"No, Your Grace. I understand."

"Good. Now, what is there to report about the prince?"

Elnok's face grew hot. He already knew what she was about to do. She would share his desire for the healing tree, using it as leverage to get her cure. It would be smart. Calculated. She didn't owe him anything. Slowly, he backed away, lungs sinking into his stomach. He needed to leave this place undetected, find Kharis, and convince him to return him back to Vutror. Better to get out of this blood-soaked kingdom and see Orym one last time than decay in a prison cell.

"He can't hold his wine," she replied, "Other than that, there's nothing impressive about him."

Elnok froze.

"Curious," the High One replied, "What happened?"

"He drank two sips and threw it up. He's only had salted rice, boiled potatoes, and water since."

The High One straightened his back. "Perhaps some fruit from the gardens would do him well. See to it you provide him some of our best today, will you?"

Sylzenya paused. "Of course, Your Grace."

"Excellent. So, no information of why he's been gone these last ten years? No reasons as to why he never returned?"

She shrugged, "If I had to guess, it was because he and his brother developed bad blood."

Elnok's eyes burned.

How did she know?

The fountain. The wine. He'd probably said something in his delirium about Tosh before he passed out last night.

Damnit.

But this was smart of her, giving the High One parcels of truth. Still, she could ruin him *and* get her cure. Surely she'd take the opportunity.

"Very well. Keep a careful eye on him. Now, go and follow through on our deal. If you do good work, I might give you the cure sooner."

"Yes, Your Grace."

They left the trees and returned to the main path. Elnok quietly retreated from his hiding place, disbelief warring inside of him. Before he could make sense of it, Elnok dashed from tree to tree, a newfound energy lighting up his veins as he found his way back to the healing pool before they did.

Closing the heavy door soundlessly, he slowed his breaths, picking twigs from his hair and throwing them across the room. He straightened his posture, hands laced behind his back as he absently studied the carved image of a monster.

The door opened.

"Thank you, Your Highness," the High One announced as he led Sylzenya in. "We'll begin our discussions about the treaty between our kingdoms in a few days. I'll have one of my Dynameis send for you."

Elnok bowed. "Of course, Your Grace."

"Excellent." He smiled at Sylzenya. "I'll see you in a few days as well."

"Yes, Your Grace." She bowed.

Once the door slammed shut, Sylzenya spun, fists clenched and smile gone. Elnok thought he liked her face earlier, the way the sun shone on her small smile.

But anger fit her well.

"Hope you enjoyed the conversation," she said, approaching the wall and slapping her hand against the sandstone. "You're lucky he didn't see you."

Elnok crossed his arms. "I'm afraid I never left this room."

"Save it," she interrupted. "I know every hiding spot in this place, and I sure as hell know when someone else is using it."

Elnok raised his hands in mock surrender, deniability always his safety net.

"Did he suspect anything?" she asked, a drop of sweat beading down her face.

"I'm not sure what you're asking me."

"Did the High One suspect I lied? That I was keeping information from him?" The shimmer in her deep blue eyes was replaced by a strained plea. "It's clear you're well-versed in spying. So tell me what you saw."

He sighed. "I think you'd know that better than me."

"*Damnit,*" she cursed, a tear sliding down her face as she scrunched her eyes shut. Her breaths slowed as she leaned against the wall. "I've never done that before."

"Lied?"

"I've lied many times," she retorted, "But… never to him."

Elnok's heart pounded as they stood in silence. Apparently he hadn't been the only one to misjudge her.

"Be wary of who you trust," she whispered, more to herself than to him.

She turned towards the image of the glowing willow, the pool's light shimmering on the wall and in her widened eyes.

"If you still want my help, I think I might know a way to find the compass," she said.

He stopped spinning his gold ring.

She could've gotten her cure by turning him in, but instead, she lied to her leader—lied to a powerful man who held her close. A precarious choice, and he knew she could feel it; if the High One found out she'd kept information from him, she might risk never getting her cure. And yet, she'd done it anyway—protecting Elnok in the process. It was something he and his crew would do for each other. He never thought this pious, radicalized woman was capable of such things.

It was refreshing to be proved wrong every once in a while.

"Well then, Your Holiness." He smirked, stepping next to her. "Enlighten me."

She smiled, and damn it all if it didn't bring him to his knees.

CHAPTER 15
TRUST

O*ne month.*

The High One had successfully developed her cure, the very thing to restore her connection with their goddess, and yet, he wouldn't give it to her for an entire *month.* And for what, a single mistake? The villagers had calmed down; she'd fixed it. And still, he punished her.

She'd known the High One to be severe at times, holding Kreenas to higher expectations than acolytes, but this was cruel. He thought he could control her, and perhaps he *had* all these years, but this time she would forge her own path.

For if he truly cared for their kingdom's wellbeing, he wouldn't wait to restore her power.

If he truly cared for *her,* he wouldn't withhold her destiny.

What do you think your leader is hiding?

She'd dismissed Elnok's accusation last night as ignorance. But now, she couldn't stop asking herself the same question.

"Are you sure we can trust your friend?" Elnok asked quietly as they walked out of the temple and through the gardens.

Last night's festivities had been promptly cleaned up. All wine glasses and barrels were out of sight, the hanging orodytes returned to the Dynami barracks, and all extra produce taken to villagers' homes. Willow branches swayed in the breeze, brushing against each other, a sound that usually brought Sylzenya peace. But she didn't feel at peace anymore, hadn't since the rite.

"Nyla will understand the severity of the situation," Sylzenya replied.

"What makes you so sure?"

She stopped underneath a large willow. "I just lied for you, and you still don't trust me?"

"Whoa, let's remember some fine details, shall we? You sticking out your neck for me wasn't just for my sake, but yours. Don't get me wrong, I'm grateful, but I'm not convinced you know who you can trust."

Sylzenya raised a brow. "You know how Kreenas aren't supposed to leave the temple?"

Elnok tilted his head. "Right?"

"Nyla and I have before."

"I thought you'd never lied to the High One?"

She shrugged. "He never asked."

He laughed. The sound was deep and full, reverberating through her own chest. She approached him, the smell of his warm skin a surprising comfort.

Lowering her voice to a whisper, she said, "It was three years ago at the annual banquet. We were approached by two Dynameis who were severely drunk. Nyla and I weren't much better, admittedly."

"You sly dog." He smirked. "A golden warrior did you in, did he?"

Sylzenya scowled. "Do you have to be so crass?"

His smile widened. "And how was it?"

She narrowed her gaze.

"Let me guess," he said, leaning in, "Underwhelming?"

Yes.

"Privacy is an important value in my kingdom, so I'd prefer you not invade such an intimate matter," she muttered.

"You brought it up," he teased. "Sounds like you had the night of your life."

Sylzenya eyed him, heat rushing through her face as she studied his physique. "I learned attractiveness doesn't guarantee much. It's all bravado and shining armor until behind closed doors."

"Is that so?" he whispered, leaning in closer, "Perhaps you just needed someone outside of your… typical scope."

Her breath caught. She collected herself, backing away, "I know you're not suggesting yourself?"

"Me? And you?" He scoffed. "I think we'd end up throwing punches instead."

"It'd be like a Dynami fighting a monster," she agreed, and yet her heart beat fast against her chest.

"Who's who?" He smiled.

"You'd be the monster. Just look at how disheveled you are."

"Then you're the prim and proper warrior? Fitting, considering how straight you stand *all* the time. Looks exhausting."

She laughed—a hard kind of laugh that hurt her belly, as if a spark of lightning had passed through her, leaving her warm and bright. But she quickly caught herself, clenching her jaw tight.

Elnok smiled, only to thin his mouth again. "But *that's* your reasoning? You two went on a secret sexual escapade?"

"Would you be *quiet*?" Sylzenya whispered. "It's one of Aretta's highest laws to not only stay at the temple, but also to never…"

"Fuck?"

Sylzenya's face burned as she shushed him. Anyone else and this conversation would've made her want to burrow into a rodent's underground home. But this man was impermanent; she doubted she'd ever see his face again after the treaty revisions.

"We could be stripped of our titles if anyone knew," she said.

"Interesting choice of words."

She pinched the bridge of her nose. "Are you capable of saying anything with substance?"

Elnok crossed his arms, his thick corded muscles accentuated in his black tunic. Sylzenya's face burned hotter, but she attributed it to the sunshine spilling through the leaves.

"You really think your High One doesn't know these little… *adventures* between your Kreenas and Dynameis take place?"

Sylzenya scoffed. "If he did, then he'd have no more Kreenas or Dynameis left."

"So *everyone* does it, do they? And has anyone ever been caught?"

Sylzenya paused. "Not that I'm aware of."

"Fascinating."

Uncertainty pulled at her mind. "It's the truth. I swear by Aretta, if anyone was found out, they'd be strippe— *removed* of their title."

He shrugged. "Of course. But I imagine it must be a *very* exciting rule to break. Adds some tension… some heat to those lustrous nights?"

It did.

"It's nothing special."

"Oh, I seriously doubt that." He leaned in even closer. "What better way to add some excitement to such dangerous and painful roles you all have to fill than having an arbitrary threat come between a person and their most primal desire? A taste of forbidden fruit *is* quite the delicacy. And there's nothing like the rush of getting away with something so spectacular."

Heat burned along her skin. "If you're suggesting the rule

is some way to distract us… *control* us… then you misunderstand my kingdom far more than I realized."

He smirked. "You can blame my guide. She's supposed to be giving me a *rich exposure*."

She narrowed her gaze. "Not the guide's fault if the pompous, radically self-assured visitor refuses to listen to a word she says."

"Pompous? I thought I was cursed?"

"I'm beginning to think you are."

Sylzenya gulped, realizing her nose was inches from his; his curved lips held her full attention. She should've stepped back, given herself more room, but it'd feel too much like defeat, as if this wasn't a mere conversation but a battle for truth.

"We can trust Nyla." She forced her eyes to meet his.

Elnok opened his mouth as if to say something, but then he tilted his head, his eyes breaking from her gaze to study her face. She refused to move. Try all he wanted, but he wouldn't unravel her. Even if the High One was acting different than usual, she'd figure it out in the end. This prince, or thief, or whatever he was, meant little. He wasn't only questioning her kingdom—he was questioning her life.

Finally, he leaned back. Sylzenya readjusted her robe, the heat in her skin refusing to ebb.

"I still don't like this plan," Elnok said, "but I suppose there's no stopping you, is there?"

Sylzenya folded her arms over her chest, the burn in her face washing away.

"We need to know the location of the compass, and the only way we might be able to do so is with a Kreena's power. Nyla's the only one I trust." She paused. "If I could do it, I would."

Elnok took a deep breath. "Then let's hope you're not wrong."

"Your faith is inspiring."

"So I've been told."

Sylzenya surprised herself with a small laugh. She quickly passed it off as a cough, but she didn't miss the sidelong smile he sent her. Her face burned again. She forced her eyes to meet his, not missing the dimpled smile he sent her; she bit the inside of her cheek as she shook herself of this conniving royal and picked her way down the path.

Willow branches brushing their arms, they passed through the entrance. Rays of golden light spilled along the path. Sylzenya's fingers flexed at the sight of the Kreenas in their designated plots. Closing her eyes, she muttered a prayer, something she knew would only bring her disappointment. She ushered in life, waiting to hear the dirt sing to her, for Aretta's blood in the soil to breathe against her palms.

She felt nothing.

She couldn't touch it, couldn't *feel* it. The cut on her back stung as a piece of her chest caved into itself.

"Sylzenya?" Elnok's voice called to her.

Fresh air swept into her lungs as she looked up, vision blurry.

"Are you alright?" he asked, brows furrowed.

She nodded. "Nyla should be a bit further down."

She was grateful he didn't ask any more questions as they walked past Kreenas, each woman's skin shining with sweat, their backs bleeding fresh blood—white robes stained with life, dripping crimson onto the dirt. Sylzenya's heart leapt from her chest as she saw the familiar dark hair and pale skin of her friend. Nyla's shoulders were burnt slightly red as she kneeled in her plot of land, a fresh plum tree wrapped in yellow light slowly but surely growing as tall as Sylzenya.

"These better taste juicier than yesterday's batch," Sylzenya said.

Nyla smiled, removing her hands from the dirt, their goddess' power retreating into the soil.

"*Syl.*"

Nyla's hug was warm and familiar. Sylzenya buried her face into her shoulder, realizing just how taxing the last day had been.

"And this must be Prince Elnok, is it?" Nyla asked as she stepped back, releasing Sylzenya from her hold and narrowing her gaze at him. "Came to the grove to put your curse on us?"

"I'd be doing a poor job if I didn't," he replied.

Nyla's narrowed gaze slowly lifted, a smile appearing in its turn. "You're not as stiff as I expected."

"No. That's her job." He tipped his head towards Sylzenya.

Nyla laughed. "One day and he's already got you figured out, hasn't he?"

Sylzenya raised a brow. He returned with a sly smile.

"I have a favor to ask," Sylzenya said.

Nyla stopped laughing. "Is everything alright?"

"No."

Nyla's smile disappeared.

"But you have to promise you won't tell anyone." Sylzenya lowered her voice. "No other Kreenas, no acolytes, and especially not the High One."

Her friend's amber eyes widened. "Syl, what's going on?"

"Can I trust you?"

"Always."

Sylzenya took a deep breath, her heart battering against her chest. "Remember how I sought Aretta through the altar room's roots?"

"Please tell me you aren't doing that again," she urged, gripping Sylzenya's shoulder, "you almost *died*."

Sylzenya gulped. She could feel Elnok's stare burning into her face.

"I learned my lesson. What I didn't tell you was that I received a vision about Aretta's Willow when it happened."

Sylzenya explained everything, including her lack of a cure and the High One's choice to withhold it. She shared nothing about the gold ring turning to blood or the bird being killed by a claw of twigs. She still didn't know what either events meant, and she feared them most of all.

"And if we're going to find the compass," Sylzenya continued, "we need to know which tree it's in. I think if a Kreena can touch the trees and usher Aretta's power, they might be able to tell if it's located in that tree or not."

Silence stretched taut between them.

"I'll be candid with you," Nyla stated. "You need to tell the High One about the vision."

Sylzenya's stomach dropped. "I tried, Nyla, but he told me Aretta's Willow was only a myth."

"And he's probably right."

"He's seen it." Sylzenya pointed to Elnok.

"More than likely a trick of the eye," he replied.

Her eyes widened as she turned to him, anger welling inside her chest. "What? But you told me—"

"See, even he understands the situation." Nyla looked to Elnok. "My apologies, Prince Elnok. She had one of the worst things possible happen to her the other day, so I would take these words of hers with a grain of salt."

"*Nyla*!"

"Sylzenya, you're not acting like yourself right now and you know it," she replied, "If the High One isn't giving you a cure right now, then we should trust that choice. And this quest for Aretta's Willow… the vision…" Her friend sighed, "You lost so much blood when you used the roots."

Fingers digging into her robe's fabric, Sylzenya said, "You think I hallucinated? Made it all up in my head?"

Nyla gave her a look that sent her blood boiling—a look of pity.

Elnok stepped to Sylzenya's side. "I know I've given Sylzenya quite the task since my foolish entrance yesterday. She wished to seek your counsel, and it seems she's received her answer."

Her breath caught as his hand touched her lower back, tracing circles, causing her skin to pimple and face to flush, her anger growing as she turned to tell him to back away—

She paused. He wasn't tracing circles.

It was a message.

S-T-O-P.

He didn't look at her, keeping his focus on Nyla, continuing to trace the letters over and over again.

"Right, Sylzenya?" he asked.

Realization draped over her like her heavy green cloak. Nyla, her best friend, the person she told everything to, had lived through some of her harshest of days and experienced the brightest of moments with… couldn't be trusted.

"Tell the High One, Sylzenya. Promise me?" Nyla pleaded.

Ever since her Kreena Rite, nothing was the same. This damned poison in her veins changed *everything.* She wasn't sure how much more loss she could manage.

Turning to her friend, she offered a feigned smile, an act she knew so well, but never did she use it with Nyla.

"You're right," Sylzenya finally said.

Elnok stopped his tracing.

Sylzenya continued, "But please, let me be the one to tell him? It wouldn't look well for me if you did it in my place. I'd much rather face it straight on, as I know I should."

Nyla's dipped brows relaxed, her thinned mouth curving into a warm grin. "Of course."

"Thanks," Sylzenya said, her spit thickening as she fought back the choke in her throat. "I always know I can speak to you about anything."

Her friend embraced her once more. "I love you, Syl. You're going to get your power back, and everything will be as it once was, alright?"

Nothing's going to be the same after this.

How is it that her friend said those words yesterday and

now sung a different tune? Sylzenya tightened her hold on Nyla, looking to the green willows for answers. A lifeless breeze returned her question.

"I believe he's still in the temple," Sylzenya said as she backed away. "Prince Elnok, my apologies, but we'll do one more stop before we head back to the village."

"Very well," he replied, his face stoic.

"May Aretta bless you both," Nyla said as she bowed, two hands placed over her heart. "Oh, and please, take a plum. They should be far better than yesterday's."

They both accepted the gift and walked back through the willow grove. Golden light flew through the air, swirling around Kreenas. Sylzenya's head ached until they finally left and arrived at the main dirt path leading back to the temple.

"I suppose you were right," Sylzenya whispered.

Elnok sighed. "I'm sorry."

"What, no humiliating comeback? No 'I told you so'?"

"No."

She turned to him, his face burdened with something terrible and haunting.

"I could see how difficult that was, and yet you did it anyways. Though I know it benefits you to do so, it also helps me and why I'm here. So… thank you."

Sylzenya rubbed her thumb along the smooth skin of the fruit. "Why *are* you here, Elnok?"

His frown deepened, fingers curling into the plum, the skin pulling and stretching.

"A dear friend of mine is sick," he said, a quiver in his voice, "Dying, to be precise. The sickness taking over the continent has no cure, but I mean to find one." He let out a breath. "I can't let Orym die."

Sylzenya could hear it in his voice, feel it in his breaths. He was desperate to save his friend, the same way she was desperate to spare her people. Maybe even more so.

"You must really love him."

"He's the brother I'd always hoped for."

Before she could respond, he bit into the plum, and then—he fell to his knees and screamed.

Sylzenya threw her plum to the ground as she rushed to him. He screamed again, deep and cracked. She called his name, but he didn't respond, as if he couldn't hear her—as if he was somewhere else entirely.

Just like the wine ceremony.

"*Tosh, stop! Please, I swear, just stop!*"

"It's ok," Sylzenya soothed as she kneeled beside him, the moist soil seeping into her white robe. "Everything's ok, Elnok, I promise."

He dry heaved. Sylzenya quickly gathered his thick hair and held it back as he released everything onto the ground. Coughing, he caught himself with his hands, a deep sob rumbling through him.

"It's ok," Sylzenya said again, instinctively rubbing his back in gentle circles. It was strangely uneven, but not just from muscle… scars, perhaps. Many of them. "You're going to be ok. Nothing's going to hurt you here." Her heart beat fast as she furrowed her brow. "I promise."

The way she said it… how much she meant it… it surprised herself.

"*Please, please.*" He whimpered into the dirt, spit and plum dripping from his mouth. "Make it stop, *please.*"

His breaths started to even out, so she kept rubbing his back. Slowly, he repositioned and sat down, away from his vomit, leaning into her touch. She moved closer, placing herself in between his legs, combing his hair and stroking his face, the same way her mother did when Sylzenya was frightened during summer storms.

"You're ok," she whispered.

He took a few more shuddered breaths. Taking her hand into his, he pressed her palm against his tear-stained face.

"Is it over?" he asked, his voice small and quiet.

"Yes, it's over," Sylzenya whispered back.

He finally opened his eyes. They were bloodshot, and yet, his green irises seemed brighter. Blinking rapidly, he sat up straighter, brows raising as he rubbed his thumb along her knuckles, sending shivers along her skin.

"Sylzenya… my apologies, I don't… I'm not sure why this keeps happening."

Sylzenya looked at the plum on the ground.

Perhaps some fruit from the gardens would do him well, the High One had said, *see to it you provide him some of our best today, will you?*

Something twisted in her gut.

"I'm not sure, but we can come back to the temple tomorrow," she replied, "Right now, let's just get some food into you and some rest."

Purple and crimson sky met them as they returned to the inn. Helena, the innkeeper, prepared another salted rice bowl and boiled potatoes for Elnok. They situated themselves back in their single room, the rope and sheet hung between them. He didn't speak as he sat on his bed. She let him eat in peace, tending to the villagers in the plaza, retelling the origin story of Aretta and Distrathrus just as the High One requested.

But it didn't matter if the High One found her worthy in this way, her preaching was only meant to keep his suspicions buried in the ground. She was going to find the compass so her people could have hope *and* a future.

And she knew where to start their search.

CHAPTER 16
EVERYTHING'S CHANGED

Elnok woke early the next morning and helped Helena make breakfast. The innkeeper had been nervous at first with him being in a space without Sylzenya's presence, afraid the "curse" might awaken if she wasn't there to stop him. But eventually she relaxed, making jokes and telling stories of her childhood as she taught him how to knead dough and fry an egg on a skillet. She even shared a few stories of Sylzenya as a child, such as the time where she chased a chicken into a lake, nearly drowning the poor creature. Apparently, she'd returned with it alive and well, although she was soaking wet with scratches covering her arms and face.

He found himself smiling, only to remind himself how his crew might be faring at this moment. They were in Vutror's castle, so they would have access to food and clean water, but it wasn't much compared to the vast amount of foods Helena prepared for her small breakfast nook. It was a strange mix of feelings—how he hated this kingdom and yet found joy in a moment like this.

He thanked her for the help and returned to his and Sylzenya's room with a plate of hot eggs, chilled fruit, seared greens, a couple slices of wheat bread with butter, and a hot tea.

Decadence.

"Morning," he announced as he opened the door, "Helena said rose tea was your favorite, so—"

"Can you *knock*?" Sylzenya yelled as she pulled one of the sheets over her.

Elnok smiled as he sauntered to his side of the room. "There's a lock for a reason, you know."

"You're horrible."

"Opportunistic."

She shuffled behind the curtain, grumbling to herself.

"Did you say rose tea?" she asked.

"I did."

She pulled the curtain away, her mouth gaping and eyes wide. She wore the Kreena robe she had on when he'd arrived. Old and bloodied. Beautiful yet stained with her pain.

"What… what is this?" she asked.

"It's called breakfast." He smirked. "And also a thank you. I'm afraid I've been quite the handful the past two days."

"Oh, Elnok, you didn't have to."

"Better take it now before I change my mind." His knuckles brushed along hers, sending a warmth into his hand and up his arm.

She laughed, a genuine, hearty sound that made his chest ache. Slowly releasing his grip on the plate and cup, he breathed in her excitement—

No.

He quickly took a step back, face burning. This was a mission, and he needed to focus. No need to form any sort of attachment with a woman he would never see again.

"It's barely a fair trade," he continued, "but it's the least I can do."

Her brows creased and her nostrils flared as a sad smile sat on her lips. "Thank you."

They stood there for another breath. He memorized the lines on her face—the ones drawn on her forehead when upset, the others at the corners of her eyes when she smiled.

"Anyways." She coughed, letting the curtain drape back across the room, "We'll go back to the temple today and see about the compass."

"Is there a reason you won't give me any more details than that?" he asked as he lifted his shirt over his head, tossing it on the bed before grabbing a fresh black tunic.

"Perhaps." She poked through the curtain. "Don't you trust me—?"

Her eyes dropped to his naked torso. It shouldn't fucking matter, and yet, he couldn't help but flex his stomach muscles —if only a little—enjoying the way his body seemed to please her.

He placed a hand on his hip and quirked a brow. "Do you ever knock?"

"Hard to do with curtains."

Elnok took the curtain and whipped it across her face. She laughed. They finished preparing for the day and left the inn with full stomachs, a sensation Elnok still found strange.

Sylzenya thankfully interrupted his thoughts, "If anyone asks, we'll say we only made it through half the temple yesterday and you wanted to know more about Aretta's power. No one will question an outsider's desire for such knowledge."

"I'm not surprised," he muttered.

She stopped, head tilting back as she gazed at the temple's high sandstone walls. "I think I'm only just starting to realize how prideful of a people we are." She dropped her gaze to the dirt, wringing her robe with her hands. "Everything seems to keep changing, and I'm not sure what to do with it."

His throat closed and his hands shook.

Ten years ago, he'd said such similar words.

He'd been an apprentice to a blacksmith, the only occupation he could find after he escaped Vutror's dungeons. It was grueling work for a sixteen-year-old, his back always sore, fingers scraped and bleeding every hour. If a customer ever proved dissatisfied, his master would hit him in the face. One hit for every complaint. Elnok had accepted it, telling himself it was better than the torture his brother had dealt him. And, after the shop had closed, he could at least sit on the cliffside and watch the ocean waves, smelling the brine of the sea.

Even then, nothing could stop the nightmares. His mother's and father's bleeding necks when he'd found them in their bed, Tosh's torture as he swore Elnok was trying to steal the throne, and his master's beady eyes every time he hit him.

Elnok had enough.

One day, he missed his shift and sat atop the cliffside. He sat for what felt like hours, knowing his master would come looking for him soon. The jagged rocks below had stuck up like spears. It was a long fall to a quick death, and then the pain would finally stop.

As he was about to step off, a voice called out to him.

"Fantastic day for a swim, innit?"

Elnok stopped, turning around to find a boy not much older than him. Moppy brown hair, wild hazel eyes, and a smile bigger than any he'd ever seen.

"But from this height, it may not be as enjoyable," the boy continued, "Why don't you join me down at shore? Maybe we can catch some fish while we're at it?"

Elnok stared, not knowing what to say. But the boy didn't seem to mind, extending his hand, a fishing pole made of wood and string in his hand.

"Come on," the boy persisted, "I could use a hand."

On their way to the shore, he'd introduced himself as Orym. They failed to catch any fish.

They traveled to a different town after, living off of other's scraps, learning the art of stealing to keep themselves full and somewhat satisfied. A few months later, Elnok told Orym he'd escaped the dungeons, but he never told him he was Vutror's lost prince, telling him he'd been a typical convict instead.

"You were framed for your parents' *murder*?" Orym asked.

"Yes. After I escaped, everything changed so fast. I'm not sure what I'm supposed to do now."

Orym had wrapped his arm around his shoulder. "To be honest, Elnok, I wouldn't know either. But I do know this, I'm grateful to have met you. And I'm even more grateful to call you a friend."

Elnok's vision blurred as he spun his gold ring around his finger.

"I'm sorry," Sylzenya said, " it's a stupid thought to linger on—"

"It isn't," Elnok replied, "It's the truth, and oftentimes, waiting to accept change can hinder us from moving forward. But you aren't one to ignore such things, are you, Sylzenya?"

Her deep blue eyes found his.

"Something tells me you aren't either," she whispered, her hands no longer scratching at her robe, her body heat touching his skin.

His hands stopped shaking. A strong instinct coursed through him to slide his palm up her arm, to let her know she wasn't alone.

"We better keep moving," he said, forming his hands into fists, Orym's sick eyes flashing through his vision, "My friend doesn't have much longer to live."

Sylzenya straightened. "Right. Of course."

They entered the temple, the priestesses and guards elated about Elnok's desire to learn more about their goddess. They ushered them in quickly, telling short tales of how their goddess had blessed them through their own difficulties—providing food, fresh water, and days of pure bliss. Elnok's patience wore thinner with each story; how ignorant did one have to be to speak to someone whose people were at the mercy of famine, drought, and sickness?

Sylzenya requested privacy so they might honor Aretta in the altar room. The priestess and guard who'd followed agreed, taking their leave back down the willow-infested hallway.

He and Sylzenya were alone.

"Well played," he whispered.

"I'll take my payment in form of another breakfast."

"Consider it done."

She smiled. His face warmed.

Yellow stained-glass spanned the ceiling, the sandstone walls at least five stories tall. In the middle of the room stood the largest tree Elnok had ever seen. Which, he decided, wasn't saying much considering he hadn't seen many trees until stepping foot into Estea.

"And this *isn't* the healing tree?" he asked, a thin line of hope running along his veins.

"This is the great willow; we're able to commune with our goddess through its roots." She pointed to the massive roots protruding from the ground like waves on the shore. "It's rare for her to respond. Even when I did it a few days ago, I'm not sure if it was her or some specter of herself appearing as a bird."

Elnok's eyes widened. "A few days ago? This doesn't happen to be the rite your friend was talking about?" He approached her from behind. "The one where you almost *died*?"

"Of course not."

Her mask faltered.

Elnok narrowed his gaze. "Whatever plan you have, we're not doing it if it's going to result in my guide bleeding out on me."

Sylzenya huffed a breath. "What I did three days ago was… foolish. I admit it. But this is different. All I'm going to try and do is connect with these roots to see if the compass is in the tree. If I can't, then things stay just as complicated as ever. But if I can, and if I'm *right*," she paused, turning to him, "then we're one step closer to finding Aretta's Willow."

"And why do you think it's in this tree?"

"I mean, look at it. It's huge, ancient— I'm starting to question why I didn't think this would be it from the start."

"So this is based off a hunch?"

She shrugged. "Perhaps."

"*Ridiculous*," he breathed. "I see why you deigned not to tell me this earlier."

"Fine. How about we go around and knock on every single tree in this temple until we find the one that doesn't sound as hollow as the rest?"

He crossed his arms. "If it's in place of harming yourself, then I might prefer it."

She rolled her eyes. "It's not even how trees work."

"What, like I should know that?"

"I thought time was running out?" Sylzenya snapped.

"That doesn't mean you should go sacrificing yourself to get a fucking lead that may not even exist."

"Do you want your friend to live or not?"

The hairs on his neck stood, a chill running along his arms. Yenna had made it clear before he left—Orym had less than a week.

"You don't have your magic," he finally said, "Isn't that why you needed your friend? Because she could connect to your goddess, or however that works?"

She took a deep breath. "Miracles are always possible, Your Highness."

"Miracles are myths."

"Then allow me to show you your first one."

The tenacity in her eyes said it all. She was just as stubborn as Orym, an idealistic view of life that was both infectious and infuriating. Orym and Sylzenya both carried an optimism he never could. And while he found it bothersome and foolish, he couldn't help but admire it.

"Just stay in one piece," he finally said.

Sylzenya smiled. "I will."

Clenching his teeth, he backed away from the tree as Sylzenya kneeled to the floor. Closing her eyes, she let out four deep breaths. Her whispers echoed along the walls, the vast willow seeming to watch expectantly.

His breaths shortened as she placed her hands on the roots. Moments passed, and nothing happened. She grunted. Still, nothing. Sweat started dripping down her back.

"Sylzenya," he said, stepping forward, "Let's think of something else—"

"Wait!" she demanded, a crack in her scar breaking, a drop of blood joining the sweat.

He shook his head as he approached her. "You're starting to bleed. Time to stop—"

Suddenly, a golden ray of light sparked from the ground and twisted around her arms. Her yell pierced his ears, then a strong wind rushed through the room, the gale forcing him to his knees. The light flowed like a fishing line, its tip sharp as it speared her back, slicing across the cut and opening her skin.

"*Sylzenya, stop*!"

But she only kept yelling, her magic flickering in and out of existence. Sucking in as much air as he could, he stood to his feet, engaging all muscles as he ran to her.

But then everything stopped. Elnok halted as Sylzenya released her hold of the tree. She turned to him, tears in her eyes, words sitting on her tongue.

She collapsed.

CHAPTER 17
THE HEALING POOL

Not here, the bird had whispered to her.

Its blue eyes stayed with her as everything turned black. She'd felt her goddess' power, the ecstasy in her body overwhelming as she reveled in the way she connected with the great willow: the depths of its roots, the roughness of its bark, the life in its veins.

Distant and faint, her goddess' heartbeat had made itself known to her, if only for a moment.

She'd sought the compass' location, only to be told it wasn't in the great willow. And then, she'd been given pain beyond anything she'd experienced before.

The price for life will always be pain.

It'd been a gift to have been shown the tree, a true miracle to have heard her goddess' heartbeat after days of silence. But now that she couldn't hear it anymore, couldn't feel the life around her—the silence was deafening.

Sylzenya.

A voice called out to her. It sounded warm: familiar.

Sylzenya.

She liked the voice—wanted to drink it in.

"Sylzenya."

She flickered her eyes open, the blue irises of the bird disappearing as she looked into a pair of pale green eyes lined with dark lashes. Thick black hair tucked behind an ear revealed an array of gold hoops. A strong, sharp jaw and chin, some dark stubble dotting his tan skin, and a look of concern that caused her heart to falter.

"Elnok?" she whispered.

He cursed. "I'm taking you to that healing pool."

The world's weight lifted from her body as he carried her in his arms. Suddenly her back erupted with pain.

"Wait," she whispered, her voice hoarse, "No one can see me like this."

"Your reputation is safe with me."

"*Elnok*," she begged, "It isn't safe—"

"Says the woman bleeding out on me."

She had nothing to counter with as he rushed her out of the altar room.

"Tuck your head into my chest. It'll make for a less bumpy ride," he instructed.

Sylzenya obeyed, curling her fingers and bunching his tunic into her hand. Worn leather and earthy musk filled her senses, his scent calming despite the pain piercing her back.

Voices echoed in the hallway.

"Hold on," he whispered.

She clung to him as he maneuvered into and through the grove of willows. Swift movements swept a fresh breeze into her face. His muscles flexed, strong and precise, as if he'd done this thousands of times.

"We're here."

A door creaked open and the familiar smell of rosewater assaulted her, the steam falling on her face as they entered the room.

"The Kreenas and acolytes will be resting today, so they won't be using the pool," she said.

Clothes still on, he carried her into the pool. She gritted

her teeth as the water met her back. Sharp pain followed by a numbing sensation had her moan with relief. Elnok gently moved a few loose strands of hair from her face, tucking them behind her ear. His chest heaved against her head, and she realized she was still nestled into him, her hand clutching his tunic for dear life.

She could move.

But she didn't.

"You broke your promise," he said, voice low.

"What promise?" she asked.

"Staying in one piece."

Her heart fluttered. "Was Prince Elnok of Vutror worried for me?"

His eyes studied her face. "You think I wouldn't be?"

Sylzenya's breath caught in her lungs. Suddenly, everything felt close… *alive*. She could feel his his heart beating against his chest—how it mirrored her own. Calloused fingers swept another strand of hair behind her ear, his skin against hers a sweet warmth that somehow gave her chills.

"What happened to your magic, Sylzenya?" he whispered.

Sylzenya licked her chapped lips, his eyes staring at her mouth as she did. He'd told her about his friend's sickness, and he'd saved her from dying on the altar room floor. If anything, she was glad he asked; she wanted to share it with him.

"It's custom that during one's final ceremonial rite before becoming a Kreena, a member of the household mimics our goddess' power and uses a branch to carve into our cut."

She stopped, words turning into molasses in her mouth.

But he didn't push. He waited patiently, his fingers tightening around her legs.

"I hadn't seen my father or mother in ten years, as is custom." Her lower lip quivered. "I was a foolish child; I despised my power, only wanting a life with them in it."

"It's never foolish for a child to yearn for their parents."

Her heart fluttered. "My people would highly disagree."

"Do you?"

She let herself lean further into him. "It doesn't matter anymore, because my father secretly coated his branch with orodyte serum and poisoned me with it."

Elnok tensed. "The same substance in your orodytes? Used to strengthen Dynami weapons? It… poisons you?"

"Yes," she replied, "Not killing me, obviously, but it takes away my power. It can take away a Dynami's power as well. It's considered an act of violence against our goddess to use it on one of us."

He furrowed his brows, "I'm sorry, Sylzenya."

She meant to reply, help him not feel sorry for her, but he didn't stare at her in pity; he stared at her in understanding. A tight knot in her chest loosened, a swell of relief rising in her body.

"Not having my connection with Aretta… There's an emptiness inside me. I used to feel how the earth moved; the way the roots connected to one another underneath my feet; the soft lull of leaves in the breeze; the thrum of my goddess' heart. But now… I feel nothing. Hear nothing. Like a part of myself is missing."

She looked up. Surprise lit her chest as Elnok's eyes turned glassy.

"We'll find the compass," he said softly, "and we'll find the tree. I promise."

Gulping, she let a tear fall down her face. Warm skin brushed against her cheek, his thumb catching the tear, slowly wiping it away. The pool's glow lit up his face, brightening his features and casting shadows with beautiful, sharp edges.

"Elnok…" she whispered, moving her hand up his chest, grazing her fingers along his collarbone.

His body shuddered.

Heat rushing into her face, she quickly pulled her hand away, turning towards the water.

He'd been indignant when they'd first met, someone she wished to be rid of. Gods, he'd even blackmailed her only two nights ago. But somewhere in between then and now, something had changed. Maybe it was his interest in their people's history, or the way he had become a steady support while everything around her crumbled; saving her *life*.

To feel seen—to see him in return. She couldn't help but admire the way he cared for his friend, so much so that he was risking a life in Estea's dungeons to find a cure. He was devious, but he was courageous, and yet she knew there was more to discover.

And she *wanted* to know more.

Cursing herself, she tried to pull herself together. But then he whispered her name. Heat rose in her body. She shouldn't — *couldn't*—

But then his forehead gently met hers. Air escaping her lungs, she found herself melting into him, needing his warmth just as much as she needed the healing waters.

"It's beautiful in here," he whispered, "Peaceful."

Sylzenya hummed in agreement, a bright warmth consuming her chest. "These waters have been a sanctuar–".

Thump.

Thump.

Thump.

Aretta's hearbeat. It was faint, barely audible just like at the great willow tree, and yet somehow there.

"Sylzenya?" Elnok asked, leaning back, putting her down. "Are you alright?"

Thump.

Thump.

Thump.

Realization consumed her, eyes widening at the pool's glow.

"I know where the compass is."

Elnok blinked, "What?"

She turned, pointing to the pool's tiles. The tiles shaped like a willow. She grabbed him, swimming to the center of the pool, the glow brightening.

"Sylzenya—"

"Elnok, why are you seeking Aretta's tree?"

"What?"

"Answer the question."

"You already know why."

"*Elnok.*"

He scoffed. "Gods, alright, to heal Orym…"

He paused.

She nodded, because she could see it in his eyes—he understood too.

"You think the compass is crafted into the pool somehow, and *that's* why it has healing properties. But, you said the vision talked of it being within a willow?"

Sylzenya smiled. "It is, just not the kind we thought."

Warmth wrapped around the cold of her face as she dunked her head underneath the water. Ears popping multiple times, they dove to the deepest part of the pool, Sylzenya's back no longer in pain. The tiles were a blurry glow in the water, but she could still see the general shape.

A willow tree.

The glow originated at the tree's trunk.

Elnok followed her as she scraped her nail along the glowing object stuck in the floor. It was too bright to tell, but she could feel it reverberate through her skin as she touched it. It had to be the compass. She dug her fingers into its sides, loosening it from the floor.

Suddenly, something slimy brushed her leg. She twisted, but saw nothing. Elnok was on the opposite side of her, so it couldn't have been him. She shook her head. No fish lived in this pool. More than likely, she was still recovering from the great willow: hallucinating. As she turned back, Elnok successfully popped the object out of the tile.

Confusion pulled at her chest as a black liquid dispersed from the tiles. Elnok batted it away as he shot up to the surface. She followed his lead, the black substance must've been algae built up from centuries.

"Well?" Sylzenya said as she reached the surface, "Is it the compa—?"

Fingers wrapped around her throat, slamming her into the side of the pool. All the air rushed out of her lungs, her back erupting in pain as she yelled. Panic rushed through her body like dark adrenaline as she clawed at the hand tightening around her neck.

"Why, human, are you immune to my toxins?" a gravelly voice echoed in her ears.

Choking, Sylzenya peeled her eyes open, terror lighting her stomach as Elnok's green eyes pierced hers; his arm muscles pulsed as his grip on her throat tightened.

"El— El—" she tried.

He tilted his head. Confusion pulled at every corner of her mind.

"Centuries have passed, and yet no one has been immune. Why you?" he asked, the gravelly voice nothing like Elnok's.

Was this the plan all along? Find the compass and then… dispose of her?

"Answer me, human!"

Human?

Something was wrong.

The Dynameis who approached her and Nyla the day of the banquet—Marlo and Westley. They'd talked about a monster in a pond… what had they droned on about? An icurus? An icythanthium?

Ichthys.

Elnok's green eyes disappeared, clouding with white and black mist.

The ichthys secretes a toxin into the water, and you don't even have to drink it to be infected. If it gets in your mouth, eyes, what have you, then the ichthys has control over your whole self. Mind, body—even soul.

No, it wasn't possible.

Monsters lived in the forest, not in Estea.

"Answer or you die!"

"I— I don't know—" she choked.

"Worthless pieces of fecal matter," he hissed.

She sucked in as much air as she could, still clawing at his hands, digging into his flesh, his blood dripping into the water.

"Are you—" she said, "Are you an ichthys?"

"You know my species," it grated. "Is that how you're able to withstand my poison?"

She shook at its response. So it was true: a monster lived in the *temple.*

And it had Elnok under its control.

"Please, let us go," she begged. "We just need the compass and we'll be gone."

"I've been this object's guardian for centuries. I've done as I've been told—stayed hidden, misdirected as needed—but then you come along and refuse to obey my demands. And now you think I'm going to let a small insignificant *human* take my treasure from *me*?" His grip tightened further as he unsheathed a dagger and held it to her throat. The sharp tip dug into her skin, a warm drop of blood dripping down her neck. "Now tell me your secrets so I may prevent this from happening again."

"*Elnok.*" She yelled as loud as she could.

The dagger dug deeper.

"Cease your incessant yelling—"

Suddenly its grip loosened, the dagger slipping from its fingers. Sylzenya grabbed the dagger, swimming away, breaths rapidly coursing through her lungs.

Elnok started coughing, dragging himself out of the pool before he dry heaved.

"*This godsforsaken male*!" it yelled, "What's the meaning of you two?"

Then, Elnok puked.

She called his name, but then she felt slimy scales brush her leg. Heart pounding, and knuckles white around the dagger, Sylzenya swam towards the edge of the pool. But, before she reached the side, a body of scales crashed into her. Water filled her mouth as she was pushed under.

A large iridescent fish without eyes or fins floated above her. Mouth open, it exposed rows and rows of sharp teeth.

The ichthys darted for her.

A giant splash from above, then Elnok was wrangling the ichthys with his bare hands. Sylzenya shot up to the surface, gulping fresh air.

She frantically splashed, uncertain how she could help. She didn't have brute strength or special skills to defeat a monster. Dynameis knew particular tactics for each creature in the forest, but she only knew the basics, and besides, she was powerless. If she was to kill it, then she needed a Vutrorian weapon and orodyte serum.

Realization washed over her. She checked Elnok's dagger. It carried the Vutrorian flag's symbol.

Please let this work.

She sliced Elnok's dagger across her palm, coating the blade in her blood. Counting the seconds and holding her breath, she waited, hoping Elnok wasn't dead.

The dagger glowed a bright yellow.

Taking a deep breath, she dove under. Elnok was pinned against the wall, wrestling the monster's jaws open, his muscles pulsing and air bubbles leaving his mouth as he kept the ichthys from biting into his flesh.

Gills flashed under the monster's belly. If what she remembered was correct, that's the part she needed to slice with her weapon. Elnok's yell rumbled in the water, bubbles leaving his mouth, the icthys' teeth close to his neck. Muscles clenched, she attacked the creature, wrenching the dagger clean through its exposed gills.

A bubbling screech echoed in the water. Elnok yanked its jaws open until it cracked. He pushed the creature away as she pulled the dagger out of its scaly flesh. It drifted to the floor, lifeless, its iridescent scales mirroring the ground, turning it invisible.

As if it had never existed.

They pushed to the surface, gasping for air as they collapsed onto the marble floor.

"Are you alright?" Elnok breathed, grabbing her shoulders. "What was that? Did you kill it? Did it hurt you?"

Sylzenya grabbed onto his arms, eyes widening at his marred skin. She quickly let him go in fear of causing him more pain.

"Your dagger was of Vutrorian make," she gasped, holding it up, the steel still glowing a bright yellow, "And I carry orodyte serum in my blood."

His brows raised, eyes wide. "You're brilliant."

Her face flushed. "If you hadn't held it down, I wouldn't have found its gills."

"And what exactly *was* it?"

"An ichthys. It… it shouldn't be here, but," she choked on her words, heart battering against her chest, "Where's the compass?"

They made their way to the spot where Elnok had emptied his stomach. Relief washed through her as she picked up the object, its gold casing just like it had been in the vision. A thin glowing piece of bark sat in its center, pointing south.

Thump.

Thump.

Thump.

Her goddess' heartbeat—it was in the compass to Aretta's Willow.

Triumph lit Sylzenya's chest as she turned to Elnok. "We need to tell the High One."

CHAPTER 18
THE DYNAMI BARRACKS

"Have you lost your mind?" Elnok questioned.

Ironic, he realized, that he'd decided to choose such words, considering a monster had taken over his mind only moments ago. He remembered grabbing the compass from the pool's tiles, a black substance floating in the water, and then everything turning cold. From then on, it was as if he had been watching through someone else's eyes—holding Sylzenya by the throat, demanding she explain why the poison didn't infect her. Every inch of his skin fell prey to someone else's eyes, his whole body thrumming with the monster's sole instinct: protect the compass.

But the monster's intent had been interrupted by the pain in Elnok's back, searing white hot until he heaved everything out of his stomach, just like with the wine and the plum.

Even now, Elnok's mind continued to be consumed by a thick fog, but he forced himself to stay focused; he needed to stop Sylzenya from telling the High One *any* of this.

"You said you saw Aretta's Willow in Lhaal Forest, so we'll need a Dynami if we're going to stand a chance against more monsters," Sylzenya said, leading them out of the healing pool room and into one of the willow groves in the main hallway. He was shivering, both of them soaked. "We can only get a Dynami with the High One's approval. And besides, he needs to know about this. What if there are more ichthys' in the pool? What if it attacks a Kreena or acolyte next?"

"There are no others," Elnok replied, the sensations of the creature's poison still fresh in his body. "It'd been there, alone, for centuries, doing nothing but guarding this compass by redirecting people with its poison. I could sense it, all of its… loneliness." He pointed to the compass in her hand. "It had every intent to kill when we took it."

"So let's perform our due diligence and inform the High One immediately."

"Look, I know you feel obligated to tell your *ever-gracious* leader everything, but now isn't the time."

"This isn't about how I feel," she argued, her voice rising. "It's about making sure no one else gets hurt."

"And I'm telling you there aren't any more monsters in there."

"Better to be safe than one of my people dead in the morning."

"It is *safe.* Anyways, we'll be thrown in the dungeons if we say anything."

She flared her nostrils. "You'd risk people's lives for the well-being of yours?"

"Ah, I see now." Elnok leaned forward, spinning his gold ring. "You've just been wanting to find this compass because you believe it'll put you in good standing with the High One again."

She scoffed. "That's not true."

He traced the gold chain on her neck before tapping the orodyte. "I'm not so sure about that."

Eyes widening, she lifted her hand to slap his face, but he stopped her, gripping her wrist before she could land the blow.

"Do *not* touch me—"

Covering her mouth with his other hand, he spun her

around, forcing them deeper into the grove, her muffled screams hopefully getting lost in the thick branches and leaves. He held Sylzenya tight to his chest.

"I need you to understand the predicament we're in," Elnok whispered into her ear, dodging her attempted head-butt, "The High One told you to never talk about Aretta's Willow, claiming it was a myth, and then we're nearly killed by a centuries-old monster guarding the one item that can lead us to the willow? And let's not forget how you proceeded to *lie* to the High One yesterday, pretending you weren't still seeking out the tree, then immediately following up with telling your friend that you were trying to find it. Do you see where I'm going with this?"

She stepped on his foot, a sharp pain rising up his ankle. A groan escaped his mouth as he cursed.

He continued anyways, "Not only is there no situation in this in which we aren't imprisoned, but none of your people can be trusted until we know what's going on."

Especially the High One.

She stopped flailing.

He didn't loosen his grasp. "If your people's lore is correct, then this tree is the last remaining source of your goddess' power, and yet, someone in Estea didn't want this compass to be found. Until we know more, we can't tell anyone, or the dungeons may be the least of our problems."

They stood in silence. Finally, her breaths evened out, her body relaxing in his arms. He slowly removed his hand from her mouth, loosening his grasp around her waist.

She turned, her eyes glassy. "I know who you think's behind this, but I promise you, he isn't. The High One would never…"

Suddenly, her arms shook, her pupils far too big.

"Sylzenya," Elnok gently whispered, "I need you to take a deep breath."

"And I need you to release me."

He held his hands up. "Fine. Just try to calm dow—"

Her eyes rolled back, her knees giving out as she stumbled on a root.

Before she fell, he caught her in an embrace. Her muscles stiffened, followed by a shudder against his chest. With a strength he didn't know she possessed, she wrapped her arms around him, fingers digging into his wet tunic while a silent sob wracked her body.

He clutched her tighter, tangling his fingers in her wet hair.

Memories of his escape from Vutror's dungeons flooded him: the way he'd fallen to his knees and rid himself of his royal cloak, praying beyond all hope no one would recognize him as he got up and ran through the dead woods; trying to find shelter before his brother's guards killed him; arriving in a village late in the night; a woman taking him in and offering him a fresh bath and a warm bed for the night. He'd cried like this, his pillow damp and his body convulsing.

And so he held Sylzenya as if he embraced a part of himself.

"It's alright," he whispered into her ear, soft and gentle, "You're alright. We survived."

But Sylzenya didn't respond, shaking harder instead, tears spilling down his neck as she mumbled words he couldn't understand.

"Everything's wrong," she finally whispered. "The High One keeping my cure from me, Nyla refusing to help us, a *monster* in the goddess' healing pool…"

He stroked her hair. "We need to be careful."

Shuddering, she took a deep breath against his neck, her warm lips grazing his skin. He gripped her tighter. As long as she was next to him, he would do everything within his power to keep her safe. He'd tackle a hundred ichthys' if that's what it took.

"If we're going to find the willow, then we need a Dynami," she finally said.

"What if I told you we already have one?"

When Elnok first laid eyes on Sylzenya two nights ago, she'd been on the temple's balcony, preaching to her people, weakness rippling across her masked confidence.

But now, he realized, it hadn't been weakness at all. As she stood next to him outside the Dynami barracks, explaining to the guards why she needed to escort Elnok into the sanctum, he could see how all her "tells" were simply an act.

In the coastal villages, Elnok had no choice but to present himself as callous and impenetrable, otherwise, thieves and pirates would raid his and his crew's supplies. But in Estea, a mask of intimidation garnered suspicion.

Esteans desires were at odds when it came to their chosen one—the Kreena destined to save them from the famine. They wanted her to be both powerful and meek—an impossible combination. And yet, she did it seamlessly, pouring power into the ground while bringing laughter to their faces.

Only moments ago she'd been shivering in shock from the monster in the healing pool; the monster she'd killed with his dagger and her blood.

It was a strange comfort, knowing that despite the carefree smile she offered the guard, she was scared.

Elnok's mouth dried as she glanced at him, a small rush of heat crawling up his neck. He issued his own carefree grin, so opposed to the sweat covering his back. A secret shared between them, as if they were the only ones capable of smelling the sharp salt in the air before an approaching storm.

And yet, despite the impending danger, Elnok ceased spinning his ring.

They would face it together.

Warmth enveloped his chest. He let his eyes wander along Sylzenya's face—her sharp features softened by her full lips, her slender neck decorated with the glimmering gold chain, the piece of clear orodyte settled between the gracious curves of her breasts. The front of his pants suddenly tightened.

He clamped his jaw, turning his gaze to the sandstone pillars, taking measured breaths. He'd known she was beautiful the first night he saw her, but everything she'd represented at the time had been everything he hated: ignorant power; thoughtless obedience. But now…

Rarely did someone surprise him as much as Sylzenya had.

"Very well," one of the guards said to her, waking Elnok from his thoughts, "While we don't believe Prince Elnok to be carrying the continent's curse of famine and sickness, we understand it's frightened the villagers. We'll allow you to escort him. We'll have the Dynami you requested meet you both in the barracks' drinking room. If you'd follow us, please."

The Dynami barracks, while still grand, were far less ostentatious than the temple. The ceilings were no taller than a typical home, and green vines draped down the sandstone walls, spilling onto the floor. Glittering streams lined either side of the hallways, the waters filled with red and yellow fish. The air smelled of newly brandished metal and lingering sweat.

The guards opened two large wooden doors, beckoning them inside. Dark wooden tables and chairs filled the large room while vines looped around stone rafters, dangling from the ceiling. Elnok counted five Dynami, three of them huddled together, discussing a serious issue over wine while two others sat at the long bar, drunk.

Great.

A large indented circle took up the middle of the room, its

surface not made of marble like the rest of the flooring, but dirt.

The guard motioned for them to sit at a table.

Cold bit into Elnok's skin through his damp clothes as he sat on the wooden chair, Sylzenya's arms pimpling next to him. They'd dried off the best they could before leaving the temple, none of the priestesses or guards batting an eye when they'd wished them farewell. The only evidence of their visit to the healing pool was the compass, which was safely stored in one of Sylzenya's pockets.

"What's the circle for?" Elnok whispered.

Sylzenya shrugged. "I know little of what Dynameis do behind their walls—"

Multiple glasses suddenly shattered, causing Elnok to flinch and reach for his dagger.

"It's a duel, then," one of the drunk Dynameis said as he stood up, his hair a tuft of orange in the torch's glow. "Unless you think you'll lose?"

The other Dynami cackled. "In your dreams."

"Careful now; we have guests." The bartender motioned to Elnok and Sylzenya.

The Dynameis halted, surprise lighting their faces.

"It can't be, can it? The Prince of Vutror *and* our most holy of Kreenas? I'll be damned." The orange-haired Dynami pointed a finger at them. "How's about whoever wins in our duel gets the lady for a night, hm?"

Elnok's insides boiled as he gripped his dagger's hilt.

"Hold your tongue," another shouted, "Such talk is meant for behind closed doors. Leave them be."

Elnok clenched his jaw.

The drunk Dynameis gawked. "It was merely a jest—"

"Do you not take Aretta's task of celibacy seriously?" Sylzenya asked, standing up. Her ash-colored hair flowed to her waist in gentle waves, her countenance as sturdy as jagged rocks on shore. "Because if you do not, I'll gladly let the High One know you wish to see a shift in such laws."

Both of their faces blanched.

"Your Holiness, it really was a simple *jest.* No harm's been done, so please, let's move on from the outrageous subject," the orange-haired Dynami stammered as he and the other Dynami entered the dirt circle.

"Very well," Sylzenya replied, returning to her seat.

Elnok left his dagger at his thigh, crossing his arms, studying Sylzenya. Her face turned red as she avoided his stare. He liked this, watching her become flustered, knowing he was the reason behind it. She'd reprimanded this Dynami for wanting to break his celibacy vow—as if he hadn't already—and yet, she'd confessed to Elnok she'd done the very same a few years ago.

Sacred and profane, holy and wicked; she danced between these elements, somehow striking a balance in their liminal space. A glorious woman, indeed.

"Prince Elnok," Kharis exclaimed, the warrior quickly making his way to their table, his green and brown leather armor replaced with a white linen shirt and dark pants, his golden hair tied in a topknot. "I was beginning to worry you'd been thrown into the dungeons with all the rumors of your curse."

Elnok rolled his eyes as he welcomed Kharis to sit. The bartender served them each a glass of red wine. Its potent stench curled along Elnok's nostrils; he pushed it aside. Sylzenya did as well.

Kharis drank his swiftly.

"So, Prince, what brings you to see me?" the warrior asked, his bright smile stained with wine.

Elnok took a deep breath, motioning for Kharis to lean in.

"We found Aretta's Willow," Elnok whispered.

Kharis's eyes widened as a sharp wind rushed by, a crackling sound flooding the room. The two Dynameis had begun their fight, their veins glowing a bright yellow, matching the orodyte strapped to their chests.

"Never mind them. It's just a duel, and these two imbeciles do it far too often," Kharis replied, grabbing Elnok's shoulder. "Where is it?"

Elnok turned to Sylzenya. Carefully, she motioned for Kharis to observe the compass underneath the table. They all looked, the golden case gleaming with the bright yellow glow.

"A compass?"

"The tree is always moving," Sylzenya whispered, "Its needle is a part of the tree's bark, and so it always points towards its home."

Bright light and crackles of magic filled the air, providing the perfect distraction from potential prying eyes.

"I'll be damned," Kharis said, leaning back and staring at Sylzenya. "Does the High One know of this?"

Her nostrils flared as she shook her head.

"Why not?" Kharis questioned.

Sylzenya took in a deep breath, "We wish to find it first and then present it to him."

"That won't do. You need to tell him immediately," Kharis replied.

Kharis' words caught Elnok off guard.

"You were the one who told me to be cautious of him," Elnok interjected.

"*Kharis* is the reason you don't trust the High One?" Sylzenya leaned forward, turning to the warrior. "But you're his closest of warriors. The greatest Dynami we've had in centuries."

"Both of you, stop," Kharis replied, "Elnok, I fear I've misguided you."

Elnok straightened his back, confusion tugging at his muscles. "Misguided me?" He lowered his voice further. "Do we need to move this conversation… elsewhere?"

Another crack of power, a wind sweeping Elnok's hair in his face.

"Elnok, the tree can't heal your friend or brother."

He stared at the warrior, gauging for any false pretenses, a signal perhaps that this was code for something else, it *had* to be. Kharis was the one who told him about the tree in the first place.

"Now you choose to humor me?" Elnok replied, "Look, now that we can locate Aretta's Willow, we need to go into Lhaal Forest as soon as possible. Sylzenya and I agree that going in tonight would be best."

Kharis' eyes turned to Elnok's full wine glass, his fingers tapping the wood table. He said nothing.

"I'm going to get a different glass of wine. I'm not too keen on this one." Sylzenya left them, walking around the fighting Dynameis and finding a seat at the wooden bar.

"You've been here three days and still refuse the wine?" Kharis questioned.

"What does that have to do with any of this? Kharis, we found the godsdamn tree. We're going to heal Orym and my brother."

"They're gone, Elnok."

Air rushed out of his lungs, like he'd been hit in the gut.

"No," Elnok stammered, shifting his gaze to Sylzenya, her eyes wide in worry as she sipped on her new glass of wine. "Orym has a few more days left. And as far as my brother goes—"

"None of it matters anymore," Kharis pressed, pushing the wine glass towards Elnok's hand. "The only reason I had any faith in the damn thing was because of a wayward dream I had when I was a child, nothing more. Even if it exists, we'll never make it in time. Besides, who's to say the tree can still heal? It's been centuries. Best we move on with our lives than linger on that which is already gone."

Heat and cold swirled in Elnok's veins, his fingers shaking

as he leaned across the table, forcing Kharis to look in his eyes. A bright light erupted from the Dynameis behind him, the two warriors yelling, one of them landing a hard punch to the other's face. It reminded him of his blacksmith master, the way the man would hit him for every mistake Elnok made. It reminded him of Tosh, how his brother seared him with fire out of madness.

If it hadn't been for Orym, Elnok would've drowned in those memories.

If it wasn't for Orym, Elnok would've jumped off that damned cliffside.

"You told me you loved my brother," Elnok whispered.

"A foolish act."

Elnok scoffed. "You see reason now, is it? Then *that* is foolishness, claiming to love someone when you would let them die without a fight." He leaned closer. "Seems as if you never truly cared for him."

He waited for the warrior's veins to pulse, for his power to ignite, for his anger to consume him. Elnok had seen the deep love Kharis held for his brother, and even though he didn't understand it, he needed a Dynami to get them through Lhaal Forest. He needed Kharis to find hope again.

"Perhaps I didn't," Kharis replied.

Elnok's heart stopped as another crack of power rumbled through the room.

"If this is to get back at me for my heinous comments about how I felt about you two, then fine, I apologize, *truly.* But we can't find this tree without you."

"Kharis, we're grateful you made time for us," Sylzenya interjected, a small smile lining her lips as she approached the table, "I can see now where I've gone awry. I'll go ahead and deliver the compass to the High One when I have my meeting with him tomorrow and allow him to decide what we'll do with it."

"*What?*" Elnok questioned. "Sylzen—"

"She's right, Elnok," Kharis said as he stood, his broad shoulders somehow looking smaller than when he had first come in. "The continent outside of Estea is nearing its end. If I were you, I'd finalize those treaty revisions and then see if the High One would allow you permanent residence here as an ambassador." The warrior gripped his shoulder, a sad smile on his mouth. "You're safer here with us."

Before Elnok could argue, the warrior dismissed himself, thanking Sylzenya as the large wood doors shut behind him with a thud. Elnok steadied himself with his chair, wrestling against the truth he wanted to ignore.

Kharis had wanted to find Aretta's Willow; he'd been fervent in making sure Elnok's brother lived a long life. He'd made it seem as if the treaty revisions were unimportant in comparison to finding the tree.

And yet, Kharis no longer wanted his brother.

But why?

"Come on," Sylzenya whispered. Grabbing his arm, she led him past the now bloodied Dynami warriors and into the sparkling hallway. "Lingering will do us no good."

Elnok lowered his voice. "I refuse to take this compass to the High One."

"As do I," she replied quietly, "so we better sit down and figure out a plan for how we're going to get through Lhaal Forest alive."

Elnok's panic eased. Heat rose in his cheeks.

"Not a bad idea," he replied.

Sylzenya smirked. "I'm well aware."

Despite Kharis' change in perspective, Elnok wouldn't let it change his goal. He needed the tree whether there was a safe route through Lhaal or not, and if there was anything he was becoming more sure of, it was his and Sylzenya's ability to do the impossible.

They would get to Aretta's Willow, and they'd do it with or without a Dynami. He'd fight all of Distrathrus' monsters if it meant saving Orym's life.

CHAPTER 19
A SALVE FOR WOUNDS

Dinner was roasted greens mixed with pepper sauce and slices of freshly baked bread. Sylzenya ate the food mindlessly while Elnok bathed, her focus centered on the compass and everything they'd gone through to get it.

It seemed impossible. There were no monsters in the Temple; *there couldn't be.* And yet there had been. The ichthys had asked why its poison hadn't affected her; why it hadn't controlled her *mind.* She didn't know the answer, could barely make sense of its existence let alone how it could ask her questions. Monsters lived in Lhaal Forest. It was their prison, much like how Estea, in its own way, had become hers.

Elnok had claimed no more monsters lived in the healing pool, but what if more monsters existed in the temple? It could really mean only one thing.

There was a worshiper of Distrathrus among them.

A chill ran up her spine. Centuries ago, there'd been a group of Distrathrus worshippers claiming he'd been the one in the right, not Aretta—that his monsters were innocent and humans were not. Legend said they tried to prove their point by living in the forest alongside its creatures.

They were killed within the hour.

Sylzenya thought back to her vision.

For life there is a price, the bird had said, *and only in pain is it made whole. Your choice has been made, and so your consequence is set in blood and stone.*

A gold ring turning into blood, filling the orodyte. The bird killed by a thicket of branches. None of it made sense to her.

This price she'd paid, had it already come to pass? It might as well have, because everything changed after she failed the Kreena Rite.

Gripping the compass to her chest, she kneeled to the wood floor. The scent of damp soil filled her lungs. Quickly, she removed a floorboard, revealing a bed of dirt. She and Elnok still hadn't figured out how they could traverse through Lhaal Forest, their chances of survival slim to none without a divine warrior by their side.

Tilting her head, she listened; the sound of water washing over skin still echoed from the bathing room, which meant Sylzenya had time before Elnok was done.

If she was to do this, she had to do it right now.

She placed the compass on the ground next to her.

Thump.

Thump.

Thump.

The familiar sound silenced her nerves. Hopefully it would help her in their time of need.

Unclipping the orodyte from her necklace, she dug a hollow hole into the dirt underneath the floorboard. Dirt crusted her fingernails as she shoveled the soil back over the stone, placing her warm palms on top of it. Taking a deep breath, she prayed a silent request for her goddess' blessing.

Help us find your willow, Aretta.

Sylzenya's fingers ached with a natural pull towards the earth. She obliged, leaning forward, searching for her goddess' power woven into the soil, the roots, all that bore life.

Thump.

Thump.

A warm tingle met her palms, Sylzenya's chest brightening at the long-awaited sensation. Golden sparks flickered from the ground, circling her arms in weak spirals. Even still, it felt like a part of herself had woken up. Excitement rushed through her veins as her goddess' power sliced into her back. It was sharper than she remembered, deeper; a cry spilled from her mouth. But it didn't matter.

Help us find your willow, she urged, sweat dripping from her brow. Her fingers dug deeper into the dirt as if she'd never let go.

The golden light flickered, the brightness in her chest fluttering away, the pain in her back sharpening.

Please, Sylzenya begged. *Please. Help us.*

Air, acidic and sweet, shot into her lungs. The inn's wooden bed frames and stone walls disappeared, replaced by a dark earthen wall. The walls glinted—cavern walls, she realized—with white and yellow specks of light, like stars in the night. But these weren't stars.

They were pieces of orodyte.

The ancient orodyte mines.

"*Sylzenya.*"

A deep, commanding voice overwhelmed her. The cavern vanished, replaced by the sight of her crimson blood dripping down her arms. Elnok caught her as she collapsed.

"Do you have a death wish?" Elnok asked, clearly exasperated. She hung limp in his arms, her blood now smearing on his freshly cleaned hands.

She gulped, trying to find words, but her throat had decidedly become parched. She shrugged instead. He swept a hand through his wet black hair, remnants of water spraying her face. It felt nice, *he* felt nice.

"She's blessed us," Sylzenya finally choked out. "The orodyte mines; that's how we can get through Lhaal Forest. There's a rumored entrance to the tunnels in the ancient Willow Grove."

Elnok's eyes widened, only to narrow once again. "We could've retraced our steps at the temple tomorrow and figured that out. You didn't need to bleed to death in order for us to learn that."

The cut felt like flames engulfing her. "Your friend doesn't have much time before he dies. Why waste more when we can avoid it? We should go tonight."

He opened his mouth, only to close it, his throat bobbing as his hands held her tighter against his chest. "We'll take tonight to rest, and leave first thing in the morning."

"I'll be fine within the hour."

"Gods, you really don't know when to stop, do you?" He sighed. "Look, I need rest too. It'd be unwise to start a journey exhausted if we don't have to."

Sylzenya scratched her palm. He was right; and she was tired too.

"Suppose one more night in a bed would be nice," she muttered.

"Come on," he said, "your turn to bathe."

After drinking water and regaining her ability to walk, Sylzenya took a quick warm bath. The soapy water stung her back, but she held in her yell.

The innkeeper, Helena, had given her a thin satin robe, detailed with intricate lace. She had said it was a gift in exchange for her teachings in the village. Sylzenya had gladly accepted it, the cool material refreshing on her heated skin. Wiping a towel over her stinging cut before putting on the robe, she sighed with relief, returning to the bedroom.

"I have a surprise for you," Elnok said as she shut the door.

She spun around. Elnok was sitting on his bed, a small box with silver edges in his hands.

"A surprise?" Sylzenya asked, a heat blooming along her cheeks when Elnok's eyes drifted to her robe.

It wasn't just a thin piece of material, it was short, with a deep "v" allowing her cleavage a chance to breathe. She would be lying if she said a part of her didn't want Elnok to see her like this, but another part of her chastised herself for being evocative. There would be nothing to come from this. He was leaving the moment he got the cure for his friend. Here and then gone.

But then his breathless smile made her heart flutter, and she was glad she wore the robe.

"Since you refuse to listen to reason and continue to hurt yourself, I've got just the thing to help ease at least some of the pain."

He raised the box. Curious, she approached him, his thin black tunic accentuating his corded arms.

"It's a salve," he said, opening the box to reveal a clear substance with a consistency of honey, "If you'd like, I can put some along your scar?"

She should say no. Only Aretta's healing waters could cure her cut, anything else typically just added an uncomfortable stickiness to her skin and ruined her clothes. But as his lips parted with a warm smile, she stepped forward.

"Interesting," she said, "I'd almost say that's kind of you."

He shrugged. "Even I'm capable of generous acts every so often."

She rolled her eyes as he positioned himself at the edge of his bed, legs spread apart; he motioned for her to stand in between them. Heart pounding against her chest, she decided this was more than likely a normal occurrence for outlanders; something he offered most people he traveled with.

So she turned around, her back facing his front.

Gently, he placed a strong calloused hand on her hip. Her breath caught, arms pimpling as he guided her closer to him.

"Is this alright?" he asked.

"Yes."

"And if you could," he paused, his fingers tightening on her hip, "move your robe a bit? That way I can reach all of it."

Chest growing heavy, Sylzenya turned to look at him. "Right."

He smiled, a confidence mixed with a gentleness in his green eyes. Slowly, she let the silk fabric fall off her shoulders, exposing her entire back. A chill ran through her skin, causing her nipples to peak. She ignored the heat burning her cheeks.

"This could sting at first," he whispered, his voice lower than before, a kind of huskiness to it she hadn't noticed.

She nodded, her breaths short as a sharp cold touched her skin. She jumped.

"Sorry about that." He laughed, deep and warm.

"You did warn me." She chuckled, stealing a glance behind her shoulder, watching as Elnok glided his hand along her skin—the part of her she'd been told was holy since she'd first ushered her goddess' power.

The part of her body where suffering originated, giving life and taking her blood in return. Elnok's face softened, and his brows furrowed—an intention in his features leaving Sylzenya at a loss for words.

"How does this feel?" he whispered, pulling her closer to him, heat rising in her lower belly as she obeyed his implicit requests.

It felt… it felt like everything. While this salve did far more than most, a strong mint leaf, no doubt, it was his skin on hers, showing her a gentleness where she typically only felt pain.

He touched her like she was sacred.

"It feels fine," she said, trying not to let her emotions show, a small sob sitting in the back of her throat.

"And how about this?"

He leaned in, pursing his lips and lightly blowing on her scar. Wings fluttered in her stomach. She leaned further into his touch. Blowing on her skin again, his lips ever so lightly grazed her shoulder blade.

Sylzenya's breath hitched.

"I see," he said in a low voice, a small smile on his lips.

Before she could respond, his other hand gripped her waist, pulling her closer to his warm body. Everything within her succumbed to him. She turned, letting the robe slip down her arms. Elnok ran his palm up to her side, his rough hands a balance to her soft skin.

"Sylzenya," he whispered, extending his face towards her, his eyes dipping to her lips. "You are…"

His words were lost in the air, in his breaths and in his touch, in Sylzenya's want for more of this. More of *him*. She leaned forward, wanting to know what his lips felt like on hers—

No.

Reality split her open like another cut on her back. Collecting herself, she quickly pulled her robe back on her body, stepping away from Elnok, his hands sliding from her waist.

He stood up, eyes blinking as he rubbed the back of his neck.

"Sylzenya, my apologies."

"No, no, it's alright."

"I'm just so tired, and things are stressfu—"

"I understand," she assured him. "Thanks for the salve and I hope you have a good night."

Without another word she disappeared behind the makeshift curtain. She ignored the shuffling of his feet as he blew out the flame.

The undeniable pulse between her legs ached with longing for Elnok. But she had to stop herself, *needed* to. There was no point in getting physically involved with this prince, or whatever he really was, because they would part once they found Aretta's Willow. This wasn't a time for distractions.

Forcing herself to forget, she closed her eyes, trying to think about the compass, getting to Aretta's Willow, escaping monsters—

But then her hip burned, the shape of his hand seared into her skin. All she could imagine was his full lips on hers, his hard stomach underneath her fingernails, his hair tangled in her fingers.

He was insufferable, yet he was kind. Dangerous and handsome. Sarcastic and courageous. She wanted that dirty mouth of his on hers, on every part of her body. He was rough when he wrapped her in his ropes and blackmailed her, but gentle as he bathed her back in his salve, worshiping the most sensitive parts of herself.

He was a living contradiction, and she only wanted more.

Damn all this pain she constantly carried. Maybe, just this once, not everything needed to be covered in her blood.

She ripped the blankets off her body, staring at the sheet hanging across their room, so much like the forest keeping his land from hers. A barrier not meant to be crossed, and yet it somehow made everything more desperate. She stood tup, blood pumping fast as she pulled the sheet aside.

Sylzenya stilled.

Elnok stood before her, shirtless, chest heaving. His linen pants hung low on his hips, eyes wild as he drank her in. His hand was outstretched as if, he too, was about to tear down this damned wall she'd built between them.

"Elnok," she whispered, all breath and no substance as she stepped towards him, "I couldn't sleep…"

But she couldn't find anymore words as Elnok grabbed her waist and dragged her against his warm skin, pressing his lips to her mouth. Everything shifted, as if the ground beneath her gave way, falling into something warm and dark, a deep pleasure burning through her skin.

"Sylzenya," he breathed, his low whisper pulsing against her skin, twisting in between her legs, "If you don't want this—"

"I want this," she whispered, tracing her thumb along his stubbled jaw, "I'm so tired of pain, Elnok."

He tangled his fingers in her hair, pulling on it, exposing her neck. He trailed kisses along her sensitive skin, his warm, wet tongue marking a trail up to her ear. A cold shiver rushed along her skin.

"You talk so much of pain, but when was the last time you felt pleasure?"

His words brushed along her ear, drawing liquid heat in between her legs. He'd been unraveling her since the moment they'd met, challenging whom she trusted, and inspiring her to choose her own path. He'd pulled a single thread on a life already falling to pieces.

And yet, it didn't anger her. While her life had shattered around her, this man stood next to her despite it. He didn't expect perfection from her, didn't expect her to save him. Didn't ask her to bleed pain so she could give life.

To him, she wasn't the holy chosen one.

She was just Sylzenya.

"Please," she gasped, wrapping her legs around his torso. His hands caught her thighs, a low rumble in his throat as his fingers dug into her skin. "Please unravel every last part of me."

He laughed, low and deep against her neck, his tongue circling her ear; a moan released from her lips.

"How can I deny such a desperate request?"

CHAPTER 20
PLEASURE & PAIN

Elnok pushed Sylzenya up against the stone wall, grateful this inn was sturdy enough to not cause a sound. She'd wrapped her legs around his torso, grinding against him, that damned robe so thin it was as if it barely covered her skin at all.

It'd driven him mad when she'd walked out of her bath wearing it. And by the look in her eyes, she knew it too. She'd wanted him to suffer.

He fucking loved her for it.

But after he'd offered her the salve, her skin so smooth and warm against his touch, his desire rising with each stroke, moments away from kissing her… she left.

It was her right to do so, even though it ached as she backed away from his advances, separating herself from him with that damned sheet hanging between them. He'd meant to let her do as she wished, hadn't meant to get up and try to win her affections back. He'd stopped himself, counting his breaths, trying to force himself back into his bed…

But then *she* moved the curtain. And as she stood there, heavy breaths and shimmering eyes on his lips, he'd been undone.

And now, as she opened her mouth to his, her tongue desperate for his taste, he had no intention of letting her go.

I'm so tired of pain, Elnok.

Her words had shook him. So much talk of pain, of blood, of sacrifice. Even as he thought of it, his back burned from his scars; he too, was tired of all this pain.

He gripped her curved hips, groaning as the wetness between her legs soaked into his pants, deepening the kiss as her melodic moans sent blood pumping into his cock. She'd asked him to unravel her—every last part—and damn him if her added request didn't make his need for her become something ravenous.

"I want you," she whispered into his mouth, "all of you."

He nipped her bottom lip. "So eager, are we?"

His groin ached at how her brows dipped, the way she nodded her head feverishly. But it was too soon to fill her. He wanted to take his godsdamn time with this woman, something he hadn't desired in many years.

"What about what *I* want, Sylzenya?" he teased, grinding his length against her.

She whimpered, clutching his neck with her fingers. "Isn't that what most men want?"

He smiled against her mouth. "Do you trust me?"

Her body stilled, breaths brushing along his lips.

"Yes," she whispered, "I do."

Desire rushed through his muscles as he carried her to his bed. Gently, he lay on his back, Sylzenya straddling him, her tits spilling against her robe, begging to be released and covered by his tongue.

But he would do that soon enough.

"Sit on my face," he instructed.

Her eyes widened, color rushing to her cheeks.

"That Dynami you fucked really didn't know much, did he?"

She shook her head, a smile peeling across her lips as her throat bobbed.

"Are you sure?" she questioned, "Because you don't have to do that for me."

"Sylzenya," he sat up on his elbows, stroking his thumb along the bottom of her lip, "I think you know by now I'm a rather selfish man, and so anything I ask of you, no matter how charitable it may sound, *always* benefits me."

Her chest heaved, those perfect tits flushed with color as her lips parted. She was hesitant, believed it was a sacrifice on his part to pleasure her. Oh, but how wrong she was. Her pleasure was his, and he needed to make it clear just how badly he needed it.

"I want to taste you," he whispered, "So *sit on my face.*"

Crawling, she spread her legs, revealing her perfect dripping cunt. He groaned, grabbing her hips and lowering her down. In one languid motion he ran his tongue along her swollen skin; the way she moaned his name was somehow even sweeter than her taste.

He'd almost decided to not live to see this day; not live a life where he would meet this woman who, despite all their differences, understood the pain of life, and yet lived it anyways. A woman whose tenacity and compassion for others had bolstered his own, someone he could speak to freely and trust with his deepest secrets.

Yet another reason to thank Orym for that day at the cliffside.

With every lick, every stroke on her throbbing lips, he felt each painful memory of his distant past disappear, replaced with her warm skin, heated breaths, and soft hair. Need stoked into unrelenting desire. Running his tongue back and forth, he circled that small, swollen part of her, his hands wandering up her silk robe and finding her full breasts.

Gods help me.

Her cries took him away from the scars seared into his

back, as if every word she spoke and touch of her body healed parts of himself.

"Please," she whimpered, "Elnok, *please*. I need you."

Her words undid him. Spreading her quivering legs, he slid underneath her. Her hands fumbled for his pants then she dragged them off his hips, his hard cock standing upright. She gripped him, slowly sliding her hand up and down his shaft, sending a moan out of his lips.

"Can I?" she asked, licking her lips.

Elnok gulped. "Is that what you want?"

She nodded. "Tell me how."

Realization thrummed through his chest—she'd been intimate before, but she'd never done *this* before. But he could tell by her determined gaze she meant what she said—she wanted his cock in her mouth. And godsdamn him, if that didn't make him pulse in her grip.

"You can start slow," he instructed, voice low, "Licking, exploring, and when you're comfortable, you can take as much of me as you want."

Fingers digging into the sheets, he couldn't stop himself from moaning; she took him so damn well.

And yet he didn't deserve this. Pain had been his companion since his parents died, marked into his skin, a sign of how unwanted he was in this world. As if she heard his thoughts, she stopped, eyes peering up through her long lashes, those deep blue eyes bringing him back to this moment—to her.

"I want you, Elnok."

Everything within him died at those words. He wanted her too, *needed* her. But he hadn't been able to afford a contraceptive medicine in years.

"If you're concerned at all, a girl's womb is turned barren the first time she uses Aretta's power."

His stomach sank. "You give so much for this life."

"And I don't regret it," she said, slowly crawling on top of him. Her calloused hand caught on his skin as she glided it over his chest, bringing it up to cradle his jaw.

"Will you regret this?"

Her eyes searched him, and he felt as if he'd asked the sea if it could survive without the waves, if its depths could still be a mystery if it was shallow.

"Will you?" she whispered.

He gripped his hardened cock, watching as she lowered herself onto him, slowly, carefully.

"I could never regret you."

She sank herself onto him, whimpering into his mouth as he claimed her lips, teeth, and tongue. He pierced into her, and she ground against him; he lost all sense of where his body started and hers ended. Pain and power and sorrow intermingled with pleasure and light and desire. They shared all of it between their skin—sweat and blood, tears and prayers.

She broke their kiss, hiding in the nape of his neck as he held her steady, any gentleness leaving them as he pulled her hair and she scratched his back, their breaths and moans echoing as their voices met together in a shared cry for mercy and pleasure.

It was as if this one moment, here with her, was all life had been created for. As they rode waves upon waves of desperate need, he couldn't remember why he would've wanted to be anywhere else.

And then everything stilled.

Pleasure rolled off of his body, onto hers, and then pooled around them in a still, quiet sort of peace. He folded into her, and she buried her face into his skin, whispering words he didn't understand as if they were ancient prayers breathed into his body—as if he was the one being worshiped when she was the one who deserved it all.

Sylzenya kissed his forehead, retreating to their bathing room and returning with cloths. He praised her body as he wiped his remnants off her, and she spoke terribly dirty things as she cleaned him. He laughed, embracing her as he fell onto the bed, tangling his legs with hers.

"Who did this to you?" Sylzenya asked, a single nail wandering along the scars on his back.

Normally he would've closed off the conversation, retreated into himself, or made some crass joke about being whipped by a past lover. But as he looked into her eyes, those deep blue irises that reminded him so much of the sea, he kissed her hand.

"My brother," he replied, intertwining his fingers with hers, "After my parents were assassinated, he went mad, drinking all the wine he could get his hands on. He was convinced that I would do anything I could to take the Crown from him, even plan to murder him. I wanted no such thing."

Her brow furrowed, her thumb brushing his. "The wine reminds you of him."

"It's an unfortunate association," he scoffed. "He kept me in the dungeons for six months, declaring me on trial for believing I'd murdered our parents. He got an iron rod shaped in our Vutrorian family symbol and used it to torture me for a confession, saying this was the closest form of a crown I'd ever receive. I finally escaped to a village on the coast where I met Orym and became quite a nuisance as a village thief. I'm sure you've gathered by now my princely duties have been left far behind me."

Eyes glistening, Sylzenya squeezed his hand. "How old were you?"

"Sixteen."

She whispered his name, wiping a tear he hadn't realized ran down his cheek.

"I suppose we both bear pain on our backs from those we love, don't we?" she asked.

His heart stalled in his chest. Stroking her neck, he pulled her in, kissing her warm full lips. Sliding closer, she ran a gentle hand along his back, his cock hardening again as he looped her leg over his hip, heat growing between them as he lost himself in her scent. She knew what he felt, understood the complexity of his life with barely a word.

A loud knock sounded on the door.

Shock ruptured through his spine as they pushed off each other. Sylzenya scrambled off the bed, finding her robe and holding it in her hand.

"Sylzenya?" The innkeeper, Helena called through the door, "You have some visitors."

Elnok turned to her, confusion set in his face.

She seemed just as confused as he did, which meant meeting with someone in the dead of night wasn't some Estean cultural expectation. They both glanced at the compass, and then back at each other.

Panic sliced through his skin as he grabbed the compass, motioning for her to say something—to stall Helena.

"Um, Helena, so sorry, I'll be right there," she said, her voice sounding as if she'd just woken up.

"Please hurry, dear. They wish to see the prince as well."

They dressed quickly. Elnok took down his rope and attached it to his belt, giving Sylzenya the compass, which she pocketed in her bloodied Kreena robe. Heart racing, he took Sylzenya's hand before she opened the door.

"We should run," he whispered.

Sylzenya shook her head, squeezing his hand. "If we tried, they'd suspect something. The best thing we can do is present just as we have the last few days. If they ask about the healing pool, we lie, for no one saw us. Even Kharis doesn't know where we collected the compass."

"This is a gamble."

"It's this or fully expose ourselves by running or hiding. We'd inevitably get caught, and there would be unavoidable consequences. At least in this we have a chance at keeping the compass hidden and sticking to our plan for tomorrow."

Elnok's instinct still screamed for them to run, but Sylzenya was right. Outside of this kingdom, hiding was simple. There were villages and ships, factions of people who opposed or supported one another, more land that stretched the distances and with it, buried names. But here, there was only the temple, barracks, village, and forest. The High One's rules were obeyed by all.

They were trapped.

"Very well," Elnok replied, letting go of her hand as Sylzenya opened the door.

Helena wrung her hands as two people stood on either side of her: a woman with dark hair and pale skin, her Kreena robe decorated with fresh blood, and her golden eyes downcast; a man donned in Dynami armor, his golden hair tied in a topknot, and the orodyte on his chest glowing a bright yellow.

"Nyla," Sylzenya whispered.

"Kharis," Elnok breathed.

"Yes, um, they've requested to speak with you both," Helena said, motioning to the only two people in all of Estea who had any information about what Elnok and Sylzenya had been planning. "There are sweets and various drinks in the breakfast nook."

Kharis coughed.

"Oh, yes," Helena said swiftly, "And wine, of course."

"Sylzenya, Prince Elnok," Kharis said, "If you would join us."

Elnok snarled at the glass of wine Kharis poured for him.

All four of them sat at a wooden table decorated with bright flowers and white doilies, Helena's breakfast nook a well of pastel colors and fanciful designs.

Elnok traced the hilt of his hidden dagger.

Kharis folded his hands as he asked Elnok, "Are you still in possession of the compass?"

Strained silence stretched between the four of them.

"We plan to see the High One tomorrow for the treaty revisions," Elnok finally answered. "It's during that time we'll give him the compass to do as he sees fit."

"I see." Kharis unfolded his hands. "I think the matter of the compass is far more dire than either of you realize, so, I'd urge us to go meet with the High One and discuss it with him now."

"Now?" Elnok laughed, "Kharis, it's the middle of the night."

"What do you mean a *dire* matter?" Sylzenya interjected.

Kharis turned to Nyla. She gave him a nod, as if they'd made a plan of how they were to conduct themselves.

"An acolyte almost died yesterday," Nyla said, "She was newly ordained and had just begun using her power. So, when she went to the healing pool, she didn't understand how it worked. A priestess had left her to heal, and when she came back, the girl was lying on the floor, her blood everywhere."

Elnok instinctively grabbed his dagger's hilt.

"How?" Sylzenya asked, but they already knew the answer.

"The healing pool no longer heals."

The compass. Its piece of bark from the tree; the pool couldn't heal without it in the water.

Shit.

Everything had happened so fast: the monster, the compass, Sylzenya's initial desire to tell the High One. They'd made an oversight.

A damn important one.

Kharis interjected, "After hearing this matter, I realized how strange it was that, just as you two had found the compass, the healing pool simultaneously could no longer heal the backs of acolytes and Kreenas. So," he paused, staring at Elnok, "I must ask we go and return the compass to the High One this instant, that way the healing pool can be restored. We'll advocate for you both, saying how it was an honest mistake, not an attempted murder."

Elnok's body turned rigid.

"Or, you can both join us as we find the tree," Sylzenya argued. "Think about it, we wouldn't have to rely on only the healing pool anymore. If we had the tree's location, we could get enough power and healing to sustain not just the current acolytes and Kreenas, but more. Maybe we could even help the outlanders; we could help fight the famine and sickness not just in Estea, but outside of it. We could finish what Aretta had tried to all those centuries ago."

Elnok's chest burned with light at Sylzenya's words. But judging by Nyla's and Kharis' faces, there would be no convincing them. Dread slithered along his spine.

"Sylzenya," Nyla urged, "now isn't the time to fantasize. We need to return this or else more acolytes and Kreenas could get hurt, myself included."

"It isn't fantasizing," Sylzenya said, revealing the compass, its needle bark glowing and still pointing south, "We have its location. We could make real change with it."

"The High One requests you bring it to him immediately," Kharis stated.

Elnok crumpled a doily in his fist. "He requests it? As in… he already knows we have it?"

The Dynami let out a deep breath. "Yes. I told him."

"*Damn it*, Kharis." Elnok slammed his fist, a well of anger he'd been holding since his meeting with the warrior yesterday spilling over. "*You* were the one who convinced me to find this damn tree in the first place. *You* warned me to not trust the High One. *What's wrong with you*?"

"You didn't get him to drink the wine yet?" Nyla asked,

looking at Kharis. "He vomited the plum I gave him two days ago."

"What the fuck are you two talking abou—?"

Sylzenya's chair screeched as she stood, grabbing his hand. "Elnok, we need to go. *Now.*"

"I wouldn't do that if I were you," Kharis said.

The orodyte on his chest pulsed a bright yellow, his eyes flickering like torches, his veins crackling along his arms and neck with magic.

"*Come on,*" Sylzenya shouted.

Elnok didn't hesitate as he dashed out of the inn with her, Nyla screaming Sylzenya's name as he unsheathed his dagger. The square was empty except for the wine fountain in the center and lightning bugs hovering just below the trees. Their footsteps echoed along the stone ground as their breaths heaved through their lungs. A door swung open, glass shattering. Elnok didn't need to look back to know Kharis was coming for them.

"We can hide in the foliage up ahead!" Sylzenya yelled.

He obeyed, running as fast as he could, the shaded pathway almost within reach, but then, light erupted and blinded them.

"Seize them!" a deep voice boomed.

Elnok blindly waved his dagger in front of him, holding onto Sylzenya's hand with all his might as footsteps rapidly approached them.

"Elnok, don't let go!" Sylzenya shouted.

He squeezed harder, fighting to stay standing and to see what was happening, but then strong hands and built bodies slammed him to the ground.

His fingers slipped.

"*Sylzenya!*"

A boot slammed into his face, sharp, abrupt pain cracking his nose. Another kick to his stomach sent the air out his lungs, but he kept fighting against the endless limbs grabbing for him.

Bright pain ruptured in the back of his head, and his mind fell into darkness.

CHAPTER 21
IN THE FLESH

Leaves gently rustled in the wind, as they always did on spring days. Yet everything was dark, Sylzenya's eyes were so heavy even her greatest effort couldn't relieve her of this blindness. Fresh loam swept into her lungs as she took a deep breath, the air crisp and cool.

Evening, then. And she was outside.

But why would she be outside? She'd been lying in bed at the inn, the scent of earthy musk and worn leather consuming her every thought.

Consumed by *him.*

Elnok.

His skin had been warm, his muscles tough as she'd dug her fingers into his shoulders and back. Pleasure had been teased out of her, slowly and deliberately, and she'd sworn her power had returned when all she saw were sparks and all she felt was light. Pale green eyes, a relaxed half-smile. He'd felt like warm summer days swimming in lakes, cold winter nights snuggled beneath blankets, and hot rose tea warming her fingers.

She wanted to see him. He was here, wasn't he? Had they gone out for a walk in the middle of the night—?

The compass.

Clenching her jaw, she cursed her heavy eyelids. Nyla and Kharis had come to talk about the compass. They'd said something strange… something that made her fear for Elnok's safety…

The wine. Nyla had sounded exasperated that Elnok hadn't drunk any since he'd arrived, even mentioning how Elnok had thrown up her plum. The wine and fruits were laced with something; they had to be. It would explain why he kept puking. But what about the monster? He'd vomited then too. How did that have anything to do with it?

"She's waking up, Your Grace," a familiar voice—Nyla's—said.

"Good," the High One replied.

Fear gripped her chest.

She remembered how she got here. Dynameis had assaulted them, pushed them to the ground, Elnok's fingers slipping through hers as he shouted her name.

Sylzenya finally forced her eyes open.

"Everything's going to be alright," Nyla whispered into her ear.

Sylzenya jolted, now realizing her arm was wrapped around her friend's shoulder, like a limp vine on a wooden terrace. She tried pushing away from her, but she couldn't; she couldn't feel anything but her face and her chest, moving up and down with her slowed breaths.

"What—" Sylzenya fought the haze in her mind. Pale light illuminated blurred trees. "Nyla, where's Elnok?"

"Do not fret about the prince, Sylzenya. He's being taken care of, trust me," the High One replied from somewhere in front of her, his figure a tall white blur.

Anger rumbled through her. Trust—a difficult flower to tend to—yet so easy to tear out of the ground. The moment the High One held the cure above her like a dangling carrot, the roots had begun to pull. And now, the flower didn't have much left to hold onto.

"And how exactly is he being taken care of?" she demanded.

Her words surprised her, but she didn't take it back. She wouldn't, not until she knew Elnok was safe.

"I brought you here to say something important," he said, approaching her with the same graceful steps he always did, "And it's to say I'm sorry."

She scoffed, heat building in her neck as she met his yellow eyes. "Rare to hear an apology from your lips, Your Grace."

"*Sylzenya,*" Nyla whispered in warning.

"No, no, it's quite alright, Nyla. I've done a terrible thing to her, and I mean to pay the price in addition to seeking recompense."

"You can do those things when you tell me where Elnok is."

"I should've never sent you away on that forsaken mission with that thief," the High One replied, his eyes turning glassy.

It made her sick.

He continued, "I've learned many a thing about him during these last few days. Pillaging villages with his notorious posse, plotting to kill his brother and take the Crown, killing multiple Vutrorian guards in his escape from the dungeons: a nightmare of a man."

She curled her fists. "You know nothing about him."

"And you do? After three days?" the High One questioned. "Come now, Sylzenya, you're being naive. Nothing's royal about him besides his blood, but enough about him. We're here so you might be given your cure."

Her heart stilled. The High One dug into his pockets, taking out a vial filled with a thick dark liquid.

"Come," he motioned for her as he alighted a small set of marble stairs, "Stand beside me and allow me to explain, and then we'll waste no more time. Your power will be restored this very night."

Nyla pushed her forward. Sylzenya stumbled, catching her balance as she gripped Nyla's robe. Her limbs tingled, prickling like needles as she took in her surroundings. Tall willow trees encircled them, a white atrium covered in looping vines, and a single white marble throne sitting underneath it. The willow she'd created fourteen years ago stood tall behind the throne, and beneath her feet was the sacred soil bordered by marble.

The Willow Grove: the place where she'd failed her rite—where her father had poisoned her.

We never wanted to give you to the temple, Sylzenya, her father had said. *It wasn't supposed to happen like this.*

His words tasted different in this moment, sounded less like a plea for her to come home and more like a desperate attempt to save her from something.

Save her from what?

A small golden light sparked from her willow tree. Sylzenya furrowed her brow, staring at the tree in a long silence.

"Sylzenya, if you would join me—"

"Did you know Aretta's Willow still lived? That it existed at all?" Sylzenya interrupted, gripping Nyla's robe, the heat rising in her skin. "Did you know about the compass? About the monster living at the bottom of the healing pool?"

The High One spun around, his eyes wide and brows dipped—as if he was hurt.

Her shoulders dropped. Guilt weighed down on her like a fallen tree, her heart faltering as the man that stood before her, the one who had comforted her in times of need, stared at her as if she'd caused him pain.

But things had changed. He'd led her to believe Aretta's Willow was a myth, sent her on a petty mission to prove herself worthy of her power, and then sent his warriors in a rampage to take back the compass which he'd sworn didn't exist.

"*Did you?*" she asked again, the force behind her words causing her own spine to shudder.

He said nothing.

Tears stung her eyes. How many other ways had he lied to her?

"I swear on Aretta's blood, I will never take your cure," she said.

Slowly, his features shifted: dipped brows relaxed into a harsh gaze; his downturned mouth a straight line; his yellow eyes sharp and poised to strike.

"Know this, Sylzenya," he said, his voice deep and grating, "things could've turned out differently tonight if you had so chosen."

The High One returned the black vial into his pocket. A familiar glimmer of light shone before he closed it.

Her heart stuttered.

The compass.

He wouldn't put it anywhere he wouldn't deem safe; he wouldn't trust anyone else to hold it, of this Sylzenya knew with certainty. He had only ever trusted her with such tasks.

The High One looked past her and flicked his head. "Restrain her and retrieve him."

Before she could react, the glowing chest plates of two Dynameis appeared out of the grove's shadows. With a flash of power, they quickly pinned her arms to her side. She cursed, not having checked her surroundings well enough to see the hidden warriors.

Her stomach dropped at the familiar red hair and freckled face, and the familiar golden skin and black hair.

Westley and Marlo.

The Dynameis who'd approached her and Nyla for orodytes the other day. Westley… the only other man she'd ever been intimate with.

"Westley, please let me go," Sylzenya whispered, "*Please.*"

But he said nothing, his grip tightening with each passing moment, his eyes distant. Nyla kneeled to the ground, burying a piece of orodyte. Their goddess' golden light erupted from the earth, encircling her body while thick vines birthed from the ground and twisted around Sylzenya's legs and arms.

"What are you doing?" Sylzenya questioned, her voice shaking.

Her friend looked up, but her amber eyes didn't glisten like usual, her mouth was thin, facial expression bored. Nyla didn't answer as the vines wrapped tighter—harsher.

"Nyla, what's happened to you? What's happened to Westley?" Sylzenya pleaded.

There are many things that I cannot say, even if I wish to, the bird in her vision had said. *But I will say this—be wary of who you trust.*

Sylzenya fought against the tightening vines and rough hands keeping her in place as she tried to help her friend remember herself.

Kharis, the Dynami Elnok had trusted, and another Kreena entered the sanctuary, carrying between them a man with dark hair, tattered clothes, and a blood-stained face.

Elnok's pale green eyes grew wide as they found hers.

Sylzenya screamed his name as she lurched forward, only for the vines to squeeze her skin until it burned.

Horror ripped through her as Elnok fought against Kharis' hold, her name falling from his lips as Kharis shoved him to his knees, directly across from her. He grunted with the impact, his face—covered in bruises—was strained in pain.

The Kreena kneeled next to Elnok, the golden light of their goddess being used to secure Elnok's wrists to the ground and to bury his feet into the soil. Their goddess' power no longer a source of life, but a weapon.

"This is *madness*!" Sylzenya shouted.

"It is retribution," the High One replied, "You are Estea's

salvation; this filth of a man has poisoned your mind away from your destiny and towards nothing but distraction and hedonistic pleasure."

"It isn't him who's been poisoning minds," Sylzenya spat.

The High One's brows raised, nostrils flaring as a cruel smile curved on his thin lips. "You've been observant."

"What's he talking about?" Elnok questioned, his eyes drooping and body swaying as if he was barely hanging on by a thread.

Face burning, she wrestled harder against the vines. "He's been poisoning the wine, *all* the wine. And since Kreenas' blood mixes into the soil while we create, it's also been infecting the vegetation. It's why Nyla and Kharis aren't acting like themselves... why Kharis kept pressuring you to drink the wine and why Nyla wanted you to eat the plum." She took a deep, shaky breath, "The wine rituals, the kingdom-wide banquet... everyone in Estea's under its influence—*his* influence. But not you, Elnok, because you can't keep anything down besides food that's been boiled."

Elnok's eyes widened.

The High One laughed, the sound causing her insides to freeze.

"And can you tell me why it is that *you* are no longer under my influence, Sylzenya?" the High One said in a dark grating voice.

The truth ran in her veins, gold and bright. "The orodyte serum."

He smiled. "A side effect I hadn't taken into consideration until I learned what you and this ruffian had done in the healing pool. But it's no matter, considering I've made sure no one will ever defect again. Not your parents, not any other Estean—not even you."

"What have you done to my parents?" Sylzenya shouted, despair lacing through her bones like a thorny vine, piercing her insides.

Westley yanked Sylzenya back, her cut blooming with pain.

"Your parents are fine," the High One replied, "Just enjoying their lives in the dungeons, drinking wine so they don't become parched. Surprisingly, it was your mother who held out the longest; almost died until your father convinced her to drink it."

Angry tears fell from her eyes. Her father *hadn't* betrayed her at the Kreena Rite… he'd tried to save her.

"Why are you doing this?" she demanded, hating how tears streamed down her face.

"You figured out the wine, found the compass, but don't know the answer to your question?" He smiled.

It was as if the earth had tilted: trees planted into clouds and growing from the sky, rain rising from the ground and soaking into the leaves, fire cold as ice burning along her arms.

"That's impossible," she whispered.

"And what might that be?"

"You don't worship Distrathrus," she argued, "You worship Aretta. You've erected statues of her everywhere. You had me create willows in her name throughout the gardens."

"A rather clever facade, isn't it? Hiding behind the deity everyone's sworn they love to no end; their creator whom they'd die for if asked." He tilted his head. "But still, you're missing a rather important detail."

"I don't understand," she choked, voice breaking.

"Can you *really* not figure it out?" He approached her, leaning in close, his cold hand brushing her cheek. "My sister protected you violent creatures, making excuses for your spears, your anger, your need to dominate. My creation was blamed for it all when it was humans who made the first kill. And then she cursed me into one of your own filthy, weak, powerless bodies to try and contain me, leashing this pound of flesh to this forsaken kingdom's soil." He gripped her jaw tight, Sylzenya's skin ripping beneath his icy touch. "Humans poisoned my sister's mind, turning her against me. I mean to end your race's reign once and for all."

"No... " She faltered, the reality too absurd, his words nothing she could've ever imagined. "You can't be..."

"Distrathrus." He smiled. "In the flesh."

Acid rose in her throat as the world continued to tilt, turning and spinning and spiraling out of control. This had to be a nightmare, nothing more. And yet, his familiar yellow gaze no longer spoke of comfort, but of insanity.

"But you..." She forced bile down her throat. "You've been like a father to me. You can't be..."

His eyes flared, a thin silence hanging in the air. "And you've been the closest thing to a daughter I've ever known."

Squeezing her eyes tight, she choked on her tears, despising how weak she'd become. How utterly small and helpless.

How much of a fool she'd been this entire time.

"Enough tears. It's time you regain your power, for I have need of it," he said.

She seethed, lifting her head and gritting her teeth. "I won't become your puppet."

"You talk as if you haven't been one this whole time."

The High One—Distrathrus—approached Elnok. He placed a long, thin finger underneath Elnok's chin, forcing his eyes up, "I was a fool to let her run around with the likes of you: human waste from the streets. You thought she could be yours, but you knew from the moment we met she would always be mine. "

Kharis grabbed Elnok's hair and pulled up. Elnok winced; his black tunic, almost ripped in half, revealed the bright red bruises on his chest. Sylzenya wanted to reach forward and cover them, bathe them in salve and whisper soothing words into his ear until the pain in his face disappeared.

"She belongs to no one," Elnok seethed.

Distrathrus clenched Elnok's face, "Don't tell me you actually… care for the woman?"

"I don't give a fuck what you do to me, just let her go."

Distrathrus laughed. The dark scratching sound echoed in the grove. He gripped Elnok's face so hard Sylzenya thought he might crack his jaw.

"A fruitless offer," he said, "besides, you'd be singing a very different tune if you knew everything Sylzenya has done in her lifetime. In fact, she's committed atrocities far worse than yourself."

Sylzenya's gaze fixed on Distrathrus, her stomach twisting into itself. She didn't know what he was talking about, and yet, something inside herself did. Something that'd been lurking just underneath the surface for years. A truth meant to stay buried.

What had she been doing as an acolyte all these years underneath this god's commands?

Elnok sneered. "You're even more insane than this kingdom's lore suggests."

"Don't believe me?" he questioned, "Kharis, your sword, please."

Sylzenya's stomach dropped.

The warrior gave Distrathrus his blade, the weapon glowing a bright yellow from the orodyte serum. Sylzenya pleaded to her goddess to save them, looking towards her willow tree behind the throne as if Aretta could somehow resurrect herself and come to their aid.

Thump.

Thump.

Thump.

Shock ran up her spine. A small spark of golden light flashed along a branch, dissipating into the night air. Surprise lit her chest as she felt it: the earth singing to her; the branches of the tree calling her name, begging her to touch it—to be in its power.

Thump.

Thump.

Thump.

She *needed* to get to that tree.

"I'm not one to tie you down and force the cure on you, Sylzenya," Distrathrus announced, "And so I'm giving you a choice." He stood behind Elnok, his white hair flowing in the breeze as the sword glowed. "Do you know why orodyte serum makes it easier for swords to slice through flesh?"

Sylzenya's insides twisted as the god in human form pressed the flat side of the blade onto Elnok's scarred back.

He smiled. "Because it burns."

CHAPTER 22

MINE TO KEEP, YOURS TO LOSE

Sweet-smelling tea drifted in the sunroom while a tart raspberry biscuit crumbled in Elnok's mouth. Brown dust blew across the crystal-cut windows, the dark brick of Vutror's castle walls shielding them from one of Druenia's heavy winds.

"Elnok, dearest, is it archery or astronomy today?" his mother asked, her thin yet strong fingers gripping her favorite black teacup.

"Archery was yesterday," his father answered gruffly, his eyes trained on a freshly delivered letter, the paper sealed with a golden Estean leaf, tied to a dark wine bottle, "arithmetic today."

"It's anthropology," Elnok replied with a quick grin as he took another bite of biscuit, "Or was it art?"

"Perhaps assholery?" The familiar voice of his brother quipped as Tosh opened the broad double doors of the room, "A subject you truly thrive in, brother."

Elnok twisted in his chair. Tosh stood with the air of a royal, black hair flowing to his chest, pale green eyes just like their father's, and a thin smile like their mother's. Elnok didn't hesitate as he threw the raspberry biscuit, the breakfast treat sailing through the air, heading right for Tosh's head.

Feigned shock followed by a quick dodge had his brother stumbling to the floor.

"Elnok!" their mother scolded, "What have we said about throwing *biscuits* of all things in the sunroom?"

But Elnok ignored her warning as he lept for his brother, Tosh's shock turning to twisted laughter as they met on the floor. Blue and red carpet pilled underneath them as they jabbed for each other's stomachs and groins. If mother was scolding them, they didn't hear her. Tosh delivered the final blow, causing Elnok to curl into himself while laughter fell from his mouth.

"Assholery?" Elnok gasped between breaths. He smiled wide at his brother six years his senior, "That's the best you could come up with?"

Tosh smiled as he stood, extending his hand with a warm grin on his face.

"I'm not the one throwing raspberry biscuits or sneaking out into the city instead of attending my lessons, am I?"

"Could do you some good."

"Just get up, you miscreant," Tosh laughed.

Elnok reached for the strong hand of his brother. Suddenly, something cold and dark wrapped around Elnok's arm, his stomach, his throat. The face of his brother shifted from mirth to terror. Heavy silence gripped the room. Elnok turned to ask their parents what was wrong only to find his mother's and father's bodies having withered into pale skeletons, turning into ash as they fell to the floor.

His mother's teacup shattered against cold brick.

"You," Tosh growled through bared teeth, "my own brother, trying to kill me… for this?"

Vutror's crown now sat on his brother's head, blue and red jewels shining like blood in the dark sea.

"No, Tosh, please—" Elnok begged as he backed away, the rug replaced with biting stone.

Tosh yanked his arm. Elnok yelled as his brother quickly grabbed his throat—

"*No*!" a woman's voice screamed, "*Stop hurting him, please*!"

Searing hot pain hissed against Elnok's flesh as reality came into focus. Sylzenya kneeled in front of him, her face covered in tears while vines wrapped around her body.

"Then you'll do as I say," Distrathrus commanded, removing the sword covered in orodyte serum from his back, a swell of relief aching in Elnok's skin, "Take the cure, and this thief will be escorted home without so much as another scar."

Panting and clenching his jaw, Elnok locked his gaze with Sylzenya's. "Don't listen to him."

"I'm not going to let him hurt you," she replied.

"He'll do it anyways, *and* he'll have you under his control."

Sylzenya turned to Distrathrus, "You promise he'll return home safely if I take the cure?"

Dread spiked in his veins. "Sylzenya, *no*."

"Of course," Distrathrus replied.

"He's *lying*," Elnok sneered.

"I'll do it."

Elnok meant to yell for her to stop, but Kharis' hand covered his mouth, his pleas muffled.

"Excellent. Nyla, you may release her. Kharis, you'll be in charge of burning him if she refuses to cooperate at any point."

Elnok threw back his head, earning a grunt from Kharis and a loosened grip on his mouth. "Sylzenya, *don't do th*—"

A vine wrapped around his mouth, pulling back until it sat between his teeth. He tried biting through it, but it was as tough as stone. Eyes widened, Elnok struggled against the vines, wishing he could stab Distrathrus in the chest. Estea's leader—the god of chaos—moved around him and towards Sylzenya, presenting her with a small glass vial filled with black liquid, the pale moonlight filtering through the trees giving it a glossy glow.

"Pour this on your cut," he instructed. "*All* of it."

Elnok shouted for her to stop, his screams and yells muffled.

Her deep blue eyes found his, a look of regret stitched into her face as she took the vial from Distrathrus' pale hand. Dread and guilt and darkness consumed him as Sylzenya uncorked the bottle, her throat bobbing as she placed it over her shoulder, the opening of her cut already dripping with blood.

She froze.

Distrathrus lifted his hand.

Searing pain ruptured through Elnok's flesh as Kharis placed the sword against his back, disjointed memories of Tosh flickering in and out of his mind's eye. Desperation laced through Elnok's veins as he begged for the nightmare to end.

"Enough!" Sylzenya said.

Elnok regained his sense of self, the vine in his mouth falling to the ground. He looked up, and everything within him turned into ice. Sylzenya tipped the vial, pouring every last drop of the black liquid into her cut. Shrieking, she fell to her knees, the glass thudding into the dirt while her fingers gripped the soil. Her veins raised against her skin—turning black.

"Very good, Sylzenya. Now, stay down. It'll take some time for you to adjust."

"You fucking bastard!" Elnok screamed. "I'm going to *kill* you!"

"So many threats, and for what?" Distrathrus hissed as he kneeled in front of him, his back to Sylzenya. "To protect a woman who's part of the reason your entire continent suffers?"

"What are you talking about?" Elnok spat.

Distrathrus smiled. "A few days by her side and you think you know her, is that right?"

"I know she'd never do anything to hurt anyone."

His smile widened. "My acolytes and Kreenas do more than create food and water for our people. They've been helping me gather the resources to resurrect my true form for centuries, Sylzenya proving the most powerful out of them all."

"You're insane," Elnok hissed.

Distrathrus sneered, digging into his robes and pulling out a piece of yellow orodyte. "Every Estean believes these store the earth's impurities, and this is how Kreenas are able to create vegetation. But it's only partially true."

Elnok's stomach soured, his head spinning.

"In my sister's last attempt to destroy me, she filled the entire continent with her power, spreading it as far and wide as possible so I couldn't use it for my restoration. But she didn't consider the other ways I could gather it." He flipped the stone in his hand. "I utilized my resources—her very people—convincing every Kreena and acolyte over the centuries to unknowingly reclaim my sister's power by storing it in these stones. I then use your generously given Vutrorian steel to perform a perfect extraction, the ore specially made by my sister's hand and the only substance able to break through orodyte." He tilted his head. "These women think they create life, when in reality, they steal it."

Elnok's chest tightened, spots forming at the corners of his eyes.

"But you know what I find most interesting?" Distrathrus continued, "In order to take life, there's always a cost, and these women don't even question the pain it brings them."

"You're the reason their backs fucking bleed?" Elnok yelled.

"You make it sound so… distasteful." Distrathrus' yellow eyes narrowed. "But that's besides the point, Elnok. What I'm very curious to know is would you still love a woman who's been stealing life from your land? The reason you have famines, the culprit behind your droughts, the origin of your sickness?" He paused, rotating the stone in his hand. "The reason your friend will die in a few short days?"

Everything grew distant and cold, the trees bent in the wrong shape, his mouth dry and parched.

"You're lying," Elnok seethed, his arms trembling and vision blurring.

"You certainly wish that were true, don't you, thief?"

Elnok didn't dare break eye contact.

"Why tell me any of this?"

The High One grinned. "Because, Elnok, before I have Kharis kill you in these next precious moments, I need you to understand that Sylzenya was never going to be yours. She was and always will belong to me." He slid his cold hand across Elnok's face. "Mine to keep, yours to lose."

Elnok clenched his jaw, a scream sitting in the back of his throat, every part of him desiring nothing more than to tear this god apart limb by limb.

"If what you say is true, then orodyte serum isn't poison, it's your sister's power. And that means Sylzenya's father put a goddess' *power* into her body, not toxins," Elnok snarled. "He meant for her to defeat you."

Distrathrus tilted his head. "Far more observant than your brother, I'll give you that much. But Theraden's plan was never going to work. I've convinced everyone—including Sylzenya—orodyte serum is poison, and once one believes in something so firmly, there would never be a reason for them to think otherwise; there's no using my sister's power without knowing the truth. Anyways, now that my undiluted blood has entered Sylzenya's body, it's eradicated all of my sister's power from her veins."

Bright yellow light suddenly illuminated the grove. Elnok turned to the source: the willow tree growing behind the marble throne surged with magic. But it was the person standing next to it that shone the brightest. Her hand was pressed onto its trunk, her hair and skin bright as the sun.

Elnok's heart leapt into his throat.

"Impossible," Distrathrus yelled, "*Kharis! Nyla!* What are you two doing standing around like that? Stop her *now*!"

Soil shifted underneath Elnok's knees. Distrathrus staggered back, yelling at the Kreenas and Dynameis. It shook again, this time so hard Elnok collapsed, the vines wrapping around his body falling limp. Fighting the tremors and untangling himself from the vines, he managed to stand.

All color drained from his face.

"Elnok, the compass is in his pocket!" Sylzenya shouted, her hair and robes floating as if she was suspended in water, one arm planted on the ground, the other secured to the tree.

Thick vines shot up from the earth, one of them close to spearing Elnok's foot. He stepped aside, heart pounding against his chest, streams of light swirling around the rising vines—guiding them. They struck like snakes, light flashing through the air as they grabbed the Kreenas, Dynameis, and then Distrathrus, twisting around their bodies and securing them in place.

"Sylzenya, I *command* you to stop this at once!" Distrathrus shouted.

"*Now*, Elnok."

Purpose surged through his body as he rushed for Distrathrus and rummaged through his white robes.

"You insolent little thief," Distrathrus spat, wrestling against the vines, "Go into Lhaal Forest, and you die. My monsters will make sure of it."

Elnok's hand slipped over the familiar cold metal of the compass. He pulled it out, the object glowing with the piece of bark at its center.

"With her by my side? I'll take my chances," he replied, "but before I go…"

Elnok picked up the glowing sword from the ground and swung it high above his head.

"*No!*" Sylzenya screamed.

But Elnok didn't care what Sylzenya said or felt when it came to this god. Distrathrus had manipulated her and the Esteans, using the Kreenas and acolyte's magic to kill Elnok's homeland. Distrathrus *deserved* to die.

Elnok speared Distrathrus in that soft spot just below his rib cage, angling it up as he pushed with all his strength. He choked, spit raining down as his yellow eyes widened, but no scream came from his mouth.

"You think a god can be killed so easily?" Distrathrus sneered, a large cruel smile forming on his mouth.

No blood poured from his chest or his mouth, just wheezing breaths as his smile grew. Gulping, Elnok backed away.

"Elnok, we have to go, now!" Sylzenya shouted from the tree, "I don't know how long my power will last!"

Distrathrus grinned. "She may be saving you now, little thief, but her power has killed countless people from your land. No matter how badly she wants to be a hero, she'll always be your ruin."

Elnok shouted a curse as he ripped Kharis' sword from the god's human body and ran for Sylzenya, the cold compass in his hand no longer pointing south, but east. Sylzenya released herself from the tree, the vines still holding everyone as she grabbed his hand and led them out of the grove.

They ran through forest, sprinted across meadows, and dashed past a lake until they made it to the large white wall. They sneaked their way around the wall guard, his patrol taking him far enough away for them to pass through unnoticed.

As they ran into the shadows of Lhaal Forest, Sylzenya stumbled to her knees, the magical glow emanating from her body blowing out like a candle at its wick's end.

Elnok caught her as she lost consciousness, heaving her up into his arms.

The chitters and scraping sounds of the forest sent shivers up Elnok's spine as he stumbled forward. Exhaustion swept in, his body aching from being beaten and burned; he couldn't go much further. At last, he spotted a cave, carefully and quietly, he approached before laying Sylzenya down on the cracked dirt. He sat next to her, hand steady on the sword's hilt, the other holding the compass.

The longer he sat in the darkness, the more everything that'd just transpired became real, became *heavy*, like boulders stacking on his shoulders. Sylzenya's chest rose and fell, her breaths harsh and quick. Her magic had been beyond anything he'd witnessed in his few days in Estea, so much so that Distrathrus seemed surprised as well.

Elnok's stomach dropped.

Her cut.

Quickly, he rolled her to her side, set on tending to her back, only to find it had scabbed over. Dried blood clung to her skin—far too much of it. Yet she still breathed.

Sweat built along his neck, a new sense of disgust rising in his throat.

What if she'd depleted more resources from Druenia?

He shouldn't be feeling this way. She didn't know what she'd been doing all these years. She didn't know she and her people had been making his and everyone else's lives a fight for survival. She didn't know Distrathrus had been using her magic to kill. Hell, she'd been consuming a poisoned wine keeping her under a god's suggestive will.

And yet, his anger and disgust remained.

He slammed his fist into the ground. No matter how he spun it, the truth remained—Druenia's famines, droughts, and sickness were due to this kingdom's godsforsaken magic.

And Sylzenya was at the helm.

He didn't know what to do with this. All he knew is that he

wouldn't be able to look at her the same, and gods, he hated himself for it.

As he rested his head against the cave's wall and spun his gold ring, he contemplated how Distrathrus' existence and plan to dominate fucking *humanity* changed Elnok's goal.

But did it?

He'd meant it when he told Orym he would get his medicine, and he sure as hell wasn't going to let this god get in his way.

The key to finding Aretta's Willow wasn't just the compass anymore, but making it through this forest; he needed Sylzenya's magic as their protection, even if her utilizing it meant depleting resources in Druenia—even if it meant a few more people died. Distrathrus said Sylzenya wasn't a hero, but neither was Elnok. Stealing was his occupation, and there was no room for mercy in such dealings.

All that mattered was his and his crew's survival. He'd get Orym's cure, get out of Estea, gather his crew, and then sail far away from this place.

Once Sylzenya woke, they'd escape this hell once and for all.

PART TWO

CHAPTER 23
NOT MY OWN

Red and gold flowers swayed in the warm summer breeze. Green grass poked at Sylzenya's exposed legs, her white linen dress soft and light as she leaned her head against Elnok's warm skin.

"I never knew days could be like this," Elnok said, the smile in his voice causing her to look up.

Her stomach fluttered as she looked at his lips. Elnok surveyed the lake sprawled before them, his green eyes shimmering in the sunlight. She found it difficult to remember when they'd gotten here, or how they'd arrived. Yet she smiled, for it didn't matter how, only that they were here—together.

"Like what?" Sylzenya asked as she leaned further into him.

He ran his calloused palm up her arm, cupping her jaw, bringing her gaze to meet his.

"Full of life," he said.

Warmth flooded her body as she gripped his black tunic, bringing his lips to hers. He tasted of worn leather and musk, sending heat into her core, every part of her body wanting him.

Needing him.

He wrapped a strong arm around her waist. She giggled as his soft laughs feathered her mouth. She straddled him, deepening the kiss as she felt his hardness press against her.

"And I'll make sure your people know nothing less," she breathed, lightly biting his lower lip. His whimper sent heat between her legs.

"*Our* people," Elnok replied breathlessly, twisting her hair in his hand, a light tug causing her nipples to harden, "There's no other woman I know who could provide Druenia with life like you can."

"And yet I know next to nothing about any place outside of Estea."

He gripped her neck, sending a delightful shiver up her spine as he leaned back, his green eyes searching her face.

"You're Estea's most renowned Kreena. Your very presence will calm storms and win hearts. You'll be a beacon of hope." He kissed her neck softly, slowly. "Just as you've been for me."

Everything within her melted into his touch as he slid her linen dress up to her waist. Sylzenya gasped as she clung to his neck.

Suddenly, as if the grass was fake and the flowers were frauds, everything blurred, only to sharpen again as she smelled Elnok's skin.

"How can someone say such sweet things and yet act in such a foul manner?" she teased with a grin, rocking against him slowly.

He stopped.

"Do it for me," he whispered as he stroked her hair, "Show me what life you will bring to Druenia."

Sylzenya didn't question the request as she dismounted his body. He looked at her expectantly as she kneeled in the soft grass. A clear orodyte sat in front of her. She dug a hole in the ground and placed the empty stone in it, covering it and sealing it with her hand. She closed her eyes, breathing deeply as she ushered Aretta's power.

It answered her.

A sharp sting ran along her back as golden sparks lit her hands, her arms, her entire body. She called upon life, a sprout poking through her fingers, curling into a flower. Yellow petals unfurled with flowing grace. Sylzenya smiled wide as it opened itself towards the sun.

Towards her.

But as she lifted her gaze, her heart stopped.

Elnok no longer stared at her with those shimmering green eyes. Instead, he laid crumpled in the grass, his body naked and thin, his flesh a cruel color of jaundice.

"*Elnok!*"

She crushed the flower under her feet, rushing to his side. Falling to her knees, she held his head in her lap, his eyes sunken and lined with deep purple.

"You…" he struggled to say, his arm reaching for her face, his fingers dry and cracked, "You did this."

Her stomach dropped.

"No," she whispered, shaking her head furiously as she brushed his thin black hair away from his face, "I didn't mean to, I swear—"

"You don't bring life," he choked, red blood dripping from his mouth and onto the earth. "Druenia's been dying, and it's your fault. *You've taken from us.*"

Panic gripped Sylzenya's chest as the green grass and colorful flowers faded into dust. Breaths shortening and heart pounding, she turned. The lake was no longer filled with water, but cracked with brown dirt. Warmth turned into unbearable heat as the sky took on an orange hue, bathing the dead meadow and dried lake in what looked like charred smoke.

"Elnok," Sylzenya whimpered, tears forming in her eyes, "I didn't mean for any of this. Please, you have to believe me."

But he said nothing in return, his hand falling to the earth, eyes fluttering shut.

Sylzenya's throat burned as she screamed.

"It is finished," a grating voice echoed from behind her.

She turned to find the High One in his white robes, his long hair floating above him in the shape of a crown.

Not the High One.

Distrathrus.

"Help me," Sylzenya pleaded as she held Elnok's dead body in her arms.

Distrathrus dug into the earth, pulling out the orodyte stone that now glowed bright with yellow light.

"You've done well," he crooned as he crushed it in his hand.

But the stone didn't shatter; it became liquid, flowing to the earth and coating the ground in orodyte serum.

"Please," Sylzenya begged, "*Save him!*"

Distrathrus laughed, the sound echoing all around her as if he was not one, but many.

"You are truly Estea's most renowned Kreena. Aretta's most *devout*," he said as he swiped his finger in the serum, creating a strange pattern. "If it wasn't for you, my plan would've taken another century to achieve. I'm grateful, for now we get to behold this beauty you've brought to the world." He lifted his yellow gaze to hers, motioning his hands to the death that lay before them.

"This wasn't my doing," she breathed.

His smile widened, "Oh, but it is. You and every other woman who has filled orodyte with Aretta's power." He ceased tracing the orodyte serum as he tilted his head, "But I still need you, Sylzenya. There's one more task to accomplish, and I'm in need of my most powerful Kreena. So please, come home." He pressed his hand to the earth, "Come home to me, your *true* god—the one who has never abandoned you—so I might finally be set free."

Rage rose up her neck as she spat, "Why would I *ever* come back to you?"

"Because," he whispered as he rushed to her, too fast for her to react. He gripped her face with one hand, his eyes flashing between yellow and black. "*You are mine.*"

Everything spun, her screams echoing as darkness melded with golden light; a ring that turned into blood and a bird crushed by branches. The bird's warning rang through her mind over and over and over again…

For life there is a price, and only in pain is it made whole. Your choice has been made, and so your consequence is set in blood and stone.

"*Sylzenya.*"

She bolted upright, her hands sweating and chest heaving. Darkness surrounded her on all sides. Terror speared her insides. She tried to shuffle away from whomever was holding her, but her body ached in ways that had her fall back into their arms.

"We escaped," Elnok's familiar voice echoed, his warm calloused hands gripping her arms. "We're in Lhaal Forest now."

Worry and uncertainty filled her as she opened her eyes. The dim, familiar outline of Elnok's broad shoulders and sharp face came into focus, accompanied by his scent. She relaxed her shoulders.

"Your scars," Sylzenya whispered as she slowly cupped his jaw in her hand, remembering how Distrathrus had pressed the sword into his scarred back, the hissing of his flesh still echoing in her ears. "Are you alright?"

"Not nearly as painful as my brother's methods, although he did give it a worthy try, didn't he?" he replied, sarcasm biting at the end of each word.

Before she could reply, he withdrew from her, the absence of his skin sending an icy shiver up her arms. The compass' golden glow dimly lit his face, casting sharp shadows across his features and against the cave walls. His eyes were puffy, the skin underneath them a deeper color than usual.

"You don't have to pretend like that," Sylzenya said, reaching out to touch his arm, "If you have your salve on you, I can apply some to your scars."

He flinched at her touch. "I'm fine."

Gulping, she tucked her hand into her chest. "It's clear that you aren't fine."

"Sylzenya, please, just…" He took a deep breath, his thumb spinning something—a ring, by the looks of it—on his pinky finger, "I'm relieved you're awake, but we need to focus on finding Aretta's Willow."

Vision blurring, she held herself together. Now wasn't the time to cry, nor was it the time to try and recover everything Distrathrus had torn from them. Surely these were his desired outcomes, that Elnok would lose trust in her, and that she might lose all faith in herself as well.

"How long was I out for?" she asked, sitting up straight and blinking back the tears until she could see clearly.

"Over an hour."

She cursed. "Has the compass changed direction at all?"

He nodded. "It's pointing east."

"Shit," she whispered, "any monster sightings?"

"Not yet."

Sylzenya took a deep breath. "I don't know much about Lhaal, but I do know that's not normal, not when we don't have a Dynami with us. The monsters can sense their power and are more apt to avoid than attack, but you and I…"

She trailed off, observing her hands, remembering what it'd felt like to touch her willow tree she'd created while they were trapped in the grove. It'd burned her with life, a song she'd never heard rushing through her veins. It wasn't just the roots and leaves opening up for her, but it was her own blood and skin. It was everything in her veins and under the earth, flowing through her body like glittering streams of water populated by buzzing dragonflies.

The orodyte serum.

Everything had fallen away, desperation taking hold of her as she called on the roots and vines of the ancient forest floor to obey her every whim, calling them to rise, to come to life—to fight.

But the "cure" she'd been given—Distrathrus' blood—had fought against her at every moment.

Never in her life had her cut bled so much.

Surprise found her as she gently ran a finger along her scar, the wound had already scabbed over.

"How did you do that, back at the grove? Using your power?" Elnok asked.

She furrowed her brow, the compass in Elnok's hand pulsing with golden light. She pressed her palm to the ground

Thump.

Thump.

Thump.

The compass and her goddess' heartbeat pulsed as one.

"It seems that whenever I'm near something filled with Aretta's power, I'm able to connect to it. My willow seemed to have more of her power stored within than I'd thought."

Elnok looked to the compass, then to her. "Let's see if your theory is right."

Breathing in deep, she closed her eyes, letting her goddess' heartbeat thrum through her, the song of the soil running through her veins again.

Dried plains, fire-charred sunlight, Elnok's dying body.

She yanked her hand back.

"I can't," Sylzenya stated, sweat sliding down her temple.

"What?" Elnok questioned, leaning forward, "It doesn't work?"

Sylzenya gritted her teeth. "No, it does, but… you heard the High On—" She paused. "You heard Distrathrus. When I use my power, it depletes Druenia—takes away your crops, rivers, even invokes sickness on your side of the continent."

"With *orodyte*," Elnok argued, "You steal life from the continent and put into those stones. He never said using it without the orodyte did that."

"Orodyte or not, it's *power*, and it *always* comes with a price." She stared at her hands. "I won't let any more death be met by my hands."

Elnok ran his hand through his hair, exasperated. "It isn't just your life that's on the line right now, Sylzenya."

She grimaced. "You'd tell me to use my power, knowing I might be killing people in your land, just so *you* can live?"

"And Orym. And my crew."

She scoffed, digging her fingers into her robe. "Didn't know how little you cared about people's lives."

"What can I say?" He grinned as he spread his arms wide. "I excel in disappointing others."

"You know what?" She stood up, grabbing the compass. "Just because you bear some scars on your back doesn't mean you get some kind of free pass to disvalue the lives of others."

"Look who's talking." He replied, standing with her. "You have no idea what it's like to kill to survive: seeing them face-to-face, forced to watch the light leave their eyes, to know you probably just stole a parent from their child, a lover from their spouse, a man from his father. But you? You've killed without even knowing it, taking entire villages in one sweeping measure according to Distrathrus' little confession." He sneered. "So before you go questioning *my* choices, *my* life, I'd spend some time doing some self-reflection."

A bright wave of anger flooded her veins. "Fuck you, Elnok."

He raised his brows. "Careful, Your Holiness, you're losing that piety pretty quick."

"Last night was a mistake."

The words left her mouth before she could stop herself,

but she meant it. She'd been unknowingly causing suffering for an entire decade, and now that she knew it and could stop, he was asking her to intentionally put the lives of others at risk so they might survive. She should never have trusted him with her body, no matter how badly she'd wanted him.

"Well then," his smile faltered, eyes mirthless. "Glad we can finally agree on something."

He walked past her, swiping the compass from her hand and unsheathing the glowing sword he'd stolen from Kharis as he left the cave.

"*Elnok.*" She rushed after him, grabbing his shoulder. "What're you doing?"

He held up the compass. "Orym has about two days left to live. I'm finding his cure."

"But you'll die out there."

"How generous of you to care." He turned to her. "Good luck living the rest of your days in this cave."

"Elnok, *wait*—"

"I think you're beginning to learn something, Sylzenya," a deep voice echoed from somewhere in front of them, the dark fog obscuring them from sight. "Prince Elnok doesn't have a very patient temperament."

Three Dynameis pushed through the fog, swords unsheathed and bodies glowing with the power of their orodyte stones.

Sylzenya's limbs grew cold.

It was Westley and Marlo–the two Dynameis that approached her and Nyla only days ago–flanking either side of Kharis.

Elnok stretched his arm over her body, forcing her to take a step back. She grabbed his wrist, her fingers picking up on his increased heart rate.

"This is pretty shitty of you, Kharis," Elnok seethed. "I'm not even sure if Tosh would approve of you pursuing me like this."

"Tosh is nearly dead and there's nothing that can be done. I've accepted that," Kharis replied, sending his sword into a wide arc. "I'd recommend coming back with us peacefully, and maybe Distrathrus will show some kind of mercy."

Elnok scoffed. "*Mercy.* Right."

Sylzenya stepped forward, Elnok's muscles tensing as she pushed against his arm. "Kharis, you're under his influence right now. Look deep within yourself and see the truth for what it is. Help us. Help Westley and Marlo."

"You speak as if it's something none of us wanted, but this is as it should be. As *you* should be, Sylzenya. Don't you see that he needs you? That he made you? That you belong to him alone?"

Elnok held up his sword as he stepped fully in front of her. "Over my dead fucking body."

"Don't be a fool," she whispered, her cheeks suddenly warm.

Elnok didn't respond, nor did he back down.

Kharis let out an exasperated breath. "If that's what must happen, then so be it."

As the Dynameis stepped forward, a loud crunch echoed from within the cave. Kharis stopped the other two warriors, his eyes focused at his feet. Sylzenya strained her gaze; a thin, translucent material shimmered in the fog.

"*Serpentum,*" Elnok whispered.

Suddenly, the ground shook violently, bringing Sylzenya and Elnok to their knees; the Dynameis managed to stay on their feet, their stances wide and swords readied.

A loud hiss slithered along Sylzenya's bones, her stomach dropping as six large clouded eyes glowed in the darkness of the cave. Elnok grabbed her arm, stumbling as he dragged her away.

"I'll take the serpentum, you two get the prince and Kreena," Kharis yelled over the tumbling of rocks.

"Still not going to use your magic?" Elnok asked.

Sylzenya grabbed Elnok by his tunic and led them away from the Dynameis. "Not if I can help it."

"What if I'm about to die?"

"*Don't you dare.*"

"That's answer enough," he replied.

She gaped as he ripped his arm from her grasp, shoving the compass into her hand and running straight towards the Dynameis—the deadliest warriors on the continent—while three serpentums slithered out of the cave.

CHAPTER 24
SERPENTUMS

Sylzenya had grown up learning about Lhaal Forest, had stared at its crooked treeline from the temple's balcony, its black shadow an ever-hanging presence surrounding her kingdom. She'd read books about its monsters, listened to Dynameis discuss their adventures in harrowing details.

And yet, nothing could've prepared her for this.

Three giant serpentums emerged from the yawning cave, each of their body's thicker than ancient oak trunks. Their length was beyond anything she'd witnessed—a never-ending tube of white iridescent scales. Black tongues licked the air and clouded eyes glowed yellow.

They were slow. Poised.

Sylzenya had read enough to know these creatures were cunning, severe, and most importantly, the hardest to kill. Even a sword with orodyte serum struggled to slice through their scales.

And they were moving straight towards the Dynameis.

And Elnok.

Damn that man. *Damn him to hell.* She was a protector of people, not a destroyer—not a killer. And yet, she'd been unknowingly killing people on the other side of the forest for ten long years. Crops had been stolen under her power, rivers drained, people made sick.

She knew what had to be done: let Elnok fight for his life while she continued her journey to the tree. Druenia had lost enough from her.

Easy decision.

And yet…

"*Elnok Rogdul,*" she yelled, falling to her knees, "*I hate you.*"

One palm pressed firmly into the dry forest soil, Sylzenya concentrated on her goddess' power. She turned her other palm turned up towards the tree tops. Digging deep into her veins, she remembered how it had felt when she touched her willow, how her goddess' heartbeat had thrummed through every crevice in her body.

Thump.

Thump.

Thump.

Bright gold water flowing through her body. Power shocking every nerve until it woke. Vision sharpening.

The orodyte serum: *Aretta's power.*

No, it was more than her power… it was Aretta's blood. She could sense it now, the way it flowed under her skin. Gold light peeled out from her opened palm, spinning itself around her arm like a powerful thread. With a tilt of her head, she sent it into the ground.

But then her mind ruptured.

Instead of light, all she could see was darkness as black as the liquid she'd poured into her cut.

Her goddess' heartbeat ceased.

Sylzenya, a chilled voice whispered, ***have my monsters finally arrived?***

A deep cold slipped in between her bones, freezing her to the earth.

Distrathrus' voice wound in and out of her head then in between her muscles. She fought against the cold, urging Aretta's blood, warm enough to thaw the thickest of ice caps, through—but it was more than cold and heat. A barrier had been erected between her and Aretta's power.

Your power has never been your own. And now, my blood flows through you. Without my permission, it will remain dormant, trapped behind my blood.

"*Bastard*," she breathed.

She tried clawing through the barrier within her, scratching at the hard surface, desperate to unite with her goddess' thrumming heart. But it was impossible, Distrathrus' presence hovering over her like a thick fog, deafening her ears.

It was as if she'd never escaped him.

"Swords up!" Kharis shouted.

A sudden flash of white scales pierced her eyes.

Streaks of light blurred as the serpentums struck, the Dynameis utilizing their orodytes to fight the monsters, slicing at impenetrable scales. Sylzenya's heart faltered: Elnok stood in the middle of the creatures, dodging the serpentums' strikes. His speed was impressive, especially for someone without power, but he wouldn't last long, even with the Dynameis weakening the creatures.

Your poor little thief will be the first to go.

Sylzenya gritted her teeth, refusing to speak to him as she pounded against the barrier, writhing against Distrathrus' blood.

"*Don't stop, Elnok*," she shouted, sweat dripping down her neck as she dug her nails into the dirt.

He picked up his speed. But then, two serpentums simultaneously struck. Their fangs missed, but the impact sent him into their wall of hard scales. Blood spurted from his mouth, his body sliding to the ground.

"*No*!" she screamed.

Tensing her muscles, she fought harder, trying to climb the barrier only to lose her grip, falling into darkness.

Distrathrus' voice snaked through her, ***Time's running short, and I need you to return home.***

"*Let me through,*" she demanded.

Silence met her instead.

"Aim for their throats," Kharis shouted as he raised his sword, the orodyte shining bright on his chest plate.

One of the warriors fell from the air, landing on the ground with a loud thud. His torso was torn in half, entrails spilling out into a pool of blood.

Marlo.

Westley stood back to back with Kharis, yelling in anguish for his dead friend.

"You'd let your own warriors be killed for this?" Sylzenya shouted.

I've killed many things for you, Sylzenya.

Dark dread dripped down her throat.

"Westley, *focus*," Kharis commanded, "Let the prince fend for himself. Distrathrus only needs Sylzenya alive."

Her insides burned bright and hot—power and blood.

And yet, her power wasn't enough.

I'll let you save them, Distrathrus' whisper seeped into her mind, ***because I care for you. I want you to understand this above all else.***

"You've never cared for me," she seethed, fighting back tears.

How far from the truth you are.

Suddenly, the barrier crumbled, a rush of golden power overflowing into her limbs.

Thump.

Thump.

Thump.

Gold light circled her arms, her torso, her entire body, digging deep into the flesh of her back. She held back her scream, commanding Aretta's power through the air and sending it into the ground, the heartbeat pulsing with the compass' light.

Time was running out. Gritting her teeth, she stood up, the earth connected to her not through touch, but through her being.

Blood and blood.

Life.

She opened her hand to the darkened sky, light erupting from both her palms, warm blood pouring down her back.

All three serpentums stopped their attacks, turning to her as if they knew she was about to send them to their graves. In one swift movement, they abandoned the men, jaws unhinged and fangs dripping with black poison as they lunged for her.

"I will never be yours," she whispered to Distrathrus.

His laughter cackled in her ears, far away, disappearing into the darkness.

The putrid air froze.

A thick glowing root shot up from the ground, piercing a serpentum's jaw up into its head. Warm, rotten breath brushed her face, the creature's black poison dripping at her feet, its fangs hovering over her body. Its shriek rang through the air, its body flailing only to fall limp. More glowing roots shot up, the other serpentums' screams filling her ears as scales gave way to flesh.

Curling her lip, she stared into the yellow clouded eyes of the dying serpentum.

"Praise be to *Aretta*," she growled.

Distrathrus' voice was nowhere to be found.

Clenching her jaw, Sylzenya circled the monsters, all three of them staked to the ground.

But then her stomach dropped.

Westley's feet didn't touch the forest floor, his body elevated by the thick root speared through his lower back and out of his mouth. Acid rose in Sylzenya's stomach, her hands shaking as she rushed forward, her legs losing their strength.

Grabbing his slick, bloodied hand, she shook her head; she couldn't have done this. She wasn't a killer—

But she was, wasn't she?

"Westley…" she whispered.

"*Sylzenya*," Elnok's weak voice called

A new wave of panic sliced through her. She left Westley, searching for Elnok, praying to her goddess that she hadn't speared him too. She circled a serpentum, her heart faltering; Elnok lay on the ground, one leg underneath the massive creature. Strained smile on his face, he waved her over as if it was a casual afternoon.

"Could use some help," he said, pulling at his leg.

Rushing forward, she stopped, mouth twisting into a horrible grimace.

"You're a complete and utter *fool*," she spat.

"Look, you can berate me all you want *after* my leg isn't being crushed."

"What did you think was going to happen?" she interjected, "that you were going to kill all the Dynameis and serpentums in one go? What, just you and your fancy rope and glowing sword? I hate to break it to you, but if it wasn't for me—"

"I would've died. Yes, I'm well aware of the situation, Sylzenya." He grunted as he tried freeing himself. "And I still might if I lose this leg."

"Perhaps you should lose a leg. Then you might learn a lesson."

"So you're volunteering to carry me the rest of the way to Aretta's Willow, then?"

Tilting her head to the darkened sky, she said, "In your dreams, *thief*."

"Well then, we're a few minutes away from watching my dreams come true."

Sylzenya gritted her teeth as she gripped the heavy body of the serpentum, using all her strength to lift any weight she could off of him. It was barely enough, but after a few attempts, he slid his leg out, caressing his knee as he let out a relieved breath.

"Where's Kharis?" Sylzenya asked.

"You didn't spear him, if that's what you're asking," Elnok replied, wincing as he stood up, "He fled once he saw what you did to the serpentums. Left his men, too. Coward."

"He isn't in his right mind," she replied, "much like yourself if I might add."

Elnok raised a brow. "He instructed his men to leave me to die. I think I can call him whatever I'd like at the moment."

Sylzenya meant to reply, but instead she staggered, her vision blurring as she fell to her knees. Everything swirled around her, different colors and smells overwhelming her senses. Acid rose in her throat, and she couldn't stop herself as she released it onto the ground. Elnok gripped her shoulder, sweeping her hair out of her face before she could sully it.

"You're losing a lot of blood," Elnok said, "Wait here."

"Not much else I can do," Sylzenya replied, spitting out the foul taste in her mouth.

Elnok returned with rags, waterskins, food packs, two leather pouches, orodyte serum vials, and another sword. Quickly, he placed the rag on her back, the cloth stinging. She gritted her teeth, fingernails scraping dirt.

"It's not going to stop," she said, "I need you to use the blunt side of the sword."

"I'm not going to burn you," he argued.

"Then I'll bleed to death."

Elnok grunted, grabbing the sword and steadying it over her back. Sylzenya bit the inside of her cheek, readying herself for the inevitable burn.

"Hold on, let's try something else," Elnok said.

Exasperated, Sylzenya turned around to find him holding the compass instead, its dim glow still pointing east. Slowly, Elnok placed the compass on top of her cut. It felt like cold running water laced with gentle mint leaves, soothing her hot, flaming skin. She groaned in relief as he slid the compass along her cut, the skin knitting back together, the pain silencing into a dull throb.

Sylzenya whispered in relief as she hung her head.

Bark from a healing willow: she'd been blessed beyond measure.

"I'm grateful, by the way," Elnok said as he put the compass away, wetting a cloth and applying it to her skin. "You're right, if it wasn't for you, I would've been dead."

"You didn't give me a choice," she sneered.

"But now you know what you're capable of."

"I didn't want to know, Elnok."

Silence spanned between them. "Then what do you want?"

Sharp as a dagger, her cut flared again, the pain so vibrant she grabbed Elnok's forearm, squeezing his muscle in her hand. He didn't flinch, letting her work through the flames until they died down into a smoldering ember; pain she'd lived with ever since she stepped foot in the temple.

"The only reason I was able to do… any of this… was because *he* let me."

Elnok kneeled next to her. "What are you talking about?"

Dirt wedged into her fingernails.

"He's in my mind, Elnok. In my body. Distrathrus has control over me because I poured his blood into my cut. It's why it took me so long to use my power. He *let* me save you."

Shaking his head, Elnok let out a low growl. "No, he doesn't control you. You're stronger than him—"

"You understand *nothing* about this," she shouted. "He's been using me for *years*, Elnok. He's been using *everyone.* That godsforsaken bird even warned me not to trust him. But why wouldn't I? I've followed him for a decade. I did everything *for* him, *because* of him. He shaped me, and I let him. He's the only reason I have any power at all."

Elnok's green eyes searched hers. He didn't back away, didn't refute her, didn't try to change her mind.

Instead, all he asked was, "So, what are you going to do about it?"

She paused, her anger surging deeper and wider than she'd ever allowed it. Tears stung her eyes; she let them roll down her face, dripping onto the earth, same as her blood.

So much sorrow and pain.

And Distrathrus was the reason for all of it.

"I need to find Aretta's Willow." Sylzenya whispered, "It's what the bird was trying to tell me all along: if I don't, I won't just lose my power, but Distrathrus will try to destroy all of humanity."

"Then the only way we're going to find it and survive is if you use your power," Elnok said.

She looked at Westley, his corpse drenched in blood. "And that doesn't bother you? That I've been draining your land's rivers and drying your people's crops?"

"We're in a forest filled with monsters trying to kill us," Elnok replied. "Philosophical ideals are a bit arbitrary at the moment."

Allowing the stench of metal and rot to fill her nostrils, she took a deep breath.

"All I've worked towards in my life has revolved around protecting my people, and I mean to continue that endeavor," she replied. "And your people deserve protection too. The war between Aretta and Distrathrus never stopped, and in war, there are casualties. The only way we save more lives is by stopping Distrathrus. *However,* I'm only going to try and use my power when *absolutely* necessary." She sat up, pointing her finger at him. "So don't go running into battles we don't need to fight. Understand?"

He raised his hands in mock surrender. "I wouldn't dream of it."

"Swear to it."

He lowered his hands. "Trust me, I don't want any more death for Druenia either, even if I didn't give that initial impression. It's just..." He took a deep breath. "I can't get Orym's medicine without you."

"Without my power, you mean, which I'm not even in control of at the moment."

"Well, yes, if we want to talk technicalities."

Sylzenya knew it shouldn't matter, but she *didn't* want to talk technicalities. She wanted to know if Elnok still cared for her even after their argument earlier. Would he defy his morals to make sure she could fill air in her lungs, just as she had?

But, how could she expect him to care for her in the same way when she'd been the reason his life had been famines and droughts? The reason his friend was dying? It was her responsibility to right her wrongs, and so, she would. She would help him get Orym's medicine from Aretta's Willow.

And if she truly cared about Elnok, then she would leave it at that.

"We should get moving before any more monsters show up," Sylzenya suggested.

Elnok's throat bobbed—hesitating. Sylzenya held her breath, a small bout of hope rising in her chest. Instead, he nodded, gathering the supplies he'd taken off the dead Dynameis and situating them in one of the two leather pouches. Her hope doused as quickly as it came.

She accepted the other leather pouch, filling it with a vial of orodyte serum, five strips of dried meat, two large clusters of nuts and berries wrapped in leaves, and a half-full waterskin.

Barely a day's worth of food.

Her hands shook as she took out the compass, the reality of everything she'd just done starting to consume her. She had killed Westley—*murdered him*—with her power, slayed three serpentums, lost track of Kharis, and possibly took away an entire field of crops on the other side of the forest.

And Distrathrus still held her in the palm of his hand.

Acid rose in her throat again.

"Be honest, what do you think?" Elnok asked, interrupting her thoughts.

Sylzenya looked up. He had belted another scabbard around his waist, sheathing a second longsword on the opposite side of his first. Both of the swords tipped just above the ground, as if he had two legs made of steel.

"What are you doing?" she questioned.

"I think it's pretty obvious. I'm asking for your opinion of my new look."

"Now isn't the time." Her voice wobbled as she turned her gaze to Westley's body.

"Sylzenya."

The smell of blood dissipated as his warm hand gripped her chin, tilting her face to meet his while his other hand took her shaking fingers.

"Don't look at any of that," he said, his gaze steady and determined. "Now, tell me, what are your thoughts?"

Falling apart wasn't an option, not in Lhaal Forest, and not when their goal was so important. She was tipping over the side of a cliff, about to become undone, and Elnok could see it.

She straightened her spine. "You look like a youngling who thinks he could be a Dynami when he's actually destined to run a floral shop."

He smiled, a blessed vision in the wake of her carnage. "What a diabolical assessment, as if you assume I wouldn't thoroughly enjoy owning a floral shop."

"The problem is that you'd probably run it to the ground," she replied, a smirk crawling along her mouth.

"Well, guess I'll have to prove you wrong on all accounts someday."

Surrounded by blood, death, and destruction, she laughed. It felt wrong, and yet it felt right as Elnok joined her. A strange knot had been tying in her chest, but it started to loosen. His half-grin took her away from Westley's pale eyes, Distrathrus' cold voice, and the lingering pain in her back.

Her hands no longer shook.

How did he do that?

"We need to be watchful," Sylzenya said, removing her chin from his hand while she stood, "I doubt Kharis is gone for good."

"I agree. Let's not linger."

Sylzenya grunted in agreement as she led them forward through the dark fog, the glow of the compass and Elnok's sword illuminating the barren path. Sylzenya offered a prayer to Aretta, seeking her guidance, and requesting the tree stay in its current location before Elnok's friend ran out of time.

And that, by some miracle, it held the answer to stopping Distrathrus.

CHAPTER 25
THERE ARE NO HEROES

Elnok knew he'd made a gamble when he sprinted away from Sylzenya and towards the Dynameis. He'd been far outmatched, the warriors' magic enough to kill him in a blink of an eye, the serpentums even more so. But at the end of the day, he trusted Sylzenya, and he believed she would sooner use her magic than forfeit his life, even if it meant putting others in danger. And he *needed* her to use it. Her magic was the key to making it through Lhaal Forest alive, and he couldn't let her guilty conscience get in the way.

The night they'd spent together may have been a mistake, especially since the truth of her magic had been made known, but he couldn't deny the thin web spun between them, its material threaded with the strength of Vutrorian steel.

Even if he was supposed to hate her, he wasn't sure he could find the will to do so.

"We should rest," he finally spoke, voice hoarse from thirst.

They'd walked somewhere around ten miles, and he could tell Sylzenya was feeling the strain as well. Her speed had significantly decreased in the last mile or so.

"We don't have time," she replied.

"If we keep this pace for much longer, we'll lose our strength and only further delay ourselves."

Sylzenya glanced over her shoulder, the yellow glow of his sword illuminating her face in such a way she looked like a goddess amidst the dark crooked trees. Her eyes looked determined, her full lips set in a calculated line, and her muscles shifting in the shadow and light. Of all the times for his cock to get hard, of course it would be in a deadly forest with a woman whose magic had been stripping his land of its ability to survive.

"Inconvenient" was an understatement.

"Fine, but it'll need to be short," she replied, "We can't risk the tree changing locations."

"Agreed."

They traveled a little ways further until they found a small clearing. Quietly, they surveyed the trees, careful to identify any serpentum skins or arachni webs. They found none. Head teetering on the brink of a throbbing ache, Elnok sat, leaning against a petrified log as he took two large gulps of water from the stolen waterskin. The dead warrior had only carried one waterskin, suggesting he'd thought they'd capture him and Sylzenya with ease.

They didn't take into account just how powerful she'd become.

Idiots.

At the thought of Kharis' escape, the headache won. Sylzenya was right—they hadn't seen the last of him. Perhaps he'd come back with more reinforcements, or perhaps even Distrathrus himself. He took a bite of the dried meat. Although it was stringy and caught in his teeth, it didn't make him puke like the rest of their godsdamn food.

"So is he… talking to you?" Elnok asked. "In your mind?"

Sylzenya sat across from him, eating a cluster of nuts and berries.

"Not since I killed the serpentums," she replied.

Elnok swallowed the meat. “Suppose that’s good news.”

She met him with cold silence.

“You seemed to have figured out Distrathrus’ poisoning of the wine long before you admitted it in the Willow Grove,” Elnok said, tearing at another piece of meat.

“I’d begun to suspect something, but I wasn’t sure what until Kharis and Nyla came to take the compass.”

“You could’ve told me you had your suspicions,” he paused, spinning his gold ring, “You *should’ve* told me.”

“I didn’t want it to be true, so I ignored it.” Sylzenya sighed. “I chose to ignore many things.”

“You certainly did,” Elnok muttered.

Her eyes drifted to a dirt pile in the center of the clearing, her forefinger scraping at her thumb, a drop of blood blooming from the cut.

“I should’ve never doubted my parents,” she said, her nose crinkling and eyes shining, “what kind of daughter abandons her love for those who gave her life to a man who only cared about the power she possessed? I was a fool. A young, naive, idiotic fool.”

“You were manipulated by a centuries-old god who’d poisoned everyone to be on his side,” Elnok retorted, “you probably would’ve been killed if you’d seen through all of his bullshit from the beginning.”

A tear fell down her cheek. “Doesn’t excuse anything I’ve done.”

Elnok stopped spinning his ring, leaning forward. “You’re right, it doesn’t.”

Sylzenya didn’t respond, her eyes glazing over, her mind traveling somewhere else. Taking a deep breath, Elnok tilted his head back, eyes fixed on the dark treetops.

“But just because you’ve committed atrocities doesn’t mean sitting around and sulking is the answer,” he continued.

“Then what should I do?” she whispered.

He looked at her face, but she turned away. Another tear fell down her cheek, dripping onto her robe.

"I think you already know the answer to that question."

She paused, taking a heavy, shaking breath. "Even if we somehow find the willow and it gives us a way to stop him, it doesn't take back all the damage my people and I have done to yours."

"The more you linger on the past, the harder it will be to see that there's a future worth living for."

"What if there isn't?" she replied, "What if it's my fault?"

Elnok sighed, leaving his petrified log to sit next to her. Her fingers fidgeted with her white robe, the fabric stained in blood and caked with mud. Grabbing her hand, he brushed his thumb over her skin. She turned to him, but he kept his stare on her dirt-covered fingers.

"You want so badly to be a hero, and it terrifies you to think you've failed," Elnok said, "But heroes are just people who tried their best and fucked up along the way. The more time passes, the more their story is made into one of perfection and glory. No one wants to remember the awful things they did to get where they wanted to be. No one wants to acknowledge they were just as selfish as any other person in the end."

She shook her head. "I just want to make sure my people are safe. I just want to make sure this *world* is safe."

"Why? And don't bullshit me by saying *it's the right thing*."

She let out a hushed breath, her back muscles constricting as she sat up a bit taller. "I suppose… I want to feel like I did something meaningful. I need to know I did something worthwhile, otherwise my life will amount to nothing. And what's more valuable than saving my people when they need it?"

"Then you're right," he replied, "You did fail. Pretty miserably, too."

Her body stilled, fingernails digging into his skin. "I didn't mean to. That has to count for something."

"Sure it can, but it doesn't change anything. Everyone fails, even you, it's just that your mistakes cost a whole lot more than most."

Silence.

She removed her hand from his. "I'd hoped for something a bit more… comforting than this."

Elnok sighed, "Would it have actually been comforting to hear me tell you lies? That you're a hero in shining armor with so much good intention it'll wipe away all the sins you've committed in your temple? All the devastation you've sown on this continent?"

"By Aretta's blood, I get it, Elnok."

"No, I don't think you do," he retorted. "You aren't a good or bad person, Sylzenya. You're just… human. A human with magic, which means your consequences reach farther than mine ever could. Ever since I first heard you on your temple's balcony, I saw what Distrathrus was trying to display: that you're different. Special. And in ways, you are, just like anyone is with their intricacies. But even with all your magic and pageantry, you were still no better than anyone else down in those gardens." He paused, swiping his thumb along his gold ring. "You're not separate from this world like Distrathrus wants you to believe, you're a part of it."

She sat in silence until she said, "Are you always this scathingly honest?"

He huffed a laugh. "No, actually. But I guess… I really believe in you." His eyes caught her gaze. "And I suppose I feel like I can be honest with you because of that."

"Well, it hurts. A lot."

He smiled. "Good. Because if it didn't, then I'd be concerned."

The scowl on her face relaxed, her rigidness melting away. "How are you doing that? Tell me what a fuck up I am and yet still look at me like you don't want to see me dead?"

"It'd be hard to have a conversation with a dead person," he chided. But all humor left his bones as he sat up straight. "I'm with you until the very end of this, Sylzenya. We're going to find that willow."

Slowly, she lifted her head.

"Do you promise?" she asked.

He could feel the hopelessness in her words, the loneliness in how she hugged her knees to her chest. This woman who'd commanded roots out of the ground and killed three serpentums now sat as if she held no power at all. For the first time since meeting her, he finally saw in full clarity what Distrathrus had done to her:

Reduced her to believe she was nothing without him.

Every wall Elnok had built around himself crumbled. Suddenly he was back by the cliffside, his tears mingling with the rain; his own body trembling as he grasped for a reason to continue listening to his heart beat instead of throwing himself into the sea.

"I promise."

A stream of tears trailed down her face, meeting the faintest hint of a smile on her lips.

Elnok brushed her hair away from her face before embracing her, his hand sliding up and down her arm. He knew he should've kept his distance, her naked body still fresh on his tongue, but what kind of person withholds comfort in these moments? He wanted to whisper to her how everything would be alright, how they'd defeat Distrathrus and life would become something beautiful and wonderful. But it wouldn't be the truth, for they still hadn't found the tree and they didn't know what it would take to stop a god from destroying humanity.

He warred with himself, holding her close. If it wasn't for her and her people, he might've lived a normal life free of hunger and pain.

And yet, he didn't want to let her go, hadn't since he'd first seen her smile talking about her people's history; since she slammed her fist into the wall and decided she would find the compass instead of bow to the High One's threats; since he'd first heard her laugh in the temple gardens; since she'd removed the hanging sheet between them and touched his body as if he'd been everything she'd been looking for.

And he'd be lying if he denied feeling the exact same way about her.

Fingers digging into his shoulders, she leaned back, her shimmering eyes searching his. Gently, he brushed the remaining tears from her face, wiping them on his cloak as if to say her burdens would be his.

She whispered so soft he barely heard her, "I want to be free of him."

He leaned forward, unable to stop himself as he combed his fingers through her hair.

"Your power far outweighs Distrathrus', can't you see that?"

Her eyes dipped to his mouth as her fingers traced his chest. Heat rising in his body, Elnok leaned down; her mouth slightly parted, and damn him because he didn't want to hold back. If last night was a mistake, then why had it felt so right even after learning the truth?

"No, I can't," she whispered.

She removed her hand, turning away.

Elnok gently grabbed her chin, tipping her face to meet his.

"I can," he said.

He studied her face with his eyes—her strong chin, slender nose, deep blue eyes, and full lips. Silence hung over them both, her breath dancing along his mouth, a fire lighting in his body.

"Last night was a mistake," she whispered, her half-lidded eyes staring at his mouth.

Everything within him ordered him to back away. Nothing would come of this. He knew this, and so did she. Once they found the willow, he'd part from her and go to Orym, and she'd stay.

Best not to get more attached.

And yet, as he brushed his thumb along the column of her throat, her soft skin sliding under his touch, his heart betrayed him.

"Yes," Elnok agreed, "a grievous mistake."

Her eyes fluttered shut, her throat bobbing against his thumb. "A horrible mistake."

"The very worst."

She paused. "I think I like making mistakes with you."

Heat and want rushed through him at her words. As he gripped her throat, angling her lips to his—

A shrill screech pierced their ears. Everything between them broke into iced veins and dark fear as they pushed off one another, fumbling for their leather pouches and weapons. Elnok swiped his sword through the air, a trail of thin glimmering threads wrapping around the blade.

Webs.

"*Fuck*," Elnok muttered.

Eight glossy eyes blinked from the shadows, multiplying into numbers he could hardly fathom.

Arachnis.

Metallic chitters echoed through the trees. Elnok slowly stood up, lifting his sword, the yellow glow piercing through the shadows and crooked forest. His blood turned to ice as bulbous bodies black as obsidian twitched in the light, the arachnis' long sharp legs piercing into the earth as they each snapped their fangs together.

It was far too dark, even with the lit blade, to determine their number.

Elnok turned to find Sylzenya sitting perfectly still.

"Sylzenya," he urged, placing a hand on her shoulder, "now would be the time for your power."

"I'm well aware," she replied through gritted teeth as she stood, pressing her back against his.

A shriek shattered the air as one of the arachnis skittered forward, its glossy sheen shining against the sword's light, black liquid dripping from its fangs. Elnok's chest squeezed.

"They're most vulnerable at the juncture between their legs and body as well as their throats," Elnok said as another arachni twitched forward, its eyes scanning them frantically.

"Have you killed one before?" she asked.

"Almost."

Sylzenya cursed as he felt her body heat rise, her back seeming to convulse against him.

"I can't do it," she gasped, "Distrathrus' blood. It's blocking me."

Blood drained from his face. "You can do this. I *know* you can."

"He isn't letting me this time," she grunted, "I can't get past him."

This would be it then.

Gulping, he said a silent prayer to whatever deity might listen to him that Orym would be saved and that, by some miracle, this wouldn't be his and Sylzenya's last stand.

"Doesn't matter," he replied, readjusting his grip on his sword and handing her his extra blade, "We stick together and we fight until we can't any longer, understood?"

She cursed again, taking the sword with a trembling hand. "I can barely hold this damned weapon."

Elnok's arms dared to shake, but he forced his body to remain poised. The monster that lived within himself roared to life—death or not, he would take as many arachnis to their graves as he could manage.

If he was to fight, it would be to his last breath.

"We can do this," he breathed, for while he knew Sylzenya

was no warrior, she needed to believe she could be. "Are you with me?"

Her breaths shook as her muscles tensed against his back.

"Always," she replied.

He grabbed Sylzenya's wrist and wrenched her to the ground with him, both of them barely dodging an arachni as it flew over their heads, colliding into one of its own.

Their screeches reverberated along his bones, sending panic into his heart. But his fear became fire as another arachni skittered towards them. Eyes wide and focus sharpened, he jumped to his feet, sword ready to pierce the monster through its jaw.

It vanished.

Shock ruptured through his spine. Then, he remembered.

They can move in and out of sight, Kharis had told him. *It's not due to swiftness, as they're rather slow creatures, but they're able to render themselves invisible.*

A gust of air whooshed past him.

"*Sylzenya,*" he shouted, "Watch out!"

But it was too late. She screamed as it crashed into her, its fangs aimed for her chest.

Instinct pulsed through Elnok as he swiped the sword through one of its legs, amputating it from its body. It sliced through easily, as if it was nothing more than a piece of thin cloth. The arachni shrieked, falling to its side. Elnok cut off another leg, and then another, yelling at Sylzenya to move.

A weight heavy as an anchor crashed into him from behind. All air left his lungs as he slammed into the musty earth, his shoulder cracking on impact.

"*Elnok!*"

He quickly flipped to his back, the arachni screeching above him, jaws wide. Black slimy liquid dripped onto his face. He gripped his sword, aiming to slice it through its mouth—

Red filled his vision as pain ruptured through his arm.

He screamed.

Sylzenya raised her sword, aiming to slice the leg that speared through his bicep, but she was too late; the arachni's fangs dug into his chest. The last thing he saw was Sylzenya's ash-colored hair fluttering through the air like a silver wave crashing against a wall of jagged rock, and then, pain consumed him.

CHAPTER 26
WEBS & SWORDS

Power flickered in Sylzenya's veins. Though her goddess' blood rushed in her body, it couldn't push past Distrathrus' impenetrable barrier, as if his long crooked hand was crushing her veins, denying any blood from flowing to her heart. Like a muscle refusing to tense, a root unable to soak up water, a flower's petals dying in the relentless heat…

Agony ripped through her as an arachni crashed into her. She hit the dirt, her sword spinning out of her hand. The creature aimed a sharpened leg for her heart. Rotted dirt filled her mouth as she quickly rolled through the dust, the thud of its leg a hard tremor in the earth. She reached for her sword, but the monster swiped it away.

Terror laced through her veins, the sword's light revealing countless arachnis skittering in the clearing.

Sylzenya dug her elbows into the earth as she crawled for the weapon, only for a sharp pain to spear her calf. A desperate yell escaped her lips as she reached for the sword, her fingertips brushing its hilt, only for one of the creature's legs to pin her hand to the ground. Tears flooded her vision as she screamed for Elnok.

A low voice echoed through the clearing.

Do not kill her.

Sylzenya ceased her screams, lungs burning. She'd recognize that voice anywhere—the one that once comforted her, told her pretty lies, and shaped her into a monster.

I need her, as do you, Distrathrus commanded. ***Leave her and I will collect.***

The arachni seemed to have heard the god's words, removing both its legs from her flesh. She groaned in pain, the flaming sensation flooding her skin as the arachnis chittered together.

Suddenly, one of them shrieked.

She lifted her head. Unlike the others, it skittered towards her, fast and unrelenting.

Do not harm her, Distrathrus' voice raged in her mind.

The other arachnis jumped for it, attacking their own kind. But this one was strong and evaded every attempt, its speed quicker than the others. Fangs dripping heavy black poison, it leaped into the air, aiming for her neck.

She was going to die.

Sylzenya, reach for your power, Distrathrus commanded. ***I'll give you the strength you need.***

Thump.

Thump.

Thump.

Hope flooding her heart at the sound of her goddess' heartbeat, she pressed her palm to the ground—but then she stopped. Her life, which she'd thought to be one of grandness in which she saved her people, in which she brought life to her kingdom, had been nothing but death and destruction. Distrathrus needed her to carry out his plan, so perhaps her death would be a blessing.

Maybe he wouldn't be able to take the continent if she was gone.

"I don't want your strength," she whispered.

Distrathrus' voice echoed all around her. ***Sylzenya, your people need you.* I *need you—***

Her breaths slowed, as did everything around her. Distrathrus' barrier vanished, his presence absent while her goddess' power flooded over her.

Thump.

Thump.

She didn't respond. Instead, she retreated into her own body.

The arachni looked sluggish as it flew through the air, like it was gliding through water. Something warm surged through her body, her limbs, and her veins. Strange. She'd thought her moments before death would be quick, perhaps a brief remembering of her life. Or maybe this was simply a moment to offer one last prayer.

Aretta, save Estea. Save Druenia.

She closed her eyes.

And please, save Elnok.

Silent darkness ruled over her senses.

Silence and darkness.

Silence and darkne—

Thump.

Sylzenya ignored the heartbeat.

Thump.

The heartbeat grew louder.

Thump.

Sylzenya gasped a long, arduous breath. Bright, dangerous power sung through her body—her limbs, her veins, her blood.

The dormant muscle twitched. The dying root soaked up the surrounding water. The withering flower petals opened up to the burning sun. Every ache in her muscles disappeared; the exhaustion in her body vanished. Sylzenya opened her eyes and watched as the rogue monster stayed suspended in the air, as if time had stopped for her.

She hadn't called upon any power, had she?

Thump.

Thump.

Thump.

Sparks lit up her veins, her vision sharp. Lifting herself up from the ground, she stepped to her blade, picking up the weapon in one hand with ease. It no longer felt like lifting an oversized boulder, but like picking a sunflower stalk. An easy, light weight.

Had the sword changed?

No.

The earth didn't sing to her. The roots beneath the earth didn't obey her. Instead, it was her own blood which sung a powerful, effervescent song, her muscles firing underneath her skin. Not a death, but a rebirth.

This wasn't the power of a Kreena.

This was the power of a Dynami.

Impossible.

Only men could access this power, and yet she knew it to be true—could sense it in every part of her being. She'd read enough texts to know how this power worked. It was all instinct. While Kreenas trained to harness their power through the earth and into orodyte, Dynameis learned how to undo themselves, giving all their faith to the orodyte strapped to their chest plate. The more a Dynami thought out their movements, the less effective they would become.

She had to trust her own power if she was to get her and Elnok out of this alive.

Your power far outweighs Distrathrus', can't you see that?

Sylzenya gulped as she steadied the blade in her hand, gripping the hilt tight as she stared into the arachni's glossy eyes, imagining Distrathrus' yellow gaze instead.

"I will tear you apart until there's nothing left," she hissed.

Except for the steady, thrumming heart of her goddess, she was met with silence.

Rage surged through her as she charged the arachni, every limb screaming for survival as her veins glowed and sword pulsed as bright as the sun.

All at once, time caught up with her, the arachni's shrieks shattering her eardrums. But it was too late for the creature. She pushed the blade through its jaw and up into its mouth, its fangs dangerously close to her arm. Sylzenya yelled as she ripped the sword free, splitting the creature's head in half, picturing Distrathrus screaming alongside his creation. Black blood and poison poured into the earth.

Sweat slid off her nose, dropping onto the earth. She'd never felt so alive in her life.

Adrenaline and power spiked through every crevice of her body as she raced towards the arachni poised over Elnok, its fangs still deep in his chest. But another arachni skidded in front of her, blocking her path.

Sylzenya considered how never learning how to fight was a blessing, for she had no choice but to trust instinctual power.

She didn't stop her pursuit, allowing her goddess' power to overtake her as she slid to the ground on her hip. Energy rushed through her as she slipped under the arachni's body, slicing its belly open with her sword. The creature crumpled to the ground right as she cleared its body, its loud chitters echoing as it died in a pool of its own blood.

Despite impending danger, the arachni continued poisoning Elnok, relentless in its task.

Sylzenya jumped, cold air rushing past her face as she landed on the monster's back, blade aimed for its head; she pierced it. Shrieks shattered the clearing as Sylzenya yanked the sword out of its skull, pulling the creature to the side to avoid it falling on top of Elnok.

She gasped.

Elnok was pale, his breaths labored; black web-like veins crawled up his neck and along his face. Two holes marred his chest. The distraction cost her.

Air pushed out of her lungs as she was slammed into the earth, the sword sliding from her grip.

She reacted quickly, grabbing the two poison-filled fangs before they sunk into her skin. Uncanny strength surged through her body, her muscles contracting as she fought against the monster. Poison dripped onto her skin, the creature's eyes frantic and hungry as it squirmed to end her.

Out of the corner of her eye, she watched as another arachni dashed for Elnok.

No more of this.

A loud crack echoed in her ears as she twisted the arachni's head. The monster's body fell limp. She dodged the massive weight about to trap her as she jumped to her feet, grabbing her sword and slicing three limbs off the arachni charging for Elnok. It fell to the side, screeching.

She grabbed Elnok and covered him with her body.

Her heart faltered as more arachnis skittered out of the shadows.

They needed to retreat.

Without another thought, she flung Elnok over her shoulder and ran. Everything around her slowed, the arachnis moving in a sluggish manner. She swung her sword at every creature blocking her path, slicing limbs, stabbing eyes, and evading poisoned fangs.

She didn't look back as she cleared the horde, running faster than she knew was humanly possible.

She ran until her body gave out, collapsing to the earthen floor. No more shrieks filled the air, the skittering of sharp legs gone. Sweating and shaking, she placed Elnok on the ground, her heart cracking as his breaths slowed further, eyes closed, the poison continuing to crawl through his veins.

They needed Aretta's Willow—*now.*

She rummaged through his clothes, pulling out the compass tucked in his chest pocket. A moment of terror took her as the needle spun, a golden glow pulsing until it finally settled on the direction they needed to take.

Still east.

Elnok's eyes slowly peeled open.

"Sylzenya," he whispered, voice raspy and weak.

Her vision blurred as she tucked one hand underneath his head, propping him up as she held his hand.

"It's alright," she said, "You're safe now."

His throat bobbed as his eyes studied her face.

"You look… awful." He paused, clenching his jaw as pain riddled his features. "Am I dead?"

"No," she replied, "But you were poisoned. We need to get to Aretta's Willow as soon as possible."

Elnok blinked. "How long do I have?"

Sylzenya bit her lip to keep it from quivering. Based on what she'd learned in ancient scrolls and the discussions she had overheard from Dynameis, less than a day. And they still had no idea how close they were to the tree.

"You'll make it," she said, keeping the tears behind her eyes.

He laughed softly. "You've never been good at lying, you know."

She squeezed his hand tight, rubbing her thumb over his fingers, the cool metal of a ring sliding under the pad of her finger.

A gold ring.

"What is this?" she whispered, eyes wide.

"My signet ring," he replied, "gods know why I kept it all these years. Suppose I knew it'd come in handy one day."

Twisting it in between her fingers, dread gripped her chest, constricting until she couldn't find any air. A gold ring turning into blood, filling an orodyte. The ring from her vision.

The price for life will always be pain. The bird had said. *But you will regret choosing this path. I have seen it.*

The price for the compass, the price that'd been hidden from her since the start…

Was it Elnok's death?

Everything she'd come to know as truth had been shattered ever since her failed Kreena Rite. And even when she thought it couldn't get any worse, it did. So much worse. Not only was she to blame for the famines, droughts, and sickness in Druenia whenever she used her magic, but her godsdamn vision she had of the bird… the bargain she made to gain this compass…

She'd traded Elnok's life for it.

My fault. All of this is my fault.

"No, no, no," Sylzenya breathed, dropping his hand and cradling his face. "You're not going to die, do you understand?"

His face twisted into something between pain and amusement. "I can barely feel my legs, Syl."

A new wave of determination struck her as he said her nickname.

Quickly, she took the compass and ran it along his neck. Nothing happened. The black webbed veins didn't heal, not even the skin stitched together. She cursed as she ran it along her own wounds. The cuts healed, blood no longer dripping down her spine.

She had to find the damn tree. She needed to ensure Elnok lived. She'd find that stupid, prophetic bird and barter herself instead if that's what it took.

She hooked Elnok's arm over her shoulder, ignoring his protests as she moved them forward, the lone sword lighting their way. It wasn't until much later that Sylzenya noticed her power had vanished; sweat drenched her back and her muscles ached, the continual readjustment of Elnok to ensure his feet didn't drag taking its toll.

She didn't complain; didn't even consider the notion, because this was all her fault. Distrathrus' betrayal, losing her powers, having the vision and making a bargain, learning the truth of all the destruction she'd caused—it wasn't just her life that'd been shattered into a thousand pieces.

As Elnok's breaths labored, all she craved was his laugh; she wanted to listen to his stories of Druenia and his crew, hear his crass jokes, and watch his eyes light up as he droned on and on about his rope being a superior weapon. Gods, there was so much she still didn't know about him. She wanted to hear about what he liked, what he disliked, his dreams, his fears…

She wanted to know everything, even if she didn't deserve to.

And this man, the one whom she would readily trade her own life for so he might live, had people waiting for his return. If he meant this much to her after only a handful of days, then she could only imagine the bond between him and his crew.

Sylzenya moved forward through the dark twisted landscape of Lhaal Forest with Elnok stumbling next to her, praying to her goddess that the tree would draw near before the poison killed him.

CHAPTER 27
A BRAVE COWARD

The air tasted of foul rot and dampened mold. Coughs spurted out of Elnok's mouth, trails of red and black dripping from his tongue as he leaned his entire weight into Sylzenya. Despite her powers having run their course what must've been miles ago, she continued on, heaving him more and more onto her shoulder as they stepped over cracked roots and avoided dead trees.

He wanted to tell her to stop, that she needed to let him go, but he'd seen the look in her eyes—had felt the desperation in her tone.

She wasn't going to abandon him.

Despite the poisoned chill that gripped his chest, a small light of warmth dipped into his stomach. Sylzenya was strategic, this he'd seen numerous times in the few days they'd spent together, and yet, she chose to take him with her—a risk that could cost her life.

Elnok thought back to their time at the inn. He'd assumed their groping and desire for one another had been nothing more than lust and heightened emotions.

Perhaps, at the time, it had been just that.

But this… this was different. Deliberate. Sylzenya cared

for him, and he wanted her to know he felt the same before he died.

"Syl—"

But his voice gave out. If he could curse, he would.

Sylzenya studied the compass for what had to be the hundredth time, her ash-colored hair a tangle of braids and flyaways. Her dark ocean eyes glared at the object, her jaw flexing as she shoved it back in her pocket.

"Are we close?" Elnok managed to choke out, the trees blurring as his vision swam in and out of focus.

"Yes."

A lie. They both knew it, but it felt good to hear it anyways.

Elnok couldn't help but think this tree had only been a trick of the eye, a trivial pursuit made for dreamers. But Sylzenya bet her life on it. If she believed that this tree existed and could save both Orym and the continent, then he would follow her. There was little choice to do otherwise, but even if there were, Elnok had a sense he would follow Sylzenya to the end of the world if she asked it of him.

"This way," a familiar voice echoed amongst the trees, "I see drag marks. One of them is injured."

Elnok's stomach dropped.

"*Kharis,*" Sylzenya whispered as she lifted Elnok's legs into her arms. Elnok felt her knees buckle as she did so, and he wished beyond anything he wasn't so fucking useless.

She stumbled through branches and in between trees, twisting and turning, still heading east. Twigs and branches bit at Elnok's face, but there was no pain, his entire face numb as he fought to keep his breaths even despite this newfound panic.

"*There,*" Elnok wheezed, pointing to a hollowed-out tree.

. . .

Sylzenya gave a quick nod and rushed for the crooked tree. Rot and mildew assaulted his senses as she squeezed them through the narrow opening. They quickly assessed the hiding place; small insects crawled up and down while black, tar-like mold layered the tree.

"Don't touch any of this," Sylzenya warned as she placed him back on his feet, "It could be just as poisonous as the arachni."

Elnok grunted in affirmation.

Slowly, she guided his numb body to the ground He wished he could feel the warmth of her touch against his aching skin, but all he felt was the steady sharpening pain splicing through his veins. She cradled his head in her arms.

They were in total darkness together, their only sword now sheathed and losing its glow. The poison continued to push into his feet, his eyes, his mind.

"They're somewhere nearby," Kharis' voice echoed from somewhere off in the distance, "Set up camp here and search. We need rest, and they couldn't have gotten far."

Fucking Kharis.

First he fell in love with his brother, and now he was hunting him. While he knew the man was under the influence of Distrathrus' blood, it—his brother's lover sent out to kill him—still felt all too real. He should never have trusted Kharis.

His thoughts were brought back as he felt Sylzenya's body shake. Despite the feeling of daggers slicing into his skin, he managed to lace his fingers with hers. Her breath caught as she squeezed back.

By the gods themselves.

He needed her. He had needed her since the moment he met her outside the temple. Life had slowly grown colorless over the years, more so than he'd realized. Waking up, scrounging for food, thieving for other necessities, and then doing it all over again the next day. And while he loved his crew, loved Orym so much he was willing to face an arachni and be poisoned to death, he'd never met someone who'd seen him so clearly as Sylzenya had.

There were parts of himself he'd always kept hidden, and yet she saw them; he *wanted* her to see them.

It comforted and terrified him.

"Syl," he whispered, so low he wasn't sure if she could hear him.

But he felt the lightest of touches on his jaw, running up his cheek, finding the lone tear that trailed down his face.

"It's alright," Sylzenya whispered back, "We're going to get you to Aretta's Willow. I need you to keep going. We're so close."

Elnok closed his eyes so tight another tear ran down his face.

"I already told you, you make a terrible liar."

He felt her chest convulse as she replied, "I need you to stay strong."

Elnok squeezed her hand tight, her chest convulsing again as he felt a hot tear fall onto his forehead.

"Don't let the Dynameis find you," he said.

"*Elnok.*"

"You know, all I used to want was to survive. I played it safe after I left Vutror, hiding in the shadows, masking myself behind aliases; a life unnoticed. And while Estea is where it'll end for me, I'm glad I did it." Elnok gulped as his voice threatened to fail, "I'm glad to have done something for once in my life, and I'm glad I met you."

Her hands began to shake. He stayed steady, slowly rubbing his thumb across the soft skin on her knuckles, an ache ripping deep in his chest as he did.

"You're going to live," she said breathlessly into his ear, "I'm going to make sure of it."

He ignored her pleas, because she knew just as well as he did that this was the end for him.

"I need you to get the medicine to Orym," he said as he traced his hand up her forearm, her skin shivering from his touch, "In a world full of selfish people like myself, it's people like Orym who deserve to live another day."

Sylzenya wiped loose pieces of hair out of his face.

"Do it yourself," she whispered.

He scoffed. "I'm dying and giving you my last wishes. That's what needs to happen in times like this—"

"No, I need you to stop talking and listen to *me*," she retorted, her lips brushing his ear, "Do you know the one thing that's harder than dying?"

She waited in silence.

"What?" he asked.

"Living," she said, "living is much harder, and I need you to choose to do the harder thing right now."

Elnok's lip quivered. "It's poison, Syl. It's not that I want to die."

"Then stop talking like you're giving up."

"I'm not giving up, I'm being realistic."

"You're being a coward."

"For *fuck's* sake," Elnok grunted, a cough laboring out of his chest. "I'm just a thief. A low life who steals from others to get what he wants. I've always been a coward."

"No," Sylzenya replied, leaning back, "No one is ever that simple, not even you. You came all this way to save your friend, knowing this kingdom had its secrets. You crossed Lhaal Forest and didn't turn back despite its dangers. You risked telling me your plans so you could save your friend, knowing I might betray you." She paused. "So don't tell me you're selfish or a coward, Elnok Rogdul. You're the bravest person I've ever met."

His heart leapt into his throat.

"But I swear to the gods, if you decide now of all times to be one, I'll strangle you myself."

A choked laugh left his mouth. "Will you now?"

"Yes, I will. So stop talking and focus on your breathing while I come up with a plan."

Elnok fought every screaming muscle in his body as he lifted his head, gripping her face in between his hands as he brushed her hair behind her ears, whispering her name softly. Her nose brushed along his before she placed her chilled forehead against his own.

Elnok couldn't find words, so he brought his lips to hers instead.

Her mouth was cold, but it was more likely he was feverishly warm. Her tongue found his—the only part of him that hadn't turned completely numb yet—causing his body to shiver. This was nothing like the time in the inn. That had been all fire and heat and want. This was yearning and sorrow, shared tears dripping into their open mouths, tasting of salt.

Her silent sobs echoed into his chest. He pulled her closer, refusing to let this final moment with her end. Combing his fingers through her hair, he wondered what it would've been like to take her on a ship and journey through Druenia with her by his side; to hear her laugh around the nightly fires and have her share her own stories alongside his crew. And then, once the embers died out, he'd take her into their bed, and he'd taste her until her sweet whimpers sent him to a blissful sleep.

He wanted to live a life with her. *Damn it*, he really did, didn't he? He wanted it more than anything in his short, sad life.

She whispered into his mouth, "This is all my fault."

"You have nothing to be sorry for."

"Yes I do."

"Distrathrus tricked you." He gripped her hip tight. "He betrayed everyone here and on this continent, and if you had known, he might've gotten rid of you. He would've killed you."

"I would've deserved it," she whispered.

"No," Elnok growled, wishing he could see those dark eyes of hers. "You didn't deserve anything that bastard did to you. Not the scar on your back, not the pain in your body, not anything else you were forced to do in order to serve this kingdom. You deserve all the joy and happiness this world can offer you."

An aching silence spread between them, her fingers digging into his shoulders.

"You're so much more than your cuts and bruises and pain," Elnok said as he caressed her face, "You're brave and courageous and compassionate. You of all people deserve a life where you can laugh to your heart's content and create life without sacrifice—a life where you can be free. I'd do anything to give that to you."

He slowly wiped the tears running down her face, his heart slowing down—dangerously so. He wanted to tell her he felt the same as her; he wanted to know what a life with her could be like outside of this hellish war they'd been caught in. But he felt the desperation in her touch and he wouldn't dare cause her to do anything rash. It'd only make this parting worse than it needed to be.

A slice of pain ran up his neck, his grip tightening on her as a quiet groan escaped his lips. Air refused to enter his lungs, his throat feeling as if it was closing in on itself.

"I wish we had more time," he whispered, his hands sliding to the ground.

All he could perceive was Sylzenya's frantic breaths, her fingernails digging into his skin.

"Then I'll get us more," she whispered.

Dread gripped his throat.

"Syl," Elnok weakly whispered, "there's nothing that can be done."

"You're not going to die," she seethed, rummaging through her leather pouch, "We need their help."

"*Their* help?" Elnok sputtered, "If you expose us, Distrathrus will take you. Torture you. Force you to become his weapon—"

"If he wants me, he's going to have to save you first."

"*No,*" Elnok begged, "Sylzenya, you're not thinking clearly right now. Please, *don't do this.*"

"I have a plan," she argued, "Trust me."

But he didn't trust her, not right now.

Glowing compass in her hand, he could finally see her clearly. Her eyes were wild and bloodshot, her face ragged and tired. Sleep had evaded them for an entire day. She'd lost an ample amount of blood, and she'd barely eaten anything besides a few nuts and berries. His body was failing him due to poison, but her mind was collapsing under over-exhaustion.

"Let's face it, I won't make it to the tree at this point either. We need help." She fished out a vial of orodyte serum from her leather pouch. "You said Kharis told you about the tree. He was on your side before coming back to Estea and drinking Distrathrus' wine, right?"

Sweat built along his neck. "The bastard had fallen in love with my brother, so yes, but he's too far gone now."

"Not if I get this in his blood." She held the vial between her fingers, a faint laugh leaving her mouth. "Suppose I really am my father's daughter after all. It'll at least give him a chance to fight against Distrathrus' blood. And if it works, he'll help us get to the tree."

"For gods' sake." Elnok coughed. "And how are you going to do this? He's clearly brought reinforcements. You can't risk getting caught."

"And you can't die."

Her words silenced him. He'd had this conversation before, but it wasn't with Sylzenya—it'd been with Orym. And he'd been the one to say Sylzenya's exact words.

"Damn your high morals," he whispered, Orym's voice echoing along his bones, the poison sinking deeper.

All this effort to save his friend, only to die from his own sickness in the end.

"No more wasting time," she whispered, gently settling his head on the ground. "I'll be back with Kharis, alright? Just hang on a little longer."

"*Sylzenya*—"

"Promise me you'll hang on," she interrupted.

Her bloodshot eyes watered. Elnok knew the promise was futile, but she wasn't looking for the truth.

She wanted hope.

"I promise," he wheezed.

Wiping a tear from her cheek, she left to battle Kharis and his Dynameis, leaving Elnok to his own fight of filling his lungs one breath at a time.

CHAPTER 28
WARRING BLOOD

Desperation.

Sylzenya thought she'd experienced it before, like the time she begged her father to take her away from the temple, or the time when her and Nyla evaded priestesses as they sneaked back to their rooms after her sexual escapade with Westley, or even the time when the High One—*Distrathrus*—had ordered her to create ten willows in one day and she had been close to failure.

But desperation wasn't a single flower struggling to bloom. No, desperation was a hurricane. Rain, wind, and chaos billowing everywhere, threatening to uproot ancient trees and send them toppling onto unsuspecting homes. Desperation was crawling through a deserted plain, mouth parched, only to discover the oasis was a mirage.

Sylzenya had never been desperate until now.

She'd left Elnok dying.

From poison.

In a tree.

Godsdamnit.

And now, she needed to somehow cut open Kharis' skin—the most well-trained warrior in *all* of Estea—and dump orodyte serum into his blood. If she was going to save Elnok and, hopefully, the entire continent, then Kharis needed to be woken from his poisoned stupor.

The thought sent her exhausted head spinning.

Flames from the campfire cast dancing shadows on the surrounding trees. Quickly, she hid behind one, its drooping limbs smelling of rot and sulfur. She crinkled her nose, forcing a cough to stay inside her throat.

Ignoring the sharp scuttles of insects, she maneuvered behind a bush, orodyte serum in one hand, sword in the other. She counted three Dynameis, all sitting on a log, the man in the center sporting Kharis' golden hair and tight topknot. *Strange.* She'd assumed Kharis would return with an entire battalion.

She snarled her lip. It was a message for her—Distrathrus saw her as his own. Malleable. Under his control.

Closing her eyes, she placed a palm to the earth, her other hand upturned towards the trees. She breathed in her power, feeling the way it connected to the roots beneath her feet and the rotting leaves of the cursed forest; her body became one with it all.

Thump.

Thump.

Thump.

Distrathrus' barrier was gone. Aretta's power flowed freely.

Hope lit her chest. Whatever had happened when she'd fought the arachnis had broken Distrathrus' hold.

Elnok had been right.

She was stronger.

Rubbing her thumb along the compass, she closed her eyes.

Thump.

Thump.

Thump.

Gold light erupted from her palm, wrapping around her wrists and her shoulders, the sharp sting along her back opening and blood dripping. She gritted her teeth, placing all her focus into the roots writhing underneath the ground.

But what if she was stealing a life from somewhere in Druenia?

She silenced the thought as quickly as it came. There wasn't time to consider how she might be stealing a village's only source of fresh water. She couldn't linger on the sickness she might be sowing into a piece of soil in Druenia.

How far I've fallen.

But she was human, not a hero. Choices stood before her: to save the one or to save the many. Even if a part of her was disgusted by her decision, she chose the former. She chose to be selfish.

Eyes steady on the Dynameis, she clenched her fist.

Roots illuminated with yellow sparks sprung from the ground.

The Dynameis jumped up, but they weren't fast enough, not even with their glowing orodytes. Power surged through her veins as she grappled all of them, slamming them back onto the log.

Elnok would make it to Aretta's Willow.

She'd make sure of it.

She approached the men. Tilting her head, the roots tightened around their arms and legs, their eyes widening as they found her. But then she stopped. The Dynami with blonde hair looked nothing like Kharis. In fact, Kharis wasn't here.

Cold steel bit into the back of her neck.

"Impressive work, but I think you missed one." Kharis' voice said from behind, his sword pinching the skin.

Sylzenya's mind was lost to exhaustion and desperation, so she smiled wide.

"I can fix that," she replied, the roots writhing underneath her feet.

Clenching her fist, the roots shot up.

Kharis successfully dodged, landing on a branch a single story up from the ground. The orodyte on his chest plate—a larger stone than most—glowed bright.

Power against power.

He dropped to the earth, swinging two glowing swords. "Where's our prince, Sylzenya? He can't have gone far, not with how injured he seems to be and how protective you've become of him."

"Kharis," Sylzenya started, holding her hands at eye-level, "I only want to help you."

"Interesting, because that's what I was going to tell you."

He charged for her. Quickly, she erected a wall of roots. He slammed into them, cursing as he used his glowing sword to cut through them. Stumbling back, Sylzenya gripped her sword and orodyte serum vial, commanding the vines to capture Kharis as he walked through them.

He swung his two swords in consecutive arcs, like a waterwheel of power, slicing the roots down until they were nubs. Sylzenya summoned more roots, but his speed outmatched hers.

Shit.

There was a reason Kharis was considered the best Dynami in Estean history. Why did she think she could beat him?

Elnok.

He was going to die, might already be dead…

No. She wouldn't let that happen—*couldn't.* A fresh hurricane raged through her limbs as she urged her power into the dying trees surrounding them. They fought against her, their energy far more difficult to connect to than the lively roots underneath the ground. Still, she drew the trees down, five of them bending precariously over Kharis.

"Distrathrus has you under his control, but you don't have to give in," Sylzenya yelled, the Dynami slicing away at her upturned roots.

"There's no one else I would rather serve. You used to understand this." He smiled, his veins glowing a bright yellow.

Sylzenya continued sending vines and roots at him, attempting to overwhelm him, but he sliced and sliced and sliced. She was slowing him down, but she needed more time before the trees obeyed her completely.

"What about Elnok's brother?" she asked, "The man you love? Is it worth abandoning him to serve this god?"

Kharis' smile faltered, the light in his veins flickering. "The price for life will always be pain, even if it means giving up a dream."

"Would he give up on you?"

Kharis missed a root, the sharp point slicing through a layer of his leather armor. Wincing, he continued his fight. Sylzenya held her ground, commanding more and more roots. Pain, heavy and sharp, sliced deeper into her back.

This needed to end *now*.

"Does he know you've deserted him?" she asked.

Kharis' power shifted. It no longer flickered, instead glowing brighter, his blades moving faster.

Shit.

Blood and sweat dripped like rain down her skin. She needed to uproot these trees and send them on top of Kharis, and she refused to give in to the pain until he was subdued.

"I'm afraid that if anyone should be questioned for their abandonment, it would be you," Kharis replied, "You abandoned Distrathrus at his most important moment. You abandoned your decade of work because an outlander showed up in your life and convinced you of his lies." His eyes softened, the light dimming, "I understand the temptation. I know exactly how you've felt, but you need to learn as I have that they aren't worth it in the end."

Flames billowed along her cut, harsh and unrelenting.

Just one more moment, and the trees would smother him.

One more moment.

"Consider my words carefully," he continued, "Do you truly believe Elnok will forgive you? After learning of all you've done to his land? His people? The man isn't dull. He wants the medicine to cure his friend, and he knows he can't make it through this forest without someone with power by his side."

Curling her hands into fists, she ignored his words. Instead, she forced more roots out of the ground, willing the trees to bend and bend and bend.

"Why waste your time with a man who sees you as a means to an end when you have a god—a *father*—who sees you for everything you are?"

All at once, Distrathrus' dark barrier slammed down on her, breaking her away from the roots and trees.

Her goddess' heartbeat ceased.

Aretta's power vanished from her fingertips.

Sylzenya, why won't you listen to reason? Distrathrus' cold voice slithered along her spine.

"*No,*" she gasped, but it was too late.

The earth's song faded, the roots falling limp as she crumpled to her knees. Skin slick and head pounding, Sylzenya dropped the orodyte serum and sword, the vial hitting a sharp rock and shattering—her only way of turning Kharis… gone.

The lack of Dynami reinforcements, her access to her power… it'd given her the confidence to try and beat Kharis.

A trap, and she fell right into it.

She hadn't overcome Distrathrus' hold.

He'd only allowed her to *think* it.

The thief is nearly gone, he whispered into her mind. ***You'll thank me one day for such a mercy.***

"*Don't you dare touch him,*" she shouted.

Distrathrus' blood pushed further into her body. Yelling, she gripped her head, her back burning and mind throbbing. Kharis stopped spinning his swords, sheathing them as he approached her.

I can't stand to see you get hurt any longer. Let Kharis bring you home. This fight can be done once and for all.

"*You* are not my home," Sylzenya whimpered.

If not me, then who?

"I-I-" Sylzenya couldn't find words.

There were none to say, because she had no answer.

Where will you go after you find my sister's tree? With the thief to heal his friend?

Cold tears fell down her weary face.

You weren't made for his world. You weren't made for my sister's either. You were made for mine, always mine.

Kharis grabbed her throat. Sylzenya struggled, but his strength outmatched hers as he slammed her to the ground. She cried out, dirt and gravel wedging into her open cut, burying into her skin.

Even with Aretta's blood in her veins, she couldn't beat them.

She would never be strong enough.

Distrathrus was right. She was his, had been before she'd been dedicated to the temple, and had been since she'd been born on this side of Lhaal Forest. Her destiny had been carved into orodyte. Land scorched, rivers desolate, people dead—she'd done it alongside the other acolytes and Kreenas. No amount of good deeds could change it. Distrathrus had been her master, and she'd trusted him—*loved* him. She'd trusted and loved a monster so much so she let him turn her into one.

Digging into his leather armor, Kharis pulled out a clear glass vial full of black liquid.

Distrathrus' blood.

"*No,*" she gasped, ripping at his skin, "Please, don't do this. *Please.*"

"It's going to be alright, Sylzenya." He popped the vial

open. "You'll feel much better after your body partakes in more of his blood. I promise."

Struggling against his hold, Sylzenya pushed and clawed, but he wouldn't budge. Her power had been spent, her head throbbing in pain, her back engulfed in flames, and now, her transformation would be complete.

She'd belong to Distrathrus mind, body, and soul.

Memories flooded through her as Kharis steadied the vial over her cut: the times when her and her father would watch butterflies flutter among the flowers in early spring, her mother's bright hazel eyes as she taught her how to knead dough and pour wine, and those lazy summer nights when the three of them sat around a fire and stared at the treetops until the sun rose.

Pale green eyes flashed through her vision. Elnok's touch as he traced her hips with his calloused fingers, his warm breaths caressing her ear, his musky earth and worn leather scent reminding her of home.

A crack in the dark barrier. A thin film of gold power slipped through.

Thump.

Thump.

Quiet and faint, her goddess' heartbeat slowly swelled.

Kharis' orodyte glowed brighter and brighter, his fingers digging so deep he drew blood as he started to tip the vial. Thoughts jumbling, heart racing, and throat gasping for air, Sylzenya closed her eyes.

She thought of Elnok's smile.

I'm with you until the very end of this, Sylzenya.

Thump.

Thump.

Her mind stilled, focusing on the single crack through the barrier; the single source of power running through her veins.

I promise.

Thump.

Clenching her fists and teeth, she searched underneath her, calling upon a single root—any of them.

None responded.

I promise.

Thump.

The thin crack in Distrathrus' barrier grew wider, power spilling over. She called upon the roots again, breathing through her blood and veins, sending her power deep into the earth.

She needed to push more, to concentrate more, to feel *more*. This new plan forming in her head was a gamble, but it was all she had left. She'd made it this far, and she wouldn't fail this time. Elnok's life depended on it.

Another breath.

Everything will be back to normal after this, Sylzenya, Distrathrus whispered. ***Your power will be fully restored, and you'll be back by my side.***

A single root writhed in response.

Her breath caught.

She sent her golden light down, diving after it, encircling it, guiding it up from its home, driving up and up and up.

We'll be together again—

She yelled as the root pierced clean through her upper shoulder, her blood splattering on Kharis' face as the root continued its path and pierced into the gap in Kharis' armor, just between his collarbone and neck.

Distrathrus' distant yell echoed all around her, dying into the darkness. The barrier remained, but his presence was gone.

Kharis yelled, stumbling back and dropping the vial of Distrathrus' blood. Sylzenya quickly rolled to the side, missing the vial and its contents as it spilled onto the earth.

"What-What's happening?" he shouted, rolling on the dried forest floor, the root lodged in his flesh. "*What did you do to me?*"

"My blood is now in your blood." Sylzenya gasped as she cautiously stood, throwing his swords out of his reach. "Both Aretta and Distrathrus' blood live within me, and now they live in you."

"*Traitor!*"

"You need to remember yourself. Remember your love for Vutror's King. Remember why you were so desperate to get Elnok's help to find Aretta's Willow. Remember that you *don't* belong to Distrathrus, but to yourself."

He slammed a fist into the dirt. "*I serve him. I belong to him.*"

She kneeled next to him, holding him down as blood seeped from her shoulder. "Orodyte serum isn't poison, Kharis. It's Aretta's blood—her power—and now it flows in your veins just as it does mine. Feel it within your own skin and blood, not through your orodyte. *It's a part of you.*" Gripping his shoulder tight, she forced his eyes onto hers. "Elnok is dying. He won't survive unless you *wake up*. Distrathrus is going to eliminate all of humanity. Your king—your lover—is going to *die* if we don't stop him."

"No, *no*—" Kharis grimaced, his face twisted in pain, the yellow light in his eyes fading and turning black. "*Tosh*… no, not Tosh!"

Sylzenya ripped the orodyte from his chest. He reached for her hands, but to no avail, unable to get a firm grip on her arms as he screamed and fought with the two bloods battling for control in his body.

"Come on, Kharis," Sylzenya begged. "Don't let Distrathrus win. Don't let him take our lives from us anymore than he already has."

Kharis grabbed her arm. Sylzenya meant to rip herself away, but she stopped as his pleading gaze found hers, black clouds threatening to overtake his vision; Distrathrus' blood threatening to overrule him.

Estea's greatest Dynami needed Estea's greatest Kreena to help him fight.

"*Remember*," Sylzenya yelled, grabbing his hand and squeezing tight, "Your life is more than following orders. You can defy Distrathrus." She gulped, tightening her grip further. "We can defy him together. We're stronger."

Kharis' eyes rolled to the back of his head, his body convulsing and hand squeezing Sylzenya's so tight she couldn't stop the yell spilling from her lips.

Finally, he stilled, body slumped to the ground and eyes closed.

His hand slipped through hers.

"Kharis?" Sylzenya whispered, the sudden stillness causing her heart to pump loud in her ears. "Kharis… no, no, no. Please. *Oh my gods*—"

"Get up," a low, grating voice demanded from behind. "*Now.*"

Heart lurching in her throat, Sylzenya turned. Her power had left her, and now, the three Dynameis were free, surrounding her with glowing swords and harsh stares.

She'd failed.

Two men's deaths, bleeding from her hands.

"I said, *up*," the Dynami shouted.

But everything turned numb, her body unable to comply. Two of the Dynameis grabbed her arms and hoisted her up. No tears fell from her face as Kharis' body lay on the dusty ground, the root covered in her blood still lodged in his skin.

Her hands had never brought life, always death.

Always, always death.

She didn't fight as they clamped her wrists in chains—

A flash of golden light and harsh air whipped across her face.

The cold metal chains dropped from her wrists, the three Dynameis dropping with them. Blood dripped along their necks, vacant eyes staring up at their killer.

Kharis.

He stood over them, breathing heavily, a glowing sword in

hand. Sylzenya couldn't move, her feet rooted to the ground as he turned to meet her gaze. His eyes weren't clouded black, nor were they glowing gold. They were a deep hazel, tears streaming from them and down his face.

"Sylzenya," Kharis whispered, his voice scratched and welling with emotion as he dropped the sword, "Where's Elnok?"

CHAPTER 29
TIME'S RUNNING OUT

Throat closing with each breath, Elnok stared into the darkness of the hollow tree.

A dying tree. A dying man. A dying land.

It was familiar—the stench, the dread, the way his heart slowed and breaths fought in and out of his lungs. He wanted out of his clothes. Everything was so feverishly hot, like he was wrapped in a cloth made of flames.

A warm glow, like the torches from Vutror's castle, slid down the tree's bark. He could see the dust-paned windows, the thick curtains of his parent's bedroom, the large oak bed as the guards allowed him to enter.

"*Morning, sleepyheads,*" he'd said with a wide smile, carrying a cup of rose tea in his mother's favorite black teacup. "Don't tell me you both forgot we'd planned to go out to the dried gardens to celebrate Tosh's birthday today?"

Neither of them moved.

"Mother? Father?"

Still, nothing. Elnok's lungs squeezed.

Heart slowing, he removed the thick comforter. Black porcelain shattered onto the stone floor as Elnok stumbled backwards. Two necks bleeding deep crimson, dried blood covering the white sheets and blending with the maroon comforter. He meant to yell for the guards, but he couldn't speak, wheezing too much, lungs unable to hold any air.

Vacant eyes. Pallid lips. The faces of his dead parents staring into the heavens. The bright hazel of his mother's eyes blown out like a candle.

"Elnok?" Tosh's warm voice sounded from the door as guards rushed in. "What's the meaning of this?"

Another glass shattered on the floor.

He turned to Tosh, his brother's green eyes wide, his body trembling. Guards yelled as they swarmed the bed. Elnok backed up until he slammed himself against the wall, clawing at his face.

"No." Tosh choked. "Elnok, how?"

Shaking his head, Elnok slumped to the floor, unable to form words.

"Elnok…" Tosh held onto the large doors as his legs gave out. "This… this wasn't you, was it?"

Elnok whipped his head to his brother. "What the fuck are you talking about?"

"The guards didn't know. You came in and now… now they're…" His brother's eye twitched. "They're dead."

"How can you even suggest that?" Elnok yelled, returning to his feet. "What's wrong with you?"

He shoved past him, sprinting down the hallway, his mother's blank hazel eyes haunting him as he ran until hot, scorching sun coated his skin, burning his neck as he ran through the dusty, cobblestone streets.

Suddenly, darkness swallowed the sun, its heat gutted into cold, damp stone walls, a single flame burning in the corner. Heavy chains dug into his wrists, blood dripping from his chapped lips as he scrambled away from Tosh.

"You killed them." Tosh whispered, the iron rod's tip a glowing ember, a wine bottle in his other hand. "And you're going to kill me, aren't you? You're going to slit my neck and take the Crown for yourself, aren't you?"

"Tosh, just listen to me!" Elnok begged. "The guards confirmed the windows had been tampered with. Someone, or maybe multiple people, broke in and killed them. I don't know how they got past the guards outside, but I didn't kill our parents and I'm not going to kill you. I don't even want the fucking Crown—"

"Liar!"

Skin searing with flames, Elnok yelled into the darkness as his brother's green eyes spilled over with tears. Their voices echoed against the stone walls as they both cried for their mother and father.

Breaths labored, heart slowing down until he only had a few beats left, the memory faded into poison black as ink. He'd wanted death all those years ago… maybe this would finally bring him the peace he'd been reaching for ever since his escape.

Maybe, all this time, he'd still wanted to die.

"By Aretta's blood," someone's deep voice echoed somewhere far away from his burning flesh, "He's almost gone, Sylzenya."

"Then pick him up and *run,* Kharis. We're making it to that tree."

That voice. *Her* voice. He wheezed a deep breath. He couldn't control himself as tears spilled from his eyes.

Sylzenya.

She'd survived. She'd survived and somehow turned Kharis. Her plan had *worked.* And just as he'd accepted his death, Sylzenya showed up in time, just like Orym.

The flames in his back ebbed as her familiar touch ran across his numbing face. She whispered words he couldn't understand, his reinvigorated will to live causing his lungs to burn and heart to beat faster; it took every ounce of will to just breathe. *Pain, pain, pain.* But he wanted to live, godsdamnit—for the first time in his life, he wanted to fucking *live.*

He wanted to see her face, kiss her lips, fuck her breathless. He wanted to adventure across every sea until they'd drunk all the salt and travel through every piece of land until she had filled them with flowers. Life amidst death. Laughter amongst tears. He wanted to experience it all, and he wanted to do it with her.

"The compass is still pointing east, but it looks like it's shaking," she said, her breath brushing his ear as Kharis' strong arms hoisted Elnok from the ground, "What if it's about to change locations?"

"Then we make it before it does," Kharis responded, "I'll carry him, and you hang onto me. Elnok, this is probably going to hurt."

He meant to tell him there was nothing to hold, especially since his arms were shit, but all he could manage to spit out of his numb mouth was:

"*You fucker.*"

Kharis sighed. "I'm sorry. I was supposed to help you find this tree, and I was supposed to protect you, but I failed."

"You're just like him," he wheezed.

Just like his brother.

Kharis' mouth opened, but he said nothing.

"You two can fight all you want when we've gotten to the tree, alright?" Sylzenya interrupted, "We have to go, *now*, Kharis."

Elnok didn't think his skin could feel any hotter until Kharis' veins glowed gold. Gritting his teeth, Kharis whispered another apology as he grabbed Sylzenya's arm and dashed forward. Elnok's stomach dropped, muscles screaming in pain. Air rushed past him, slapping his face and rushing into his lungs as he choked on his own saliva. Dark trees blurred past them as if they were strokes of black paint on canvas, monster growls and chitters coming and going; they wouldn't have a chance to attack with Kharis' speed.

"*There!*" Sylzenya yelled above the whooshing of air.

Craning his neck, Elnok's blurred vision distinguished a ball of light in the distance—yellow and sparkling.

Glinting in and out of existence, like a star about to leave the night sky.

"*Faster, Kharis!*" Sylzenya screamed.

Elnok fought down gulps of air, Kharis panting and chest heaving as they rushed towards the magical willow, the distance closing. Its glow faded in and out, in and out—

"*Come on!*" she cried.

Elnok fought for another breath.

"*I can't go any faster!*" Kharis yelled back.

Another yellow light glowed, and Elnok's stomach flipped over a second and third time. Sylzenya screamed, her eyes glowing and her veins crackling like lightning as she ran with him.

Powerful. Beautiful.

A true goddess.

Aretta's Willow flickered for another moment, then it faded into the darkness.

"*No!*" Sylzenya and Kharis yelled. They stopped, the air flat and smelling of rotten flesh. Coughing blood and poison onto the ground, Elnok's heart sank.

This would be it, then. He looked towards Sylzenya, her face covered in dirt, blood, and tears. Those beautiful dark blue eyes so like the ocean. He wanted to tell her she would be alright, they'd find the tree without him. She had Kharis to help kill Distrathrus, and if anyone could do it, they would.

"Syl," he wheezed, "Sylzenya—"

A golden light flashed before them. Elnok shut his eyes, the light so oppressive it burned his vision. Air rushed into his face again as Kharis dashed forward. The smell of rotten flesh vanished. Everything felt cool, as if fresh, chilled water had doused the flames in his body.

Opening his eyes, Elnok gasped. Gold sunshine filtered through green leaves while butterflies and birds fluttered over a field of flowers. A woman with bright hazel eyes and hair black as night stared at him.

A woman he hadn't seen in ten long years.

"Welcome, Elnok Rogdul of Vutror." His mother smiled. "You've made it just in time."

Sorrow, confusion, and relief welled inside him as she waved a hand over his face; he fell into a deep sleep.

Sucking in a long breath, Elnok woke. Sunlight burned his eyes. Memories of his mother floated in his head, her gentle hands pressed on his chest, a strange prayer chanting into the golden air, butterflies fluttering along her white robes.

A dream.

"This is no dream, Elnok Rogdul," his mother's familiar voice assured.

Sitting up, he gripped his chest. Bright hazel eyes stared deeply into his, the crinkles deepening around her mouth as she smiled.

"Mother?" Elnok whispered, a sob crawling up the back of his throat, "Did I die?"

His voice surprised him. Small, like a child.

"You're very much alive, especially now that the poison has been extracted," she replied, "But I'm not your true mother. I'm Aretta—the goddess of life."

Elnok gulped, his chest twisting, confusion pulling at his mind.

She continued, "As the goddess of life, I appear as the one who gave life to you."

He stared long and hard at her, the details so exact and

precise he wasn't sure how he was supposed to believe her. He wasn't sure if he should embrace her or run.

"Where are Sylzenya and Kharis?" he inquired.

She waved her hand, motioning behind him, her long white robes flowing like water. He turned, a meadow full of red and yellow flowers rested among a willow grove. It looked endless—unchanging.

The light wasn't from the sun, rather, it was everywhere. No horizon in sight, as if a wall erected of light circled them. Rivers of gold flowed from ground to sky. Yet there was no sky, only more pulsing light. Gray and white birds flew through the air, their songs filling the space as they landed among the willows and rested in the meadow.

Kharis sat leaning against a tree, hair falling to his chest, leather armor tattered, his belly slowly heaving up and down. Next to him, Sylzenya also slept. She was sprawled among the flowers, the reds and yellows framing her dirtied and bloodied face. Her white robes were ripped apart, barely covering her body, and her hair was muddied. A sudden urge to touch her skin overwhelmed him, needing to know she was safe. He tried to stand up, only for a sharp pain to run along his chest.

The arachni bite.

"Careful," Aretta spoke softly, gripping his arm and guiding him back to the meadow floor, "You're still healing, and they need to rest. All of you do."

"Where are we?" Elnok whispered.

"My prison of paradise. My willow."

Fighting to find words, he turned to his mother—the goddess—and gripped the green grass poking into his skin.

"We made it?" he checked. "We made it to Aretta's Willow?"

She nodded. "You three are the first to have found it."

Elnok's uncertainty transformed into hysterical laughter as he looked up into the sky, the glowing walls, realizing it was the bark of a tree.

They were *inside* the magical willow.

"Oh my gods," he whispered, smiling wide, "*We did it.* I honestly thought it was just a figment of legend. But, I… I need medicine for my friend, Orym. I'm not sure how to ask for this, but, I was told you have the cure."

"Elnok Rogdul, you barely survived arachni poison, and now you wish to get onto business? Please, let's take a few moments to breathe before we jump into why I ushered you three here."

"Ushered us?" Elnok laughed. "You make it sound like you handpicked us or some bullshit."

Bird song filled the silence.

"And what if I did?"

He furrowed his brow, turning to her, the picture of his mother difficult to reconcile as a centuries-old goddess.

"You said it yourself—you've been trapped here," Elnok replied, "We all had our own agendas for finding your tree. You didn't do any of that."

Lacing her hands behind her back, she stared past Elnok —towards Sylzenya—in silence.

"I'm here for Orym's medicine, that's it," he said, "He doesn't have long to live, so I don't have long to sit here and discuss things with you."

Aretta sighed. "I understand this was your main goal, but we have a far more dire situation at play than your sick frien—"

"I'm going to get him healed and then get off of this damned continent you and your brother ruined."

"I am a *goddess.* How dare you speak to me like this?"

Elnok scoffed. "A goddess trapped in a fucking *tree.*"

The birds stopped their songs. The breeze, which Elnok hadn't noticed until now, stopped brushing his hair across his face.

"Nothing will save you from my brother's wrath," she said carefully.

"You'd certainly like me to think that, don't you? Get me caught up in your little war like you've done to this kingdom? I came here for Orym. I was told you had his cure and..." He took a deep breath, realizing bartering with a goddess was a poor time to not wear a mask, even if she was trapped in a magical tree. "Please, it's the only reason why I came to Estea in the first place."

She sighed, kneeling next to him. "I know your heartaches, Elnok. Your brother, your parents, the damage it's caused you. But you need to know the truth of what actually happened."

"Unless the truth can bring them back, then it doesn't matter. They're dead, end of story."

"Your brother isn't."

"He is to me," he argued. "I'm not here for an explanation about my family history, who did what or why. And I'm not a part of your fight."

"But you are," she replied. "Elnok, it was Distrathrus who warped your brother's mind. It was his wine—his blood."

Elnok's heart raced, his hands clammy as he crawled backwards, away from her touch. Sharp pain sliced into his neck. Of course it'd been Distrathrus. He'd been too busy trying not to die to fully accept it.

She shook her head, "But that's only the start."

"I don't need to know," Elnok sneered. "Besides, weren't you the one supposed to destroy your brother? Be the savior of this world? So, in reality, I should be blaming you for my brother's crazed state."

Aretta's nose flared.

He continued anyways, "Orym has less than two days, maybe even less than a day until he's dead."

"What of Sylzenya?" she pushed.

"What about her?" Even as he said the words, something in his chest twisted. He'd made it this far, was this close to getting Orym's medicine, and he'd do anything to retrieve it.

Just because he'd imagined a life with Sylzenya—*wanted* a life with her—didn't mean he could have it.

Not if it meant sacrificing Orym's life in the process.

"I thought you cared for the woman?"

"It doesn't matter."

"*Fool.*" She shook her head. "Wasn't Orym the one who told you that, even if you find medicine, he wouldn't take it unless you had enough for everyone? I don't have the power to heal all your people, and you knew this. So why come all this way knowing it would amount to nothing but his inevitable death?"

"You know, I really don't appreciate how much interest you seem to have taken in *my* life while being caged in this paradise of yours," he growled. "Orym will take the medicine, even if I have to force him."

"I'm sure that will go well," she retorted, "but you're avoiding my question, Elnok. Why are you really here?"

"I already told you—"

"If I'm going to give you the medicine, you need to be honest with not just me, but yourself. Why are you here, Elnok Rogdul of Vutror?"

Rage and sorrow collided into him like a fresh storm off the coast, lightning and thunder raging all around him, his brother's face cast in shadow as the waves crashed over Elnok, tasting like dark putrid wine.

"Because I'm not going to lose Orym like I lost my brother!"

Fresh tears ran down his face. The goddess' face—his mother's face—stared at him unflinchingly.

"Since you seem to know *everything*, then you already know I've lost everyone I ever loved," he said, his salty tears thick on his tongue, "and I won't lose anyone else."

He stared into the face of the woman who had sung nighttime lullabies, tended to his cuts and scrapes, and taught him that, in order to be a decent human, he needed to be there for those who needed him most.

He'd failed his brother.

He wasn't going to fail Orym too.

Aretta pressed her palm to the grass, her eyes fluttering shut as golden light sprung from the ground, circling around her arms the same way it did to Sylzenya. But unlike Sylzenya, there was no cut sliced into Aretta's back. As she pulled her hand from the ground, a glowing glass vial formed out of the earth, the contents a bright white.

The magic vanished as she opened her eyes.

"Have your friend drink this, and he'll be healed," Aretta said, "But first, you, Sylzenya, and Kharis are going to hear what I have to say."

Elnok grasped for the vial, but it vanished from her hand. He'd found it—Orym's medicine—and he still couldn't have it.

"I'm not joining in your sibling fight."

"And you don't have to," she replied, kneeling next to Sylzenya, "but I doubt you want to go through the forest without these two."

Elnok couldn't refute that statement. The goddess used magic to wake up Sylzenya, the golden light highlighting her face, her dark-blue eyes deep and full as she opened them. Before he met her stare, a gaze that would surely be his undoing, he reminded himself why he came here.

He couldn't stay, no matter how badly he wished to.

Even if he was falling in love with Sylzneya, because he had no doubt that's what this was, he needed to save Orym, return to his crew, and get them off this continent before Distrathrus could take more from him than he already did.

Elnok wasn't a hero, and he certainly didn't plan to become one now.

CHAPTER 30
ARETTA'S WILLOW

Gold light swirled above Sylzenya's head, power circling and dancing in the darkness. A fluttering echoed in her ear, followed by a flash of gray and white feathers.

There is more pain than that which carves into your back, Sylzenya Phatris.

Haziness ruled her mind as she tried to sit up. The bird's wings fluttered faster in her ears, the gold light pulsing and crackling, the darkness growing heavier with each passing moment.

You will regret choosing this path. I have seen it.

Heart beating fast, Sylzenya fought for more breaths, unable to locate the bird despite its echoing voice.

There are many things that I cannot say, even if I wish to. The creature continued, its deep blue eyes piercing through the darkness, *But I will say this—be wary of who you trust.*

Sylzneya tried to speak, yell, even scream. Nothing but pain sliced through her throat.

For life there is a price, and only in pain is it made whole, Sylzenya Phatris, the bird shrieked into her ears. *Your choice has been made, and so your consequence is set in blood and stone.*

Sylzenya bolted upright. Warm light bathed everything around her. Willow branches swayed in the warm breeze, red and yellow flowers dotted the grass hugging her skin, and a familiar woman kneeled next to her, the ash-colored hair spilling onto her exposed knees.

A choke caught in Sylzenya's throat.

Mother.

Yearning and confusion rolled through her stomach. Memories of love and abandonment. Love and expectation. Hot and cold. Even though Sylzenya knew her mother and father had been under the influence by Distrathrus' blood all those years ago, the sting of abandonment still hadn't left.

She wasn't sure if it ever would.

"Sylzenya Phatris, welcome to my willow. While to you I bear the image of your mother, my true identity is that of Aretta—the goddess of life—and so, I appear as the one who gave life to you."

Sylzenya blinked hard, the image of her mother and the goddess' words disorienting. In all her years of study, she'd never heard of Aretta appearing as such, but then again, the goddess' image was never made known. She'd been depicted as a woman of all body types, all hair lengths, all skin tones. Surprised, she realized how accurate these depictions had been.

"Aretta?" Sylzenya asked, "The legends say you… died."

"The same is said about my brother, Distrathrus, and he's very much alive. And yet, in many ways, we're both dead," the goddess replied, a sad smile on her lips. "I understand my brother's blood flows through you, blocking your power and allowing him access into your mind. He has no such access here, in my tree."

Sylzenya relaxed her shoulders, a well of buried excitement rushing to the surface.

She was in the presence of *Aretta*. The heartbeat she'd always found comfort in.

“My apologies,” Sylzenya quickly said, getting on her knees, placing both hands over her heart and bowing. “Praise be to you, oh goddess of life. May my life reflect your glory and bring you honor above all things.”

“Please, Sylzenya, you may rise,” Aretta gently chided, a soft hand alighting on her shoulder. “Formalities don’t befit the situation, not with the tasks laid before us.”

Smiling, Sylzenya lifted her head. “It brings me joy to know you were never dead, my goddess. Your life has given me life; your heartbeat has given me my own. I never thought in my wildest dreams I’d behold you.”

Aretta’s smile softened. “I’ve been keeping a close eye on you, Sylzenya, ever since your first day at the temple.”

“You have?” Sylzenya brightened.

“I have. More so than you know, but I’ll explain more of this soon. First, I must wake Kharis and offer you all some sustenance. You’ve gone through much to get here and we haven’t much time.”

Sylzenya turned to find Kharis fast asleep, leaning against one of the willows. Relief overcame her, then realization hit. She thought they’d miss the tree, the willow vanishing right before they dashed for it, but then it reappeared just in time. Otherwise, the arachni poison would’ve…

“Where’s Elnok?”

Aretta smiled, pointing towards a small clearing surrounded by white-flowered bushes. Sylzenya didn’t hesitate as she ran. Everything in her body burned from soreness, cuts, and bruises, but she didn’t care. She needed to see Elnok with her own eyes to know he hadn’t died.

Jumping through one of the bushes, her heart nearly collapsed as Elnok’s pale green gaze found hers. He was sitting, his olive skin no longer crawling with black webbed veins. With his typical dark disheveled hair, he gave her a half-smile that had begun to feel like home.

“I’ve got to admit, I’ve always thought your bloodied white

robe needed a good wash, but now I don't think you'll be able to salvage a single piece of it," Elnok chided, his voice gravelly as if he'd only just woken up. "But I'd be lying if I said I wasn't enjoying the lack of material."

Sylzenya shook her head as she kneeled next to him. "Even after almost meeting your death, you're somehow more shameless than ever."

"I like to think people enjoy it."

"Most people think you're detestable."

"But what do you think?" He smirked.

Sylzenya smiled, running a hand along his stubbled jaw. "I'm just glad you're alright."

His throat bobbed, his calloused hand finding hers. Mouth parting, his eyes dipped to her lips; heat built in her stomach as she leaned in—

"Ah, well, I have you to thank for that." Elnok's smile disappeared as he pulled away, dropping her hand. "I think we better listen to what your goddess has to say so I can get what I need and leave as soon as I can."

Sylzenya gulped, a sudden, unwelcomed warmth crowding her cheeks.

"Oh." She slipped out the word like an afterthought.

A silence hung between them, as if they were back in the inn, Elnok's rope stretched across the room, the sheet draped over it—separating them.

"Orym," she whispered, the realization finally dawning on her. "You'll need to go straight to Vutror once you've gotten the medicine."

"Yes." His eyes looked anywhere but at her.

"What…" she paused, steadying herself, "What will you do once he's been healed?"

"Probably get a boat, sail away from this continent." He ran a hand through his hair. "Keep my crew safe from whatever's about to happen."

Leave.

He was going to leave. Far, far away from here. From her. She shouldn't be upset; it was a smart move. Calculated. If Distrathrus couldn't be stopped, then getting away as quick as possible would be the safest route. And yet, hearing it out loud…

It felt like a cold gust of wind on chilled skin; the reopening of a deep wound; an abandonment at the steps of a temple.

"So that's it then?" Sylzenya asked, "You get your medicine and leave the rest of us to deal with this mess?"

Elnok straightened, brow raised. "It's certainly not my mess."

"Well it isn't mine either."

He scoffed. "None of this would've happened without you, your kingdom, or your blessed goddess—and, by the way, why the fuck does she look like everyone's mother? It's… it's creepy. Unnatural."

Sylzenya bristled, leaning back. "She's the goddess of life. And— no, that doesn't matter right now. You promised me you'd be here until the end. Now you're going to walk away?"

"This is the end for me. That was the plan, Sylzenya. From the beginning, this was *always* my plan."

"*Great.* So, what? Everything else you've said to me was just one of your thieving acts? All that talk of believing in me, caring about me— it was all just a means to one of your fucking ends?"

The words slipped out before she could stop herself. Hot tears formed at the corners of her eyes. The anger was misplaced, she *knew* this, knew he'd meant his words about how he felt for her; knew he needed to save his friend; knew his land had been dying because of her and her kingdom. She wanted him to save his friend. Wanted him and his crew to be safe. But she hadn't been prepared to say goodbye. Godsdamnit, she was falling in love with this man, and he was going to leave once he got what he wanted.

And what he wanted wasn't her.

"Sylzenya, you *know* that's not true."

"You're right. This was the plan and I got distracted." She got up, wiping the tears before they fell. "Let's just get your medicine. Then I don't have to deal with a man vomiting all over the place while carrying him on my back."

His mouth thinned. "Tell me how you really feel."

"Just because you don't have any god-gifted power doesn't mean your actions don't affect anyone besides yourself, Prince Elnok Rogdul of Vutror."

His mouth gaped.

Aretta and Kharis approached.

"I'm afraid your lively discussion will need to be finished," Aretta said, "please take some time to time to clean yourselves up as I have fresh linens available. And then I need to share the truth with you all, and why I brought each of you here."

CHAPTER 31
A GODDESS

Sylzenya stood next to Kharis and Elnok as she finished her last bite of plum and dried meat, swallowing it all down with a second filling of water from her waterskin. Sylzenya was grateful for the fresh linen tunic and pants she'd been given. Her tattered Kreena robe was floating in the river somewhere, lost in the foreverness of the enchanted tree.

Aretta sat before the three of them, her face mirroring that of her mother's—all their mothers'—in the middle of a red and yellow meadow. Her white robe flowed into the grass, melting into it as if it pooled into water.

"You come here bearing many questions, some of utmost importance, some bearing no consequence," Aretta said. "Ask your first question, and we'll begin."

Sylzenya stepped forward. "How do we stop Distrathrus?"

Aretta smiled. "You cut to the heart of matters, my dear Sylzenya. Very well."

Waving her hands in the air, a swirl of petals surrounded the goddess, her body glowing and her eyes looking to the golden sky.

"As you've all come to learn, my brother Distrathrus has been using Kreenas and acolytes to store up my power in orodytes." She twirled a flower. "In our final battle five centuries ago, I dispersed my power away from him and into the land. While we can't interact with each other's power, others have the ability to do it for us. He's always been clever, so he discovered he could use Esteans to collect my power for him."

A breeze rushed by them all, Sylzenya's hair fluttering in her face.

"You three are not the first I've called here," the goddess continued, picking another yellow flower and twisting in between her fingers, "but you three are the first to have succeeded in not only finding the compass, but finding my tree."

Tossing the flower into the air, everything shifted. No longer were they in a meadow filled with golden light, but a sandstone sanctuary glowing with yellow-stained glass. A large, grand willow stood in the center of the room, its roots so big they cracked through the floors.

"The altar room," Sylzenya whispered.

"Yes," Aretta replied, "but this is the altar room two centuries ago."

A woman with black hair and dark brown skin stumbled into the room, her eyes wild as she kneeled to the floor, grasping onto one of the roots with both hands, her body erupting with magic. Yellow light circled her, cutting into her back. Gritting her teeth, she spoke words Sylzenya couldn't understand.

"'*Seek Aretta's Willow. Find the compass hidden within a willow, and you will save your people.*' This is what I had one of my birds tell this woman in a vision two centuries ago, the only information I'm able to communicate thanks to my brother's enchantment. She was a gifted Kreena. Enough power to seek me out, and yet not enough to stand out to Distrathrus. She was the perfect candidate to find my tree and destroy my brother, or so I thought."

The vision shifted, the woman using her power as she walked from willow to willow in an alcove in the temple.

"What's the meaning of this?" a familiar voice echoed along the sandstone walls.

The woman turned to find the High One at the end of the hall, fingers laced behind his back. His yellow gaze was bright, as if it were piercing through a shadow. Sylzenya could feel his cold hands on her shoulders, his voice whispering to her.

You're mine. You're mine. You're mi—

Elnok's hand gripped hers, bringing her back.

"You're alright," he whispered.

Quickly, she released his hand. "I know."

He sighed, thankfully not reaching for her again. She placed her focus back on her goddess and the vision, stepping closer to Kharis.

"Your Grace," the woman in the vision said, bowing deeply, "Some of the acolytes were observing the willows and I was checking to make sure none of them were damaged."

Distrathrus raised a brow. "Were they?"

"Not that I can tell."

He breathed in deep, his yellow eyes sharp. It sent a chill up Sylzenya's spine.

Distrathrus said, "You already know we have priestesses for such purposes. So, tell me again, what is it you're doing?"

The woman gulped, sweat shining on her brow.

"I've noticed you haven't partaken in the wine ceremonies this past week. Is it not to your liking?"

The woman backed up a step. "I've been taking a little break."

He smiled, revealing a glass of wine in his hand. "Let's be done with that little break then, hm?"

"I'd rather not, Your Grace, if that's alright."

"It's, in fact, not alright, my dear. So please, have a drink and we'll forget this ever happened. Unless you find something wrong with my wine?"

The woman looked at the wine, then at Distrathrus.

She broke into a run.

He caught her robe with his long, thin fingers, slamming her into the wall. She yelped. Gripping her jaw, he forced the glass to her lips and spilled the wine into her mouth. She screamed, attempting to spit it out. She kicked, but he dodged every attempt. Sylzenya's heart raced as the woman finally slammed the wine glass away from her mouth, the glass shattering to the floor.

Yellow eyes flaring, the High One spun her around, kicking the back of her knees with such blunt force she screamed and crumpled to the ground. Quickly, he pulled out a dagger and sliced open her Kreena cut. Sylzenya gagged; Elnok gripped her shoulder. Distrathrus uncorked a vial full of black liquid and poured it into the woman's open wound.

Sylzenya remembered what it'd felt like, Distrathrus' blood spilling straight into her cut when he'd trapped her and Elnok in the Willow Grove. Torturous black flames consuming her bones, her muscles, every living thing inside of her until she was sure she'd been turned into ash.

The woman's scream drowned out as the vision dissolved.

They were back in the temple's altar room, the same woman standing before the great willow tree, her eyes clouded. Distrathrus stood behind her with a wide smile.

"Clever, sister. Very clever. But not enough, I'm afraid." He motioned to the Kreena. "Destroy it, so my sister can't communicate with anyone else ever again."

Kneeling down, the woman gripped a giant root, her power shooting out of her body, wrapping around her, the roots, and the entire tree. Wind rushed through the room. Sylzenya could feel it brush her skin, her hair flailing with the woman's as a giant crack ripped through the great willow.

The woman crumpled to the floor. Her face was hollow, cheeks sunken into her bones and eyes bulging from her skull. Blood pooled around her as Distrathrus' shadow covered her.

Sylzenya's stomach revolted against her, but she kept it down, staring into the dead eyes of the Kreena.

Aretta finally spoke, "My brother had finally disconnected me from my creation, using my own people to destroy the roots connecting my current prison to the willow in the altar room. I'd tried many times prior with different Kreenas and acolytes during the first few centuries of my imprisonment, but after this woman, he'd finally had enough."

The temple's altar room suddenly flooded with numerous women dashing in and out of its hall, like ghosts, running on top of each other, using their power to gain a vision from one of Aretta's birds. Suddenly, the image shifted to different locations in Estea—the gardens, the temple hallways, the healing pool—where Distrathrus met each one of the women with a glass of wine and a vial of his black blood, forcing it into their open cuts.

"*No,*" Sylzenya whispered, stepping back, Elnok squeezing her tighter.

"This is *cruel,*" Kharis finally shouted.

Aretta raised her hands, the vision dissipating, returning them to the meadow. "I finally stopped my endeavors a century ago. I was wrong for inflicting such harm on my own creation. Even so, Distrathrus gained more of my power each day, getting closer to his goal of resurrecting his body and taking the land—*our* land—as his own."

The meadow disappeared again, replaced with darkness.

"But then," Aretta continued, "I had a vision of my own. A foretelling of how to defeat Distrathrus, and it involved three people. First, a Kreena with insurmountable power."

An outline of a woman erupted with golden light, a great willow rising above her head.

"Second, a prince who ran away from his crown." The next outline carved into the darkness, this one of a man holding a crown, throwing it into the shadows and running towards the woman.

"And third, a Dynami who fell in love with a king." The third outline was a man in armor, reaching out his hand towards a robed figure with a scepter in his hand.

Sylzenya stared before turning to find Elnok's brow furrowed, his finger spinning the gold ring on his pinky finger.

"In the vision, it was clear only these three could defeat my brother." Aretta continued, "And so, I stayed connected to the roots throughout the continent for an entire century—watching carefully. Low and behold, it was my brother's desperation that started it all. Elnok's parents began to stop shipping Vutrorian weaponry. They took away the only instrument capable of extracting orodyte serum for my brother's resurrection. In his inability to negotiate politically, he issued the assassination of Elnok's parents. He then sent shipment after shipment of wine, so that the next king, Tosh, would stay under his control and never limit their trade again."

Sylzenya watched as Elnok spun his ring faster and faster, her insides twisting as if she was the ring spinning around on his finger.

"It was the king's crazed state governed by the wine that drove Elnok away from his crown. And it was because Distrathrus sent more Dynameis to Vutror for trade that Kharis met King Tosh, the king's anguish over what he'd done to his younger brother softening Kharis' heart to the point of intimacy."

"You don't know anything about Tosh and I," Kharis whispered.

Elnok spun his ring even faster; Sylzenya couldn't stop herself, she held his hand. He didn't refuse her, only squeezed her hand.

"And then, when Sylzenya met her hands to the earth only a day after Elnok's escape from the dungeons, I knew. I could feel the way her power surged through the roots, the way her body could hold more power if it was given to her. I knew this was her—the Kreena needed to perfect the triad. And so, when she created her first willow, I pushed more of my power into her hands. I helped her create that first willow, gave her even more power than she had already possessed, and Distrathrus took immediate interest in her. A risk, but my vision foretold his obsession with this Kreena would be pivotal. But, I knew you'd still need more. My blood needed to flow through you; your father's willingness to carry out the deed on your ceremonial day was the final piece of the puzzle."

"*You* involved my parents?" Sylzenya spat. "They've been starving in the dungeons because of this."

"I did what had to be done," the goddess replied, "Your parents understood well enough when I visited their dreams. They did as they were told: they stopped going to the wine ceremonies, and were able to smuggle a vial of orodyte serum undetected."

"I thought it was Distrathrus who made a weapon out of me." Tears welled in her eyes as she clenched her fist. "Not *you.*"

Aretta held up her hands. "Before you start blaming prematurely, listen to what I have to say. You three are from my vision, the ones foretold to finally end my brother's plan. And so, I helped each of you by preparing you and orchestrating a way to find my tree."

Elnok stepped forward. "I can understand how Kharis and Sylzenya came into this—they worship you. But you had no guarantee I would ever step foot in Estea. I didn't have a reason until Orym became sick."

Aretta became silent, picking another flower from the meadow—a red one.

"Sometimes we must do things we aren't proud of for the greater good."

Elnok scoffed. "What the fuck are you…"

He paused. Sylzenya's lungs squeezed.

No, she wouldn't have. She was the goddess of life, not death, she couldn't… *wouldn't*—

"Just as I gave Sylzenya power, so I can take away. It's a tiring effort, and I can only do it every so often, but I needed you to seek a way into Estea, and you needed a purpose. So, I figured out what would motivate you."

Elnok's hand squeezed Sylzenya's so tight she held back a scream.

"You're the reason Orym's sick," he whispered, "the reason he's going to die."

Laying the red flower in the grass, the goddess looked up.

"Yes, Elnok," she said, "I am."

CHAPTER 32
TWO IN ONE

Hot, molten rage drowned out all other thoughts. Elnok barely noticed Sylzenya's hand in his, the comfort she brought while everything around him dissolved into fire, anger, and nothingness.

The reason he'd been looking for this damned, magical tree was to find Orym's medicine. And yet, it was this very tree, the goddess residing in it, that was the cause of Orym's death sentence. A full circle. A full fucking circle and he walked it like a blubbering idiot.

"How *dare* you," Sylzenya shouted at the goddess.

The goddess, Aretta, sat in the middle of a meadow decorated with yellow and red—orodytes and blood.

"You're the goddess of *life*," Kharis added. "How could you put someone's life on the line for this?"

Aretta raised her hands. "This is war, and like Sylzenya said the other day during your journey, casualties are expected." She looked to Elnok. "Weren't you the one who told her to keep using her power even if it killed people in your land? Does your humanity only start and stop with people who've saved you, Elnok Rogdul?"

Elnok sneered, unable to keep his body from shaking. "You don't deserve to look *anything* like my mother."

"You can place all your blame on me, or you can see who the real culprit is. My brother motivated my actions. It's *his* bloodlust that's caused my hand to move in such ways."

"Why?" Sylzenya said, letting go of Elnok's hand and stepping forward, "What happened between you two? What *really* happened?"

The goddess stood, twirling yet another flower in her hand, Elnok's stomach growing sick the longer he looked at her face.

"A lot of what he's taught you is true. We created this world together, and we loved each other while doing it. Brother and sister. Two born of one whole. But when I made humans, I discovered a joy I hadn't felt yet." She paused, a small smile peeling along her mouth. "I fell in love with one of the humans."

"I fucking hate it here," Elnok growled.

"I had children—Esteans. It's why you and Kharis can wield my power. But it caused my brother great jealousy. One night, one of my grown children went out for a night hunt, and they came across one of my brother's creatures. They were terrified, convinced it had been tracking them to kill them." She paused, crushing the flower in her hand. "In the end, they both killed each other. Both were afraid of one another, but my brother was convinced that my daughter killed his creation out of bloodlust. And so, he decided to destroy every human he could find."

Silence filled the meadow as she folded her hands. "He and his monsters needed a swift end, otherwise my creation couldn't exist in peace."

"You're right, we *can't*. And we have you to thank for that," Elnok retorted.

"But he was your brother," Sylzenya interjected, "couldn't

you have discussed the matter? Made sense of it some other way? Come to a peaceful solution instead of involving us?"

"The price for life will always be pain."

"*Bullshit,*" Elnok muttered.

Kharis tapped his empty chest plate. "But you wanted us to go to war, didn't you? You wanted to fight, and you wanted to put us to the test against his monsters; to prove we were better—that you were in the right, and he was in the wrong."

"He *was* wrong," the goddess argued. "He demanded I end all of your lives over a misunderstanding. I tried to save you."

"By threatening to do the very same to his creation," Sylzenya said, "you can't honestly stand here and blame him for everything when you had the chance to fix it."

The goddess shook her head. "I underestimated how much of a hold he has over you. Even in your right mind, you defend him over me."

Elnok's rage clipped as he ran towards the goddess, stomping on her damned flowers. "Let's get one thing straight. This isn't just your brother's fault, it's yours. *Your fault.* You were the one who fucked one of your own creations and started this. You got all those Kreenas killed. You stole my friend's life to get me here—"

"*Silence,*" Aretta boomed in a voice dark as thunder.

Harsh winds blew through his tunic, landing like a punch to the stomach, flinging him backwards into Kharis. The Dynami caught him, the man grabbing Sylzenya as well, sheltering all of them as dark clouds formed over the meadow.

"None of you seem to understand what this world is about to become—what Distrathrus is capable of." The goddess waved her hands, the clouds consuming the golden light until all that was left were her eyes—yellow glowing stones in the darkness.

Screeeeeeech.

Elnok jolted, but Kharis kept him close. All three of them breathed hard, slowly backing away together. Another shriek, this time from behind, the sound metallic and blood-curdling. Wings flapped from above, Elnok's heart racing as a guttural laugh echoed from every corner.

"*Finally, it's all mine.*"

Red light flooded his vision. They weren't in Aretta's tree anymore, nor were they in the temple's altar room. Instead, they were in a throne room, the familiar dark gray stone causing Elnok's insides to twist into themselves.

The Rogdul Castle.

But it was all wrong. The roof had crumbled, large bricks and stones littering the throne room, a dark red sun positioned overhead.

Upon the throne sat a skeleton, its crown ladened with red and blue jewels, its white shirt stained with wine. Tattered and frayed, the shirt barely hung onto what was left of his brother.

"*Tosh!*" Kharis yelled, letting go of him and Sylzenya to run forward. He collapsed at the skeleton's feet, taking its hand into his. "No, you can't be dead. This can't be real."

"That was the last of them, Your Grace," Sylzenya said, her voice distant and sharp.

Sylzenya's mouth gaped as she stumbled back, staring at the entrance of the throne room. Two figures walked in, one tall and wide, black eyes a stark contrast to white, pasty skin, the other—

Sylzenya.

But she looked different. Not lithe and strong, but skinny and pale. Sickly. She was dressed in all white, blood seeping from her back. Her deep blue eyes were gone, replaced with a clouded gaze. She placed her hand—spotted with red and black blisters—above the one held out to her — a blanched, pasty, decrepit hand.

"No more humans," Distrathrus sighed, taking the sickly

Sylzenya's hand into his. The white cloak he wore was ripped in the back, revealing sharp horns that protruded from his spine, each horn as sharp as arachni fangs. His skin looked scorched, peeling as if it was molting, the skin underneath an iridescent white and red.

"Your creation roams free," the other Sylzenya replied, her voice monotone and distant.

"And we'll rule this place together, Sylzenya, just as I dreamed we would."

"Yes, Your Grace."

Anger billowed in Elnok's chest.

"I've seen enough," the real Sylzenya said, shaking next to him.

A horde of arachnis skittered into the throne room, covering the ceiling, chittering and shrieking as Distrathrus hooked his hand underneath Sylzenya's jaw. Elnok's blood ran hot as he grabbed his rope and dagger, breaths increasing as Distrathrus forced Sylzenya's face to meet his—

"Aretta, please, that's *enough*," Sylzenya yelled.

But the goddess was nowhere to be found. Elnok clenched his jaw, watching Distrathrus drag his mouth across Sylzenya's pale neck, his clawed fingers gripping her hair and yanking her head back, her clouded eyes looking towards the arachnis crowding the ceiling.

Rage burned into fury, Elnok gripping his dagger so tight his knuckles hurt, Sylzenya screaming for the vision to stop.

"She's had *enough* of this!" Elnok yelled, spinning in circles, trying to locate the goddess.

Distrathrus ripped Sylzenya's robe down the middle, exposing her naked flesh, the god's hands running down her body.

Elnok couldn't watch any longer.

Running towards Distrathrus with his dagger in hand, Elnok cursed all the gods and their blatant treachery and their fucked up ideas of life.

But then, a scream shattered his ears as Sylzenya—the *real* Sylzenya—ran in front of him, Kharis' sword in her hands. She struck through the vision of Distrathrus before the god's hands defiled the sickly Sylzenya's body any further.

The vision dissipated, like a wave falling into the sea. Distrathrus no longer stood before them, but Aretta with the sword embedded in her chest.

The birds ceased their songs.

The goddess smiled, the same smile as his mother as she dropped to her knees, gold liquid dripping from her mouth.

"No," Sylzenya whispered, "No, I didn't mean to. I just… I couldn't watch any more of that…"

"This sword is the one you must use to pierce Distrathrus' heart—it's how he will form his true body he's attempting to resurrect." The goddess wheezed, grasping the blade with her hand, more gold liquid dripping from her palm.

Sylzenya let go of the hilt, her eyes wide. "Why didn't you stop me? *You should've stopped me.*"

"Two halves of one whole, Distrathrus and I," Aretta continued, "and so our deaths must be met in the same way. This, too, was foretold in my vision, for only through my death can my brother be killed."

Elnok stepped to Sylzenya's side, gripping her shoulder as she kneeled and held the goddess' face in her hands.

"You tricked me," Sylzenya sobbed. "*Why?*"

"You wouldn't have killed me otherwise, and it had to be you," the goddess whispered. "I'm the one who must thrust this burden onto you, and it's I who must die knowing I couldn't save my own creation." She looked up, her dying gaze staring into Elnok's with a sharp intensity. "The medicine is yours, Elnok. Your task of bringing Sylzenya here has been completed, and if you leave now, you'll save your friend. I've a gift for you, use it and you'll make it out of Lhaal Forest quickly and safely."

The vial of white medicine appeared next to her. Elnok

grabbed it, lingering on his mother's hazel eyes as she offered a sad smile. Some part of him thought to express his gratitude, but he thought better of it. This goddess didn't deserve it.

She laughed. "You're not wrong, Elnok. I don't deserve anything else from you."

He said nothing as he took the vial.

She turned to Kharis and Sylzenya. "You've been taught that only women can be Kreenas and only men can be Dynameis. It's a lie my brother concocted for more control over you all. You're both capable of every power I possess. And while his blood is powerful, my blood is stronger." She smiled. "You're *both* stronger."

The goddess looked to the golden light pouring in from the tree's power. "My birds have the gifts I've crafted for each of you, one of which will show you where my brother is currently preparing for his resurrection." She coughed, gold liquid seeping onto her white robe. "You must leave as soon as you can. There isn't much time left. With or without Sylzenya, he will find a way to resurrect himself, and he'll do it soon."

"Aretta," Sylzenya whispered, wiping the gold blood from the goddess' face, "If I go to him willingly and he gets a hold of me..."

"His love for you mirrors the kind he had for me—what we once had for each other."

Sylzenya reared back. "You and Distrathrus? You were—"

"Lovers," she confirmed.

Fluttering his eyes closed, Elnok ground his teeth. Of course they were.

"You both buried so many lies in our soil," Sylzenya whispered.

"Forgive me or not, it changes nothing. We were once one and then split in two, brother and sister. Lover and lover. Because of the power I gave you when you made your first willow, you have a piece of me always with you. Whether he realizes it or not, he recognizes it—recognizes the love we once shared. You can use this to your advantage, for while he can use his blood to stop your power, you can do the same to him, although in lesser measure." She coughed. "Going to him will be a risk, just like me giving you my power was a risk. But it's the only way, or the future I've just shown you will come to pass."

"You're a *real* piece of work, especially to those who fucking *worship* you," Elnok seethed.

Sylzenya raised her hand to him. Elnok took a deep breath and stepped back, letting his anger fume.

"I can stop his power?" Sylzenya questioned.

She nodded. "You've already done it once, in the Willow Grove when you and Elnok escaped him. You interrupted his control of the Dynameis and Kreenas, your desperation pushing into their minds, commanding them to let you escape."

Sylzenya nodded, but Elnok didn't miss the way her mouth quivered. She was angered at her goddess, and she had every damn right to be.

"If we stop him, will Tosh live?" Kharis inquired, kneeling next to the goddess.

"I can't be certain," she replied, "All my visions have shown me is that, if he's defeated, the depletion of the earth will stop, and there will be a chance to revitalize the land."

"*If* is a very important word you keep on using," Elnok growled.

"Indeed, Elnok, it is."

The way she said his name sent a shiver down his spine.

Aretta turned to Sylzenya, her breaths fading. "For life there is a price, and only in pain is it made whole, Sylzenya Phatris. Your choice has been made, and so your consequence is set in blood and stone."

"What's the consequence?" Sylzenya asked. "I still don't

understand it. Why is the gold ring turned into blood and stored in orodyte? Why was the bird in my vision killed?"

The goddess smiled, wiping a gold bloodied hand across Sylzenya's face. "I'm so sorry, Sylzenya. For everything."

The goddess' hand fell limp as she crumpled to the earth.

CHAPTER 33
FAREWELL

Sylzenya squeezed her goddess' hand until the golden light left her eyes.

Heart pounding, palms sweating, and mind reeling, Sylzenya wept. Her goddess hadn't been who she'd thought; she'd been ruthless, cunning, but most of all, desperate. In her efforts to save humans, she'd killed many, and Sylzenya couldn't blame her for such a choice. She'd been making the same decision throughout her entire time in Lhaal Forest.

But Aretta had also lied to her, shaped her to be someone Distrathrus would want for more than just power: sadistic love. A warped and twisted sort of yearning. It disgusted her. This goddess was supposed to be a deity she honored and worshiped, but she turned out to be worse than any human she'd encountered in her lifetime.

Gripping the hilt to the point of pain, Sylzenya cursed her goddess. Whether she loved or hated Aretta, she now held a sword in her hand, given a burden far heavier than any she'd felt before. Providing for her people was one thing—that she knew how to do—but to kill a god with brute, tactical force?

She didn't know how she could possibly accomplish the task.

Despite Aretta's death, the golden power of the tree didn't diminish. Her birds flew down from the sky, landing in the meadow next to her, Elnok, and Kharis.

Each of them drew shapes into the grass, the shapes glowing brighter until they raised from the ground and solidified into objects. One of them was a shield, gold-plated with intricate designs carved into its metal. The bird who created it pointed its beak to Kharis. The Dynami stood, his face stoic as he took up the shield.

"I believe I'm to be your shield, Sylzenya," Kharis said as he turned to her, his hair blowing in the soft breeze, "I'll protect you until my last breath—until Distrathrus is killed once and for all."

Sylzenya gave him a nod, yanking the sword out of the goddess' body; Aretta's flesh flickered with yellow light, transforming into sparks of power before drifting into the air.

A bird poked its beak on Sylzenya's thigh. She looked down. A compass laid in the grass. The cool outer casing was set in gold, the needle of the compass glowing a bright white.

Looking closer, Sylzenya recognized the needle's sharp shape.

"The tip of an arachni fang," she whispered.

The needle spun in circles until coming to a complete stop, pointing west—Distrathrus' location.

Taking a deep breath, she placed the compass in her linen pant's pocket, using all her strength to lift the sword she'd inadvertently used to kill a goddess. A goddess whom Sylzenya now realized she'd never known at all.

"Elnok, you've been given something as well." Kharis pointed to another bird, the creature sitting atop something aglow.

Elnok slowly approached it, the bird watching him intently until he kneeled down and observed the object. The bird flew away, the object's glow dissipating, revealing a black leather whip accented in gold.

"She certainly knew your taste," Kharis managed to laugh.

"I hate to admit it, but this is *much* nicer than my rope," Elnok replied, examining the weapon and pocketing the vial of medicine.

He's going to leave me.

Sylzenya shook away the thought as she stood. "Kharis, we better go. Elnok…"

But she couldn't finish her words as he turned to her, his face suddenly downtrodden.

"Look," Kharis interrupted, "I'm going to make sure we know where the entrance is to this tree. I suggest you two clear the air before I find it." He turned around, a heavy sigh as he continued, "Don't leave things left unsaid, trust me."

He disappeared behind a thick grove of willows.

Despite being surrounded by unparalleled beauty, it felt like they were back at the inn, the draped sheet splitting them apart.

"You were right, Syl, I'm breaking my promise to you," Elnok finally said, as if his words were trying to pull the sheet away, "You have no idea how much I wish I didn't have to leave—"

"You need to save Orym," Sylzenya interrupted, not wanting the sheet to come down again. She couldn't bear the idea of doing this without him, and yet she needed to. "I understand. He needs you more than I do."

Elnok's throat bobbed. "Just be careful."

Sylzenya blinked away the tears threatening to form in her eyes. "We'll do what we can."

"That is… less than reassuring."

"I'm not sure what else I can say. Aretta's dead, and she's left me with an impossible task. Yet, there's no other course of action I can take."

Elnok cursed as he left his new whip on the ground, taking a step towards her. She took a step back, not wanting to feel his touch, because if she did, she knew she'd beg him to stay. Any courage she could muster in this moment to go and defeat Distrathrus could be swallowed whole by this man's gaze alone.

"Syl, promise me you're going to make it out alive."

She shook her head, tilting her head to the glowing sky, the tears threatening to fall.

"I'll make it out alive, Elnok, I promise."

His footsteps crunched in the grass. She slowly backed away, unable to look at him, at her hands, at the sword—only the sky was safe.

"Look at me," Elnok pleaded.

"Elnok, I can't—"

"Please, Syl."

"I can't—"

"Sylzenya, *look at me.*"

Turning her gaze to him, the tears spilled down her face. Elnok took her hand, his green eyes glassy and his half-smile gone. It was a face she wished she hadn't seen, the kind that makes someone doing everything they can to hold themselves together only fall apart faster.

Sobs replaced her confidence as she threw her arms around his neck. Strong, tense arms wrapped around her, Elnok holding her so close she found it difficult to breathe. The tears wouldn't stop falling, everything coming to a head, the task ahead of her far too great.

Elnok had become a cornerstone over the last five days. Her life had been ripped to shreds, and now, during the most trying moment of all, he was leaving.

And she'd more than likely never see him again.

Elnok whispered her name, soft and hushed, the same way her mother and father used to when she was frightened. But it only made her hold him tighter, cursing her inability to keep herself together. Her goddess had a vision that Sylzenya would be the one to kill Distrathrus with a sword, but how could she possibly complete such a task when she could barely stand on her own two feet?

"Talk to me," Elnok whispered, his breaths brushing along her ear.

Burying her face into his warm skin, she said, "I can't do this."

"Yes, you can," he said, his fingers digging into her back. "But just because you can doesn't mean you have to."

She took a deep, shaky breath. "What do you mean?"

He paused, trailing a hand down her hip, pulling her closer. "Come with me."

"What?"

"Come back with me to Vutror. You and Kharis. We'll heal Orym, get my crew, and then we'll find a ship and get off this damned continent."

Birds chirping and dragonflies buzzing, Sylzenya considered his words. She *could* go with him, away from this daunting, impossible task, and she could live a life far away from here. She'd heard of the ocean, had seen pictures in books; it was treacherous more often than not, but it seemed Elnok felt confident his crew would navigate it well enough.

"We could," she whispered.

She felt his smile against her neck, a calloused hand wiping hair away from her face.

"Your goddess did this, not you. She can't expect her creation to clean up her messes."

Squeezing her eyes shut, Sylzenya rubbed her forehead on his shoulder. He was right—everything between Aretta and Distrathrus was a product of their own selfishness, not hers. It was unfair to bestow this on her shoulders.

And yet, there was no one else.

Monsters would kill every last human on the continent while she sailed away, leaving everyone else to reap the destruction she'd had the chance to prevent. It didn't matter that she shouldn't be responsible for killing Distrathrus. The fact remained that, according to Aretta's vision, only she could kill him.

"I can't," she whispered. "His blood still runs through my veins, and enough people have died by my hands. I wouldn't be able to live with myself knowing I could've prevented more from dying."

Elnok tensed. "But this isn't your fault."

"It doesn't matter," Sylzenya retorted, straightening and leaning back, staring into his eyes. "I've killed a lot of people, Elnok. Stolen their lives without a second thought. I may not have intended it, but my intentions don't change anything. Aretta thought she was making the right choice, but it turned out to only make matters worse." She stared at his tunic, the black texture glistening in the golden light, purples, oranges, blues, and reds shimmering. "What kind of person would I be to walk away knowing thousands of lives could've been spared by my hand?"

His shoulders drooped, his hands squeezing her arms as he shut his eyes.

"But what if you die?"

Light filtering through the surrounding willow trees, Sylzenya flexed her hand. The earth—this strange earth within this powerful tree—sang to her. But this melody was different—soft and aching, a yearning for home. It flitted through her hair, danced along her skin, and melted into her flesh.

A strange sense of calm wrapped around her veins, like vines covered in salve. If she was going to die, then she would make sure Distrathrus died with her. No more destruction by her or her people's hands; no more taking what wasn't theirs; no more death.

She needed to end it once and for all.

"Then I'll die knowing I finally did what I've always wanted." A small smile peeled across her mouth. "Being here for my people—and for the continent—when I'm needed most."

Elnok no longer stared at her. Instead, his gaze turned to the ground, his body shaking as shimmering tears fell. Filled with a new sense of purpose and longing, Sylzenya tilted his chin up. His bloodshot eyes searched hers as if trying to find some way to change what had to be done.

"Then I'll go with you," he said, standing tall.

Sylzenya shook her head. "We both have our own responsibilities. You have Orym and your crew while I have—"

"The entire fucking continent," he muttered.

She laughed, wiping the tears from his face, the stubble of his jaw rough against her fingers. She'd miss it—miss him.

"Same thing, really," she chided, brushing stray strands of hair from his face.

A harsh laugh mixed with his sobs. "And here I thought I was going to be the one to comfort you. I should've known better."

She tilted her head. "Why's that?"

"Because," he leaned down, his breaths evening out as they brushed her lips, "you persevere, even when no one has the will to do it. And while I hate your goddess to the deepest, darkest pits of hell, she couldn't have chosen anyone better to see that Distrathrus finally gets what he deserves."

Lower lip quivering, Sylzenya's smile wobbled. Her heart, her nerves, and her resolve steadied, and she didn't question herself as she said her next words.

"I'll never forget you."

Elnok's brows dipped, his grip squeezing her arms tight. A small warm silence floated between them. She wanted him to understand that, if it had been possible, she would've gone with him to the ends of the earth.

"How dare you undo me like this," he whispered.

Before she could reply, he pressed his lips to hers.

Yearning and desire spiked through every crevice in her body as she breathed him in. It was as if air no longer existed, only his calloused fingers as they caught on her smooth arms;

his heartbeat pulsing in rhythm with her own; his scent of worn leather and earthy musk draping and melting into her skin.

Sylzenya gasped as Elnok pressed her up against one of the willows, its branches and leaves a thick canopy, enough privacy even if Kharis returned. He placed his thigh in between her legs, a whimper leaving her lips as she arched her back, his large hand pulling her closer to his chest while instructing her to do as she pleased. Desperation laced through his lips, his tongue, his hands; she grabbed his tunic and ran her fingers through his hair.

"Even if this is all the time we were given, I wouldn't have traded it for anything."

Slowly, she reached for the waist of his pants. "Neither would I."

He laughed, warm and deep, a yearning already building in her chest knowing she'd never hear it again.

"Tell me what you want, and I'll give it to you," he replied, running his hand along her rib cage, stopping just beneath the swell of her breasts.

"I want to remember this moment," she whispered into his mouth. "I want to remember you like a new scar running along my body, opening whenever I think about you." She brushed her finger along his stubbled jaw, "I want to remember how, even in these past few days during my darkest moments, you inspired me to live."

"*Sylzenya*," he breathed.

But no more words left his lips, nor did they leave hers. There simply weren't enough words to describe this weaving together of their flesh as they stripped one another, the naked hardness of his skin like an ushering home as he slid into her. They were no longer separate, sharing a moment holy and strong enough to mark their souls—one they both chose for themselves. She ran her fingers along the scars on his back, careful to keep her touch soft and delicate while his strokes inside her were anything but.

She whispered ancient prayers of devotion into his ear for the last time.

One last time.

She'd offer him her worship, because he deserved it more than anyone else. And maybe it was sacrilegious of her, the highest form of blasphemy she could partake in, but her entire life had been a single heresy, bowing down and praising death and destruction. Surely, worshiping this man who loved others more than he loved himself, was the most holy thing she'd ever done in her life.

Golden light peeled from her skin, wrapping around them both as his cries joined hers. Colors flashed before her—purples and yellows and blues—a life with Elnok playing across her vision. Everything they could've been if this life had been different; if she'd never been born in Estea. If the gods had never gone to war.

Hers and Elnok's children dancing in the meadows while they sat underneath a lush willow, reading books and drinking sweet wine, laughing at whispered crass jokes and dancing under moonlit skies.

Everything burst into glorious light, Elnok whimpering her name as she held tight to his neck, grazing her lips on his throat. She bowed into him, pleasure like blooming flowers opening to the warm rays of sunlight. And then the pleasure gave way to calm, the visions of a different life fading, their last moment passing by them in fleeting colors and bitter whispers.

What they'd done together these last five days hadn't been enough—would never be enough.

She could move on, but a piece of her would always be missing.

"Alright you two, I found the entrance," Kharis yelled

through the grove. "Please, don't make me come in there and separate you both. I've suffered enough as it is."

Staring into Elnok's pale green eyes, she offered a sad smile. Elnok brushed her hair from her face, kissing her forehead for a long moment.

They quickly cleaned and dressed themselves, the euphoric moment slowly fading away, their final fleeting glances causing the new scar within her heart to break and bleed.

Sylzenya grabbed the heavy sword, its blade glowing brighter than any she'd ever seen. Elnok picked up his whip, and together, they walked through the grove. Kharis was waiting for them at the edge of the meadow, the golden light of the tree shimmering in the shape of a door. Without another word, they followed him out of the goddess' willow, entering the darkness of Lhaal Forest once again.

Elnok stepped out last.

The tree vanished.

Kharis gripped Elnok's shoulder. "May I have a quick word before we part ways?"

Elnok agreed, the two men discussing in hushed tones. Taking a deep breath, Sylzenya studied the hilt of the sword, the weight of its make causing her to feel off-balance. She readjusted herself, cracking her neck and reminding herself of everything Aretta had told her.

Her powers weren't just that of a Kreena, but a Dynami as well. Perhaps she could discuss the skill with Kharis, learn some tips to access it again so she could overcome Distrathrus' barrier.

The men returned, the two of them embracing for a moment longer than she'd anticipated. Despite the animosity she'd witnessed on their way to the tree, it seemed they'd made up their differences.

"Syl," Elnok said, releasing Kharis and grabbing her hand, "I believe in you—both of you."

Chest filling with air and hope, Sylzenya nodded, words unable to find the tip of her tongue. They stared at their intertwined hands. Calling upon every point of will in her body, she let him go, her fingers slipping through his, her heart aching until she swore a part of it cracked.

"You see the path?" Kharis asked him, pointing towards a cleared portion of trees, "It'll take you all the way out of the forest and set you straight to Vutror. It's all flatlands once you get out of here. You'll see your kingdom in the distance."

Elnok nodded, his nostrils flaring as he patted the whip on his hip, the object glowing a bright yellow.

"Here," Sylzenya said, "I want you to have this."

She dug into her pocket, taking out the compass that had led them to Aretta's Willow. The piece of bark no longer glowed.

Elnok half-smiled. "Thank you."

He took the compass, rolling it in between his hands—those hands she wished she didn't have to let go of.

As he turned, a cavern opened in her chest. He walked into the darkness of Lhaal Forest, his footsteps receding until all she could hear were the chitters and screeches of the monsters waiting for her at the other end of the forest.

Waiting with Distrathrus.

CHAPTER 34
A CHOICE

The further Elnok walked down the path of crooked trees, the more his heart faltered. He'd already stopped multiple times, turning around, considering what it would mean to run back to Sylzenya and Kharis—to help them fight.

To stay with her until the end.

But he couldn't.

Staring at the glowing medicine vial, a sweet relief etched itself into his bones; he'd done it. And yet, as the fog billowed around his thighs, the momentary relief vanished, replaced by a deep chill settling into his veins. He cursed. Sylzenya and Kharis had to fight a *god*.

How could he leave them?

For Orym.

For Orym.

A shock ran up his spine as he touched the leather of his newly gifted whip. His breaths came easier, his vision sharpened, and his limbs grew stronger. He unwound it, letting it slap against the forest floor with a loud *crack*.

Uncanny. This weapon felt less like an object and more

like a part of himself. An extension, as if he could feel the ground quiver in his veins. Perhaps he shouldn't be surprised, considering it was crafted by a goddess, but he'd never felt anything like it. He'd always gotten along fine with his sword, rope, and dagger, but now… now he had *power.*

"Power like Sylzenya," he whispered.

He shouldn't have uttered her name. It wasn't that his heart was misguiding him, but rather his heart had been split in half. Gods, he was going to return to Orym and heal him, but at what cost? Leaving behind someone he'd grown to care for just as much as his crew? And what of his role in helping humanity as a whole?

Fuck.

Sylzenya's righteousness had been rubbing off on him. Humanity's plight wasn't his to care for. Those who were closest to him… that was his humanity to save. Sacrifices had to be made to do so, and his obsession with this woman was no exception.

Fool.

This wasn't an obsession. If it *was*, he could say his unyielding desire for her was a problem.

But she wasn't a problem—far from it.

He laughed to himself. He'd gone as far as thinking she was his personal hell, and she had been at first, but it'd changed so quickly. She'd gone from devoting her life to a crazed lie to denouncing everything she'd ever known and saving his life in the process. She'd understood his pain—met him in it. They'd laughed together, cried together, held each other.

She'd been so easy to be with. He didn't just tolerate her… he *liked* talking with her, looking at her, just *being* with her.

He shook his head. Dreams were dangerous in this world. He should've known better than to grow so attached.

Turn around.

Don't let them fight this alone.

He ignored his thoughts. Instead, he ruminated on the conversation he'd had with Kharis.

"I promised I would protect you," Kharis had said, "that as long as I was by your side, no harm would come to you. And I failed, much like your brother."

Elnok had explained to Kharis he understood why.

"You forgive me because I wasn't in my right mind. Does this change anything now you know your brother wasn't either? That Distrathrus had him under his control with his blood wine?"

Perhaps it should've changed his perspective, but it didn't. Under a god's control or not, Tosh wasn't a stranger he'd met days ago—he was his brother. His protector. He'd decided to drink the wine when their parents died, and it'd been his hands that put the scars on Elnok's back.

"You never have to forgive Tosh," Kharis had replied, "I just need to tell you what he won't share with you."

The Dynami had proceeded to explain how once a year, Tosh hosted a month-long vigil in Elnok's honor, putting on multiple festivals, and scraping the last of their trading reserves to make Elnok's favorite food—raspberry biscuits. Vendors would share their fondest moments of Elnok, all the while, Tosh sat and listened, eventually retreating to the castle and crying himself to sleep. Kharis had ran into him on one of those nights, and it'd led to their relational spark.

It'd taken everything within Elnok to not break down out of anger and sorrow. He missed his brother, and hearing this made him remember what their brotherhood had been before their parents died—before Tosh went insane. His brother had always been more intentional than he ever needed to be.

Yet even this didn't change anything.

No amount of guilt or remorse could smooth over what Tosh had done to him.

"You don't need to forgive him," Kharis repeated, "but

you do need to move on. Both of you do. Whatever it means to you, do it. Never talking to him again, forgiving him and pursuing a sibling-ship… just let him know what you decide. Let the past be what it is, but don't let it take away from your future—the joys, the happiness, the excitement. You deserve more than that. And Tosh does too."

Elnok had pulled Kharis into an embrace, confessing that, even though he couldn't stand Tosh, he was glad Kharis made his brother happy.

Kharis had smiled. "We'll see each other again someday. I have no doubt about that, Elnok Rogdul. And if you can, let Tosh know I love him before you depart for your life on the sea."

Elnok had promised he would, had turned and hadn't dared look back, because if he did…

For Orym.

For Orym.

Elnok, Orym's voice echoed in his mind, *if you don't come back in one piece—*

I will.

Elnok's head swam with memories…

Let the past be what it is, but don't let it take away from your future, Kharis' voice echoed.

If I'm going to give you the medicine, you need to be honest with not just me, but yourself, Aretta had said.

I don't think I would've laughed half as often during this gods-damned famine if it wasn't for all our misadventures, Orym had confessed. *But good things must come to an end, even if it's sooner than we had hoped. And just because I'm gone doesn't mean your life stops too, Elnok.*

Elnok's breaths stalled. Sylzenya's deep blue eyes and full smile burned in his vision, a light in the darkness of Lhaal Forest.

I'll never forget you, she'd whispered.

Grinding his teeth until his jaw hurt, he cracked the whip

against the ground again. And again. And again. He hadn't told her how he'd been falling in love with her, hadn't because if he was willing to leave her like this, did he actually love her?

Orym hadn't asked him to get the medicine. Orym hadn't wanted Elnok to get it in the first place. Looking up into the shadowed sky, realization flooded him as if it was raining on his skin. He'd chosen Orym's fate for him. He'd decided he wouldn't die, not listening to what Orym kept trying to tell him:

That Elnok's life mattered too.

His choices, his wants, his decisions—they mattered to Orym, so much so his friend would probably kill him if he returned. He could hear him even now…

You left the most beautiful, intelligent, and bravest woman you've ever met to defeat a god of unparalleled power bent on destroying humanity? All because you wanted to save me? *Elnok Rogdul, I mean it when I say this—I've never been more disappointed in you in my entire fucking life.*

Learning Elnok could've helped save humanity wouldn't just make Orym mad, Orym would take it upon himself as the reason humanity was in jeopardy. He'd twist Elnok's words and motivations and think it was his fault, not Elnok's. Orym would be healed, but he'd be a guilt-ridden mess for the years to come.

As much as Elnok hated to admit it, he would be too.

I'll never forget you.

Sylzenya's eyes, full and constant as the sea.

I'll never forget you.

Her strength an anchor in his body.

I'll never forget you.

Her love a salve on his twisted, broken heart.

Taking one more look at the glowing medicine vial, Elnok spun around.

Dozens of glowing red eyes shone through the shadows, a small chorus of chitters echoing along the branches, flitting through the trees.

He dug in his pocket and took out the compass to Aretta's Willow. Hope sparked in his chest—it'd begun to glow again, and he knew it wasn't pointing towards the tree. It would be pointing towards the one who had killed the goddess, the one who had her power.

It was pointing to Sylzenya.

CHAPTER 35
TOGETHER

Sylzenya stepped over a collapsed tree as she and Kharis made their way through Lhaal Forest. She held the new compass flat on her palm, the direction never shifting nor shaking, the archni fang's tip pointing west.

Towards Distrathrus.

Silence deafened her ears. Not only were there no signs of monsters, but the god hadn't attempted to speak into her mind since they'd left Aretta's Willow. It worried her greatly.

"He knows we're coming," Sylzenya whispered, gripping the hilt of her new sword—the sword that would kill him.

"You sound surprised," Kharis replied, eyes glowing with power despite his chest plate empty of orodyte. He'd learned to access Aretta's blood in little to no time.

Sylzenya hadn't tried yet, afraid she might welcome Distrathrus and his poisonous words into her mind again.

"I wish *we* could've been the surprise," she mumbled.

Kharis chuckled. "Would've been a nice advantage, but I'm afraid we won't have many of those with this fight. Although, if Aretta says we'll be able to do it, we should trust that."

"I find it hard to trust her at all."

"Then why are you doing this?"

Sylzenya turned to him, his golden hair shining against the glow of their swords.

"Because what other choice do we have?" she asked.

He grunted in affirmation. Tapping her fingers against the sword's hilt, she slowly gripped it and tugged—it's weight far too much.

"How are you able to do it?" she inquired, "Your power, I mean. I managed it once by accident."

"Do as I do," Kharis replied.

He took a deep breath. Sylzenya did as well, the rot and mold in the air causing her to cough. Kharis patted her back, a small smile on his mouth.

"Again."

He took a breath. Sylzenya took a breath. This time, it stayed down. They repeated this another four times, her heartbeat slowing, her focus caught on a tree up ahead. The limbs, long and spindly, reminded her of reaching fingers.

"Good. Now *feel* your body. What are your feet saying? What are they experiencing right now? Your knees? Your thighs? Hips?" He continued his list until he got to the crown of the head. "Did you consider them all?"

Sylzenya took another deep breath. Her feet walked upon the dry earth, aching from the journey. Her knees wobbled, her thighs asking for rest. She continued until she reached the crown of her head, wishing she hadn't asked what it was thinking.

Elnok.

Elnok.

Elnok.

She shooed his name away. "Yes, I've considered them all."

"Now, bring them together as one. Let them speak to one

another, support one another, find strength in one another. Let your body be together."

She furrowed her brow. "I'm not sure what you mean?"

He tilted his head. "My chest is heavy from exertion, while my feet are light as a feather. I bring them together, and now I'm allowing them to aid each other. I do this with each part of my body, and then—"

Bright yellow crackled along his skin, his veins, and into his eyes. Smiling, he rushed in front of her, becoming mist.

"Understand?" he asked, appearing by her side again.

Sylzenya put her hands on her hips, raising a brow. "This was less of an explanation and more of a demonstration. I still don't understand."

"Just give it a try."

"Easy for you to say."

Kharis laughed. "You really did spend a lot of time with him, didn't you?"

Something caught in her throat. "What do you mean?"

"You just sounded a bit like Elnok, that's all." His smile faded. "From what I can tell, you did everything in your power to keep him safe, even fighting me, *helping* me, really. You did what I couldn't. I'd heard the rumors of how Sylzenya Phatris was a powerful Kreena, but it seems your power doesn't just stop at your abilities."

Sylzenya's face burned. "I disliked him at first. Strongly, I might add. He had no respect for our culture, no reverence for everything I'd dedicated my life to…" she trailed off, the image of his half-smile and pale green eyes flashing through her mind. "But he'd been right, in the end."

"What a bastard."

"The worst of them all," she agreed.

They laughed, the heartache easing a little.

She continued, "So… deep breaths, letting my body talk to itself, and then connecting it together? That's your secret?"

"Afraid so."

The last time she accessed Dynami power, she'd been able to escape Distrathrus' presence. Perhaps this is how its power worked, and if it did, then she needed to know she could harness it at any moment.

She needed to know she could stay in control of her power when facing Distrathrus.

She followed Kharis' instruction. Calling upon each part of her body, she led them together, pushing them to work with one another, to aid each other's burdens; she needed to trust every part of herself—a strange feeling.

Thump.

Thump.

Thump.

Her goddess' heartbeat thrummed against her skin. No longer did it bring her comfort, but it would bring her power, and for that reason alone, she would continue to reach for it.

Suddenly, a shock rushed through her veins. Opening her eyes, she could see deeper into the forest, as if some of its shadows moved aside for her. Ears perking up, she realized the forest wasn't silent, there were chitters and screeches somewhere far in the distance. With each step, her muscles no longer spoke of tiredness, but of anticipation.

The dark barrier of Distrathrus was nowhere to be found.

This time, she wouldn't celebrate. She would remain cautious of his tricks until the very end.

"Of course you'd be a natural." Kharis smiled. "Estea's greatest Kreena, indeed."

Blinking quickly, she let out a breath, her heightened senses dissipating, the power flowing out of her body and into the ground.

"Alright then, your turn," Sylzenya offered, motioning to the ground. "Is Estea's greatest Dynami ready to harness the earth's power?"

He listened intently as she described her method.

"Think about it as if you aren't trying to get your body to

work as one, but rather, your body is a part of something more, something bigger than yourself. Feel how similar the roots underneath the earth are to the veins running along your arms. Or how the dirt covers the layers beneath it like our skin covers our blood and organs. You aren't separate from it, but rather, you are whole because of it. But most importantly, listen for Aretta's heartbeat. She might be dead, but her blood still lives within the earth, and it's through this you'll be able to create."

"You have no liberty to make fun of my instructions when yours sound this absurd," he said.

She scoffed. "Absurd? I don't think I could've been any clearer. Do you know how many acolytes I've had to aid in a given year?"

"Three?"

"Try all of them. Now, *just give it a try*," she mocked.

Suddenly, the earth tremored. Sylzenya smiled, Kharis' eyes wide as he turned to her.

"And you say *I'm* a natural."

Kharis shook his head. "That wasn't me."

Sylzenya turned to find trees shaking and then crashing in the distance.

"Fuck," Kharis said, unsheathing the sword Elnok had given him, "Do you think you can spear the serpentums with your roots like last time?"

Digging her shoes into the dirt, she felt for the earth. "I can try."

"I hope you can turn that *try* into a *yes, Kharis, of course*."

"Why?" Sylzenya questioned, her palms sweating.

Kharis arced his sword. "Because if I had to guess, we've got about ten headed our way."

Her mouth gaped. "*Ten?*"

Metallic chitters split the air, echoing through the trees and filtering across the dirt.

"Great. Arachnis too." Veins crackling and eyes glowing,

Kharis readjusted his weapons. "Suppose this will be our first test to see if we can kill a god, won't it?"

Arms shaking and legs wobbling, Sylzenya felt for the earth, her goddess' heartbeat thrumming heavily through her body. The roots writhed underneath the ground as yellow sparks erupted from the ground, circling her arms and slicing into her back—that familiar pain grounding her.

"I suppose so," she muttered under her breath.

A tree to their left crashed to the ground, the earth shaking violently under their feet. Sylzenya remained upright, Kharis keeping her steady with an outstretched hand. A large iridescent figure slithered over the toppled tree. Clouded eyes blinking, the serpentum tasted the air with its black tongue, directing its head downwards—smelling them.

More trees collapsed. Two. Three. Five. Seven.

Ten serpentums.

Tree branches shook, the sound of skittering on the forest floor sending pumps of adrenaline into Sylzenya's limbs. Large bulbous arachnis crawled over the serpentums' bodies. A shriek sounded from above. She turned skyward; a myriad of dark beady eyes glistened against the dark leaves. Sharp legs splayed like skeletal wings attached to bodies as black as obsidian and as large as boulders.

They were surrounded.

Kharis cursed. "Sometimes, I really hate being right."

Sylzenya felt for the roots beneath their bodies, feeling for what little life still remained in this deadened forest, for there wasn't enough to create, only to use.

A serpentum struck.

On instinct, Sylzenya raised a single hand in the air.

Roots shot up from the ground, aimed for its throat, but it dodged. The sharp branch clipped its scales, a thin cut appearing along its neck. It hissed, turning around and flicking its large tail for her chest. Kharis picked her up, jumping backwards with a quickness that left her breathless.

"Thanks," she gasped.

"Less talking, more roots," Kharis commanded.

She called upon the earth again, sending her power deeper into the soil, curling her fingers as she directed the roots to become sharper—deadlier.

The serpentums and arachnis charged.

Kharis left her side.

Sharp, pointed roots emerged from the ground, sweat beading along Sylzenya's forehead as five of them successfully found their targets. Two serpentums and three arachnis shrieked as they fought to free themselves from the roots lodged through their throats, spearing their mouths, and protruding from their heads. A third serpentum barely dodged the attack, shaking the ground more with its quick movements.

"Keep going, Sylzenya!" Kharis yelled from somewhere above.

She looked up; the man's glowing veins shone against the serpentum's head as he struck the monster clean through its snout. Kharis yanked the sword out of its head, disappearing into a light mist as he struck the arachnis jumping for him.

He appeared again, another serpentum snapping at him. Sylzenya sent an attack, missing the large creature by a hair. The warrior dodged, falling to the ground with a thud. Sylzenya felt for more roots, crafting their heads into sharper points than before—

Crack.

Wind whipped past her as she skidded across dirt, her tunic ripping against sharp rocks. She coughed up saliva and blood, spitting it out quickly as she placed her palms on the ground. A serpentum and four arachnis charged towards her, their jaws wide and poison dripping from their fangs.

"Come on!" she cried, the roots responding far too slow.

She'd expected to hear Distrathrus bait her, whisper into her mind how he could save her—but she heard nothing.

Perhaps Distarthrus had given up on her. Perhaps he *would* let her die after all.

"*On your right!*" a voice yelled.

Sylzenya looked up, heart battering like a bird trapped in a cage. A man with disheveled black hair flew through the air, his body blazing with golden power.

"*Could use a vine or something!*" Elnok yelled.

Her breaths faltered.

He came back.

New adrenaline pulsed through her as she slapped her hand against the ground, grasping not for roots or vines, but for the dirt itself. If all of Aretta's creation could obey her, then so could the dirt. *It had too.*

And so it did.

A pile of solid earth rose up—a pedestal—and Elnok didn't question it as he used it to jump even higher. He unleashed his glowing whip, cracking it across the serpentum's jaws, the weapon hitting once, twice, three times with thunderous cracks.

The serpentum's head fell in pieces, sliding in opposite directions. The monster collapsed to the ground. Elnok landed in front of her, that damn half-grin plastered on his handsome mouth.

"Miss me?" he said through panted breaths.

"*Damn you,*" Sylzenya breathed, the smile on her own mouth wide and impossible to hide. "I thought you left?"

Elnok smiled, sliding his hand over her arm, her skin electrified despite the chaos around them.

"I came back," he said.

"*Obviously.* But why?"

"You know why."

Tears burned her eyes. "What about Orym?"

"I couldn't—"

A serpentum appeared from behind Elnok, jaws extended as it rushed in. Sylzenya stepped in front of him, raising both hands into the air. The roots from before finally shot up from the ground, piercing the serpentum through its jaw, its throat, and all the way down to its belly.

She turned around, Elnok cracking his whip as he sliced another serpentum straight through its jaw, the mouth crashing to the ground, the serpentum writhing on the forest floor.

"I hate to admit it," he said, "but your goddess makes some damn good weapons."

Kharis landed in between them, grabbing their shoulders with such force Sylzenya almost slipped. Sweat slid off his body in rivulets, his veins glowing golden.

"Look, this is all very sweet, but we need to prioritize," he said, voice like that of a commander, "Let's finish off these last serpentums and arachnis, and then we can chat, hm?"

Elnok clapped his back. "Right."

Sylzenya sent her power into the dirt again. "Ready when you both are."

Kharis smiled. "From here on out we work together. Elnok's whip is the most effective besides Sylzenya's roots. Sylzenya, how are you doing with those?"

Her back stung and her head had become fuzzy. She wanted to fight through it, but the blood dripping down her back said otherwise.

"Not great," she admitted, "Getting them up and out of the ground takes a lot of power."

"That's fine. We need to save you for Distrathrus, so don't go for the big kills. Just assist us where you can. As for Elnok, slice up these monsters as much as possible. I'll do what I can to steady them and give you a good shot."

Elnok grinned. "Sounds like fun."

Kharis smiled even wider.

Jumping high into the air, Kharis soared towards one of the monsters. Sylzenya called upon the dirt and sent a mound of it up to meet him. He used it the same as Elnok, stepping on it and sending himself up and over until he landed on top of a serpentum headed their way.

"Have I ever told you how sexy you look when you use your magic?" Elnok yelled as he ran towards the serpentum.

Sylzenya smiled, shouting, "What else can your whip do besides slice through monsters?"

He cackled. "What do they teach you at that temple?"

Digging into her bones, she timed his jump with the dirt, pushing him up with her power. Kharis had sunk his sword into a serpentum's head, the monster writhing but steady in one spot. Elnok flew forward, cracking his glowing whip across the serpentum's head, jaw, and throat, nearly hitting Kharis.

"By the gods, *are you serious?*" Kharis yelled as he jumped off, "Nearly removed my legs from my torso!"

"Would you hate me if I told you I've only been aiming for their necks this entire time?"

A shriek sounded behind Sylzenya. Whipping around, she wrapped her power around some of the protruding roots, the ones that had missed the serpentums in her first attack, and pushed them forward. One hit a serpentum's clouded eye, black liquid seeping from their eye sockets while another root found its way down a second serpentum's throat, impaling it from the back of its neck out into the rotten air. Another speared through three arachnis

"Keep going!" Kharis shouted.

Sylzenya moved quickly, assisting Kharis and Elnok where she could, providing them stepping stones and digging up roots whenever she could find the strength.

Suddenly, the shrieks of the final handful of monsters changed, no longer high pitched, but lower, a resounding call that made the earth quake. Before she could react, the final serpentum and arachnis retreated into the trees, scattering in different directions. Slowly lowering Kharis and Elnok down on a mound of dirt, Sylzenya crumpled to her knees, a sharp, pulsing pain in her back spreading into her limbs.

Elnok cursed as he rushed to her, lifting her tunic.

"That's a lot of blood," he whispered.

Kharis let out a cry, falling next to Sylzenya, his eyes wide and breaths coming in fast.

"My back," he breathed. "I don't remember a serpentum getting me."

Elnok lifted his shirt as well. "It wasn't a serpentum."

Sylzenya's mouth gaped, the pain still riding along her own back. "Did he get his own cut?"

"He did."

"What?" Kharis yelled. "I have a Kreena cut?"

"You have both Distrathrus' and Aretta's blood in your veins, like me," she replied, "They don't play well together, and life demands a price from you now because of it."

"*Shit,*" Kharis cursed. "Elnok, I need you to cauterize it."

"I have a better idea," Elnok replied.

Vision blurring in and out, Sylzenya dug her fingers into the dirt. Elnok rummaged in his clothes, pulling out a glowing object—the compass to Aretta's Willow.

"Well, Kharis, I guess I can name you an honorary Kreena now," she breathed.

"This is worse than getting slashed by an arachni."

"You know, it's nice to hear a Dynami say that." Turning to Elnok, she said, "Heal him first. A new cut is barely tolerable. I'm fine."

Elnok huffed a laugh. "Gods, you're incredible."

A smile found her mouth while Elnok pressed the compass to Kharis' back, the Dynami yelling in relief as his first cut healed; the first man in Estea to have ever gotten one.

Elnok moved over, pushing the compass against her skin, the chill causing her to yell in surprise.

"It's alright," Elnok chided, running the object along her back.

The cold felt good.

Sylzenya asked, "So it still works? The compass to Aretta's Willow?"

"It's what led me back to you."

She turned, pulling her shirt down and staring long and hard into his face. His beautiful, wonderful, handsome face she thought she'd seen for the last time.

"I still don't understand. Why did you come back?"

Getting on his knees, Elnok gently grabbed one of her hands, running his fingers over her knuckles, the gesture so normal it made her skin warm.

"Orym told me to come back in one piece, and I realized I wasn't going to be able to do that." He looked up, eyes locking with hers. "Not without you."

Despite the chill of the forest, Sylzenya swore a warm breeze brushed along her skin, like a fresh summer day after a long winter freeze.

Perhaps it was the exertion of her power or maybe the near-death experience, but Sylzenya couldn't hold herself together as she grabbed him into an embrace. She hadn't wanted to admit it, but his absence had reminded her of the day her parents gave her to the temple. So much love, so much desire to be with someone, only for them to walk away because of "duty." It'd killed her inside when she was a child, and she thought she'd understood it better as an adult. She was hungry for the love and affection she'd willingly given to someone else. And while Elnok had walked away, it'd only been for a moment.

At the end of it all, he did what no one else had done.

He came back when it mattered most.

He breathed into her neck, cupping her head with his hand. "And I'm not letting you and Kharis fight this god alone. We need to see this through together."

Together.

Together.

Together.

She squeezed him tighter. The sweetness of that word, the comfort and safety it sang in the air, gave her a strength she didn't know she'd been needing for this final confrontation with Distrathrus.

"Together," she breathed.

Elnok released her, looking up to Kharis and extending a hand. "You too, Kharis."

Kharis stepped next to them, taking Elnok's hand, resting his other on Sylzenya's shoulder. She smiled, grabbing his hand.

"Who would've thought it'd be us three?" Kharis asked, taking a knee, "I supposed Distrathrus has taken something from all of us."

Her parents and childhood. Elnok's family. Kharis' lover.

"Bastard," Elnok agreed.

"Then let's end this." Sylzenya said, standing up.

The forest looked to have been trampled by giants, most of the dead trees sprawled on the ground, creating a pathway to the end of the forest. She checked her compass.

The path led straight to Distrathrus.

"Of course that's where he is," she whispered, grabbing the hilt of her sword.

All three of them walked along the path, finally arriving at the Willow Grove. Sylzenya's first willow tree stood tall, its green leaves a luscious waterfall.

But Distrathrus' marble throne was gone.

Instead, a great hole sat in its place, a flight of stairs leading down into the earth, glowing orodytes lining the path.

"The passage to the orodyte mines," Sylzenya said, her heart pounding as she stared into the steep stairwell, "Distrathrus wants us to meet him down there."

"Is there no other entrance?" Elnok inquired.

"No," Sylzenya said. "This is it."

"Then we march forward and remain wary of any traps he's laid out for us," Kharis said.

“A fairly sound plan, given our circumstances,” Elnok said, rubbing the back of his neck.

Sylzenya rolled her shoulders, gripping the hilt of the only weapon able to kill Distrathrus’ god-form. The only weapon that could end him—the god who’d controlled her since the day she stepped into the temple—once and for all.

“Well then,” she finally said, “let’s go kill a god, shall we?”

CHAPTER 36
A CELEBRATION OF BLOOD

Orodyte cast a soft glow on the marble steps, the path growing steadily steeper as they continued down into the earth. Sylzenya fumbled her hand over the sword's hilt, practicing a quick grasp while trying to remember Kharis' instruction on how to use power like a Dynami.

Distrathrus still hadn't spoken into her mind since Aretta's Willow. The dark barrier hadn't been erected, her power flowing through her with ease, her goddess' heartbeat loud and clear.

He was expecting them.

And as they walked deeper into the earth, she couldn't help but imagine him waiting for them down in the mines. He'd be sitting on his throne, an evil, cruel smile on his crooked face. Monsters surrounding him, all evil, no light.

Sylzenya took a shaky breath.

Elnok's warm hand intertwined with hers.

No one spoke. It felt as if anything they said from now on would be heard by him, used by him, taken by him. And yet, the silence felt far more deadly than any word they could've spoken to one another.

"Sylzenya?" a familiar feminine voice said, echoing along the walls.

Heart stopping, Sylzenya halted. Straight black hair catching the orodyte's light, Nyla's amber eyes shimmering against her pale skin. Her Kreena robe was ripped to the seams. Blood was splattered everywhere and her arm was bleeding onto the steps.

"*Nyla?*"

"Fuck," Elnok muttered.

"What happened?" Sylzenya meant to step forward but Kharis and Elnok held her back.

A trap. This *had* to be a trap. But her friend was hurt—badly.

Nyla stood before them, shaking. "So much blood. It isn't stopping, Sylzenya, so much blood…"

Her eyes rolled back. Sylzenya lunged forward.

"*No,*" Kharis demanded.

"She's *hurt,*" Sylzenya said.

"It's what he wants."

But Nyla was about to fall down the steep stairs.

Freeing herself from Kharis and Elnok, Sylzenya ran forward and caught her friend.

"What happened?" Sylzenya asked.

"A celebration," her friend whispered.

Her eyes distant.

Clouded.

Vines crashed through the ceiling. Nyla gripped Sylzenya's shoulders. Sylzenya tried to break away, but she wasn't fast enough; roots and vines wrapped around her, digging into her skin.

"*Syl!*" Elnok yelled, lunging for her.

But more vines and roots launched out of the ceiling, grabbing Elnok and Kharis.

"He's been expecting you three," Nyla said, a wide smile on her mouth.

"*Nyla!* Listen to me, you're not yoursel—"

Vines wrapped around her mouth, digging into the sides of her lips.

"Follow me," Nyla commanded.

Vines bit into her flesh, cuts and scrapes blooming with blood. The vines moved in response to Nyla's silent commands, forcing Sylzenya down the stairs. Elnok and Kharis followed, their grunts echoing along the stone walls. Sylzenya turned the corner with Nyla, and then light flooded a large, open cavern.

Massive clear orodytes lined the walls, ceilings, and floor like the stained glass in the temple. Falling from the ceiling were large wispy roots. More small clear orodytes dotted the deep brown branches, twinkling like stars.

The legends had been a lie.

Orodyte was still produced here.

Underneath the roots stood a tall orodyte pedestal, something large, dark, and pulsing sitting atop it. It thrummed rhythmically, a heart bleeding on stone.

Distrathrus' heart.

Dark liquid dripped down the large piece of orodyte, pooling into a moat filled with glowing, golden liquid–*Aretta's blood.* A sudden urgency rushed through her veins. It was right there, the thing she needed to spear through with her sword, and then everything would be done.

Distrathrus would be dead.

Clank.

Sylzenya jumped. A Dynami stood next to the heart, a large, glowing hammer in his hand. Muscles rippling, he swung the hammer down onto a table attached to the pedestal, another loud clank ripping through the cavern.

Sylzenya's breath caught.

On the table was a yellow orodyte.

Another loud clank and the hammer shattered with the orodyte. The gold liquid spilled off the table and into the moat, gurgling and hissing as the pieces of stone and steel disappeared into its depths.

"Ah, Nyla, thank you for welcoming our long-awaited guests," Distrathrus announced as he stood.

In the center of the strange cavern was a long golden table. Countless wine glasses littered its surface, chairs lined the table…

Filled with people.

Distrathrus' pale skin shone in the dimly lit cavern, his white robe etched with gold and splattered with wine—or maybe it was blood. Long, white hair fell to his waist, his straight nose seeming to bend in the stark shadow and light. His yellow, severe eyes pierced into her.

Welcome home, he whispered into her mind.

Sylzenya shivered, biting her tongue so hard she tasted metal.

"Dynameis," Distrathrus said, "would you please remove their weapons? This is a celebration, after all. No need for more bloodshed."

Elnok and Kharis cursed. Sylzenya closed her eyes, trying to connect to the vines.

But the barrier had returned, taller than before—thicker. No cracks were in its surface.No heartbeat thrummed through her body.

This had been a mistake.

Three Dynameis approached, each of them wearing bright glowing orodytes on their chest plates. One by one, they took their weapons, Sylzenya's sword last. Desperation laced her veins as she lunged for it, only for the vines to pierce her wrists, hips, and thighs.

"Perfect." Distrathrus smiled. "Nyla, if you could escort them to their seats? Except for Elnok, of course. Dynameis, you may restrain him."

Elnok fought against the men as the vines released him, but the warriors were too fast and strong. Without his whip,

Elnok was outmatched. Sylzenya's stomach dropped at the realization.

"Sylzenya, I think you'll be happy to see who I invited to join us tonight." He said.

Sylzenya frantically searched the table; it was filled with Kreenas, each one with clouded vision and a gaping mouth. But it wasn't until she turned her gaze to the two seats placed on either side of Distrathrus that she lurched forward. A woman with long ash-colored hair and dark eyes, and a man with a strong chin and her same deep blue eyes.

Her mother and father.

"*Sylzenya—*" her mother began, but Distrathrus shushed her. She obeyed.

The vines unraveled as Sylzenya and Kharis fell into their chairs. She made to stand up, Kharis following her, but Distrathrus raised his hand, halting them.

"Look a bit more closely, Sylzenya and Kharis."

Dynameis stood behind her parents, each of them holding a glass vial filled with black liquid.

Distrathrus' blood.

She turned to Kharis, his face losing all color.

"I've kept my word, your parents are in good health. I'd hate for that to change."

Nyla sat down next to Sylzenya, her twisted smile never leaving her mouth as Distrathrus continued. "Now that everyone is finally here, let's get onto the celebration, shall we?"

He began pouring wine into empty glasses.

"What celebration?" Sylzenya asked, her parents trembling as they stared at their wine glasses.

"Oh yes, we practiced this, didn't we, Theraden?" Distrathrus looked to her father. "Why don't you tell Sylzenya what's happening tonight, hm?"

Throat bobbing, her father turned to her, fear riddling his eyes. "Tonight—" he stopped, turning to Distrathrus. The god smiled, clapping her father's shoulder. Her father winced. Sylzenya clenched her fists.

"What have you done to them?" Sylzenya demanded.

Distrathrus held a finger to his lips, the Dynameis with the blood vials stepping closer to her parents in response. Sylzenya scraped her nails along the table.

"Tonight, Sylzenya," her father turned back to her, his mouth trembling, "Distrathrus will use our goddess' power through a Kreena to free himself." Sweat beaded down his face as he glanced at Distrathrus. "And you're to be the one to do so. A great, wonderful honor."

Distrathrus continued pouring the wine. "See? A celebratory night indeed!"

"I won't do it," Sylzenya stated.

Distrathrus' smile vanished. "Sylzenya, this is your great purpose, the one I've been preparing you for ever since your parents left you at my temple's steps. Remember that, Theraden? How she begged to go with you but you made her stay. With *me*?"

Her father's lips curled.

"Don't you dare speak to him like that," her mother hissed.

Quickly, one of the Dynameis took her shoulder, uncorking the vial.

"*No!*" Sylzenya shouted, her heart deflating as she turned to Distrathrus, hating how he'd already placed so much power over her. "Please, leave them alone."

He smiled, motioning the Dynami to stand down.

She gulped. "Distrathrus—"

"*Your Grace*," he interrupted.

One of the Dynameis stepped to her father, uncorking the bottle. Her father trembled, leaning away. Sylzenya stopped, digging her fingernails into her palm.

"Your… Grace." The words grated out of her throat. Painful and sharp.

The Dynami stepped back.

She shoved the anger down.

Brute strength was gone. Now, all that was left was tact.

While he can use his blood to stop your power, you can do the same to him, although in lesser measure.

It explained what happened back in the Willow Grove when her and Elnok had escaped—she had dulled Distrathrus' power, the control he had over the Kreenas and Dynameis in the grove, allowing her to get to her willow tree and use her power. She hadn't stopped his control entirely, but rather, she'd disrupted it with her own demands.

She'd taken them into her own control.

Glancing over at Elnok, she hoped he would catch on to the distraction she was about to pull. Elnok furrowed his brow at her, but she looked away before Distrathrus could take notice.

Straightening her posture, she laced her hands on the table, willing each Kreena to turn their head and stare at her hands as a test.

They did.

"Your Grace, I met your sister, Aretta," Sylzenya said.

He continued pouring. "And how is she?"

"Dead."

The wine poured over the glass, spilling onto the table. "Yet another reason to celebrate."

"You loved her. Deeply."

He continued pouring, the wine dripping onto the floor.

"She betrayed me, Sylzenya. You know this, as did she. I never harbored any love for her."

She knew what she needed to say—what she needed to bring to light. And if her plan worked, then she'd command the Dynameis to release Elnok, buying him time to slip out of their grips and grab the sword.

She'd have to keep Distrathrus' undivided attention on herself for as long as she could.

"And yet, love is why this all started in the first place," Sylzenya replied, "You were jealous of her humans, how she took one as her lover."

Her parents and Kharis stared at her warily, but Sylzenya remained poised.

"She was a *traitor*," he shouted, yellow eyes flaring.

"You *loved* her. More than just as your sister." She paused, breaths shaking. "You two were lovers. Intimate."

The wine poured onto the floor, splashing at his feet.

Perfect.

She continued, "But she loved her creation more than you. She treated you poorly, Your Grace. She treated you like scum of the earth when all you wanted was her love."

He stopped pouring, mouth trembling. "She told you the truth."

"Yes," she confirmed. "How you two were one and then split—brother and sister, lover and lover. And then, one of her humans and one of your monsters killed each other. How she should've treated you differently—better. She regretted it. And both of us," Sylzenya pointed to herself and Kharis, "told her she treated you wrongly."

Furrowing his brow, Distrathrus set down the pitcher, tapping his fingers on the table. "And what did she say?"

Sylzenya gulped, not daring to glance at Elnok in case Distrathus noticed. By the looks of the Kreenas, their hands hanging limp by their sides and their eyes wandering, her plan was working.

"That she had no other choice," Sylzenya said, "because she seemed to believe neither of you could fix what was broken through anything but war."

"It's the only way."

"Not always, Your Grace."

Distrathrus cackled, staring at the ceiling. Sylzenya couldn't stop herself as she glanced at Elnok.

He'd escaped.

The Dynameis were swaying, hands at their sides, their gazes empty and wandering as Elnok silently moved through the shadows. He was mere feet away from the Dynami holding their weapons when he turned, finding her eyes, mouthing for her to keep going.

Maintaining her steady breathing, she looked back to Distrathrus.

"And what is it you propose, Sylzenya?"

"You could change the will of your creation," she said, her words slow, trying to buy what time she could, "have them treat humanity with neutrality, and we can do the same. We could live in harmony as it was always meant to be."

His laughter stopped, smile falling from his face. "How intriguing."

Standing up, he walked around the table, stopping behind her, his cold hands gripping her shoulders. She refused to flinch, needing to play this all the way through—needing Elnok to grab the damn sword.

"You were right," Sylzenya said, willing her hands not to shake. "This is my home, and we can make it a home for your creation as well."

His breath brushed her ear as a bead of sweat trailed down her back.

"You sound just like my sister," he whispered, gripping her tighter, "right before she betrayed me."

Her stomach dropped as Distrathrus rushed for Elnok. Without thinking, she stood to stop him, but her body halted of its own accord. She tried moving her leg forward, but it wouldn't.

Panic gripped her chest.

What was happening?

Distrathrus grabbed Elnok by his hair just as his hand brushed the hilt of the sword. Pulling his head back, Distrathrus commanded the Dynameis to aid him. They raced to his side, holding Elnok down by his shoulders.

"You must think me simple, Sylzenya," Distrathrus shouted, turning to face her, eyes wild, his smile unnerving. "Just as you can feel when I'm limiting your power, I feel when you're limiting mine. I know your mind's been poisoned away from me. I've seen it, *felt* it. This bastard of a thief and my whore of a sister have done it to you thoroughly."

Sylzenya tried to speak, but her tongue refused to move, her mouth sealed shut.

Distrathrus kept smiling as he turned back to Elnok. "You've been a thorn in my side long enough, *Prince* Elnok Rogdul of Vutror."

Elnok grinned. "Strange. I feel the exact same way about you."

Distrathrus yanked Elnok's hair back further. Elnok winced. Sylzenya tried to yell, but it was useless.

"How about we duel to solve this problem?" Distrathrus suggested.

"Duel? With swords?" Elnok asked. "Not very god-like of you."

"I could snap your neck and have it be done with, but you deserve something a bit more… *exciting*." He leaned in close, running his nose up Elnok's cheek, the sight causing the hair on Sylzenya's neck to rise. "I want your blood to decorate mine and Sylzenya's home. I want it to stain and serve as a reminder for what happens to those who try to take that which is *mine*."

Elnok seethed. "It won't be my blood on this floor."

Distrathrus smiled. "Dynameis, bring us some weapons. Seems this celebration will call for blood after all."

"Let me use Sylzenya's sword," Elnok argued. "What's the point in a duel if there's no real chance of killing you?"

The god smirked. "Your confidence is… endearing."

"Or perhaps I'm wildly naive."

"Perhaps you are." The god raised a brow. "You may use

the sword my sister cursed to kill me." He turned to Sylzenya. "We'll do it right here so everyone can watch."

Panic seized her, but she couldn't do anything. Not even her body shook in fear for what was about to take place. She'd never witnessed Distrathrus' sword abilities, but he was confident.

That worried her greatly.

A Dynami with clouded eyes approached Distrathrus, offering a sword glowing fresh with orodyte serum.

"It's not for me," he smiled, pointing to Sylzenya, "it's for her."

Her stomach dropped.

"You said *you* wanted to duel me," Elnok retorted.

"And you will, through her." Distrathrus grinned wider. "Sylzenya, take the sword."

Sylzenya tried fighting against it, but she was no longer her own, only her thoughts and her pain stayed with her. The barrier didn't just stand between her and her power any longer—it prevented any connection with *herself*. It wasn't so much a barrier, but a large endless pool, and she was drowning in it.

Power and pain rushed up her arm as she took the sword, its cold hilt like ice in her hand.

"Very good, Sylzenya," Distrathrus said as he approached her, "You see, the closer you are to my heart—my beautiful piece of flesh resting atop the orodyte pedestal—the more effectively I can control you. A little secret I purposely kept from my sister." He paused, stroking a piece of hair behind her ear, "Now, let's show Elnok why you're *mine*."

CHAPTER 37
SACRIFICE

Sylzenya's hands moved without her wishing it, her body stolen from her. Perhaps it'd never been hers to begin with, being born in a kingdom where she would be destined to be given to Aretta's temple.

Given to Distrathrus.

It all felt strangely poetic, the way she gripped the cold, sword's hilt in her hand instead of dirt caught underneath her nails. A strange mockery of her life that the person who hadn't sought to control her, hadn't asked anything more of her besides to be who she was, failures and all, now stood across from her with a glowing sword in his hand. Sweat beaded down his face, shouting at Distrathrus that he refused to fight her.

But Elnok was going to finally learn what she always knew to be true: Distrathrus—the High One—played by his own rules. There would be no stopping him.

Aretta's vision had been wrong.

Distrathrus' laugh echoed. "If you wish to kill me, Elnok Rogdul, then you'll have to start with her."

"*Coward,*" Elnok shouted, "Too afraid to fight your own battles, god of chaos?"

There was no time to prepare herself for what happened next. Pain shot through her legs as she sprinted forward, sword aimed for Elnok's chest as she lunged for him. But Elnok was a far more skilled swordsman than her and Distrathrus.

He dodged her attack, but he didn't counter.

"Syl, you need to snap out of it," Elnok begged.

Body surging with power, she lunged again, this time for his neck. He parried, sliding a foot behind him as he caught her weight. Yellow light clashed as he spun under her sword, grabbing her shoulder from behind.

Sylzenya didn't miss the growl reverberating through Distrathrus. She could feel it in her veins, the grip of Distrathrus' blood turning into ice; realization thrummed through her.

His true form was exposed, and Elnok was proving more deadly than he'd thought.

He was afraid.

Her lips finally undid themselves. "I need you to hurt me. Once you do, use the sword to kill his heart."

"*No.* You can stop this," Elnok said.

Before she could argue, her mouth sealed itself again. She gripped his wrist, and in one smooth movement, she whipped him over her shoulder. Elnok grunted, stone cracking underneath the force of his body. Blood ran down his arm, her nails biting into his skin.

Elnok spun, an outstretched leg colliding with both of hers. She tumbled, metal scratching stone as her sword clattered to the floor. Elnok jumped on top of her, gripping both her arms as he pinned her to the ground.

"I'm not going to hurt you," he panted, "so you better get your act together and regain control from this weakling of a god."

Hot fire stoked in her chest as she pushed against him, the anger coming from elsewhere—from Distrathrus.

But Elnok held her fast.

A voice, deep and guttural, released from her throat, "Your days were numbered the day you entered my kingdom, Elnok Rogdul."

Elnok's eyes widened as her goddess' power transformed, no longer golden light but black flames. Veins turning dark as ink, Sylzenya launched Elnok off of her. He flew through the air, sword still in hand as he slammed into the cavern wall. Orodyte crumbled from above as he slid to the ground.

She wanted to retch.

"Up, Sylzenya," Distrathrus commanded from behind her, "I've had enough of his insolence."

His control wrapped around her like vines. Gripping her sword so tight her knuckles cracked and bled, she stalked towards Elnok. He was still slumped to the ground, his head bleeding.

She tried fighting against Distrathrus' barrier, the pool of blood she was drowning in, no longer able to find purchase within herself.

Get up, she thought, trying her best to shout it at him. *Get up, Elnok!*

He turned his gaze to her, sorrow filling his face.

No, she shouted into the void. *Get up! Please, dear gods, get the fuck up!*

Teeth clenched, Elnok slowly rose to his feet.

"I'm not going to hurt you," he breathed.

Her lips loosened as she screamed, "Stop acting like a prince and think like a godsdamn thief. Do what needs to be done."

"*No.*"

"You're the better fighter," she yelled. "Stop letting me get the upper hand and end this. End me, if you have to. Think about your people, about Orym—"

Her mouth closed again. She cursed herself. Distrathrus was doing this on purpose; he was allowing her to say the words he knew would keep Elnok in this fight. Digging deep into herself, she fought for her body—fought for the golden power to overtake his blood and flow through her veins. She clenched her jaw, pain slicing into her back, down her spine, and up her neck, cracking into her head.

She drowned further still, yellow glowing eyes staring into hers.

You're mine.

She launched forward.

Metal against metal screeched in her ears. Elnok's pale green eyes filled with anguish as he pushed against her. She stared at him, pleading with her own eyes—he needed to end this. To end her.

Hope ignited in her stomach as she stumbled back.

He jabbed. She parried. He spun with a quick slice to her thigh, but she caught it before it could touch her. Elnok was gaining ground, his movements growing faster, his sword close to finding its mark. He was going to do it. Sylzenya begged it from him, that he might kill her if it meant Distrathrus would finally be defeated.

Elnok parried one of her blows and, instead of dodging, he crashed into her, pinning her to the ground with the sword at her throat.

Do it. Please. Release me from this hell.

Elnok growled, "Do you really want me to hurt your most powerful Kreena, Distrathrus?"

A dark laugh filled the cavern as Sylzenya's tongue loosened.

"Do you wish to kill the one you love, little thief?"

Elnok's grip faltered.

No.

Sylzenya tried to stop herself, but it was too late. Elnok's moment of hesitation was all Distrathrus—all Sylzenya—needed.

She drove her sword into Elnok's stomach.

"*No!*" Sylzenya screamed, her mouth now free.

"*Elnok!*" Kharis' yell came from somewhere behind.

Blood filled Elnok's mouth, dribbling from his lips as he fell. Sylzenya scrambled to her knees, her body her own again, bile rising in her throat. Her blade protruded out of his back, red blood dripping onto the clear orodyte floor.

"Syl—" he breathed, grabbing her hand, "Sylzenya."

"No, no, no," she repeated endlessly as she gripped his head, his hand, her eyes telling her the truth but her heart denying it. She hadn't stabbed him. Elnok wasn't dying. This was just a nightmare she would wake up from, and he would be next to her, fast asleep and perfectly healthy.

She hadn't killed him.

"I—" he choked, fingers squeezing hers. "You need to end this."

"You said we'd do this together, remember?" Sylzenya sobbed. "So you can't die. Just— Just stay with me, alright? *Please,* stay with me."

He coughed up blood, his hand sliding up her face.

"Sylzenya, I love you."

His hand fell limp, his gold signet ring slipping from his finger, tumbling across the clear orodyte floor, mingling with his blood before falling into a thin crack.

For life there is a price, and only in pain is it made whole. Your choice has been made, and so your consequence is set in blood and stone.

Tears welled in her eyes as she gripped his face.

Her fault. *This was all her fault.*

A long shadow consumed her as a spindly hand settled on her shoulder.

"See, little thief?" Distrathrus grated, "She was always mine to keep, yours to lose."

Red filled Sylzenya's vision as she grabbed the sword out of Elnok's hand—the sword Aretta cursed to kill Distrathrus—and spun around, shoving it into the god's stomach.

Suddenly, her body became rigid. Tears stopped running

down her face as she stood, her hands still gripping the sword, the pale-faced, yellow-eyed god of chaos staring at her—smiling.

"Wrong body, I'm afraid," he hissed, yanking the sword out and dropping it. No blood ran into his white robes.

"*Save him*," Sylzenya yelled. "If you ever truly cared about me, then you'd let him live."

"My sister said the very same thing when I killed her human lover," he snarled.

"*You're out of your godsdamn mind.*"

"No, Sylzenya." He gripped her jaw, pain cracking along her mouth, "*I* am a *god.*"

Rage and hatred swirled in her mouth as she spat her blood on his twisted face.

He took a deep breath, wiping it off, "We're celebrating tonight, remember? You're going to resurrect my true form while our little prince-turned-thief decorates our home with his blood. Now, let's not waste any more time."

He grabbed her arm. Elnok's breaths were nothing but wet gurgles, but she couldn't escape the god's grasp.

She'd failed Elnok, Kharis, Nyla, her parents, her people… she'd failed everyone.

Distrathrus forced her to her knees before his altar.

"Now," Distrathrus hissed into her ear, "place your hands in Aretta's blood, and *create life.*"

Tears clung to her face as she took in a deep breath, willing herself to fight—but there was nothing left to hold onto.

It was over.

She released the breath, shoulders slumped and hands dipping into the gold liquid surrounding the altar.

"But there's no soil," she whispered.

"You won't be needing it."

Power ignited in her veins, that of Aretta breathing life again, but it wasn't the same.

Thump.

Thump.

Thump.

Distrathrus' heart thrummed through her, dark and heavy. His claws ripped into her mind, in her limbs, moving through her veins. He was using her as he always had.

As he always would.

"*Sylzenya!*"

She looked up. Nyla's amber stare found hers, the cloudiness in her gaze drifting in and out of focus. Dried blood trailed down her face, her body hunched over as she kneeled with all the other Kreenas before the altar, circling it.

"He's going to kill us!" she screamed.

"*Silence,*" Distrathrus commanded. "Create life, all of you."

Suddenly, a bright yellow light flooded the cavern, the vat of orodyte serum blinding like the sun. All the power he'd collected over the centuries, stored at this altar, was now being used to resurrect him.

Every Kreena screamed, their shouts echoing off the walls as blood poured out of their backs and onto the ground.

Sylzenya's heart stopped.

She wasn't going to just help resurrect Distrathrus' body through the orodyte serum—she was going to be extracting every Kreena's power with it.

Blood for blood.

Life for life.

"All life comes with pain," Distrathrus whispered into Sylzenya's ear. "And with it, a sacrifice of great price. But that's what these Kreenas have been made for, their power enough to help you push my sister's blood into my heart. Just enough to form my true body to what it once was." He slipped a piece of her hair behind her ear. "But while they'll die, you'll live. And don't worry, Sylzenya, I'll help you forget all these people. All this death. Even the scar on your back. I'll give you a blissful life by my side, as I always promised. No more pain ever again."

No more pain.

She could forget… he would help her forget. No memory of all the horrors she'd committed. No more pain slicing down her back. No more pain plaguing her. No more memories of the lives she'd stolen. No more slow torment blooming in her heart, twisting around her like vines, swallowing her whole. All her life she'd been in pain.

She didn't want it anymore.

She ignored Nyla's desperate cry, silently hating herself for it. Distrathrus would make her do this one way or another, and she was his anyways. Diving deeper into the pain, she let herself drown, allowing Distrathrus complete control. Sparks of light bloomed from the orodyte serum, but she found no beauty in it.

All she saw was death.

The liquid crawled out of the moat slithering like a river of snakes up the sides of the pedestal, and flowing into the large exposed heart.

Pain sliced into her back, and she screamed. The heartbeat of Distrathrus' bloodied flesh boomed louder. More orodyte serum flooded upward, through the crevices of the stone, covering the altar more and more until it and Distrathrus' beating heart glowed with power.

Kreenas all around her cried out in agony.

She glanced towards Nyla. Light leaked from her friend's hands, her skin turning paler and paler, cheeks turning hollow and blood dribbling from her mouth.

"You will forget all of this," Distrathrus whispered, "I promise."

The amber in Nyla's eyes turned white and lifeless—

A loud crack sounded, Distrathrus' cold grip leaving her as he fell to the floor. A gold shield clanked to the ground.

The shield Aretta had crafted for Kharis.

Sylzenya no longer drowned.

The orodyte serum stalled. Pulling back from the pedestal, Sylzenya splashed her hands out of the moat. The Kreenas' screams ceased, replaced with heavy breathing and cries of relief.

"*Hurry*," Kharis said as he gripped Sylzenya's arms.

She wobbled to her feet, clutching Kharis as he helped her walk towards Elnok, the cursed sword lying next to him.

"*Shit*, Dyna—" But Kharis couldn't finish his thought.

Glowing figures appeared before them, tackling Kharis and shoving Sylzenya away. Too weak to fight back, she crumpled to the floor, her back aching and bleeding.

Elnok's pale eyes found hers, his blood pooling around him. He moved his mouth, forming words she couldn't hear. She reached for him–

"*Sylzenya*," Distrathrus shouted, "I'm done with these delays."

Body turning rigid, Sylzenya stumbled back to the pedestal, placing her palms back in the orodyte serum, the power within her reconnecting to it. She tried yanking her hands away, but it was no use.

A flash of motion, then, "*Get away from her!*"

Sword still embedded in his stomach, Elnok jumped in front of her. He staked the cursed sword through Distrathrus' neck.

The god fell, Elnok on top of him.

"*Elnok!*" she shouted.

He looked to her.

"End this," he cried, pulling the sword out of the god and spinning it to her on the floor.

Her fingers shook as she gripped the hilt.

"You're more powerful than him, Syl. He's nothing without you, *that's* why he needs you."

Distrathrus' spindly fingers gripped Elnok's throat. He

sputtered blood, his eyes closing shut as he scratched at the god's hands.

"Why won't you just *die?*" the god yelled, ripping out the sword in Elnok's stomach.

Distrathrus smiled as Elnok's blood poured over him.

Head reeling, Sylzenya's fear transformed into rage.

Thump.

Thump.

Thump.

Aretta's heartbeat. She looked up. The roots hanging from the ceiling… they were from a willow.

Sylzenya's first willow.

CHAPTER 38
YOU WILL BE A GODDESS

ONE YEAR AGO

Thump.

Thump.

Thump.

Sylzenya dug her fingers deeper into the damp soil, the golden light of her goddess' power trailing wide circles around her wrists, up her forearms, and slicing deep into the soft flesh of her back. Cold sweat dripped from her brow, trailing down her nose and watering the earth as a green sprout rose from the dirt.

"This is your last creation for the day," the High One announced, "Yet it should be just as fresh and sturdy as your first. Do not cease until it is so."

Sylzenya pressed her palms with more force, her arm muscles aching. Green leaves pushed out from the ground. A golden trail of light spun around the leaves, guiding them upward, raising them to the sky. Green gave way to brown, soft bark cracking into place, forming a tall treek trunk. Awe filled Sylzenya's lungs as bright green fronds burst from the top of the trunk, yellow light sparking outwards and filling the sky with what looked like stars. Lush shade hid away the sun.

"Very good, Sylzenya," the High One said, his bare feet stopping in front of her, his pale skin glowing against the gold power. "You may cease."

Sylzenya released her hands, her goddess' power retreating into the dirt. Her third willow of the day was complete.

"I tried something new," Sylzenya said, the warm blood from her cut seeping into her white robe, "I produced more leaves than the one from this morning. I wanted the acolytes to have more shade when they practice."

The High One smiled as he touched the soft green leaves. "I dare say you succeeded."

The willow stood tall in the temple's garden, providing shade on a patch of grass overlooking a small pond filled with water lilies and silver fish. Bright sunshine gave way to a crimson red evening, a soft breeze brushing along her skin, stinging the open wound on her back.

"Let's see your stone."

Sylzenya obeyed, pulling away the dirt that surrounded the willow's trunk. A yellow glow fought through the soil, lighting her eyes once she dug far enough to retrieve it. Carefully, she wrapped her fingers around it, the once clear stone now pulsing with a yellow light.

"Your Kreena Rite is only one year away. Has it truly been nine years already?" he asked.

Sylzenya smiled as she joined him, the water's smooth surface broken by fish splashing, sending ripples across the pond. The orodyte glowed in her hand, its sharp edges pricking her skin.

"Of course not, Your Grace. I'm still a youngling of fourteen years with twin plaits in my hair and dirt rubbed on my nose."

The High One laughed. "A day I will never forget."

Her smile fell at the High One's words.

"You still miss your parents, Sylzenya?"

"Of course not, Your Grace," Sylzenya replied with a feigned smile, a sharp sting running along her cut.

"Not often do you lie to me, but when you do, it's clear. Ever since the day you stole that plum and blamed the squirrels years ago, I've known."

"The squirrels did steal them, I swear," she urged, a small laugh leaving her mouth.

He laughed with her, their voices filling the night air.

"I am sorry, Your Grace," she finally said, smoothing her white robe.

"The squirrels will forgive you," he jested.

"Squirrels might, but will you?"

The High One's wrinkles deepened as his brow furrowed. "My life is lonely, Sylzenya. It's not often that I think about family. When I do, it's of our priestesses, our Kreenas, and our acolytes. That is my family, and so it's been yours these last nine years. We must remain as such."

She rubbed the pad of her finger along the sharp edges of the orodyte.

He continued. "To have your parents dismiss your wishes and leave you at the temple all those years ago… It's never an obligation for a child to remain here, and yet they did so anyways. It was selfish of them. Cruel. This is how you feel about them, is it not?"

"I feel no such things, Your Grace," Sylzenya replied, the ache in her back growing as she closed her hand around the orodyte. "It would not be our goddess' way."

A few stars began to burn in the night sky.

"Nor is lying."

Sylzenya closed her eyes, begging the cut on her back to cease burning.

"My parents gave me to the temple out of love and duty."

"And yet, pain does not go unnoticed," the High One replied, his hands behind his back as he stared at the pond. "It is meant to be felt. It's the price for life, and it aids you. Feel it, let it be with you, and you'll find greatness."

Crickets and the croak of frogs bathed the night air.

"Is that how you found greatness, Your Grace?"

He stared into the sky, a small silence spanning between them.

"Was it not you who told me you were going to become Estea's greatest Kreena one day?" he inquired.

Sylzenya's lips thinned. "The words of a child."

"The dream of a goddess."

She turned to him, his yellow eyes glowing as bright as the orodyte.

"And so you shall be one, Sylzenya," he said, eyes lost in the burning stars, "You'll be the goddess this kingdom has needed for centuries. By my side, we will see Estea survive this famine. Together, this land will become as great as it once was."

CHAPTER 39
THE PRICE FOR LIFE

Sylzenya's first willow sang to her, the muffled thump of her goddess' heartbeat reaching out through its roots.

Thump.

Thump.

Thump.

The final act of Elnok's life was giving her power—the object to destroy the god who controlled her and everyone on this continent.

She wouldn't let Elnok's final moment be in vain.

She ran for the altar, sword in hand.

"*Stop, Sylzenya,*" Distrathrus shouted, throwing Elnok's lifeless body to the ground.

But Sylzenya breathed deep, connecting every part of her body until they worked as one, unparalleled strength ripping through her as light crackled along her skin.

Power thrummed fast and hot through her body as she landed on Distrathrus' bloody heart, sword high and ready to plunge into its beating flesh—

The dark barrier crashed down on her.

She shouted in anger as the sword grew too heavy, its

weight throwing her backwards. Strong fingers gripped her shoulders, pulling her off and slamming her to the floor.

The sword clattered away.

The thrumming heartbeat of her goddess ceased.

Eyes wild, Distrathrus steadied a sharp dagger to her throat. "You were supposed to resurrect me, Sylzenya, not *kill* me."

Sylzenya gripped his arm, scratching and screaming for him to let her go, her windpipe slowly crushed by his grasp, black stars appearing at the corners of her vision.

"How could you do this to me?" he asked, tears spilling from his eyes, dropping onto her heated skin. "You… you were everything to me—"

"*You're a fucking monster!*" she shouted, the vision of Elnok's lifeless eyes causing her vision to blur.

Distrathrus' yellow eyes widened. He dropped the dagger, releasing her throat and cupping her face instead.

Wheezing, Sylzenya tried to break free from his grasp, but exhaustion pulled at her like a heavy anchor. Her hands frantically felt for the sword—it *had* to be nearby.

"*My Sylzenya,*" he whispered. "I should've put my blood into your cut years ago so I had complete control of you… it was my plan, but I didn't. I *couldn't.*"

Confusion pulled at her mind, her fingertips fumbling until she found the cold hilt of the sword.

"What are you talking about?" she choked, grabbing the blade.

He shook his head, smile wide and crooked. "You were devoted to me. You adored me, even when my blood's potency in the wine grew weak. Out of thousands of Esteans, you *never* left my side. And now… I almost killed you. *My* Sylzenya."

She stilled.

Sylzenya recalled those moments where they'd laughed together and walked in the gardens during fresh spring days, discussing new vegetables to create and different ways to provide for Esteans. He'd committed atrocities, controlled her and everyone around her, and yet... She finally saw what he'd been hiding in plain sight this entire time—even from himself.

"You—" Sylzenya faltered, searching his eyes. "You grew to care for humans."

His smile fell. "No. No, I didn't. No, no, *no*—"

"You once told me the priestesses, Kreenas, and acolytes were your family. You said I was the closest you'd ever had to a daughter."

Elnok's blood coated his face, mixing with his tears as his body shook.

"Distrathrus, you can let us live," she begged, keeping him focused on anything but her desire to see him dead, "you can be better than your sister."

Yellow eyes searched hers. His smile cracked. Tears streamed down his pale face.

"No... *no.*" He shook his head and yelled, "Can't you see? I don't care about humans; everything I did, it was for you. For *us.* So when I took this world, we would create something new out of it. You and me. Just you and me, how it was always meant to be."

She pulled her face out of his grasp, crawling backwards. He didn't pursue her. Sylzenya surveyed the chaos surrounding them. Kreenas bleeding into the floor, gasping for air. Kharis held down while a vial of Distrathrus' blood was poured into his cut. Elnok's lifeless body lying in a pool of his own blood.

Distrathrus extended his arms, pleading for her to return to him.

If her heart could crack and spill, then it would've. This was Distrathrus' fault, Aretta's fault—and it was hers.

"I'm not your sister, Distrathrus," she whispered. "I'm not Aretta."

"But you're a *goddess,*" he shouted, "*I made you.*"

Sylzenya called on her muscles to work as one again, but there was no response. Her power was still blocked.

"I'm not a goddess, Distrathrus. I'm not separate from my people or this world, no matter how much you want me to be," Sylzenya said, gripping the sword with both hands. "I may have power, but at my core, I'm just a human."

She spun, screaming at the weight burdening her arms as she lifted the sword high in the air, her shout a final prayer ushered into the sanctuary as she pierced his heart.

Black blood spilled and sputtered, its warmth coating her hands and face.

Distrathrus' yellow eyes flickered as he fell to his knees, reaching for her. "But…" he gasped, his fingers catching her clothes, "But you were *mine,* Sylzenya."

"No," Sylzenya said through stray tears. "I belong to no one."

A contorted grimace took over his face, a strange laugh leaving his lips. Sylzenya backed away, a shiver running down her spine.

"It's too late for this land," he croaked, his laughter growing louder, "My sister's blood will be consumed by my dying heart thanks to the power you've already given it. All you humans will die with me and my creation. If I can't have you or this world, then *no one can.*"

Sylzenya dropped the sword, turning back towards the pedestal.

Impossible.

The large heart's rhythm had slowed, but it continued to absorb Aretta's golden blood. The Kreenas surrounding the altar started screaming again, their bodies shriveling as their bodies continued to drain of blood.

Sylzenya looked at her hands, her power still dormant, his blood still controlling her.

No more of this.

Climbing onto the altar, Sylzenya fell to her knees,

Distrathrus' heart squelching underneath her weight. Ignoring the stench, she dug her fingers into its flesh.

"What are you doing, Sylzenya?" Distrathrus gasped.

Her neck twitched remembering Distrathrus' words to Elnok, *you thought she could be yours, but you knew from the moment we met she would always be mine.*

Curling her fingers, she pushed past his damn blood, a crack rupturing in the barrier of her mind.

You must prove yourself ready, and so far, you've only proven how far from it you are.

Gold light circled her arms, her torso, her entire self as she commanded more of Aretta's power through her body. Distrathrus' barrier cracked more, power pushing through.

"*Sylzenya!*" he screeched.

Your parents proved who they were—who we always knew them to be—delirious, selfish, and hostile. Wasn't it I who told you these very things?

Gritting her teeth, she leaned forward, Distrathrus' heart thrumming against her skin as if it were frightened of her.

After all these years, why are you choosing to doubt me now, Sylzenya?

She cried out as pain sliced through her back, golden power dragging along her skin, passing into Distrathrus' heart—both of them seeping warm blood down the altar.

A looming silence fell on her.

You're mine.

Sylzenya clenched her jaw. "Not anymore."

The barrier shattered into a million pieces. Gold power consumed her, a scream pushing out of her throat, tears streaming down her face.

Thump.

Thump.

Thump.

Distrathrus' blood fled from her body. Freedom filled her lungs.

Bright golden light flashed under her palms. She thought of Druenia, all she and her people had taken from them. She thought of Elnok, his half-smile and pale green eyes bringing a smile to her lips.

No matter what she did, she'd always been enough, with and without her power. She'd loved, she'd cared, and she'd destroyed. Digging deep into her nerves, she called on that power that had killed so many, transforming it into something different—something that could heal.

Elnok had been right. She would never be a hero, but perhaps, she could cease being a monster.

She'd give back everything her and her people had stolen.

A harsh gust of wind whipped around her, so powerful it could topple ancient trees. Her fingers dug into the soft beating flesh, sending the orodyte serum out of Distrathrus' heart and back where it came from.

Into all of Druenia.

She screamed, the pain no longer in her back but in her heart—ripping and tearing as she pushed harder than ever before. Light blinded her as golden power spiraled out of her, into the air, into the earth, and around her body.

Then, she thought of Distrathrus. The control he had had over her, the way he had used her, abused her—her and all her people.

She allowed herself to feel the emotions for what they were.

Rage and sorrow. Betrayal and joy. Dread and freedom.

Roots of her willow climbed down to the altar, surrounding her, spearing Distrathrus' heart. More orodyte serum spilled from it, her power continuously pushing it back into the earth.

Distrathrus' screech reverberated through her ears, his sharp nails clawing at her skin. Her willow roots formed a cage of branches, separating her from Distrathrus.

From everyone.

Suddenly, sharp pain shot through her chest. She didn't stop. Another shot of pain ripped through her leg, her torso, and into her neck.

"*Sylzenya!*" Elnok's familiar voice shouted, "Stop!"

A familiar scent rushed past her nose. Musky earth and worn leather.

He was alive.

She screamed a cry of relief. It didn't matter how or why Elnok no longer lay in his pool of blood, but she couldn't stop. This needed to end.

Everything became shadow as the roots closed in on her, crushing her; Distrathrus' dying heart beating frantically underneath her. The heart's acrid black blood spilling all over her body, into her mouth as she became flush to the sulfuric scent. Piercing blue eyes flashed through her vision—the gray and white feathered bird from her vision crushed by twigs, its face shifting in and out of focus, melting away until it transformed into something else, something human—

She looked at a reflection of herself.

Her head became dizzy, her power fading…

Thump.

Thump…

Thump……

Her goddess' heart beat slowed with hers, dying with her—

No. That wasn't right, it didn't *feel* right. This wasn't her goddess' heartbeat, but her own. She felt for Aretta's heartbeat one last time, needing to feel it, hear it…

Thump.

Thump.

All she could hear was her own, and yet, her last remaining power echoed with it.

Realization thrummed with the heartbeat, slow and steady against her chest:

The power she used to receive her vision in the altar room,

to escape the Willow Grove with Elnok, to fight in the forest… *to kill Distrathrus.*

Ever since Aretta's blood had been seared into her back at her Kreena Rite…

It hadn't been her goddess' heartbeat she'd been hearing.

It'd been her own.

Her own power.

Disthrathrus' scream consumed her as his beating heart ceased, her last breath leaving her body with it. Even if it was only in this moment she finally understood, she couldn't stop the smile peeling across her lips: Elnok had been right.

She'd always been stronger.

She let the truth she learned as a child wash over her. All her life, she'd known life came with a price.

This time, she would let it be hers.

CHAPTER 40
IT IS FINISHED

Elnok screamed for Sylzenya, the light from her body blinding him. Her yells echoed in the cavern, filling it with her pain and power. A rush of wind threw Elnok away from Distrathrus who had been poised to strike her with a sword.

The god erupted with golden light.

Sylzenya's yells ceased.

"*No!*" Elnok shouted as he rushed for her, the pain of dying nothing compared to the sight of Sylzenya's body being crushed by her own creation. "*Sylzenya, stop!*"

Blood no longer spilled from Elnok's chest, his limbs strong and his lungs gulping in air. He swore he'd been dead, but somehow he was back. Now, all that mattered was saving Sylzenya. He moved for her, his hand reaching out as the thick roots covered the heart—covered her.

But it was too late.

The large heartbeat ceased. Distrathrus' screeches turned silent as the god's human body convulsed, eyes rolling to the back of his head. Black liquid oozed out of his yellow eyes. A cut suddenly ripped down his face, throat, torso, and both legs. A lone piece of orodyte fell out of his chest and into the stream of blood.

Yellow light pulsed once, twice.

Then it turned clear as crystal.

Elnok growled. That damned goddess hadn't tried to kill her brother all those centuries ago. She'd kept him alive this whole time—gave him her own blood in an orodyte.

Damn her.

A great trembling shook the earth, sending Elnok backwards with a thud. Yellow sparks floated in the air, dancing like bugs on a warm summer night.

The wind stopped.

Silence ensued.

And then the silence fell as a familiar voice yelled for him. Elnok turned to find Kharis running towards him, his eyes aglow with power and veins crackling with light.

Kharis slid to his knees, staring at Elnok's stomach with wide eyes.

"You're healed," Kharis exclaimed.

Elnok lifted his blood-stained clothes. He placed his hand over his stomach, the skin smooth and even.

"She saved you," Kharis said as he turned to look at the large cocoon of roots, "Sacrificed herself for all of us."

Elnok grabbed Kharis by the collar, "Help me get her out. She doesn't die, not after this."

Kharis didn't argue. Hot adrenaline rushed through Elnok's veins as he climbed the thicket, splinters from the roots pricking at his palms.

"Elnok," Kharis said, "if she didn't make it—"

"Less talking, more digging, Kharis," Elnok seethed.

A woman's voice called from below, asking for Sylzenya's whereabouts.

"She's under this somewhere," Elnok yelled back.

To his surprise, the woman climbed too, worry lining her face as she started to tear apart the roots with them.

It was Sylzenya's friend—Nyla.

Elnok broke apart what had to be the hundredth root when he finally saw it—ash-colored hair.

"She's here!" he yelled.

Kharis and Nyla dug with him, breaking roots and throwing them to the orodyte floor as more ash-colored hair was uncovered. Sylzenya's body was coated in black blood. Elnok grabbed under her arms and Kharis gripped her waist as they lifted her up and out of the mess. Elnok's throat constricted at what he saw—roots pierced through her back, her leg, and her neck.

His mouth went dry as they quickly lowered her off the altar.

Her chest suddenly moved, eyes fluttering open.

"Elnok?" she rasped, blood dripping from her mouth. The branch piercing just underneath her clavicle moved with her breaths, causing her to grit her teeth.

"I'm here," he breathed, "You're ok, everything's going to be ok."

"Is he dead?" she whispered, her voice weak.

Elnok nodded, tears forming at the corners of his eyes. Nyla placed a hand on his shoulder.

"You killed Distrathrus," Nyla spoke, her voice shaking, "You stopped him, and you saved us."

Sylzenya's eyes brightened, the deep blue burning like sapphires.

"Nyla." She reached out a hand. "You're alright?"

Nyla cried. "Yes, yes, I'm alright. But by the gods, Sylzenya…" She broke down, squeezing Sylzenya's hand tight. "What do we do? How do we save her?"

Breaths short and hands shaking, Elnok looked to Kharis.

The warrior's mouth thinned. "I don't know."

"It's alright," Sylzenya said, "As long as Distrathrus is dead, that's all that matters."

Elnok cradled her head, his lip quivering. "I didn't die on you, so you better return the favor."

A faint smile graced her lips. "I wish—" she coughed, her eyes pinching in pain before she continued, "I wish we had more time."

A watery laugh came out of Elnok's mouth. "Don't go stealing my lines like that. It's not very original."

"Now you know how dramatic you sound."

"Syl…" He breathed her name as a tear streamed down his cheek.

"These branches," she choked, "they hurt."

Elnok's breaths hitched.

"I don't want to be in pain any longer," she said.

Nyla reached for the one piercing her clavicle. He stopped her.

"Prince Elnok, you may not understand, but us Kreenas have endured lives filled with pain," Nyla said, "I don't want this either, but it's the least we can do."

Elnok bit his tongue until blood filled his mouth. "She'll die sooner."

Sylzenya gripped his hand.

Fluttering his eyes closed, he gave a small nod. This was her choice, not his. He clenched his jaw as Nyla carefully wrenched the branch from her flesh. Sylzenya groaned, blood running down her sternum.

Elnok cursed as he gripped the one stuck in her stomach, ripping it out quickly. She winced, squeezing his hand harder.

"Where are my parents?" she asked.

"Right here, flower bud."

Elnok turned, struck by the similarities Sylzenya bore to her parents. He needed to let them have their final words.

Her parents took her hands, whispering words of love and some unknown prayers over her. Sylzenya's smile grew despite the red blood pooling around her.

"Elnok," Kharis approached him, "Do you still have the compass? Or the medicine Aretta gave you?"

Elnok's heart skipped. He cursed himself for not thinking about them sooner. Quickly, he rummaged through his pockets, the compass's cold metal meeting his fingers. He pulled it out, but the needle was nothing more than an ordinary splinter now.

Elnok cursed.

He searched his pockets again, the soft fabric pilling in his hands until he found the cylinder shape of the medicine vial. He held it in his hand. The substance continued to glow a bright white, pulsing with Elnok's heartbeat.

"I assumed it was made specifically for Orym. You think it can heal her too?" Elnok inquired.

Kharis shrugged. "It might."

"But he could still be alive when we get back." Elnok replied, "He could've beaten the odds and I still might be able to save him."

Kharis said nothing, staring at the vial.

"I could give this to her and it might not work," Elnok continued, "then both Sylzenya and Orym will be dead."

"You're not wrong."

"*Fuck you*, Kharis. I want some help here."

"The price for life is pain," Kharis replied, "but you better decide now. She's almost gone."

Elnok took a shaky breath.

Save one. Doom the other.

Or possibly doom both.

The truth washed over him. He already knew his decision, had known it since he turned around and came back instead of returning to Vutror.

"Sylzenya," he spoke softly, kneeling next to her, "I have Aretta's medicine."

She turned to him, tears staining her face, a small smile on her mouth. "That's for Orym. You should take it to him in case he's still alive."

Elnok shook his head, uncorking the vial. "If he's still alive, he'd want you to have it."

Her mouth gaped, more blood dribbling down her chin. "Elnok, no, I can't—"

"He'd refuse this the moment I brought it back; I was a fool to think I could force him to live just because I wanted him too." He cradled her head. Her tired eyes fluttered shut as she leaned into his hand. "He has terrible survival instincts."

Her parents touched Elnok's arm, their faces splotched red.

"It's selfish of me," she whispered.

"Oh fuck that to hell, Syl," Elnok breathed. "Now's not the time to be heroic. You already did that by killing Distrathrus."

Her laughter sounded like death. He held her head, the medicine vial balanced at her lips.

She grimaced. "The price for life will always be pain—"

"I swear, if I hear *one* more of you say that damned line…" His hands shook, his desire to see her live overwhelming. He let out a breath. "I'll only do it if you want me to. I've let you know my choice. Let that consequence rest on me, alright? But it's still your decision, no one else's."

Eyes fading, limbs falling limp, she stared at the glowing liquid.

"I don't want to die," she whispered, looking deep into his eyes.

"You don't have to." He squeezed her hand. "And I don't want you to die either, if that was ever in question."

She smiled. Sweat dripped down his face.

Finally, she gave a gentle nod. Taking a relieved breath, Elnok poured the medicine into her mouth, the bright liquid disappearing behind her tongue, her throat bobbing as she swallowed it all.

Silence filled the cavern, time slipping by, her skin growing paler, her lips turning blue.

"Please," he whispered, burying his face into her cold neck. "*Please,* stay with me."

Lower lip quivering, Elnok tightened his grip, tangling his fingers in her hair.

"Elnok," Kharis said, his hand gripping Elnok's shoulder. "I don't think—"

Suddenly, a golden light flared from her shoulder. Sylzenya's eyes burned a bright yellow as light weaved in and around her skin, closing up the holes made by the roots. The light danced around her, spiraling around her body, whipping her hair and clothes. She sucked in a long breath.

The sparks faded, leaving dried blood and perfectly healed skin.

Tears filled his vision as her parents squeezed his arm.

Her veins glowed bright, crackling with power, her eyes that same deep blue he could drown in. Elnok pressed his forehead to hers, her smile wide as she gently swept her fingers across his jaw. A resounding chorus of cries and sobs echoed in the cavern.

A miracle.

"I'm glad you listened to me for once." Elnok laughed as he stroked her face, her hair, her freshly healed skin.

"You *did* stay alive for me, so I suppose it would've been unfair if I didn't do it for you," she said, lacing her fingers with his, her brows dipping as she wiped the tears from his cheek.

He searched her face, mouth trembling as he brought his lips to hers. She ran her fingers through his hair, her mouth warm and tasting of life as she laughed. He tightened his hold on her lower back, promising himself he would never let go of her again.

"You did it," he whispered into her mouth. "You killed Distrathrus."

"I couldn't have done it without you or Kharis."

She softly grazed his ear with her lips, her heart beating in rhythm with his. His smile peeled wide as he laughed against the warm skin of her neck.

Sylzenya leaned back, her eyes glimmering as she looked at Elnok, her parents, Nyla, Kharis, and the surrounding Kreenas and Dynameis. Her parents dove in for their daughter, and Elnok stood up, giving them space to be together.

"What now?" Elnok asked Kharis.

Kharis raised his chin, observing the dead heart seeping through the roots on the pedestal and the dead body of Distrathrus split in two, the clear piece of orodyte next to him.

"Can someone burn that?" Kharis shouted.

A Dynami grabbed a handful of candles from the banquet table, using the small flames to burn what was left of Distrathrus.

"We need to inform the kingdom of everything," Kharis said to Elnok. "I checked with all the Kreenas and Dynameis here, and they agreed to help spread the word." He took Elnok by the elbow, dragging him away from everyone celebrating Sylzenya's resurrection. "Multiple Kreenas told me they were on the precipice of death, three of them swearing to me they *had* died, like you."

Elnok tilted his head. "What do you mean?"

"I mean, I think Sylzenya healed everyone in this room, even bringing the dead back to life."

Elnok went to spin the gold ring on his finger, but it was gone.

A strange wave of relief overcame him. He'd been given a second chance to live; a second chance to do something with his life, but this time, on his own terms.

It'd been a rebirth–a change.

He smiled at the thought, letting his fingers rest, placing his hand in his pocket.

"We can ask her about it when she's more rested," Elnok

stated. "We should probably leave before Distrathrus' burning body makes us all want to retch. And, I need to make my way back to Vutror."

Kharis agreed. "We'll need to take an entourage. If Aretta's vision was correct and the continent is truly saved from Distrathrus' curse, then Esteans might be able to help revitalize the land."

"Revitalize the land?" Elnok questioned, the words coming out slow, "You think that could work?"

"We won't know unless we try."

Suddenly, the sound of wings echoed in the cavern, bird song filling the air. Elnok looked up. Golden light spilled through a crack in the ceiling, a handful of gray and white feathered birds flying through, their soft songs echoing. The sun shone onto the clear orodyte floor, a vast array of colors reflecting onto the walls.

Elnok found Sylzenya's eyes as she embraced her mother. Her bright smile made his knees shake, his heart ache, and a deep laugh to spill from his mouth.

And then everyone started to laugh. Not the kind of laughter that felt strained or constricting, but the kind that felt warm and full. A laughter weaving in and out of everyone's hearts, connecting each of them to one another, joyful tears spilling from their eyes.

For the first time in a very, very long time, Elnok felt something he didn't think he'd feel again; not since he lost his parents or endured the dungeons with his brother; not since he'd been abused by his blacksmith master; not since he became nothing more than a thief in a dying land.

For the first time in ten, long years—he felt hope.

CHAPTER 41
HOME

Golden sunlight filtered through the green treetops. A soft sort of light, gentle and beautiful, mixed with the smell of fresh leaves and earth. Elnok admired the sweet-smelling air as he continued taking down his makeshift linen tent.

They were less than a day's walk from Vutror, having set up camp at the edge of Lhaal Forest. No longer did a heavy shadow hang over the trees, nor did fog spill out of its dense branches. Instead, birds sang songs and squirrels jumped between healthy branches.

"I still can't believe it," Sylzenya said as she approached him, lacing her hand in his. Warm, soft—*home.* "I never thought Lhaal could ever look like this."

"It's beautiful," Elnok breathed. "Although I could do without the lurking monsters."

She squeezed his hand. "You've done just fine with your special whip."

He smiled. "So much better than my rope."

"Hm, I'm still fond of that rope." She smirked, letting go of his hand and walking back towards her tent.

"Sylzenya *Phatris*," he growled, grabbing her waist and

pulling her against his chest, nuzzling his mouth against her ear.

A small laugh fell from her lips, one he caught with his mouth before it could slip away.

"We're supposed to be cleaning up," she teased, secretly running her hand along the outside of his pants, brushing her palm along his length, which, not to his surprise, had already hardened for her.

"Oh, but you *know* you can't just say things like that and get away with it." He smiled.

She bit her lip. "*What?* I had no idea."

It took every ounce of restraint in him to not fuck her this very moment. Judging by her smile, the thought burned in her mind just as brightly.

"Elnok, Sylzenya, if you both could please focus this morning, my ears would greatly appreciate it," Kharis yelled from the center of their small encampment, putting out the last of the burning embers. Their breakfast had been berries, roasted squash, and ample dried meat.

Rolling his eyes, Elnok claimed her mouth again, filling his lungs with her before they resumed taking down their equipment.

Outside of Lhaal Forest, the same barren lands Elnok had left still painted the hills, mountains, and valleys. Every so often, Sylzenya, Nyla, and a group of five more Kreenas would disperse and use their magic to create grass, trees, and other spots of life.

Despite the continued bareness, they proved it could be revitalized.

"It'll take a long time and a lot of work," Sylzenya remarked as she took a long gulp from her waterskin. "But if enough Esteans can commit to learning how to harness their power and help the land, then we can at least start bringing it back to its original state. Perhaps even better."

Elnok stared at her back, her Kreena cut a soft pink, the healthiest he'd ever seen it.

"What's it like?" Elnok asked as they and their party walked between two cliffsides, "Creating without your cut opening and bleeding?"

She smiled, something she'd been doing often on this trip. "It feels… right. Like this is how it was always supposed to be. And yet, it still feels like something is missing." She turned to him. "I grew so accustomed to the pain, it almost feels like the life I make is somehow unearned."

Nyla jumped in between them, her black hair tangled and full of leaves. "Don't listen to her, Elnok. She's far too philosophical about all of this. How it actually feels is *amazing*. And way less messy. I mean, by the gods, we were bleeding constantly. It feels good to create without pain or blood. Although, I'm far more interested in learning how to harness my Dynami powers."

Elnok laughed as Sylzenya shook her head, taking twigs out of her friend's hair.

"You'd make quite the warrior," she teased.

"Just you wait, Syl– *Oh!* We should create some trees over there, don't you think?"

Sylzenya rolled her eyes, giving into her friend's request as they rushed ahead of the group, creating a small ravine and oak trees next to one of the canyon faces. Despite her smiles, Elnok hadn't missed the sadness in her eyes. She hadn't talked about it yet, but he knew she still felt guilt for what their magic had done to the continent.

Suddenly, the ground started to quake.

"Serpentum!" Kharis yelled from the front of the line. "I'll take care of it. Continue forward."

Kharis rushed ahead of the group, his veins and sword aglow.

"Suppose Dynameis will need to keep vigilant," Theraden said as he stepped next to Elnok.

Sylzenya's father wore a plain white tunic and brown linen pants, a leather bag wrapped around his chest and hanging from his back. Gray hair tied in a small tail at the nape of his neck, he pointed towards Elnok's whip, "Do you plan to help them rid the continent of the loose monsters?"

Elnok shrugged. "To be honest, I'm not sure what I'll be doing after this."

"My daughter will want to revitalize the continent," he said, "she's told me many times since we started the journey."

"She's told me as well."

The man readjusted his bag. "While I want to spend as much time as I can with Sylzenya, I know she won't want to stay in one place for too long. Her heart's too large for that. Her ambitions will take her many places my body won't be able to join."

"You have a compassionate daughter, Theraden," Elnok remarked.

"A blessing I don't deserve," he said, eyes glassy.

"Something tells me she didn't get that particular quality from Distrathrus."

A small smile spread across his mouth. "You love my daughter very much."

Elnok laughed. "I fear I make that a bit too obvious sometimes."

"You do."

Sylzenya rejoined the entourage, talking with the Kreenas at the front of line. Kharis returned soon after with black blood dripping from his sword, the group welcoming him with hurrah's and shouts of accomplishment.

"Take care of her, will you?" Theraden asked, his voice low and serious. "I just… I gave her away to someone who didn't do that and… it kills me. Probably always will…"

His voice trailed off, his eyes becoming distant.

Elnok turned to him. "She forgives you, you know. And her mother too."

"I know, it's just… please."

Elnok nodded. "I could promise to take care of her, but she's pretty damn good at it herself. With or without me, she'd find her way." Rubbing his neck, Elnok grinned. "But as long as I'm by her side, I'll always be watching out for her, just like she'll be doing for me."

Theraden cracked a smile, patting his shoulder. "You're a good man, Elnok. Thank you—for everything."

Elnok couldn't stop the warmth inside his chest from blooming through his limbs.

A good man.

Never in his life had he considered himself such a thing. He still wouldn't, but he liked the idea.

Elnok stopped in front of the stone drawbridge. Kharis had ushered him to the front, Sylzenya as well. He hadn't seen Vutror's drawbridge in ten years—hadn't been anywhere near Vutror since his escape.

Sylzenya laced her fingers with his.

"You'll be alright," she whispered.

His throat bobbed as he gave a slight nod.

"We sent someone ahead to let them know of our arrival," Kharis said, returning from talking to the guard, "they'll let us through when they're ready."

Waiting felt like an eternity.

Finally, the drawbridge creaked and yawned, lowering slowly until it thudded against the dry ground. Sylzenya squeezed his hand.

The sunlight burst forth as they passed through, entering the kingdom's walkway. Gray stone buildings lined the path, their window panes full of dust and debris.

Doors slowly opened, people stepping out of their homes and exiting their vendor stands, swarming at the entrance of the kingdom. Elnok stared at them all. A small rumble of conversation slowly built into shouts before erupting into cheers and applause.

Elnok's mouth gaped, his hands shaking.

Small pieces of colored paper sailed through the air, falling onto his hair and face. He looked up. People threw confetti from their windowsills, chanting his name over and over again.

But then, the crowd slowly parted before him—all the air in his lungs left him. Walking towards him was the familiar mop of brown hair and warm eyes of his friend.

Orym spread his arms wide, wearing a broad smile.

Warm tears spilled down Elnok's face. Sylzenya let go of his hand, and he rushed for him. Orym ran for him as well. They collided, the force almost knocking both of them off their feet. Elnok crumpled Orym's tunic into his hands, sobbing into his shoulder.

"You made it back in one piece," Orym said over the cheering, his voice wavering from sobs, "And with quite the entrance, I must say."

"How?" Elnok said, leaning back, staring at his perfectly healthy friend. "I thought… you should be *dead*."

"Wow, those are your first words to me?" Orym jested. "Shouldn't they be something more like, *I missed you Orym*, or, wow, *look how handsome you got while I was away*."

"Fuck you." Elnok laughed, hugging him again, "I *did* miss you. But how are you not sick anymore?"

"No one's sick anymore," Orym replied. "No one in Vutror; no one in the nearest fishing village. Everyone's been cured."

Realization thrummed through Elnok as he leaned back, turning around to Sylzenya. Tears stained her face, a smile gracing her lips, a beautiful stream of colored paper decorating her long windswept hair.

"Oh my gods," Elnok whispered.

"What?" Orym asked. "Are you two… fucking? Because it certainly seems like you two are fucking."

"She… she healed everyone."

Orym stalled. "Her? She… she did this?"

"Yes," Elnok said, shaking his head, "She really did."

Suddenly, a woman barged through the crowd, her beige linen clothes catching the breeze as she yelled Orym's name at the top of her lungs.

Yenna, Orym's nurse from the coastal village.

"You forgot your damn medicine!" Yenna yelled, running into them as she shoved through people.

Elnok laughed. "Still his nurse even after his cure?"

Yenna's eyes widened as she finally noticed Elnok.

"Gods, you really made it back," she exclaimed, wrapping him in a quick hug, "Your friend here is even worse when he can walk. Can barely keep up with him these past two days. Oi! Orym! Just because you feel better doesn't mean it's all gone, alright? I swear, if you don't listen to me—"

Orym swept her into his arms and kissed her.

"Better?" he asked her.

Her face flushed, cheeks pink as she forced the medicine into his open palm, a trace of a sheepish smile lining her lips.

Elnok crossed his arms and raised a brow, a wide smile pulling at his mouth.

Orym shook his head. "You're not the only one who's been busy."

Turning around, Elnok caught Sylzenya's eye, her smile broad as she motioned for them to keep walking. He wrapped his arm around Orym as they continued the journey up to the castle gates. His crew met him in the crowd, shouting and yelling, embracing him with tears and stories of the wonders since everyone had been miraculously healed. Elnok laughed and cried with them until they reached the castle.

Standing at the entrance was Tosh.

Elnok stopped. His brother wore a deep maroon tunic, the

sleeves billowing out at his wrists. Black hair draped past his chest, shining and healthy. His face was no longer sunken in, but filled and round, a glowing olive tan on his face. A faint smile sat on his mouth, one that looked so much like their mother's.

Stepping forward, Tosh bowed before Elnok.

"Welcome home, brother."

Unwinding his arm from around Orym, Elnok stood before his brother. He sniffed the air, trying his best to detect if any wine stained his breath.

"You're healed," Elnok said.

Tosh nodded. "Happened the same as everyone else. Two days ago, everyone began to recover, myself included." He raised his hands. "I haven't touched wine since, and I feel as if I'm thinking clearly for the first time in over a decade."

"That wine you were drinking, Tosh, it wasn't normal wine. There's a lot to explain."

Tosh folded his hands. "I figured there might be. But before we go through all the grating royal welcome festivities, I want you to know what I'll be presenting to you in our castle." A servant approached him from behind, the blue-and-red-jeweled Vutrorian crown on a maroon pillow. "Elnok, my time as king has been nothing but chaos. I don't belong on the throne, and if what I think is true, that you're part of the reason our kingdom is healed, then I think the plan moving forward is obvious."

He turned to the servant, taking hold of the crown and extending it to Elnok.

"If you wish for it, you would make our mother and father proud as the King of Vutror."

Elnok stared at the gilded crown, fingers trembling. The one his father had worn during his time. The one Elnok had been accused of stealing over and over again. And now, the one his brother freely gave to him.

Elnok turned around. Orym wore a confident smile. His

crew waited in expectation. The Estean entourage seemed full of hope and anticipation.

He met Sylzenya's gaze. She smiled, giving him a small nod, quickly wiping a tear from her cheek.

She would be adventuring across the continent—reviving it. Accepting this crown would mean returning home, but "home" wasn't the gray stone castle where he was born.

Home was deep blue eyes, long ash-colored hair, skin that smelled of roses—just like the rose tea she loved so much—and long nights of conversation and pleasuring each other until they fell asleep. Home was soft skin and a pink scar running along a supple back.

Elnok faced his brother.

"Tosh, what happened to us ten years ago, it's done. Over."

His brother's back straightened, hands trembling. "Elnok, I'm so sorry—"

"It's…" Elnok took a deep breath. "Look, what happened, it was wrong. And even though you'll come to learn there was more at play… what happened can't be taken away. But I need you to know that I've moved on from it. We can't change what we did back then, but we can be different now."

Tosh's throat bobbed. "I think so too."

Elnok smiled. "Good. And I think mother and father would want you to finally have a chance to lead this kingdom like you'd always wanted to. My path lies elsewhere." He glanced back, catching Sylzenya's eye. "Let's move forward on our own paths, Tosh. I think we both deserve that, don't you?"

Tosh shook his head, placing the crown back on the pillow. "A miscreant your entire childhood, and now you show up as possibly one of the wisest people I've met. How did that come to pass?"

Elnok smirked. "Being a miscreant isn't all that bad, you know. You should try it sometime."

They laughed, warm and bright.

Elnok grinned. "Kharis! Get your ass up here, *now*."

Clanking armor sounded, Kharis' rushed footsteps reaching Elnok's side.

"Do you need something, Elno—?"

"Oh shut up, Kharis, and kiss my brother already." Elnok shoved Kharis into his brother's arms.

Elnok raised his arms and everyone erupted into elated shouts. His crew threw the colored paper they'd collected, for gods know what reason, into the air while his brother and Kharis kissed one another passionately for all to see.

"Thank you, Elnok," Tosh said, "You're a good man."

Elnok turned back around, giving his brother a nod. "People keep saying that to me, and I'm not sure how I like it."

"Well, it's true," Kharis replied, holding Tosh close, "Better get used to it."

"And you better make him your king, Tosh," Elnok said, pointing to Kharis. "I'm sure an alliance between Vutror and Estea would only be beneficial at this time."

Elnok turned back around, patting Orym's shoulder as he rushed past his crew over to Sylzenya, picking her up in his arms and combing his hands through her hair.

"Are you not accepting the crown?" she asked, eyes wide.

"That rusted thing? Never." He grinned. "Besides, why would I ever leave a woman who likes my rope just as much as I do?"

Her eyes narrowed, hands on either side of his face. "Are you certain about this? I'm planning on leaving in a few days."

"And you think you can get rid of me that easily?"

"It's not going to be luxurious. It'll be hard work, probably monster hunting involved—"

"I'd journey with you to the ends of the earth, Sylzenya. And if we made it there and you asked me if I wanted to journey to the heavens, I'd be by your side then, too."

Smiling wider than he'd ever seen before, she kissed his

lips, her tongue finding his as he spun her, the anticipation of life adventuring by her side until they were old and gray causing his heart to burst with color.

What a joy, he'd decided, it was to be alive.

EPILOGUE

THREE MONTHS LATER

Sylzenya washed her hands in a water basin, cleaning off the dirt caked underneath her nails. The two men she'd been training joined her, their fingers stained with blueberry juice. They'd come a long way in creating blueberry bushes in only a few short days, and she was grateful for their eagerness to help the fishing village.

Salt carried in the air, a scent Sylzenya still wasn't accustomed to, but she liked it nonetheless.

It was different, and she liked different.

"Tavern?" One of the men asked, clearly too tired to say any other words.

"Please," Sylzenya replied, the sound of beer—or anything that *wasn't* wine—a relief.

They trudged through the village, children laughing and running around the wooden homes. The repairs Elnok and his crew had been working on for roofs and shattered windows had started to show after spending a little over a week in the village. Warm torchlights cut through the maritime fog as they approached the dimly lit tavern.

Opening the door, Sylzenya groaned in relief at the scent of hearty stew and malty beer.

"Ah, there they are!" Nyla shouted from the other end of the tavern, standing at a table closest to the bar.

The men Sylzenya was training rushed ahead of her and sat with Nyla and the rest of Elnok's crew. Sylzenya followed, Nyla's face lit up as she motioned for her to sit with her. One of Elnok's crew members grabbed her stew and beer. Sylzenya hummed with satisfaction at the taste of starchy potato and warm spicy broth.

Nyla stood up again, waving her hands as she continued a story they must've interrupted.

"And then Elnok unleashes his whip and, thwap," Nyla slapped her hand against her thigh, the veins in her arms crackling with yellow light, "the arachni screamed so loud I swear to the gods my ears bled!"

"What'd you do with the body?" Orym asked, slurping on his stew.

"Carried it to the ocean," Nyla replied, sitting back down, "Didn't want to take our chances with whatever the kids would do with a dead arachni carcass."

Orym laughed. "Yeah, those kids really did a number to that other one in the last village."

Sylzenya shivered. "What'd they do with the eyes again?"

"Stuck them on wood poles and paraded them through the town telling everyone to *worship the great arachni killer*."

Sylzenya rolled her eyes, waiting for Elnok to chime in on how he and Nyla *should* be worshiped for such endeavors, but it never came. Searching the table, she placed her spoon down. Elnok wasn't at the table.

"Wow, that took you longer than I thought," Nyla said.

"I believe that's five gold coins for me," Orym sang as he held out his hand to Nyla.

"You bet on how long it'd take me to realize Elnok wasn't here?"

Everyone laughed. Sylzenya sighed.

"Yeah," Nyla replied, "and thanks to your tiredness, I lost five gold coins to this *thief*."

"Ah ah, this was a simple bet. I'm a law-abiding citizen now, remember? We all are."

The crew cheered, sloshing their beers together and taking long drinks. Sylzenya joined, finishing her glass.

"Where is he then?" Sylzenya asked.

Orym's smile vanished. "He's just over the hill behind the inn, a cliffside that looks out to the ocean. I'm sure he wouldn't mind some company."

The way Orym's body stiffened made questions tumble through her mind.

"I'll go check on him," she said, standing.

Orym gave her a wary nod. She told Nyla to use her coin to buy herself another drink and she left. Walking up the small hill, Sylzenya smiled as the fog lightly wet her face. The sun welcomed her as she crested the hill, its light shining on the glittering sea.

The cliffside came into view, a person sitting on its ledge.

Her heart beat faster as she approached Elnok, his black hair tied at the nape of his neck, his black tunic exposing his strong arms as he leaned back, staring at the warm sky.

"Heard you had quite the tussle with an arachni today," Sylzenya said, sitting next to him, the cold stone seeping through her linen pants.

"A pretty aggressive one," he noted, his voice gravelly and low. "I know it might sound crazy, but I feel like it was one we might've fought back in Lhaal Forest."

Stroking a finger along the two scars on his chest, he shivered.

"When we were attacked by that horde?"

He chuckled. "Now that you say it, I do sound crazy."

"Well, most of the times you are," she jested. "But not with this."

A small silence sat between them.

"Sometimes I dream about it," he said, leaning further back, the orange glow of the sun striking on his handsomely carved face. "Dying in that tree. The poison almost taking me. I even sometimes think about..." he trailed off, placing his hand over his stomach.

Sylzenya knew exactly what he was thinking about.

"When I killed you," she said.

"I'm sorry—"

"No, don't be sorry. It wouldn't make sense for you to simply forget that ever happened." Sylzenya took a deep breath, leaning back with him. "His eyes still haunt me. Sometimes I'm talking to someone and I swear their eyes start glowing yellow, and I hear his voice, feel his cold touch."

A sharp shiver ran up her arms, her skin pimpling. Elnok placed his hand over hers, rubbing his thumb over her knuckles.

"He's dead, but it still feels like he's alive somehow," she whispered.

"I wish we could forget it all."

They stared at the sun as it slowly melted into the horizon, oranges and pinks blanketing the sky.

"Perhaps if we forgot it all, then it'd feel like something else would be missing," Sylzenya said. "For all the destruction and damage Distrathrus caused everyone, he really seemed to be doing everything because he loved his sister."

"A *very* twisted love."

"Well, yes," Sylzenya agreed, "Still. It's like you told me back in Lhaal, it's those with power who have consequences that reach furthest. He had more power than anyone on this continent, and so his mistakes cost everyone." She tucked her knees into her chest. "As did mine."

Elnok rubbed her back, careful to avoid her scar. "What's it been like, helping communities thrive? Giving them food and water?"

She picked at a piece of lint on her pants, staring at how it glinted against the sun.

"It's been satisfying in some ways, and yet unsettling in others." She sighed, letting the lint float into the evening breeze. "To see their smiles when I create new vegetation, fill their ravines—there's nothing like it. But knowing why they were absent in the first place… Knowing me and my people are the origin of their misfortunes… it feels like a dagger to my chest every time."

Elnok wrapped his arm around her shoulder. "And yet you still do it."

She draped her legs over his. "Just like you still kill arachnis."

"They're really scary, aren't they?" he said, a small laugh in his throat.

"Terrifying. I'd hate your job."

"Maybe we'll switch one of these days."

"I'd rather do *anything* else."

"*Anything* else?" he chided, running his hand through her hair, causing her eyes to flutter closed, "Even clip off all the blisters on Nyla's feet?"

"Even that."

"I don't believe you."

Sylzenya nudged his shoulder, tracing his jaw with her finger. "You know me pretty well then, don't you?"

He grinned. "Sometimes I think I do, other times all I want to do is dig and prod until I figure out how such a delicious woman can be so intelligent *and* daring all at once."

He hooked her chin with his thumb and brushed his lips along hers. She sighed into his touch, greedily taking another kiss from him, tracing a tongue on his lips.

"What's something I don't know about you?" she whispered.

He ran his thumb over her mouth. "What do you want to know?"

"This cliffside. What does it mean to you?"

Chewing the inside of his lip, he considered his words carefully. Sylzenya smiled as she watched him think.

"I suppose it means a lot of things," he started, running his eyes along her face, down her neck, "It was home for a time, a place of peace. It was also a place of unrest, of war. And then it became a place of hope."

"Can it really be all those things?" she inquired.

"Of course it can. Just like you're both intolerable and yet the most bearable person I've ever met."

She laughed. "What in the world is that supposed to mean?"

"Contradictions. You're full of them. I am too. So are Orym, Nyla, Kharis, Tosh, everyone in my crew." He brushed a hand through her hair. "Your parents. Aretta. Distrathrus. If places can be many things, why not people? Why not gods?"

"Contradictions," Sylzenya repeated, "Like my power used to be. Life and death."

"Exactly."

"So then," she said, "what does this place mean to you now?"

Grinning, he pressed his mouth to hers, sliding his hand up her tunic and onto her cold skin, gripping her hips. Warmth spread through her body, surprise lighting her core with fire as she tangled her hands in his hair, pulling down the deep "v" in his tunic and touching his chest.

He breathed deeply, and she responded, falling on top of him and straddling his hips. His large rough hands gripped her ass, guiding her as she rocked against him. Yearning thrummed through her chest, needing to feel him everywhere all at once.

His thoughts, his dreams, his hands, his cock, his eyes, his mouth. She wanted every last part of him, and she wanted to give every last part of herself to him. All her contradictions for all of his.

Biting her lower lip, he slowly pulled away, his breaths heavy as he leaned his forehead against hers. She reached for him, but he wouldn't allow it, his hand digging into one of his pockets, pulling out something gold and shimmering.

A ring.

In its center, a deep blue gem glinted against the sunset.

"I was thinking," he whispered, "this cliff side could also mean new beginnings."

Tears burning in her eyes, she smiled. "Why blue?"

"Guess."

She smirked, "My eyes?"

"Your eyes," he confirmed.

"You're a bit of a cliche sometimes, you know?"

Pulling her in for a kiss, she sank into him. "And you love it."

"I do," she admitted, letting him slip the ring onto her finger, "And I love *you*, Elnok Rogdul."

"I haven't loved anything or anyone more than I've loved you, Sylzenya Phatris."

He pulled her in for another kiss, but she stopped him.

"But I don't have anything for you," she said.

"Don't need to."

"Yes, I do," Sylzenya said, sitting up, staring out at the sunset, and then at the layer of soil on the cliffside.

An idea sparked in her chest.

She got off him, running over to a patch of dirt. Kneeling down, she dug her hands into the dry earth, feeling for her blood inside her veins, connecting it to the blood in the earth; her heartbeat thrummed through her body.

Thump.

Thump.

Thump.

Power erupted from her hands, golden light circling her arms, her torso, her back—but no pain struck her as a small green sprout poked between her fingers. Awe took over her, just like it did every time she used her power. Breathing in life, she watched as the sprout grew into dark brown bark, bursting with golden sparks into an array of bright green willow leaves. Smiling, she pressed her palms deeper, the earth singing a new, wonderful song as the willow grew until its leaves reached the cliffside.

Placing her palm next to the tree, she called upon more roots to grow, laughter bubbling up in her throat as golden sparks fluttered across the dirt, tickling her hands. Green grass popped up from the ground and flowers of every color unfurled in splendid succession.

Satisfied, Sylzenya released her palms, her power retreating into the dirt. Looking at Elnok, concern furrowed her brow; tears streamed down his face.

"Elnok?" she asked, slowly approaching him, "Is this not what you wanted?"

Shaking his head, he grabbed her arm, pulling her into his chest and pressing his mouth to hers, salty tears mixing on their tongues as he wrapped his arms around her. She gripped his tunic, meeting his desire and passion with the same vigor.

They broke the kiss, his breath short as he whispered, "It's more than I could've ever dreamed of."

They cried and laughed together, her blue ring glinting in the sunset while the willow tree waved in the soft breeze.

The price for life would always be pain, and by the gods was it worth it.

Acknowledgments

First off, I want to thank my family of origin—dad, mom, Owen, Eric, and Morgon—for being simultaneously the nerdiest and yet most physically active people I know. You each taught me, in your own ways, that I can do anything I set my mind to. To my dad who talked me through some of my initial world-building and read my very first draft—that was a truly brave endeavor. And to Morgon: your affinity for storytelling will forever inspire us. We love and miss you.

Second, a very special shout out to my beta team who read the very first draft of this book back in 2022. Tabitha, Pierre, Mick, Jared, Kevin, and my dad. Each of you read my beginning attempts at writing a novel—some of you even read the second and third drafts. I'm forever grateful for both your honesty and graciousness. You each gave me exactly what I needed at that time: informative feedback and the encouragement to keep going.

Next, my unending gratitude to Bardsy. This organization has single-handedly influenced the way I tell stories. Adam—you push me to view storytelling in a way I'd never considered. I'd been struggling with one-dimensional characters, boring dialogue, bloated world-building, confusing plotlines, and conflict-less chapters when I tried my first few attempts at this story. But with your guidance, coaching, and encouragement, you showed me my potential. Allie Oleander—you ask some of the most insightful questions that allow me to clean up inconsistencies; not to mention your own writing inspires the hell out of me. Sam Traina—not only are you what true friends are made of, but you are never shy to tell me what's working and what isn't, and for that, this story has greatly benefited.

To my copy/line editor, Ashley Postmman-Keller, aka Aspen Editorial: thank you for your exceptional attention to detail. You took the time and energy to understand my vision for this story, and your edits improved it tenfold. You helped make this story accessible to its audience, and for that, I can't thank you enough. Getting words on the page is lovely, but having them make sense? That's an entirely different beast, and you make taming it look effortless.

To my beta reader and critique partner team who read the final version of this story: Sofi, Amanda Sims, Teegan Stine, P.C. Nottingham, Alex Bree, Jaci M. Lunera, and Kaela Woodruff. You each brought invaluable critiques to the table and solidified the pieces that were working in the story. Not to mention all of your reactions to Elnok's sassiness made my revisions highly enjoyable.

To my cover artist team—FlavulousArt. I expected a professional encounter and a well-done cover, but I ended up with so much more. Bo—thank you for sharing all your expertise and making some very important calls that made the cover's composition simply perfect. Flavia—your talent ceases to amaze me. Thank you for collaborating so intentionally with me and creating a piece of art that beautifully introduces the reader to the story. Thank you both for the support, professionalism, and shared love of D&D and *LOTR*.

Finally, I want to thank the three people who were each my anchor in this swirling, ravenous sea of writing as I started and finished my first ever romantasy novel: Emily Elmerick, Jackie Snow, and my spouse, Paul. Emily—your excitement for this story spurred me on when I would've rather thrown in the towel and called it quits. You brought up tough critiques I needed to hear in order to make this story's spot in the fantasy genre as grounded as possible. Without you, I fear I would've made some decisions that would've pushed this book back another few years. I'm endlessly grateful for your steadfastness and belief in this story, always reminding me that it deserves to be shared. Not to mention that you've read every single draft I've written. *I owe you.*

Jackie—you're the writing partner everyone dreams of having, and we have the luxury of living only a few streets away. We went from making silly, romantasy book fan account videos on social media to waking up early on Saturday mornings with laptops humming and coffee mugs steaming while discussing character motivations and how to write romance beats. Not to mention the late nights of drinking hot toddies and white russians at the nearby pubhouse, hands dusted with powdered sugar from beignet donuts, discussing book boyfriend traits we love while diagnosing the road blocks our stories were inevitably bumping up against. This book surely would've been lost in a Google Doc back in 2021 if it wasn't for you. Thanks for being my number one critique partner and, more importantly, my friend.

Paul—my spouse. My life partner. I'm not surprised Elnok was so widely loved because so much of what we love about him came from pieces of you. His ability to look at his world critically and ask insightful questions, his affinity of making jokes even in the most dire of circumstances, and most notably, his undying belief in Sylzenya. Your belief in not only my endeavors, but simply in me, have been an anchor in the stormiest nights. You championed my desire to write a story from the first little snippet I asked you to read. Not once did you tell me I should stop, even if I told you I think I should; even if there were days where I was grumpy as hell all because I stayed up way too late "just finishing up a chapter". Some of my fondest memories during this time were when we went across the street to our favorite bar and talked for hours about our stories. In good times and hard times, I love you, always.

And lastly, but certainly not least, thank you to my readers. This story was written and made for you. Thank you for taking a chance on this debut book, and thank you for trusting it enough to invest both your money and time into it. May you keep finding magic and purpose in all the stories you read.

About the Author

With a master's degree social work, A.J. Braun finds a deep fascination in how people make sense of their world, relationships, and themselves. This, in combination with their deep love for the fantasy and romance genres, inspired Braun to tell their own romantasy stories. When they're not pouring over their manuscripts, you can also find Braun hanging out with their spouse and friends, cuddling their two black cats, participating in local sport leagues, and playing D&D into the wee hours of the night.

www.ingramcontent.com/pod-product-compliance
Lightning Source LLC
Chambersburg PA
CBHW032000080125
20085CB00005B/38

9798990705401